King of Cruelty

Saint and Sinners, Volume 7

Ruby Vincent

Published by Ruby Vincent, 2025.

Prologue

Genny and I sat in the stolen cab, watching her apartment building. I was surprised, angry, and disgusted when I saw her in that picture. As we sat in that car, I felt none of those emotions. Honestly, I felt nothing at all. My feelings were wrung out and splattered along the road from the Fairfield to her building. I just wanted this done with.

"We need to get inside," Genny announced for the fourth time. "Waiting around hoping she comes out is idiotic."

"Sunny once told me that you don't follow an assassin to their house. They're the only one in the room who knows where all the weapons are hidden. What we know about this woman right now is that we don't know a damn thing about her. She got in bed with a rapist, sex trafficker, and child abductor. Underestimating her is a mistake," I said, also for the fourth time. "Let her come to us."

"She's got five minutes."

Genny was in her war gear. I was calling it that because ripped jeans, fishnet stockings, fishnet top, and a red bra were what she changed into after peeling herself off the couch.

"Gen, you bribed the doorman to tell you she comes out every morning to walk her dog in the park. Dogs have to do their business every day—rain or shine. She's coming."

"Four minutes."

I sat up straight. "Don't need four minutes. There she is now."

Genny was out the door before I finished.

Wild Springs Apartments was in one of the swankier parts of Leighbridge. The building stretched to the sky, carrying luxury apartments and penthouses to the top floor. Beside it was Wild Springs Park—a patch of green nestled among a concrete paradise. Walking trails, biking trails, a water fountain, a playground overrun with laughing kids—it had everything. We trailed her into the perfect spot with so many people going about their fun, they wouldn't notice one random woman disappear off the trail.

She rounded a hedge, setting down one of the walking trails. A little toy fox terrier trotted beside her.

"Not too close," Genny said. "You need to be close enough to see them, but not so close that they can turn around and clock your face."

"Thanks for the tip. Now here's yours: don't shove your gun down her throat. Just knock her unconscious and we'll take her to Astoria. Afterward, we'll tell the guys the truth."

"Surprised you agreed to keep this from them in the first place."

My voice hardened. "This is between me and the bitch that would've sold my baby. The more I think about this, the scarily clearer my past becomes. I don't need anyone trying to protect me from this. And for better or worse, Genny, you'd never stand between a woman and her target."

"I like you more and more every day, Blaine. Please, feel free to kick the bitch's teeth in. I'll hold her hair."

The path lined with hedges and trees—gifting the parkgoers with a green and flowered maze. She and the dog disappeared around a hedge and we let her, keeping well back as she headed for a small tunnel bridge.

"As soon as she steps inside the bridge, we run," Genny ordered. "I'll go around and catch her in the front. You come in from the back. No one will see us take her."

I glanced down at my hands. *Perfectly still.*

"Got it."

She got closer... closer... closer. We sprang into action the moment she stepped into the tunnel.

Genny sprinted across the lawn and up the hill, disappearing around the other side of the bridge. I left my usual boots, skirts, and handmade labels at home, opting instead for jeans, a simple shirt that concealed the zip ties, and rubber soles absorbing the strikes carrying me down the path into the tunnel.

Genny and I burst inside at nearly the same time and came face-to-face—

—with each other.

The tunnel was empty.

"What the fuck!" Genny bellowed. "What the hell happened?"

"That's my question."

I whirled around, shock snapping a band around my throat as Madison James appeared behind me, her yappy little puppy tucked under her arm.

"Why are you following me, Mackenzie?" She flicked over her shoulder at Genny. "And you. Shouldn't you be in the back of a prison van?"

"That's my question," Genevieve mocked.

"Excuse me?"

I slid back a few steps, putting some distance between us. I was standing in front of one of the most devious, sociopathic monsters ever spat out of a womb. I didn't know what she would do, but I wouldn't be in striking distance when she did it.

"We know, Madison," I said. "We know everything."

She cocked a brow. "Everything about what exactly?"

"Don't you fucking stand there acting innocent!" Rapid footsteps echoed in the tunnel. "When I'm done with you—"

I shot in front of Genny, glaring into her eyes. "Don't stand in the way," I said simply.

A thousand emotions warred on her face. There was no question Madison did horrible things that hurt her family, but she started with mine first.

"Fine." Genny gestured for me to go ahead.

I turned on Madison. The amusedly confused mask on her face was getting better by the second.

"Here's how it's going to go," I began. "I'm going to tell you what I know. You'll deny being a psychotic, evil bitch. Then I'll show you our proof. After that, you get to explain just how you got to be this way. Prep that sympathy defense for the jury."

She laughed. "Oh my gosh, Kenzie. You're just as crazy and desperate for attention as Lyla said. I do not have time for this, but whatever." She shrugged. "I'm kinda interested in how I'm a *psychotic, evil bitch* and what proof you have of that besides the voices in your head?"

My lips stretched to match her smile. "You used to work with a man named Luca Adams, also known as Digger. He supplied you with kidnapped children, and you put them up for *adoption* through a fake agency called the Sunshine Adoption."

"Hmm, no," she said, scratching her puppy behind the ear. "Never heard of the place."

I went on like she hadn't spoken. "Luca was able to supply you with children and babies, because he owned a string of cheap housing with his pick of women and single mothers to prey on. He tricked or forced them into prostitution, then handed their kids to you.

"I don't know how you hooked up with Luca. He was handsome and charming, so maybe he seduced you like all the others. But instead of putting you through hell, he realized you were soulmates. You were both dead inside.

"With your sweet act, pretty face, and clean background check greeting couples at the door, you had no problem making over a million dollars off of those poor women and their misery."

Madison just looked at me like this was boring and she was waiting for me to skip to the end.

"The Brotherhood didn't approach Luca." I leveled between her eyes. "They approached you. The Brotherhood recruits enemies of the Merchants who can be useful to them. You were in the building where their clothes were packed up and shipped. That put you in the perfect position to slip a little something inside. Tell me, did you come up with the idea for the trackers, or does a brother get the credit?"

"I really have no idea what you're talking about. But can you hurry this up? Poppy needs to make."

"I guess it doesn't matter who thought of it. You did your duty for the cause by tampering with all the clothes going out to the Johnsons. As for Luca, you made the case to the Brotherhood that another psychopath would be good for the organization. Who knows, maybe they liked how easily he made women... disappear."

Madison put her dog down, letting her run off to sniff the grass. "You're spinning a scary story, Kenzie, but it has nothing to do with me."

"It has everything to do with you, Madison," I forced through gritted teeth. "See, you were always different. Back when we started the internship and you became a part of Lyla's bitch crew, you didn't always blindly follow along with what she said and did. You weren't a nice person, but every now and then you openly contradicted her—earning yourself a glare or a kick under the table.

"I used to think 'she's an asshole, but at least she's an asshole that thinks for herself.' I thought the same thing the day Lyla got me fired and you approached me as I was leaving." I flashed back to that day. Me carrying a box of my things and about to shove them into a cab when Madison's call made me stop. "You said I was done in fashion. No one in our world would hire me, and even if I deserve what I get, my kid doesn't. You dropped a business card for Allison Raines on my things, told me she helps women in trouble, and said to call the number.

"Allison was a sweet old voice on the other end of the phone that helped me get the job at the diner. And when I lost that job and my apartment, I called her again, and she sent me to Luca's apartment building. Allison was you, wasn't it?" I rasped. "It's not a coincidence that you gave a pregnant woman a card that led her right into the hands of that monster. You knew he would take me, and hand Laurel right to you."

"Nope," Madison popped, rolling her eyes. "I was just trying to help you. This is what I get for feeling sorry for you."

I grinned mirthlessly. "That's good, Madison. We're already through parts one and two. Now it's time for me to show you proof." I fished out my phone. "You say you know nothing about the Sunshine Adoption Agency. You had nothing to do with Luca Adams and the children he kidnapped. And you're just an innocent designer that knows nothing about double lives and fake identities."

I shoved the cellphone in her face. "Then tell me what the hell you're doing in that photo, *Kathleen*—smiling away as you congratulate the Forbises on their adoption of this kidnapped boy, Jake Willard." The lines around her eyes tightened. I'd never seen a smile wipe away faster.

"The Forbises are pissed, by the way. They're heartbroken that they were made complicit in kidnapping, and now they're going to lose the boy they love. My sister said by the time they left, the Forbises were on the phone with their three-hundred-dollar-an-hour attorneys and the FBI. The investigation has already started into the mysteriously vanished Sunshine Agency and the woman who ran it."

"What?" Madison screeched. "What did you do?!"

"Whoops," Genny sang. "Guess we dropped the innocent act."

"I am innocent," Madison cried. "That's not what you think. I didn't—"

"Save it," I snapped. "You met with the Forbises every weekend for three months. You don't think they remember who took fifty thousand dollars from them and then gave them the answer to their prayers? They could pick you out of a lineup with fifty of your evil clones! Admit it! You and Luca were working together! You set me up!"

Madison's gaze darted around, looking for an escape. "Okay, I did, but—"

I punched her dead in the face. Madison dropped like a stone, laid flat out on her back. "You evil piece of shit." My voice shook. "You picked me out and offered me and my daughter up to Luca, knowing exactly what hell he'd put us through. What went wrong with you, Madison? How did you become... this?"

She pushed herself up, clutching her bleeding nose. The fury in her eyes burned me where I stood. "Fuck you! Why should I give a shit about trash like you? You're the spawn of some crazy murdering psycho who shot your daddy over tea and cookies. When you faked those designs and conned your way into the Phenomenal Five, it was obvious you didn't fall far from the criminal tree."

"Ah. Here we are," I said. "Part four. Before you continue explaining why you're justified, you should know I didn't fake or steal anything. I was set up by Damien and your buddy Lyla."

"Oh, please," she scoffed. "No one buys that crap. If you've never done a thing wrong, why are you shacked up with her family! Another band of crazy murdering psychos! No, Kenzie. I saw you for exactly what you are. There was no saving you, but there was still a chance for your kid. Whatever Luca did to you was his business, but I knew he would give me your kid, and I'd place her with a proper family. I would've been doing that kid a favor."

I bristled. The urge to punch her again welled in me so strong, I cut my palm clenching my fists. "Who gave you the right to decide? No one asked you to be my baby's fairy godmother."

"Someone had to be," she shouted. "Someone had to look out for those kids and give them a better life. You weren't going to do it, and the Merchants sure as fuck weren't either."

Genny stepped forward. "What does my family have to do with any of this?"

"You have everything to do with it! My mother got involved with the Merchants. She was like you, Kenzie. A fake. A fraud! She used to run scams and cheat people out of their money. And of course, any criminal that operates in the Cinco city limits pays a tax to the Merchants." She spat the name like it tasted foul on her tongue.

"When she was my age, she quit the life, changed her name, and met my father, Richard James. Our life was good," she cried. Her whole body shook. "We lived in a penthouse in Leighbridge, and had two other homes overseas. I went to the best schools. My best friends were the sons and daughters of models and movie stars.

"Too bad dear old Mom missed the thrill. She started up again, but this time didn't tell the Merchant overlords that she was back in business. Eventually, they found out and you know exactly what they did, don't you?" Madison didn't give me a chance to answer. "They ordered her to cut them in or they'd shut her down. Mom refused and the Merchants gave her up to the police! While she was fucking being arraigned, they hacked her secret accounts and drained them."

I asked, though I could guess, "What happened to you?"

She lifted her shoulders, eyes dull. "Dad paid to get her off, but after the charges were dropped, he was done with her. He invoked a clause in their prenup that left her with nothing... except me. Just like that, I went from penthouses and private schools, to living in a Rockchapel dump. Unfortunately for Mom, she wasn't running any scams after her face ended up on the news. She had no choice but to take a string of dead-end jobs just to make rent. In the end, she fell into depression and killed herself." She jabbed a bloody finger at me. "Your precious Merchants did that to us. They destroyed my life for nothing!"

Madison stood up, lifting her chin high. "When Luca suggested we partner up, he told me about the kind of women that came through his buildings. Alone, on drugs, drunk, with more baby daddies than they can count, and just as twisted up with the Merchants as all the criminals in this city. The Sunshine Agency was his idea, but it was a good one.

"I've lived these kids' lives. I know the hell of crime and poverty. The families I placed them with were the opposite in every way. These parents are wealthy, responsible, stable. They're giving those children everything they could ever want and more. If those mothers really gave a shit about them, they'd give me an award. I did what they couldn't do—give their kids a decent life."

One moment I was six feet away from her. In the next breath, I tackled her to the ground. "How dare you!" My hands were around her throat, throttling her as burning corrosive hate shattered my self-control. "We weren't trash to be thrown away because of money! Because of our pasts! The lives we'd give our children were not less because we couldn't send them to fucking private schools or summer in St. Tropez! How dare you decide I wasn't worthy to love and raise my daughter! How dare you! You crazy, evil bitch," I screamed into her reddening, bulging face.

At that moment, I hated her more than Damien. More than Lyla. More than my father. She handed me the card that destroyed my life and put my daughter in the path of a beast like Luca Adams, and she didn't have the decency to be sorry. I could *kill her*!

And Genny just stood there as I knew she would, letting me deal with the demon who haunted my life from the shadows in my own way.

But not this way. Sense broke through the fog. *Madison has more to answer for now. She has information that will help the men I love. And who knows, maybe after she and I make a video, she'll stab herself in the neck.*

It was an ugly, vicious thought, but I had nothing less for the woman who plotted to sell my child while she was still in my womb.

"Madison." I released her throat and flipped her on her stomach. She sucked in deep lungfuls of air, hacking and choking. "It's too bad you didn't take a hint from your mother about what happens when you piss off the Merchants. Good thing for you, they'll give you a chance to make it up by telling us everything you know about the Brotherhood."

"Never!"

I wrangled her hands behind her back. Genny was there before I said anything, helping me secure her in the zip ties.

"You can't do this," she bleated. "I'm not going with you!"

"You are and so is little Poppy." I hauled her up. "Laurel is going to be so excited when she meets her new puppy."

"I'd die before I betray the Brotherhood." She thrashed like a wild animal in my grip. Genny had to help me keep a hold on her. "Their cause is just. It's right! The Merchants have bred criminals in this city like rats, so they could appoint themselves the judge, jury, and executioner. They don't care how many innocents are ruined to keep their power."

Madison flung her head back. I jerked to the side, nearly catching her skull on my nose. This *sister* was not going down easily.

"They're loyal to nothing and no one," she shrieked. "You Merchants are the crazy, evil bitches. Your precious Cardinals will curse your name, Genevieve Hunt, when one is slaughtered for every day you hold me captive!"

Genny dropped her arm in shock. "What did you say?"

"You heard me. If I disappear, my brothers and sisters will know it was the Merchants. You got a taste of what happens when you defy us. What was that bitch's name? Oh yeah, Bugsy."

I strained to hold on to her. "Genny? Gen, what's wrong? Help me."

"She can't help you. Oh, did *Genny* not tell you that we cleared her bar of the trash? The Cardinals are all enjoying new accommodations with the Brotherhood, and they're not comfortable."

"What?" I whispered, eyes widening. "That's not— You're lying!"

"She knows I'm not."

Genny stood still, her face melding into the tunnel's shadows.

"I'm your only hope," Madison said. "Let me go and surrender to the Brotherhood. If you serve us faithfully, your Cardinals will be released unharmed—"

"Stop listening to her! Genny, grab her arm and help me get her to the car."

Madison shouted over me. "Or you can prove everything I know about you people is true! So much for protecting the women of Harlow. It's the Merchants over everyone else."

"Kenzie," Genevieve rasped. "Let her go."

"You can't be serious." I held even tighter, dragging her back away from Genny. "She doesn't just want to get away with helping the Brotherhood throw Sunny off a bridge and put a bomb in Liam and Tricky's car. She wants you to give yourself up to those bastards. They'll kill you!"

"Of course we'll kill you." Madison's amusement was back. "But only after we've used you to kill the rest of your family. With the Merchants all dead, there's no reason to kill your gangs. The Cardinals will be freed, Hunt. The women you swore to protect. What's it going to be?"

Genny shook with every word. "I said let her go, Kenzie!"

"No! You're grieving and you're not thinking straight. They can't make you choose between your friends and your family. Evil psychopaths that would force such a choice aren't going to keep their word! They'll kill the Cardinals anyway." I moved us back again, chilling under Genny's dead gaze. "Trust me, Genny. We'll get her back and question her. She'll tell us where they're holding the Cardinals."

"No chance of that since I don't know where," Madison breezed. "I just know that we have them."

"Kenzie." Genny took a step. Then another. "It takes strength to put others' needs above your own even while it destroys you. We need that courage to protect the people depending on us." Her speech that day fell from her lips, leadening my bones. "Because there's no forgiveness if we fail."

"Please don't do this. They're your family."

She flinched. "They are my family. The Merchants are the toughest sons of bitches in this whole damn country. I could give the Brotherhood every secret they have and it'll never be enough to take my bros down. They will win this fight, and I'll be back in my borough with my girls—using her brothers and sisters as target practice.

"Let her go, Kenzie. I won't ask again."

I tightened around Madison's wrists, refusing to let go. Genny seized my shoulder and threw me. I hit the ground hard—chest stunned as air fled me.

Madison's smile swirled in my vision, taunting me over the sound of the zip ties snapping.

"Good," she purred, standing my hairs on end. "Now just one more thing.

"Kill her."

"What?" Genny shot away. "No!"

"I said kill her! I won't have this bitch running her mouth about me."

"Hey, dumbass." I pushed up on shaky knees. "My sister. And my boyfriend. And the Forbises. And their lawyers know all about you. Even if you kill me, the truth is out."

Madison flushed a nasty purple. "Kill her!" She snatched up her dog's leash and shoved it at her. "Strangle her. Do it now, or those biker bimbos—"

Genny flashed. She snapped the leash around Madison's bruised throat and knocked their foreheads getting in her face. "You don't give me orders, bitch. If anyone dies here today, it'll be you, so *don't tempt me.*"

She shoved Madison away, and turned on me. "But still, I can't have you following us. You'll tell my brothers where I am, and they'll bust in with some cowboy shit before I can get my girls out of this." Genny advanced on me. "I'm sorry, Kenzie."

"No, Gen, wait— No!"

The last thing I saw was her fist flying at my face.

***

Poppy, my busted nose, and I trudged out of the elevator. The door flew open as I reached for the knob.

"Yes, Thatcher. She's here."

"Sun—"

He grabbed me around the waist, carrying me inside to the waiting horde. Thatcher's alert went out to the whole building.

"Oh my gosh."

"Kenzie, are you okay?"

"Who did this to you?" Liam demanded.

"When I get my fucking hands on them," Sunny barked over Lizzie's giggling. "I'll kill them!"

Bane shoved through them both. "What happened?"

"Uh, well." My voice was barely above a croak. "Good news first: We have a dog now." I tried for a smile and didn't get one back. "She's actually quite friendly, which is good because I didn't feel right leaving her at a shelter. Plus, she deserves much better than her current owner—"

"Forget about the animal!" Sunny took Poppy and promptly handed her to Elizabeth. The little girl ran off squealing happily. Good. I didn't want her to hear the bad news. "Who did this?"

I flicked over their heads, landing on Sienna. She raised her brows—questioning. Meeting her gaze, I smiled.

"It worked," I said, grinning though it hurt something fierce. "The plan worked."

"What plan?" Fuller asked.

"I should start from the beginning." I moved around them and eased my-self onto the couch. I'd be sore all over in the morning. "Sienna discovered who was putting the trackers in your clothes."

"Wait. What?" Sunny dropped next to me. "Why am I just now hearing this?"

"Because Genny was grieving and beating herself up. I wanted her to be the first to know it wasn't all a waste. It turned out to be Madison James. She..." I told them the entire story from the day she handed me that card, to the Forbises and the discovery of the Sunshine Adoption Agency.

"After I told Genny all of this, she finally told me the truth," I continued. "The Brotherhood stormed Barbarella's and abducted the Cardinals. Bugsy— I mean, Laura's death and the horrible way we found out about it was punishment for not obeying their first order to denounce Vito's video."

"Holy shit," Bane breathed, rubbing his head. "How did we miss this? Why didn't she tell us?"

"Because your violent, frustrating, wonderful sister does everything to protect the people she cares about. She couldn't accept that she failed. And I couldn't either. So, Genny, Sienna, and I came up with a plan—"

"There are many people missing from that list," Liam said, voice hard. "Three to be exact."

I shook my head. "Too many things could've gone wrong. We agreed not to tell you beforehand in case you behaved like—these are Genny's words—condescending jackasses."

Liam, Bane, and Sunny geared up to say something about that until Fuller broke in. "I don't quite understand. What did you two do? And what happened to your face?"

"Genevieve Hunt happened to my face." Sienna passed me some tissues. "We had to confront Madison. After the disgusting and horrible ways they punished her for disobeying them, I knew Madison would use the Cardinals to bargain for freedom. I also guessed that if she was clever as she proved she was, she'd realize their little tracking plan was over.

"There's no way they'd sneak something like that on you guys again, so the Brotherhood needed a new money-printing machine. What better way to control you than by doing exactly what they're doing to Genny? Holding someone you love hostage."

Liam held up a hand, his jaw clenching. "Hold on. Are you telling us that Genny is being held captive by the Brotherhood right now? The same people who shot, bombed, and threw her friend's mangled body at her feet!"

Goodness, when you say it like that. "Yes. That was the plan."

They were up so fast they blew me back against the couch.

"Fuller, watch Elizabeth, please," Liam said. "Don't let her get too attached to that dog, because we're finding her owner and my sister. Now."

"Wait—"

"Where did you last see her?" Bane asked. "How long ago?"

"If you just listen—"

Grasping my chin, Sunny smooched me. "I love you, baby, but this was a terrible plan."

"I'm seeing where the condescending part comes in," I snapped. "If you all would just listen for a second, you'd realize neither of us is so stupid that we'd let her skip into the Brotherhood's lair without assurance she could get out!"

The three of them stopped in their tracks.

"What does that mean?" Liam said.

I flicked to Sunny. "You said something very accurate the other night. There are lots of places to put a tracker."

"You're kidding," Bane said. "Genny's wearing a tracker?"

"And now we get to the part where you take back everything you said and tell your girlfriend she's a genius. I figured if the Brotherhood's happy to track us, we'd give it back just as hard. Madison's going to take her back to the boss to show off their new prize." I held up my phone. "GPS says they're still driving in circles around Rockchapel. Once Madison thinks they lost any tail, we'll know exactly where the Brotherhood is holding up."

Liam claimed my phone, squinting at the screen. "What if they find the tracker? They're going to search her—twice. Then a third time."

"We thought of that. They'll dump her phone for sure. They might even take her shoes and make her change clothes, but there's one thing no one thinks to take from a woman."

"Which is?" Sunny asked.

Sienna tossed her arm around me. "Tampons." She beamed. "My idea."

"Ah," the brothers said, all looking vaguely uncomfortable. But neither one said we were wrong.

"So." Folding my arms, I stared them down. "I'll hear it now."

"Kenzie 'Candy Nipples' Blaine," Sunny said, grinning that grin. "You're a genius."

"You deserve more praise than I can express," Liam spoke up. "The car stopped moving, and this location is very familiar to me.

"We know where the Brotherhood is."

***

Genny

"Move." A hard shove propelled me forward.

I gritted my teeth, swallowing the urge to bloody my knuckles on Madison's face. She was only getting so bold because we were finally in the Brotherhood's hideout.

My gaze swept over the long hall of nothing. Madison was smart enough to stick me in the trunk for the drive. She let me out in a parking garage, then prodded me into the hallway we were walking down.

A lone figure stood at the end, waiting silently beside the only door in the hall. I studied him but couldn't place his face among my long list of enemies. Dark hair, tall, average build, average height. I bet his mother couldn't place him among all the mediocre gang fodder.

"Stop there."

I took another step just to be cheeky, smirking at him all the way.

"Arms up."

"There's no hiding anything in this outfit," I breezed. "That's kind of the point."

"Shut up!" Madison ordered. It was hard to believe a short while ago, she was playing Lyla's simpering minion. Of course I never suspected her of being the rat. I didn't look twice at Madison James.

The guard patted me down a little too thoroughly. He snapped back when he hit my back pocket. "What is that? Take it out slowly."

"Relax," I said, rolling my eyes. "It can't hurt you."

I pulled out the tampon—my face effortlessly neutral. The stupid idiot grabbed and squinted at it like he didn't know what he was looking at.

"You can confiscate the oh so dangerous tampon if you want, but between you and me, it's about that time when I need it."

He grimaced. "Whatever."

I was still the kind of woman who didn't share, but I seriously considered making an exception for Mackenzie Blaine when the fool put my tampon/tracker back in my hands.

"You will be allowed inside," he began. "The rules are as follows: no vulgar language, no disrespect, do not speak before you're addressed, do not sit unless invited to do so, do not make threats, do not speak positively of the tyrant organization known as the Merchants. Do you understand these rules?"

"Do I look like a preschooler? Go give someone else a fucking comprehension test and let me in the damn room."

A hard blow struck my back, dropping me to one knee. I slowly twisted, burning her with a look that made her step back. "When I get out of here, you're first."

"You're never getting out of here."

"You," I hissed. "Are. First."

Madison pressed trembling lips together. Good. She was learning.

A knock sounded from the other side of the door.

"You may enter now," said the guard. "Remember the rules, Merchant scum."

And you're second, I thought as he swung the door open.

I inched inside the front room. There was nothing else for me to call the space. Concrete gave way to hardwood floors topped with a small area rug, leather couches, an ottoman, and a coffee table. An entrance peeked from the other side of the furniture. I made my way to it.

"Good evening, Genevieve Hunt."

Whipping around, I fell on a person reclined on an armchair in the corner behind the door, tucked inside the shadows.

"I'm honored you could join us."

"Who are you?"

He stood, revealing inch by inch another face I didn't know—though a pleasant one if you went for the sexy, silver-fox thing. Silver salted his not-so-pepper mustache and beard. The same gray streaks swirled through his locks, granting him a look both distinguished and fake. You could almost believe he dyed it to achieve that whirlwind of ebony and silver.

Light brown eyes tracked my retreat as mine tracked his approach. He wasn't getting close to me until I was packing more than a tampon.

"We're very happy to have you with us, Miss Hunt. Though you may not see it now, you're going to help us free the chains around Cinco City and lead it to greatness."

"That sounds great, Mister..." I trailed off pointedly.

He smiled like I amused him. "But of course, where are my manners?" The man bowed to me of all things. "I go by many names, but there's only one that suits me within these halls.

"Call me Brother Abraham."

Chapter One

Sunny drove like a madman, blasting Masie over curbs, whipping her around corners, and sideswiping every side-view mirror that dared to jump in his way. All of a sudden, he didn't give a shit about the super-expensive first love-of-his-life. All that mattered was getting to Genny.

"Turn here," I cried, jabbing my phone screen. "We're half a mile away."

I pressed my face against the window, squinting at my surroundings.

Foster care took me and Sienna to a bunch of different homes around Cinco City, more than a few of them in Rockchapel, but I didn't recognize this part of town at all. "Where are we, Sienna?" I asked my sister, who was bumping and holding on for dear life in the backseat. "Do you know?"

"I know this is the part of town Diana told us to never set foot in. She wouldn't even let cab drivers cut through here as a shortcut. Remember?"

A vague memory of our old and kind foster mom, yelling at a cabbie for turning down the wrong street, flitted through my mind. I remembered her telling us, after she made him pop a U-turn, that there was nothing to be found in this part of town except trouble. No decent people loitered here. Even those unfortunate enough to live here found excuses not to go home until exhaustion left them no choice.

I watched the blue dot on the screen getting ever closer. *How fitting the worst people in Cinco were hiding in the worst place in Cinco.*

Sunny whipped around the final corner, and our destination loomed before us.

I frowned. "A movie theater?"

"Yes," Sunny ground out, his expression graver than ever. "The movie theater. I should've known."

Our three cars screeched into the empty parking lot. The five of us tumbled out, Sienna included even though I barked at her to stay.

"I'm not letting you guys go in there alone," Sienna returned. "She's my friend too."

"No one stays behind." Bane tossed Sienna a gun that she fumbled, squawking as the thing bounced from palm to palm. "We need all the firepower we can get."

"Point and shoot, Bestie," Sunny told Sienna. He pulled me close even as he put a gun in my hand too. "Point and shoot."

"Guys, are we sure about this?" I voiced it because I had to. Someone had to. "Bursting in there guns blazing. Won't that put Genny in danger?" I wasn't sure Sunny, Liam, or Bane heard me as they fanned around the peeling cardinal-painted double doors. "You're the ones who told me you don't bust in blind to an assassin's lair."

"And you're the one who said Genny offered herself up to these bastards knowing they held all the cards." Liam's eyes were hard. "Besides, we're not going in blind."

My lips parted to ask what he meant when he jerked his chin at Bane. "Let's go."

Bane busted in the doors, running in gun up with Sunny and Liam bolting inside after him. I threw my arm up, holding Sienna back until I heard—

"It's clear," Bane called. "Come in."

Slowly, Sienna and I did. We crept in—me holding the gun up and steady, and her rattling the weapon like a jumping bean as her hands shook.

We entered the darkened, gloomy space, and a chill went up my spine. It wasn't because it was old—because it was that. And it wasn't because the movie theater was abandoned—because it was that too.

I shivered because it was... *wrong*.

Old, faded, moldy horror movie posters hung in their lighted display cases. Upturned buckets of popcorn littered the floor as if their owners had suddenly dropped them in their haste to leave. Spread out beneath my boots, the worn burgundy carpet boasted a strange, swirling, repeating design that vaguely formed the shape of an eyeball.

"Sunny, stay with Mackenzie and Sienna," I heard Liam say.

I frowned, drawing closer to the movie posters.

"Bane and I will check the theaters."

I opened my mouth. "Guys—"

"You won't need to," Sienna said, dropping her gun.

"You see it too," I rasped as she fell in next to me.

Sienna nodded, lips trembling as she stared where I stared.

"What?" Liam cried, running over. "See what?"

"The posters." I pointed. "Why are they lit up? Why pay the electric bill for this dead, abandoned place only to light up these posters, and *why* these five posters? They're all horror movies."

Bane and Sunny slowly lowered their guns, coming over to see what I was talking about, but I could tell by the looks on their faces that understanding wasn't dawning.

"The monsters," I hinted. "The monsters or the evil that was fought in these movies. Do you see?"

"You're going to have to help me out, gorgeous," Sunny said. "I don't watch horror movies."

"Me either," said Liam.

"Same," Bane agreed.

That mildly surprised me but it probably shouldn't. Their lives were already steeped in blood, gore, violence, and the evil of mankind. Of course they didn't want to deal with it in their off-time.

"Okay, well then, I'm sorry," I said softly, squeezing Sunny's hand, "but in *Pan's Labyrinth*, there's a monster who's uniquely known for having eyes on his hands, not his face." I pointed to the next poster. "In that movie, everyone is under attack by a large swarm of killer bees."

"In this one," Sienna said, taking over. "The main guy is tormented by horrible, gruesome visions until he loses his mind and kills himself. And in this one"—Sienna's hand fell on the case holding a sinister poster of a wickedly grinning woman—"there's a family of doppelgangers who are secretly killing their counterparts one by one and taking over their lives."

"That's right. So if we put all that together, we have..." My shaking finger moved through the air. "Eye. Bee. See. And—"

"You," Sunny rasped, his knuckles whitening on the gun handle. "I'll be seeing you." And then Sunny shuddered too, feeling the same creepy wrongness in this space that I felt immediately.

"I'll be seeing you?" Liam repeated, his gun slowly coming up and leveling at the posters like he wanted to blow away their disturbing message. "Are you sure? It could be coincidence."

"I don't think so." Sienna backed away, slipping her hand in mine. "It's like my sister said. Why waste money running electricity to this building just to keep these poster lights on?"

"They're running electricity to this building because it's their hideout." Bane whipped around, eagle eyes scanning the gloom. "They're here somewhere according to the tracker. We need to spread out and look for any sign of them."

"Yeah," Sunny agreed, although he didn't look away from the posters. "For all we know, our folks put these posters up. Not those bastards. Plus, I didn't see *Get Out* and even I know the bad guys in that movie were a bunch of racist, body-jacking shitheads," he said, speaking of the final poster. "How does that fit into their message?"

I jumped on two words. "Your folks?"

"That's how we know this place." Liam's voice reached me through the dark. "There used to be apartments in this very spot, but they were torn down and the movie theater was built in its place. That apartment building was once our mother's home."

My brows shot up.

"She lived here when she met our dads, and then they kidnapped her away from all of this."

"Kidnapped?" Sienna asked absentmindedly. She was still staring at the *Get Out* poster.

"Oh, yeah," Bane chimed in. "Mom likes to very heavily emphasize that her first date with our dads was them kidnapping and putting her in a cage because she witnessed them committing murder. And after she says that, they all bust up laughing.

"Bunch of weirdos," he muttered, almost making me laugh.

Almost.

I rubbed my arms, somehow warding off a chill in the stuffy, overheated room. There were a million eyes on the floor, and it felt like they were all watching me. I knew I should be searching with the guys, but I didn't want to move too far from Sienna, and Sienna wasn't moving at all.

"Sienna?" I probed, but she didn't look away.

"Our parents bought the property and built this movie theater on it," Sunny continued the story as he slowly opened the theater door and shone his phone light inside. "It was a part of their effort to help the old neighborhood. Breathe life into it. Make it a safe place to live again."

"But it didn't work." I didn't make it a question, because it wasn't one. This building wouldn't be standing empty in a neighborhood I was always warned to avoid if it had worked.

"No," Bane confirmed. "A local gang started running a drug ring out of the place. Slip a few baggies in with the popcorn. Slide a couple bills in a dark theater. Plenty of people coming and going and all of them having a legit reason to be there. After all, officer, we were just watching a movie."

I shook my head. There was something criminally ingenious about that.

"All the employees were being threatened. They were too scared to tell my mom what was going on, but she found out real quick when rival gang members blew into the place and shot it up. Ten people were killed."

"Holy shit," I cried, clapping a hand over my mouth. "How come I've never heard about this?"

"It was before you were born." Bane ducked around the concession stand, gaze sweeping over stale and ancient candy. "I was three, but I remember that night. Mom came home crying harder than I'd ever seen her. She blamed herself."

"Why would she blame herself?" I tugged on Sienna's hand, silently urging her to help with the search.

She didn't move.

"Because no one was dealing drugs, being threatened, or getting shot when the place was just a run-down apartment building. She tried to help her old neighborhood and instead she kicked off one of its greatest tragedies. Or at least that's how she saw it." Bane sighed, backing out from behind the counter. "This place has been closed ever since."

"I see." My voice was flat. Dead. "That's why the Brotherhood chose this place."

"What do you mean?" Sunny asked, shutting the door on the empty theater.

"This place wasn't just owned by your parents. It's also a monument to their failure." I tossed my head. "Failure by the Brotherhood's standards. Of course, it wasn't Adeline's fault, but I bet in their eyes, this place is proof that everything the Merchants touch turns to ruin. It's proof they're bad for the city."

"Yes, Kenzie." The shadows released Liam, allowing him to step into the circle of dim light. "And that's why I should've figured it out and raided this place before. Now that we know, it's so cringingly obvious."

I could only nod. It was true. Now that I knew the backstory of this theater, it was obvious why the Brotherhood holed up in this place. This hideout, like everything they did, was a fuck-you to the Merchants.

"There are more theaters to check," Liam continued. "Plus the projection rooms and offices upstairs. The tracker says Genny is in here somewhere, so, Bane, you go with Sienna. Sunny, search with Kenzie. Anything moves, you shoot—"

"No!" Sienna burst out.

I jumped half out of my skin. "Sienna? What's wrong? What—?"

"This poster is a message." Sienna launched at it, scrabbling at the sides to pry it open. "Yes, the bad guys in *Get Out* are a bunch of racist, piece-of-shit pricks who think black bodies are objects for them to use, buy, and trade, but don't you see?" she cried. "In the Brotherhood's twisted minds, *we* are the bad guys!

"The Merchants are the fake, smiling folk who pretend to be nice and harmless, while all the while, they're gutting innocent people from the inside out and using them as pawns." Sienna finally found the latch and smashed it with the butt of her gun. "So if we're the bad guys"—*bang*—"and they're the good guys"—*bang*—"how does our movie end?"

Eyes bulging, I jumped on Sienna's train of thought. "With us dead and defeated, and the hero escaping the—"

Sienna broke the lock and threw open the case. Tearing off the poster, she revealed its hidden secret in all its horrible glory.

A myriad of green wires connected bits and bobs I couldn't name, but nestled within them was one thing I could—a tampon. It rested on the bomb, mocking us loud and proudly as the device ticked down the final eight seconds on the clock.

"TRAP!"

A hand, I didn't know whose, hooked around my waist.

"RUN!"

The world spun as one of the guys threw me over his shoulder. All I could do was scream Sienna's name as he bolted, racing for the exit.

Stabbing sunlight attacked and blinded me, washing the world in white light. Was Sienna behind us? Was Bane, Liam, or Sunny? Did they get out?!

In a blink we were flying. Crashing down behind Masie, pain jangled through my bones as we hit the ground hard.

"SIEN—!"

BOOM!

Chapter Two

I held Sienna tight, squeezing the stuffing out of her. I hadn't let her go since she grabbed my hand and picked me out of the rubble—both of us crying, shouting, and hugging each other over the ringing in our ears.

An hour later, we were in Sunny's apartment. There was nothing else to do but leave. The police would be on their way, and the last thing we needed was for them to find us at the site of a bombing.

I held Sienna tighter as my mind flashed back to my sister ripping the covering off a bomb. She was so close. *We* were all so close to being the next tragedy in that dark, gloomy, abandoned place.

I flicked to Laurel, who was sleeping peacefully in her playpen. That was the only reason I wasn't hugging and holding her too.

Out on the balcony, Sunny, Liam, and Bane argued—loudly if their lined faces and wild gesticulating were anything to go by.

I could've been out there with them, but I stayed in the living room with my sister and my baby. I could guess what they were arguing about—*me.*

I dropped my head on Sienna's shoulder, eyes squeezing shut. They didn't have to talk outside to spare my feelings. My mind was already shouting with the truth. I thought I was a clever, badass Merchant who was ready to run with the big guns. So clever, I convinced Genny to walk into the lion's den with nothing but a fucking tampon.

"I'm so stupid," I whispered, making Sienna squeeze me tighter.

"Mackenzie."

I shot up, heart pounding as I locked eyes with Adeline Redgrave—the real clever badass queen of Cinco City. The one who managed to keep her family safe for over thirty years... until I came along.

"Mackenzie." Adeline pulled up an ottoman and sat next to me. "Can we talk?"

"Uhh..." Behind her, Adeline's husbands headed out to the balcony. "Yes, of course."

Adeline's smile was kind, but it didn't touch the seriousness behind her eyes. "What happened today?" she asked, bluntly getting to the point as any mother would. "Where is my daughter?"

I couldn't hide anything from her, so I didn't. I told her everything from telling Genny all about Madison, coming up with the tampon plan, confronting Madison in the park and provoking her to take Genny to the Brotherhood's leadership, and then walking into a big fucking trap and running out with no Genny, no clues, and no idea what to do next.

Adeline hummed, sitting back in her seat. For the life of me, I couldn't tell what she was thinking. "Was there any proof Genny was ever in that movie theater?"

I blinked. "What?"

"Abandoned buildings in the middle of busy cities don't make for good hiding places," she said. "Especially not one that's been closed for over twenty years. People would notice if strange, shadowy figures were going in and out of it all of a sudden."

"Well, I... Yes, I guess that's true."

"I don't believe Genny was ever in that building, so if you're beating yourself up thinking she may have been inside when it blew... Don't." Adeline took my hand. "She's safe, Kenzie. I know it."

"How do you know?" My voice was small.

"Because of what you've just told me. From what you've said, this Madison girl isn't the brightest bulb in the box. She made herself the face, and therefore the fall guy, of a major kidnapping and trafficking ring. She fraudulently adopted out kidnapped children, and then posed in their family portraits—giving all of them a photo and description to hand over to the cops. She's an idiot," Adeline dropped. "But whoever she's working for isn't.

"I believe that Madison drove Genny to the true hideout of the Brotherhood, and it was within that hideout that the real brains realized that if you can hide a tracker in a button, you can most certainly hide one in a tampon.

"Panicking, they handed the tampon off to one of their people and ordered them to take it to the movie theater and arm the bomb so that whoever was following that tracker—"

"—wouldn't live to tell anyone about it," Sienna finished, lifting her head. "That trap wasn't new. That's why there was still dust and cobwebs on everything. The Brotherhood must've booby-trapped it a long time ago, knowing it was an old Merchant property."

She inclined her head. "Exactly. But that old horror isn't my concern. What I need to know is—"

"—what was the first stop Madison made?" I blurted, understanding slapping me over the head. "Not the last one. The first stop on the map was the Brotherhood hideout!"

"Do you remember what it was?"

"I— I uh— I need to see a map." I jumped up, snatching my phone off the coffee table. The screen was cracked from having to break my fall, but I didn't let that slow me down.

I hunched over the map of Cinco City, scouring my memory as thoroughly as I scoured all streets, lanes, and roundabouts in Rockchapel.

Sliding metal, and then footsteps sounded behind me. Liam, Bane, Sunny, and their fathers reentered the room.

"What's going on?" a deep voice asked. "Have you found Genny?"

"Not yet, but Mackenzie will," Adeline replied, speaking like it was a certainty. I wasn't going to let her down, and Hera knew I refused to.

Come on, Blaine, think. Madison was driving in circles for a long time, clearly trying to shake off the tail that was sitting right next to her. Where did she stop before the blue dot went racing to the movie theater? Where...?

My brows crumpled.

"What?" Sunny seized, dropping down next to me. "What is it, baby? What did you remember?"

"I remember... that Madison did make a stop," I said slowly. "For like twenty minutes while I was still in the cab driving from the park. But I didn't think anything of it because—"

"Because what?" Killian Hunt, Genny's dad, demanded. "If she stopped for twenty minutes, why wouldn't you think anything of it?"

"Because she stopped at a gas station." I lifted my head, meeting the heavy, intense stares bearing down on me. "I assumed she was fueling before driving in more circles around the city."

"No, my dear." Adeline shared a look with her husbands. "It's the gas station. That's the hideout."

I had to ask. "How do you know?"

"Because a gas station is everything an empty abandoned movie theater isn't."

"It's perfect," Liam hissed. "Gas stations have random people going in and out at all hours of the day. Even better, those people are always in a hurry. They don't know who's standing at the pump next to them, and they don't care. Who's going to notice a couple members of the Brotherhood?"

My stomach twisted. "Wow. That's... wow." Genny was right. If I was going to survive in this world, I needed to learn to out-think vicious, soulless criminals. Sweet, innocent, naïve Mackenzie wasn't going to cut it.

"Kenzie." Liam dropped down next to me. "Please tell me you remember which gas station it is."

"I do," I said, loosening half a dozen shoulders with two words. "I remember because it's close to Banana Tree, and I thought what a weird coincidence that was." I winced. "Another lesson for me to learn. There's no such thing as coincidence when it comes to the Brotherhood."

Liam handled my phone like the harsh breath could break it. Squinting, he pointed where I pointed on the map before handing it to his mother.

"Okay." Adeline rose from her seat. She was still the picture of calm even though I knew inside she was raging. "We've underestimated this enemy for far too long. We have to accept that, one, they're in the middle of clearing out this hideout—if they haven't already. Two, they'll leave more exploding surprises for anyone who busts in after them, and three, they've already moved Genny to another location."

"What?" I deflated like a burst balloon. "Genny's not there either? Oh no, this is all my fault. I was so stupid, sending her in there alone with a frickin' tampon." It was a sleeping Laurel that stopped me from screaming, and saying worse. "If I hadn't sent you guys racing in the wrong direction, we could've gotten to her in time, and Masie wouldn't be a burning hunk of metal in an abandoned parking lot!"

"Babe, easy." Sunny kissed my cheek. "None of this is your fault. You didn't send Genny anywhere. She chose to go, and it's because of you two that we know where one of their hideouts is. Cleared out or not, it'll have hints that will tell us more about who these fucks are. Maybe even where they've gone next."

"He's right," Saint said. "This is a victory, not a failure. You're forgetting, Little Blaine, that our Genny is dangerous with or without a weapon. With or without backup." Saint aimed a smirk out the window and into the distance. "Right now, those bastards are scrambling. They're scuttling out of their hole like the cockroaches they are, they're making mistakes, and they're doing it all under Genny's watchful eye."

Adeline smiled at her husband, taking comfort in the words meant to do just that. "This Brotherhood took the Cardinals and now Genny because they're done playing around. Every strike they've made against our family has failed, and now they're determined not to make any more mistakes." Adeline looked her sons in the eye. "I assume you boys know what to do."

The look Sunny gave me was sweet and comforting, but the grin he sent his mother was nothing but wicked. "Mumsy, this is why you kept spitting out rejects until you birthed perfection." Sunny held out his hands. "I'm your favorite for a reason, and you'll remember that reason when Genny and I stroll in carrying that Abraham fucker's head in a bag."

Adeline fondly patted his cheek. "That's my boy."

"Seriously, Mom?" Bane deadpanned. "Not even going to speak up for the rejects."

She laughed. "Come now, you know your baby brother likes to be silly. You two are my precious and perfect boys," she said, snagging their collars and towing them in for two big, flush-inducing smooches. "I'm counting on you both to watch Sunny's back out there, especially because he thinks I haven't noticed he hurt his shoulder."

"What?" I cried, shooting up.

"His shoulder?"

"He's hurt?"

"How?"

"When?"

The questions were coming hot and fast from everyone except Adeline, and surprisingly, Sienna. Sunny's grin wiped away as he stepped back from the crowd converging on him.

"I forgot your eagle eyes," Sunny gritted, rubbing his shoulder. "I swear you could see around corners when we were growing up."

Adeline was wholly unrepentant. "Tell them."

He sighed. "You tell them. Apparently you already know."

"I know you pop pain pills and grimace in corners when you think no one's looking."

My brows rose with every word.

"But I don't know why," Adeline finished. "Fill in the blanks, Sunny."

"Sunny?" Hurt laced my voice. "What's going on? When did you hurt your shoulder? Was it when you carried me out of the theater?"

"No, love, it wasn't you and it wasn't today. It's just a lingering injury from that little tumble I took off an overpass," he said, "and it's fine. I'm taking care of it, so let's all worry about the member of the family who *isn't* fine."

"Let's *all* make it through this fight in one piece," Adeline said. "Together. As a family who has each other's backs. You all have had run-ins with members of the Brotherhood. You know this enemy better than we do, so I'm trusting you to take charge and get your sister back."

"It's in hand, Mother." Liam didn't look up from his phone, or mine. "I've already got my men en route to that gas station. This'll be over before you know it."

"It'll be over in twenty-four hours," she smoothly corrected. "That's how long you have until I expect my daughter here and in my arms. If she's not, I'm taking over."

With that, Adeline swept out of the room, taking her band of husbands—each as gorgeous as the last—with her.

I flicked to the door she walked out of, and the expression on my guys' faces. "What? What's wrong?"

"Nothing's wrong," Liam said, moving to Laurel. He fixed her bunched-up blanket and gently smoothed down her curls. "It would just be best that we meet that deadline and get Genny back. Obviously, the situation was already urgent, but now it's more so."

"Why?" Sienna asked. "Because Adeline said she'd take over if we don't? Is that a bad thing?"

Sunny stroked the back of his neck, drawing my eye to the shoulder he never told me was injured. "Bestie, do you remember reading about that city-wide riot that left hundreds of people dead, caused billions in property damage, and caused such a breakdown in peace and government, the National Guard had to be called to restore order again, and again, and again."

"Um, yeah...?"

Sunny flashed her a smile that didn't reach his eyes. "That was our mother playing nicely. She'll make the Night of Tears seem like a children's tea party if we don't get that woman her daughter back.

"There won't be a single blade of grass in Cinco City left standing."

"I see," I whispered. I went over to Laurel too, reassuring myself she was still safe, whole, and perfect. "Well then, we'd better get that woman her daughter back."

***

Genny

I counted the bumps and the turns in the road, still trying to memorize our path from that freaky gas station even though I lost my way a long time ago.

After Madison dragged me through the gas station shop and into the back room, I readied to fight that bitch and put her down hard. Wherever she was bringing me, it couldn't be good.

But then she opened a door that led down, down, down to a long hallway and a solitary door at the end of it... and that door led to Brother Abraham.

He'd only just invited me to sit in that swanky underground lair of his when he noticed the tampon sticking out of my back pocket.

I didn't try to hide it because hidden things are automatically suspicious, but my attempt at reverse psychology didn't work. He *politely* asked me to hand it over, and then I had to watch as he popped the top and got an eyeful of the tracker.

He wasn't even angry—as long as you didn't consider calmly getting up, opening the door, and shooting Madison James in the face as angry.

Even my jaw dropped and eyes bulged when her scream abruptly ended with her body hitting the ground. Abraham didn't yell. He didn't shout. He didn't give her a chance to explain. And he didn't lose his bland, pleasant smile.

He just killed her.

So this is the man Vito was so terrified of, he stabbed himself in the neck rather than face his wrath.

Looking at that smiling psychopath right then... I understood Vito's final actions completely.

"Quickly, get this to the theater," he ordered his guard. "You know what to do."

The man stepped over Madison's body and took off without a word.

"You killed her," I said, voice drained of emotion. "Why? It wasn't her fault."

"I must disagree with you on that point, Miss Genevieve." Abraham flicked an imaginary speck of dust off his lapel. "She brought you here even though she wasn't given instructions to do so, and she was silly enough not to realize here was exactly where you and your tracker wanted to be.

"A foolish mistake, and I don't abide mistakes in my Brotherhood."

I hummed, reclining in my seat. I wasn't afraid of him and I wasn't going to pretend I was just to stroke his sociopathic ego. "Since you don't want me here, I guess that means the next bullet is for me."

"For you?" His forehead crumpled, giving the perfect resemblance of a human emotion. "Of course not. You are my guest—uninvited or not—and I wouldn't dream of treating you so brutishly." Abraham leveled the gun between my eyes, his own glinting with undisguised malice. "That is, of course, as long as you quickly and quietly walk out that door and into the waiting van without any trouble. Any attempt to scream or signal someone, and I shoot you and them. Understood?"

I rolled my eyes. Again with the pointless comprehension tests? I understood just fine when a psycho's pointing a gun at my head.

Fast-forward an hour, maybe even two hours later, I was rattling around in a darkened van with a cloth sack over my head. I was trying to chart our route, but if Abraham was smart, he'd be driving around in circles to disorient me.

And I had no trouble believing he was smart.

Eventually, the van slowed and then rumbled to a stop. The next thing I knew, the back doors flew open. Abraham and two men in suits stood on a red-dirt path with a backdrop of trees spreading out behind them.

We were outside the city, that wasn't in question, but where exactly? There were hundreds of mansions and cabins nestled in the forest surrounding Cinco City. I knew because Bane dragged me around to check out half of them when he was scoping out the perfect hermit's retreat.

"Step out, please, Miss Genevieve." Amazing that Abraham was still playing the wholesome gentleman act while his two goons had guns trained on me. "Walk with me."

I eyed him, and only him. The goons didn't worry me. They were basically oversized action figures. They'd only move by his power.

Abraham lifted his chin and gazed right back at me, his vision never wavering—his dark, fathomless pools giving nothing away.

People who just met me assumed I was loud, brash, and impulsive. I struck first and considered the consequences later. But someone like that didn't become the ruler of the second-most dangerous borough of Cinco, and then lived to tell about it.

I had to be hard, and I had to be violent, but I also had to be smart. I needed to assess every situation and have an exit strategy—or five—for when it inevitably went wrong.

I was assessing then. Calculating my odds of getting home with no weapons, no backup, no Cardinals, miles from home, and in the presence of a trigger-happy maniac bearing a psychotic grudge against my family, even though we didn't fucking know this prick.

Exit Strategy: Still Pending

Meeting his dead eyes, I beamed wide. "I'd love to walk with you, and after we're finished, do you think we could take a stroll over to my Cardinals? I'd love to see how they're doing."

"Of course," he replied, beaming right back. "They're eager to see you too, but, if I may, I must gently correct you. They're not *your Cardinals* because your illegal and oppressive little biker gang is hereby disbanded."

"It's a biker gang, not a *little* biker gang," I corrected right back, still smiling like a loon. "I don't know what it is with men, always having to call what a woman does... little."

Abraham's brows shot together, then smoothed out just as quickly. "Forgive me, Miss Genevieve, you're absolutely right to correct me. It was rude of me to downplay your business, and the effort you spent building it. It is never my intention to treat a woman as anything less than my equal. Especially not a woman such as you. I underestimate many people, but you will never be one of them." He bowed his head. "I apologize."

It was everything in me not to spit on his hair. His polite routine grated on my soul like a chainsaw. Never did I think I'd miss the misogynistic bastards who called me a cunt to my face. Anything was better than hiding their true hatred behind a plastic smile.

Saying nothing, I stepped out of the van and fell in beside Abraham, with two guns pointed at my skull.

"Stay here," Abraham ordered the goons. "She won't try anything."

My fist ached to punch the certainty out of him, but I didn't make a move. He was right. I wasn't going to try anything when there was a chance to save my Cardinals. After what they did to Laura, I wasn't letting them spend another day in the hands of this madman.

Abraham set off into the trees, expecting me to follow. I did with a scrutinizing glance behind me, taking in the modest, but pretty two-story house tucked away in its own part of the woods.

Heavy black curtains blocked out all the windows, and every inch of it was painted in different shades of brown. Even so, there was a nice wraparound porch boasting comfy chairs for those nights sitting out among the stars and the singing cicadas. No one passing by would ever guess there was evil lurking behind that beige door.

"I'm sure you have questions, Miss Genevieve." Abraham walked strange and stiff-backed with his hands folded behind his back and his chin pointed at the sky. I wasn't sure what persona he was going for, but all I was getting was stuck-up butler. "Ask them."

"It's Genny." I walked four feet behind him, keeping one eye on him and the other on the coming trap. And yes, I was certain it was coming.

The guy said himself he didn't want me here. Madison took the bait and offered me up to Abraham, because the discovery of the trackers in our clothes made her useless. She thought she could score points by offering up a high-value hostage, and instead she scored a bullet in the face.

So now what? If he doesn't think I'm useful to him and he can't let me go, what option does that leave him, the insane fucker? My eyes fell on the gun comfortably tucked in his waistband. *Only one.*

"Only the woman who bore me gets to call me Genevieve, and unless you brought me out here to share some shocking news, that's not you."

Abraham chuckled. "Ah yes, your mother, the Adeline Redgrave. Everything comes back to her in the end."

"I don't think it does." My tone was even. "But if you want a question, here's one: why do you think everything comes back to her? My family doesn't even know you. My mother doesn't know you."

"No, she doesn't, and that's the biggest insult," he replied, a hard edge bleeding into his voice. "She ruined my life, and she doesn't even know who the fuck I am."

I rolled my eyes behind his back. Here it comes, I'd heard it all before. The boo-hoo sob story about how my mother spilling the ledger's secrets, and getting his mommy or daddy locked up ruined his life and that was all Adeline's fault. Because naturally, it wasn't his parents' fault for being a loathsome fucking criminal—oh no! As always the bullet of blame is aimed at the messenger.

"How did she ruin your life?" I asked, not even trying to tamp down my boredom. All of our enemies play at being big and bad, but at the end of the day, they're basic.

"I'm sure you know the story." Abraham looked straight ahead, adjusting his gait only once to step over a raised root. "I'm sure your parents told it over dinner every other night while you all laughed and applauded your mother, the great hero. The one who took down Corbin Dumont."

I frowned, slowing a beat. *Corbin Dumont?*

"See?"

I snapped up to find Abraham staring at me.

"I knew you knew his name."

I definitely knew Corbin Dumont. Decades ago, when my mom was still hiding her true badass self from my chef-abducting dads, she found herself in the middle of a child-trafficking auction. An auction run by Corbin Dumont.

She was only able to save one girl that night, and that girl grew up to be my equally badass aunt, Kaylee. Kaylee took over running the circus after my grandparents passed away, but whenever she rolled through town, we got drunk and risked our necks on the tightrope. I loved her. She was the epitome of the cool aunt, and whenever I think of how she came into the family, I wanted to dig Corbin fucking Dumont up and piss on his corpse.

He didn't succeed in selling my aunt to a pedophile, but so many other children did suffer under his sociopathic greed to make money at all costs. Because of that, my parents had to capture and torture him before the fucker gave up the hotel where he was holding the other children.

They busted in there, rescued them, and Corbin thanked them by breaking out of his restraints, summoning the Kings, getting my mom captured and beaten, and then he sexually assaulted her before getting shot in the head by his boss.

That shitstain was vile from birth to death, but no, Mom didn't laugh and crow about his demise over fucking pancakes. She told me the truth about Corbin, what he did to Kaylee, the other children, and to her while we curled up on the couch late one night. I asked her how she got into this life, and if she ever regretted it... and so she told me how.

She also told me she didn't regret a thing. If she had it to do over, she'd choose to become a Merchant every time, and the Kaylees of the world were the reason why.

"The law moves slowly, my sweet girl," Mom whispered as she wrapped me up in her cloud of cocoa butter, flour, and peach shampoo. "It's all waiting, and warrants, and informants, and evidence, and not making a move unless it'll hold up in court, and while they're dotting their damn Is and crossing their Ts, little kids are crying alone in a dirty hotel room, praying for someone to save them.

"It's the cops' job to lock away the monsters. It's ours to burn them and everything they touch to the ground, and I can promise you, the latter is much more satisfying."

Resuming our creepy walk, I let Mom's voice fade as I wiped away any expression. "Yeah, I know about Corbin Dumont. What about him?"

"A lot, *Genny*." He spat my nickname like a curse. "There's a lot about him you don't know. Details left out over Sunday night dinner. You see? Your parents never told you that Corbin Dumont... was my father."

Again I rolled my eyes. The guy dropped that information like it wasn't fucking obvious where he was going with this. "Cool," I dropped, voice flat.

"And let me guess, you're mad at my mom because Corbin's old boss, Angelo, shot him in the head? Please tell me how—"

"That's a lie."

I frowned. "Excuse me?"

"That's a lie. That's a fucking lie!" he roared, whirling on me. "Angelo didn't shoot him, your blessed fucking mother did. She shot him and left his body in an alley. An alley!" Bulging eyes blew away all appearance at calm. "Like trash!"

I edged around him, making him turn on the spot and face his back to the tree root. "Who told you that?"

"Who told me this?" Abraham barked a laugh. "Not Saint Adeline, of course. No, she never had the balls to face the innocent victims she's destroyed in her reign of terror, and tell them the truth."

"Hmm. Well, to be fair, she doesn't have balls, so—"

Abraham snatched his gun from his waistband, aiming it at my head. "You think this is a joke, bitch?" he hissed. "What the fuck about anything of this makes you think I'm in a joking mood?"

I smiled. "Actually, everything about that stupid, fake, gentleman act made me think this was all a fucking joke. Finally, you're letting your real violent, women-hating, psychopath flag fly. It's about time."

"I don't hate women." His words were half snarl. "I didn't hate my mother who was forced to give me up. She was a sex worker, but it was the money Dad made that kept a roof over our heads and food on the table. After Adeline *killed* him, it all went away.

"We were evicted from our apartment and kicked out onto the streets. When I was twelve, Mom surrendered me to the state to save me from a life eating out of the trash." The gun shook in his hands. "A year later, she was dead."

"That's a sad story." I inched closer and he subconsciously took a step back, getting closer to that root. "Almost as sad a story dozens of children told the cops after my mother rescued them from Corbin's hotel of horrors."

"Never happened."

"Corbin Dumont bought and trafficked innocent children."

"No!"

"On the weekends, he auctioned them off to wealthy pedophiles, and let those rapist monsters do whatever they wanted to them!" I didn't start the sentence shouting, but I was when I finished. Abraham shook his head the whole way through.

"More poisonous lies," he forced through gritted teeth.

"It's not a lie. These are plain facts that everyone in the fucking world knows except for your ignorant, head-in-the-sand ass!" I clapped, making him jerk. "Wake the fuck up, Brammy! Your father was the lowest form of trash—exploiting children to make a quick buck. Even the Kings were so disgusted with him, his own boss killed him!" I scoffed. "But that was only after Corbin Dumont sexually assaulted my mother.

"Face it. My mother didn't kill him, but even if she had, she would've been doing you a favor—"

Abraham backhanded me across the face, cutting my inner cheek on my teeth and filling my mouth with blood.

"Not another fucking word." His gun pressed to my temple. "You're no better than the whore who spawned you, spreading your fucking lies and filth to tear down good men, and raise yourself up on their ashes.

"Want to know the truth about what happened between Adeline and my father? The truth my mother told me, but yours couldn't be bothered to tell you? Huh?!" He shook the gun, digging it deeper into my skin.

I spat blood on his shoe by way of answer.

"It was the Merchants who were in the child-sex-trafficking business," he growled. "Yeah, that's right. Your fucking parents were the ones buying and selling children to the richest pedophiles. But the money they were making from that wasn't enough for them. They wanted to take over the Kings' territory, and their rackets, so they came up with a little plan.

"They'd frame a King for the whole thing, and then abduct and lock him up. Word spread that the Merchants were out cleaning up the Kings' dirty laundry, and Angelo was forced to deal with it." He grabbed my chin, wrenching me up to meet his glinting eyes. "That day, they purposely left the door to their *torture* room open so that my dad would escape and call for help.

"It was a trick. A trap!" Spittle coated my cheek. "When the Kings rushed in to help him, the Merchants slaughtered them all." He shoved his face in mine. "So what do you have to say now, bitch? Still laughing."

"No, Brammy, I'm not laughing." Slowly, deliberately, I grasped his fingers and pried them off of me. "I'm not laughing because I feel sorry for you. Genuinely. You want so badly to believe your father was a good man—"

"He was!"

"—so you've deluded yourself into believing he was." I tsked. "Because if he wasn't a monster, then you're not one either. Both of those beliefs are false."

Abraham cocked the gun. "You think I won't kill you." The malice in his eyes said he absolutely fucking would. "Your whore of a mother spat out half a dozen of you bigamist bastards. I'm going to put a bullet through all of your heads soon enough, so it makes no difference to me if I start n—"

I heaved a yawn, slapping his gun hand away.

He snapped it back, growling as he gripped it with both hands.

"Enough of your threats and tough-guy face," I said. "If you were going to kill me, you would've done it already. You didn't hesitate or waffle on with Madison. You wouldn't be doing it with me if you were actually going to use that gun."

His eyes flashed. "Your usefulness is rapidly fading. Disparage my father's name again and you're right. I won't hesitate or waffle on." Abraham said that, but he lowered his gun.

"I don't need to disparage your father's name." My lips twisted at the vile man he was. "The dozens of children, now adults, who suffered at his hands can do that just fine. Did you ever bother to talk to them?" I asked as his grip tightened on the gun. "While you were so busy calling my dads and my mother a liar? Did you ever take five fucking minutes out of your day to talk to the survivors of the auctions and *ask* them what's true?"

"They were children, as you just said. Frightened and traumatized. They would've repeated whatever they were ordered to say as long as it meant the nightmare ended." He shook his head. "Your parents confused them. Threatened them into spreading their lies. No doubt they're still bribing them to lie to this day.

"No," Abraham said, the finality in his voice ringing clear. "I don't need to speak to a bunch of liars so they can drip the same poison into my ear that you've been sipping on your whole life. Your parents are filthy, monstrous beasts that care for nothing and no one but themselves and their empire of blood. They prove that fact every day, and as they say, when someone tells you who they are—believe them."

I happened to agree with that quote, and right then, Brother Dumbass Abraham was telling me he was a violent, ignorant psychopath that believed whatever suited his hatred, and ignored everything else.

There was nothing I could say to pry the false memory of his father that his mother planted in his head, so there was no point in continuing to try.

He gestured with his gun. "Keep moving."

"Happily." I picked up my feet, setting off in the direction we came.

"No, that way," he barked. "Turn around."

"Nope, I don't think I will."

"Hey!" He grabbed my arm and I sprung.

Twisting hard, I threw him off-balance. The bastard stumbled into the root and it swept his legs out from under him, dropping him flat on his back. I snatched the gun from his grip before he hit the floor.

"As I said," I chirped, leveling the gun on his not-so-fucking-smug-any-more face. "I'm not going that way because I suspect you're leading me somewhere specific, and you just confirmed it by freaking out when I changed directions."

Abraham glared at me from the ground, his hands slowly moving up in surrender.

"Tell me what trap you deluded yourself into thinking I would skip right into." I slowly moved the gun now to his crotch. "Now."

Of all things... Abraham laughed. Among the dirt on his back and the grass in his hair, he laughed. "You're not going to shoot me, girl. There's no silencer on that weapon. The second my brothers hear a gunshot, they'll either think you've killed me, or that you've done something so unforgivable, it forced me to kill you.

"Either way, the first thing they'll do is make your precious biker bitches suffer in punishment."

I shrugged. "Maybe they will, maybe they won't, but it won't make much difference to you since your dickless corpse will be rotting in the pile of manure you were born in. Last chance," I sang. "Tell me where you were taking me, or I make you the eunuch you're so desperate to be, *Brother* Abraham."

Blood vessels burst all over his face. His jaw clenched so hard I heard something crack. His desperation to empty his clip into my head screamed from every pore of his furious face, but the one holding the gun was me.

"A... mile in..." he forced out. "There's an underground hatch. That's where I put the miserable cunts who beg after you, and that's where I'm putting *you*."

"Hmm, no."

"What?" He frowned. "No?"

"No," I repeated. "You're lying. And for that—"

Bang!

The gunshot ripped through the forest, its cry not nearly as loud as Abraham's.

"Ahh!" he howled, curling on his side and clutching the foot I just kindly put a hole in.

"You're not holding my friends underground," I shouted over his noise. "You psychopaths delivered—no, threw Bugsy's body at me. She was bruised and bloody, but she wasn't pale, dirty, or reeking of her own fluids like she would've been if she'd been in a hole for over a week.

"Your generous use of the word *cunt* tells me you're a misogynistic pig like the company you keep, but you'd better get it through your fucking head now. Just because I'm pretty, doesn't mean I'm stupid."

I kicked him between the legs. Abraham shot off the ground, balancing on one foot, his eyes half bugged out of his head and jaw cracked as he clutched his balls—back arched like a bowstring.

"Don't lie to me again," I growled. "If the next words out of your mouth aren't the truth and nothing but the truth, I'll put a bullet through your skull and see if your friends in the cabin aren't more forthcoming.

"Where were you taking me!"

"To the hatch!" he bellowed, blood filling his shoe and dripping out onto the grass. "But your gang isn't in there! That dirty stinkin' hole is just for you, bitch!"

"Where are my girls?" I kicked him again. "Where are they!"

"In the cabin!" Abraham heaved hard, spittle flying and coating his chin. "This is... one of Luca's hellholes! Specially constructed so that there are chains in all the bedrooms... and none of the doors open from the inside."

My stomach churned, shotgunning bile into my throat. I heard all about the dirty ratholes where Luca Adams kept Kenzie and the other women he trafficked. If he had one in other cities, it shouldn't have surprised me he had one just outside of Cinco too. There was no one around here for miles.

No one to hear the girls scream.

I didn't waste a minute. "Give me your phone."

"Wha—?"

Bang!

I shot the other foot, kicking off another round of screaming and wailing that made me roll my eyes.

"Stalling by acting stupid is right up there with lying, bro. You heard me just fine: give me your fucking phone!"

Abraham flung the blood-stained thing at my head. "You're next, bitch! I promise you! I swear it on the severed heads of your disease-ridden family! You're next!"

"Yeah, yeah, blah, blah, blah." I typed in Kenzie's number.

She answered on the third ring. "Hello? Who is this?"

"Kenzie, it's me."

"Genny? Genny, oh my gosh! Are you okay? How are you? Where are you?! Sienna? Sienna!" she called. "It's Genny!"

"Genny?" I heard from the other end. "Are you sure it's her?"

"I don't— How do I know it's you?" she demanded.

"It's me, Feisty, and you'll know it for sure when we finally bed down for that threesome we've got booked."

"Yeah, it's definitely you," she muttered. "Are you okay? What's that noise?"

"It's the noise that follows me everywhere I go. The sound of grown men begging and bawling at my feet."

"Fuck you!" Abraham roared.

"As for if I'm okay..." The lightness drained out of my voice. "No, Feisty, I'm not. They've taken me miles outside of the city to some cabin he says was owned by Luca Adams, and yes," I sliced in, knowing what she was going to ask, "it's one of *those* cabins.

"I could ask this mewling bitch how many of the enemy are in there waiting for me, but I won't know if he's telling the truth until I bust inside—alone."

"Don't go in alone! Wait for us!"

"I don't have that kind of time," I replied evenly—patiently. In the nearing distance, Abraham's minions shouted for him, drawn in by his bellowing cries. "I'm not running away and abandoning my Cardinals now that I've finally found them." I gazed at the cabin peaking over the treetops. "But something tells me getting out of that place is going to be ten times harder than getting in.

"This is the bat signal, Kenzie. Find us and get us out, before I have to do it myself."

"Gen—"

I flung the phone as hard as I could, sending it soaring through the bush.

"Boss?" a too-close voice called. "Boss?!"

"Over here!" Abraham flipped onto his stomach, struggling to crawl toward help. "I'm here! Hurry up and kill this bitch—"

I stomped on the back of his neck, forcing his face into the mud. "I have no idea why everyone in your little clique is so scared of you. You were laughably easy to beat."

"I'll kill you!" he roared, growling and snarling into the dirt like a wild animal. "I'll flay the skin off your worthless bones! You'll die for what your family did to mine! You'll all DIE!"

I sighed. "Fuck's sake, dude. Wake the hell up. Your mama was a lying leech feeding off the money teat of a child-selling pedophilic pimp, but if you still don't believe me, you can ask them all about it in hell."

I shot him point-blank through the skull, putting an end to his caterwauling. His minions burst through the trees and I finished them off before they could shoot, dropping them in quick succession.

Crossing the distance, I bent over their corpses, picking their pockets clean of weapons as a faint chime echoed through the forest—Abraham's phone ringing.

There was no point searching for it to talk to Kenzie, because there was nothing more for me to say or more information to give. They'd already had all the information they needed to find me, so they'd better do it.

"Fast." I cocked my borrowed guns, narrowing on the innocent-looking cabin in the distance. "Shit's about to get real."

***

"Genny? Genny, please, pick up!" The phone kept ringing until an automated voicemail message picked it up.

I craned to see out the large, wall-swallowing window of Banana Tree. Sienna and I insisted on coming with the guys to check out the gas station, but Liam, Bane, and Sunny didn't make it very far and Sienna and I were even farther away.

Bane and Liam loitered on the sidewalk, watching as the Cinco PD Bomb Squad swept the place.

After our very close—too close—call at the movie theater, the guys weren't about to run into any more buildings that had the Brotherhood's stink on it. So, Liam called up a buddy of his in the force and told him flat out the Brotherhood blew up the theater, and the gas station could be their next target.

This was serious enough that not even my gangster boyfriends could deny the police and proper bomb-defusing professionals needed to be involved. A bomb at a gas station could take out half the city block, and put way more people than just us in danger.

Knowing that, the guys wouldn't let me anywhere near the place, and Sienna wasn't going near it without me either, so that left us sipping oolong tea at Banana Tree while half the patrons crowded around us, straining to see down the street.

Liam and Bane were only so close because they were backing Sunny up while he gave his interview.

"It was horrrrribbble," Sunny wailed. "I was picking up some snacks for my girl. She's pregnant with our fifth kid. I keep saying, 'Kenzie baby, let's slow down or at least bag up,' but she can't keep her hands off me. Wants it everywhere, all the time, any place. She loves me, man. Loves me more than all those other rejects lapping at her feet."

Sienna smothered a snort at my narrowing eyes. I shook my head at the doofus while I dialed and redialed Liam and Bane—whoever picked up first.

We had a front-row seat to my man's lunacy because his interview was being broadcast live from the scene, and it was playing on every television. All of Cinco City could see Sole Bellisario, but not as the slick, handsome, dripping-in-expensive-clothes playboy that I knew. Sole dressed all the way down in a simple pair of jeans, scuffed shoes, a shirt with a hole in it, and hair that was ratted up like he just rolled out of a bed filled with four children and a sexually voracious girlfriend.

"This one time, me and my girl, Kenzie, were getting it on—"

"Yes, thank you!" the reporter half shouted. "Please, get back to what you were saying about the man standing on the other side of the pump."

"Huh? Oh, yeah, that freak." Sunny shuddered. It was scary how good an actor he was. If more than half of the Merchants' children weren't called to a life of crime, I had to wonder what their alter egos would've done with their lives. "He was weird, dude. He kept mumbling all this freak stuff about the devil being in Cinco, and that it needed to be purified with fire.

"Just like the movie theater. He, uh... He said—" Sunny paused, scratching his chin. It was then I noticed he'd put dirt under his fingernails. No detail too small for his grand performance. "He said something about the theater being cursed with sin, so it had to go too."

"Shocking," the reporter said. "For those listening and yet unaware, only a few hours ago, the old Late-Nite Cinema in Rockchapel was the site of a bombing. That very cinema was closed down due to a shootout that tragically claimed the lives of ten innocent people. Mr. Bell, sir, do you believe that was the theater and the sin this man was speaking of?"

"I don't know. I thought the dude was just crazy and mumbling to the voices in his head. I didn't realize he was talking to me until he said I'd better repent of my sins. I ran around to tell him to fuck off, but I couldn't even get close.

"He was wearing dirty rags and his pants were wet and yellow like he pissed himself. He had old bits of food in his scraggly beard, three teeth, and brown stuff caked on his fingers that could've been his own shit for all I knew. He damn sure smelled like it—that Brother Abraham guy."

And now Sienna did laugh, busting up even amidst the seriousness of the situation. Wherever Brother Abraham was, he would not be pleased with this description.

"How worrying," the reporter cried. "But then, how did you know this guy was dangerous, or that his threats were to be taken seriously?"

"Because he said he has more gifts to leave for the sinners of Cinco, and this was just the second stop. I was going to ask what the hell he was talking about, but then he dropped his tailgate and showed me what he had in the truck bed. Bombs," Sunny rasped. "A whole bunch of fucking bombs."

The call picked up. "Mackenzie?" Liam's voice poured in my ear. "Every-thing okay?"

"Genny just called." I told him everything she said.

He was moving before I finished. "Bane, get Sunny. Let's go."

Right there on screen, Sunny fished his phone out of his pocket, read the text, and ran off. "Hope you catch the freak. See ya!"

"Wha— Wait! Mr. Bell, wait—"

"Get back!" A loudspeaker-amplified voice ripped through the speakers, making half the patrons in Banana Tree jump. "A bomb has been located on the premises! I repeat, a bomb is on the premises. Calmly and safely evacuate this area immediately!"

Calm and safe did not describe the screaming stampede that tore out of Banana Tree.

Sienna and I plastered against the corner, staying out of the way. On the screen, the cops rushed all over the place, escorting people away from the area, and barking at those not moving fast enough. One of them turned to the reporter and cameraman, and the live feed blinked out just like that.

Only when everyone else was gone did we chance going down the stairs and out into the street where the guys were waiting.

"Let's hurry, we don't have a lot of time," Liam said, leading the way to his car. "We need to get back to the compound and trace that number."

"Genny said the place was owned by Luca. It's where they're keeping the Cardinals."

"So that's why the Brotherhood kept that shitstain around," Bane growled. "They use his network of hellholes to hide their kidnapped enemies. Or disappear them completely."

Sienna shuddered. "I don't understand these people, or what they're after. They hate the Merchants—okay. They think the Merchants are destroying the city—sure. They want revenge—blah, blah, blah. But if you guys are terrible people preying on the innocent, what the hell does that make Luca, Madison, and Vito? How can they pretend to have any kind of moral high ground when they get involved with scum like them?"

We jogged across the street, consumed by the question, but neither of us having an answer for it.

It was a long drive back to the compound, but a tense one. The guys went back and forth on how to find Genny, and how much firepower they'd need to rescue her and the Cardinals. Meanwhile, Sienna and I closely monitored the news coverage of the gas station.

We were pulling into the parking garage when the bomb squad gave the all-clear, confirming they successfully defused the weapon.

"And that's another strike against these psychotic hypocrites," I said. "If that bomb had gone off at a gas station of all places, it would've taken out that entire street and killed dozens of people. Madison whined and cried about the Merchants ruining her and her mother's life, but she had no problem hooking up with Luca who destroyed the lives of countless moms and their children, and she just as likely doesn't care about all the moms and kids that would've died today from the bomb she and her buddies left behind.

"How in the world can these people think they're better than you when they're the worst most vile scum in absolutely every way?"

"Honestly, I've been thinking about that," Sunny spoke up. He climbed out of the driver seat, then came around the back to open my door. "I've been thinking about what Madison told you. I've been thinking about the women Luca targeted, and I've been thinking about where the Brotherhood has been leaving their little exploding presents.

"Maybe they're not out to *free* all of Cinco from us. Maybe they only care about freeing some of Cinco from us. The people they think matter."

I climbed out, frowning. "The people they think matter? Who?"

"Not anyone from Rockchapel for fuck sure. Not a bunch of biker chicks working out of a warehouse. Not a bunch of poor single moms. And not anyone who'd be hanging around an abandoned movie theater in a bad part of the city," he said slowly, his expression serious.

"That's why they're not going after the Rockchapel gangs. That's why they don't care about the Rat King. *That* is why the bomb was only put in your car, Liam, even though that piece-of-shit valet could've just as easily set it off in the restaurant and made damn sure. That's it!" he shouted, making me jump. "We've been so distracted by the small-time scum they've been sending at us that we've completely missed the obvious.

"How well organized they are. How well funded they are. How determined they are to take us and just us out." Sunny backed out of the still-open garage, his eyes sweeping the soaring skyscrapers. "Bane, remember what Mom used to say? That the most dangerous criminals aren't the poor and desperate ones—"

"—they're the connected ones," he finished. "The ones with a badge. The ones with a gavel. The ones in the White House, the ones with money... and the ones with privilege."

Slowly, Bane and Sunny turned to Liam.

"Wait, no," I cried, grabbing Liam's arm. "You can't think—"

"No, Kenzie, they don't." Liam laid a hand over mine. "They're not saying I'm a part of this. They're saying I'm to blame. Because the Brotherhood isn't from Rockchapel, no matter what gas stations they hide in. They're based right here in Leighbridge... and I didn't see it."

"What?" Sienna stepped forward. "But how can you be sure of that?"

"Think about it, Si," Bane said. "Think about how wanton and callous their destruction is when they *don't* care about the collateral damage. Now, think about the one time they did."

Sienna nodded slowly, eyes glazing. "You're right. I see... I see it... You're right," she whispered. "Liam is the most visible of all of you. A successful well-known businessman, but one that's always working or dining in a fancy Leighbridge business. A bomb in your nightclub could've taken you out a long time ago, but they'd never do that because *important* people go there. The only people whose lives they value."

"The Brotherhood is based here?" I rasped. "Right under our noses the whole time?"

"It's the only thing that makes sense," Sunny said. "It makes so much sense, I should've fucking figured it out before."

"I'll take care of this," Liam growled, "but first, I need to track the number that called Kenzie. It has to lead back to Genny."

"But then..." My mind was still going a mile a minute. I barely noticed when Liam slipped the phone from my hand and took off. "But then... we were wrong..."

"We've been looking at all of this upside down. We've been thinking upside down," Sunny was saying to Bane. "Remember the Conglomerate? That band of corrupt CEOs that joined forces to cover, bribe, cheat, steal, and kill for the other?"

"Yeah, yeah, yeah," Bane said. "They wound up in the ledger and ended up bribing, cheating, stealing, and killing for Keiran after Keiran. And then all of them were slapped with life sentences after the ledger went public. Their businesses were gutted and sold for parts."

"Guys, I..." I swallowed hard. "I have to tell you—"

"What do you want to bet that's what we're dealing with here?" Sunny went on. "Another band of rich fucks who are hiding behind their desks while paying C-class henchmen to attack us."

"Sunny. Bane." I tossed my head. "We were wrong. *I* was wrong."

"Wrong?" Bane turned to me. "Wrong about what?"

"Well... I mean, I can't say for sure but... But what if we were wrong about Madison?" I scowled, thinking back to every part of our conversation in that park tunnel. "I didn't realize this before, but Madison never confessed to putting the trackers in your clothes. I assumed it was her because she was working for the Brotherhood, but Madison isn't that clever," I dropped, thinking of Adeline. "She's a dumbass who let herself be the face of a child-trafficking ring. Someone that stupid doesn't suddenly come up with the plan that almost brought the Merchant family down.

"And when I think about it, she didn't even fucking say she did! All she confessed to was working with Luca. But it wasn't her," I breathed. "It wasn't her."

"But if it wasn't her, then who was it?" Sienna asked.

"If we have to think bigger, think *rich*, then we should think about who knew the Johnsons were really the Merchants, and who would hate that their upscale fashion house was basically a bargain basement bin for said Merchants. Who would be so pissed that every time a Merchant order came in, they had to make their top designers drop everything just to 'sew the housekeeper's mom jeans' and then sell it to you guys for a steal?

"Who would desperately want a family of criminals out of their business?" I met Sunny's eyes. "Who would sew a few trackers in their clothes to make it happen? And who told us to our faces that he personally does final checks on every Johnson order that goes out the door?"

Sunny's eyes narrowed to slits.

"Hollywell."

Chapter Three

Sunny whipped around the corner, sending off a blaring chorus of car horns.

We'd been speeding all over Cinco all day. Night was already beginning to beat the sun back over the horizon. My stomach screamed its hunger, my head wailed its worry, and my heart longed to just go home and hug my daughter, but no one was going anywhere and doing anything until Genny was safe from the clutches of those psychopaths.

"But I don't understand, Angel." Sunny jerked hard to the right. "You had Hollywell on your suspect list and then you took him off. Why did you think he was innocent before, but guilty now?"

"It wasn't that I thought he was innocent. It was— Honestly, I thought he was too much of a pathetic bitch to side-eye your clothes, let alone put trackers in them."

Sunny's brows shot up. "Oh? Say more, love."

I cringed. "Ugh, just think back to the day we talked to him in his office. He's got at least fifteen years on you, but he was bowing and scraping at your feet with all that 'yes, sir,' 'no, sir' stuff. It was embarrassing," I confessed. "Every other Brotherhood person we dealt with before bled with hatred for the Merchants, but this guy nearly wet himself because you yelled at him. None of that screamed evil-villain mastermind to me, so I took him off the list."

"But now it does scream evil-villain mastermind?"

"It does if it's all an act." Grave eyes took him in. "It does when you think about how desperate Hollywell is to protect the reputation of Caddell House, so desperate, he dropped the punk-ass-bitch routine for a split second, and stood up to you when you tried to make him hire a supposed fraud and thief.

"It does when you think about the fact that almost everyone in Cinco knows that the Merchants are a notorious crime family, but they *don't know* that Caddell House only exists because of that crime family. They're a global brand now. If the world finds out how they got their start, they're ruined," I said, my words rushing out in a tidal wave of certainty. "Of course they want to sever all ties and bury their dirty money, but they can't because your father made the first owner sign a binding contract stating the Merchants would be valued VIPs for life."

"But after Genny went all Blonde Bandit on the place, he closed our account, fired you, and banned the *Johnsons* from Caddell," Sunny argued. "If he always had the balls to rip up that contract, why didn't he just do that instead of joining an actual criminal organization!"

I shook my head. "Baby, Sienna said it. The Brotherhood said it! They don't see themselves as the criminals. They see themselves as the victims rising up against criminals and fighting back. Besides, he didn't rip up anything. That was just more of Hollywell's bitch-baby playacting."

The look on Sunny's face told me he didn't know what I meant.

"Think about it, my love. Hollywell was onto us from day one," I said. "Out of nowhere, Sunny Bellisario blows into Caddell House and announces that the entire family is donating their wardrobe to charity, and—surprise—we're making you hire a new designer that's loyal to our family. Hollywell knew in that second that the trackers were found, and that you were looking for the culprit, otherwise, you would've closed the account yourself and had nothing more to do with Caddell House. You don't crawl on the floor unless you're looking for a rat."

"Fucking hell," Sunny breathed, nodding slow. "He must've been scrambling. Vance couldn't give himself away to you, but he also couldn't let the Brotherhood know that he failed. That he had one fucking job and he screwed it up. But after Genny busted in there with a gun, she gave him the out he was praying for.

"He closed our account and banned you and the Johnsons from the place both to stop you digging around *and* to give the Brotherhood a valid reason for why the tracker plan was dead. It wasn't *his* fault. It was *our* fault for destroying the business relationship so badly, the only thing it made sense to do was cut all ties with us. It would've looked hella suspicious to everyone if he didn't. But," Sunny cried, jumping on my thought train for the ride. "Deep down, he's still a fucking coward, and that's why he had you deliver the breakup note instead of telling me to my face. Because he's exactly what you said, baby, a brother, and a little bitch."

"Exactly." Even in the midst of all the danger and betrayal, I couldn't help but smile. The Brotherhood thought they had us so scared. They believed they couldn't hide in the shadows and watch us scramble, but they weren't as smart as they thought they were. "You told me to think big. Big money and big motives, well, Caddell House rakes in billions in revenue every year. That's billions with a B, baby. It doesn't get any bigger than that."

"They're big because of us." Sunny pounded his chest, rage leaking into his voice. "Because my old man took a chance on a random high-school dropout with nothing to his name but a full sketchbook. He took a chance on him and gave him the money to make his dream come true, but now all of a sudden our money is dirty? They almost kill me, you, my brother, my sister, and my niece because fucking Caddell House got too good for the people who made them!"

I rubbed his arm, heart breaking for the pain belying his anger. "I'm sorry, Sunny. I know," I whispered. "I know your parents tried to help people. They tried to do good and give back to their community, and seeing one of their most generous gifts being turned into a weapon against them... it hurts."

His hands shook gripping the wheel. "They're supposed to be our enemies. The Brotherhood is supposed to be evil shits we put down hard. But if even our partners—our friends—hate us... where do you go from there?"

My chest ached wanting to answer him, but nothing I came up with was enough. "I'm sorry. I love you."

Sunny blew out a breath. Tossing his head, his smile returned. "I love you too, Angel. As much as this sucks, all I want to do right now is pull over and jackhammer your G-spot until you scream so loud, you break the windows."

I heated up like a lava lamp. Sunny would be saying stuff like this on our fortieth anniversary, and my old butt will still blush.

"I can't believe how amazing you are." Sunny laced his fingers through mine. "I've been trying to find these Brotherhood bastards for months, and then you come in and find two in two days. I knew your instincts were gold."

And now I was blushing for a different reason. My instincts were telling me something right then—Sunny and I would make it long enough to celebrate that fortieth anniversary, because I was never letting him go.

"I love your faith in me, but what are we going to do? We're speeding over to Caddell House, but there's no way they're letting us through the front door," I said. "Vance must've doubled security and plastered Public Enemy Numbers One and Two signs with both our faces."

That smirk widened. "Oh ye of little faith. Security is just as much of a myth as locked doors, baby. Nothing and no one stands between me and a little bitch begging for a beating."

My lower belly clenched deliciously. Now I was the one wanting him to pull over and jackhammer my pussy.

Soon Sole pulled into the Caddell House parking lot and we tumbled out. Bold and sexy as ever, he took my hand and strolled us both right inside, not sparing a glance either right or left at the four security guards who darted out from behind their station when we sidestepped the newly installed metal detector.

"Excuse me, sir? Sir!" A wall of muscle shot in front of us. "I'm going to need you both to step back, show me your IDs, and then step through the metal detector. If you refuse, you will be escorted out of the building."

"Hmm. Well, I'd like to thank you for so clearly stating your needs," Sunny said, his tone as light and sunny as ever. "Clarity is so important in these situations, which is why I'm going to return the favor.

"Tell Vance that he's going to invite us up for our appointment, or I'm going to hold a press conference announcing to the whole world that *the* Jonah Caddell took a loan from gangsters to start this business—a loan that I'm fairly sure never made it on the tax form—and Caddell House has been floating said gangsters perks and kickbacks ever since."

Sunny beamed in that reddening face. "And for every minute he keeps me waiting, I'll add more names to drop and more careers to ruin, and I'll start with Vance Hollywell."

The guy raked me and Sunny up and down behind his glasses, internally weighing how much trouble he'd be in if he didn't take us seriously.

"Wait here."

Slipping past, he left his three buddies to watch us while he returned to his station and picked up the phone. He said something in a low tone, then jerked the phone away as loud unintelligible shouts were his reply. He put the phone back and said something else, and then he returned it to its cradle.

He stomped back to us with a face he tried to keep neutral. "Mr. Hollywell is waiting for you," he gritted. "Go on up."

I fought a smile as we walked past four guards, a metal detector, and half a dozen staring eyes with nothing but a mild threat and a can-do attitude.

Sunny was right—bodyguards were only as effective as the weak bitch cowering behind them.

***

Genny

In typical me fashion, I went straight up to the cabin, kicked the door in, and started shooting.

I got two brothers in the chest before they could get their crotch-stinking fingers out of the popcorn bowl. I shot the third when he jumped off the couch, scrambling for his gun, and the fourth as he came running in from the hallway. But then the fifth ran in, and the sixth, and the seventh, and the eighth, ninth, tenth.

I ducked back out the doorway, diving on the deck as a hail of bullets flew past the frame. Taking off fast, I bolted around the corner and peeked past as those morons charged out the door.

Bang! Bang! Bang!

I dropped Tweedledee, Tweedledumb, and Tweedledickhead with one foot over the threshold. They dropped like dominoes, littering the deceptively pretty porch like the trash they were.

"Back," someone shouted from inside. "Go out the back! Surround the bitch!"

Not a bad plan. Maybe someone in the Brotherhood did have two brain cells to rub together.

Too bad that won't be enough.

I listened as too many heavy boots fled the front entrance and headed for the side and back doors. This place clearly wasn't just another empty rathole. There were too many people—too many armed people—ready and waiting inside. This had to be it. The real Brotherhood headquarters.

Quickly, I crept back toward the door, keeping low. "Hey!" I growled, expertly mimicking Brother Abraham's voice just like my favorite conman dad taught me. "Get out here, you fools! Help me, I'm hit! That stupid cunt bitch shot me!"

"Boss?"

"Boss, are you okay?"

"Is it clear?"

"It's clear," I gruffed. "Hurry up!"

I quickly ducked behind a deck chair as four grunts rushed to their savior's aid. I ran inside and shut the door while they were still midway through crying and shouting his name.

Sweeping the dim room, I felt the pressing weight of silence. As predicted, everyone guarding the front door went tearing off at their master's call, so I was alone. The blackout curtains and cheap table lamps didn't provide much light, but it was enough for me to see the cabin wasn't as charming on the inside as it was on the outside.

Dirt from dozens of muddy boots traipsing in and out ground into the worn once-blue carpets and turned them into an unappealing mottled brown. Not a single painting, mirror, or picture adorned the peeling white walls, and the small living room I stepped in had nothing to say for itself except for two old, smelly brown couches, a wall-mounted television, and a coffee table with a broken leg.

Slowly, quietly, I moved toward the hall—sliding my back against the wall.

It was quiet. Too quiet. The insulation was too good in this place because I couldn't hear what was going on outside, or if those bastards were on their way back. From what my brothers told me, Luca kept his prisoners in separate rooms—alone and chained to the wall. An act which made it impossible for them to plot an escape, organize, or even have a friendly face to look to while surviving hell.

My gaze traveled up. *If my Cardinals are here, they must be upstairs.*

I crept further down the hall, picking up the pace. The staircase faced the back door, and I needed to climb up it before the brothers came back and got between me and my only way out.

Gun up and leading the way, I took the stairs two at a time. Topping the landing, I came out into another too-dark hallway, squinting at the seven doors split between either side of me. I reached for the knob directly on my right, and threw open the door—my finger ready and desperate to fire off a shot.

"*Hmpgf!*"

I dropped my gun running inside.

Everything my brothers told me about that horrible place where they found Kenzie, and the sight was still worse than I imagined.

All that made a bedroom a sanctuary had been ripped out, and the only things left in its place were dirty, stain-covered mattresses, metal bars secured to the walls, a bucket in the corner emanating an eye-watering smell, and three young, gagged women chained to opposite walls.

Boo, Lils, and Nella still had on the clothes they were taken in, and that was the only part of them clearly recognizable. All three of them were beat to shit, with swollen black eyes, welts and bruises up and down their arms and legs, and split lips separated by blood-stained gags.

Rage I'd never known before filled me to bursting. Everything in me screamed to hunt down those scurrying morons outside and put a bullet in each of their skulls.

I dropped beside Boo and pulled the gag out of her mouth.

In spite of everything, she granted me a wobbly grin. "It's real great to... see you, FGH."

"Sorry I didn't get here sooner." I freed them all from their gags, but the chains were another matter. One look told me I wasn't shooting or breaking those shackles. "Who has the key?"

"A fuck-ugly, weedy little... bitch," Nella rasped. "Face riddled with... acne and his smirk dripping with incel."

Lils nodded—barely. Her head strained to carry out the command and lolled instead. "Abraham... ordered them not to rape or grope us, so instead—instead—"

"Instead he beat us." The words scraped from Boo's parched throat. "He beat us and said if we begged for his cock... he'd stop."

I was wrong. This feeling— This hatred right now... is the most rage I'd ever felt.

"He dies first," I hissed. "Well, seventh, but I'll make it slow." I glanced back. "I've got to check and make sure the others are all here. If anyone but me walks past that door, shout."

I squeezed Lils's hand as she tried another nod. "I'm getting you out of here, Lils. Today."

"Never doubted... you, boss." Her swinging head dropped on my shoulder. "Never."

I didn't mess around with emotions like guilt. I do what I do and I say what I say. When I'm wrong, I accept responsibility for it and own the consequences of my actions. Wasting time moping and crying got in the way of making it right.

But in that moment, guilt and shame ate me out like the rotted shit-heel carcass I was. These women trusted me. They gave their lives to follow me because they believed in the Merchant name and the protection I promised them.

And I failed.

I didn't listen to Sunny the first, second, and fifth time he warned me we had an unseen enemy hunting us. I thought my little bro was just making excuses for why his business was going wrong—blaming a phantom boogeyman instead of admitting he was too young to run a borough, and too proud to admit his fuckups.

I let my own hang-ups on Sunny's maturity cloud my judgement, and then my Cardinals ended up in Satan's whorehouse being tortured and starved.

This was on me. All of this was my fucking fault.

I backed out of the room before my girls saw me do something really fucking embarrassing—cry.

I went room to room, listening for a warning shout as I ungagged my Cardinals and checked them over. They were all in a terrible state—just as bad as the beaten Boo, Lils, and Nella.

They also weren't alone.

All of my Cardinals were accounted for, but there were also five other women and one man among the chained and beaten. They were all older—late thirties and possibly early forties. I got their story after ungagging them.

"My name is Wilson," the dark-haired and broken-nose man croaked. "I was hiking. Just hiking with my girlfriend when I rolled my ankle. We came to this house asking for help and... and..." Sobs crumpled his face. "Where's Jillian?" he cried. "Where is she? What... what did they do to her?"

"I'll find her," was all I could get out before taking off to open another door and find another heartbreaking scene on the other side.

I found Jillian behind that door, and when she broke down in sobs too as she told me what that monster did to her when she finally begged for the beatings to stop, my tough, diamond shell shattered, and I didn't bother to hide my bright eyes.

Three of the women confirmed they were here before the Brotherhood moved in—thanks to that evil, disgusting corpse Luca. He just left them there after giving the place to the Brotherhood, claiming they weren't "big earners" and weren't worth the trouble or cost to bring them on his big move overseas.

If only I'd been there when Sunny stabbed Luca and left him to bleed out. I'd have liked to poke more holes in that worthless sack, starting with the eyes and crotch and then stabbing my way to the middle.

I stumbled into the last room with Shug, Bee, Pixie, and a silent figure huddled and bleeding in the corner. I gently lifted her head to tug the gag out of her mouth, revealing a pretty, lined face between a sea of black, blue, and red.

She didn't react to my promise to get her out safely. She didn't do a thing at all except to drop her head, and resume her blank-eyed staredown with the floor.

"They're going to realize I'm not out there soon, if they haven't already," I told Shug and the others. "I've got to get that key. I—"

"FGH! They're here!"

"They're back!"

"Kill them!" my girls sounded off. "Fucking kill them all!"

"Oh, well, no plan as always." I drew my guns, tearing for the door. "More fun that way."

I tore out guns up and already firing before I crossed the threshold.

"There she is!" Five dicks scrambled over each other to get to me. "That Merchant bitch!"

"Put her down!"

"Kill her!"

Gunshots ripped through the cabin—only as loud as the screams.

***

Mackenzie

Vance stood behind his desk as we came in, every limb shaking as he leveled the gun on us.

Sunny's only move was to push me behind him. Otherwise, the man could've been holding a squirt gun for all the care Sunny showed.

"Hello, Hollywell. Is this how you normally greet your guests? With piss stains on your pants and guns in your hand? No wonder Caddell House is bleeding clients."

"I'm not afraid of you!" he shouted, shaking like a leaf in the breeze. "If you try anything, I'll—"

"You'll shoot me, the gunshot will be heard on three floors, the police will be here in seconds, you'll be arrested, my family will have you shanked before the prison van leaves the courthouse, and Caddell House will go down in history as that psycho brand that employed not one, but two gun-toting maniacs."

"The other one was one of you!"

Sunny shrugged—calm as ever. "Details don't matter once a story goes viral. You'll be just another disgruntled dick who decided to solve his problems with a little domestic terrorism."

"T-terrorism?" he croaked, paling. "But I'm not— I'm defending myself!"

"Defending yourself from who? An unarmed man and a beautiful, sexy, equally unarmed woman with candied nipples?"

I sighed. *This guy...*

"How do you see that going for you, Hollywell? Think a single juror is going to vote not guilty with her face and the face of the adorable little baby girl you orphaned plastered on the news every night? Think there's anything close to a happy ending for you if you pull that trigger?"

Vance's face crumpled. Spittle flying, he sobbed—reddening worse than Laurel when she's constipated. "I don't—I don't want to hurt anybody! I— Ahhhh," he wailed.

I cringed at the sight of him. No wonder the Brotherhood put an army of hitmen and bangers between them and the real members. It wasn't a pretty sight on the other side of the battlefield.

"Then, put the gun down, Hollywell. We can talk. Just talk, I promise. I won't even move from this spot as long as you *put the gun down*." Sunny's voice brokered no argument. Authority oozed from his pores. Vance was at least fifteen years older than him and armed, but the true power in this room was Sunny.

Sobbing, Vance dropped his hand, letting the gun clatter to the floor. Only then did Sunny let me come out from behind him.

Leaning in, I pressed a kiss to Sunny's cheek as I put my arms around him—holding him close. I knew my love well enough to know he came in here to stomp Vance's ass into the carpet... until he saw the gun. He changed tactics to eliminate the danger to me, and that would always blow my mind.

No guy I'd ever been with had put me, my safety, or even my feelings first. The universe was really so impatient with me for constantly choosing assholes, she finally just dropped the love of my life on my head so that he could wake me up and introduce me to the rest of my soulmates.

I hid a smile in his chest thinking of River. *Even the soulmate I was denying and pushing away.*

"Help me out here, Vance," Sunny said over Hollywell's noise. "Help me understand how it came to this."

"I didn't want this!" he roared. "I didn't want *you*! I had no idea when I took the job who the true *silent partners* in Caddell House were! Could that cold, arrogant bitch have warned me? Sure! But she was too fucking busy getting out of here as quickly as possible!"

The cold arrogant bitch was Talia, or I'd eat my shirt.

"Why didn't you just buy us out, you miserable fucker?" Sunny was done smoothing his ego. "I've seen the contract my dad drew up and your founder signed. There is a buyout clause written in language clear enough for even you to understand. If you didn't want us in your fucking business, why didn't you invoke it instead of trying to kill us!"

"Because—"

"Because what!"

"Because we can't afford it!" Vance's eyes bugged out of his head, spittle showering his glass desk. "It'd have cost twenty million dollars to buy you the fuck out! Where the fuck am I going to get twenty fucking fuck million fucking dollars!" he bellowed, blowing my brows up. "FUCK!"

"Vance, what are you talking about?" I asked in a tone much gentler than he deserved. "It's not like you'd be fronting the bill. The company would've paid."

"The company can't pay." He threw up his hands, pacing like a caged animal. "Caddell House is broke."

"Wait, what?" I cried.

"Broke! B.R.O.K.E. Broke," he blared. "We're two fucking seconds away from bankruptcy!"

"How is that possible?"

"How we stayed in business for this long is the real question." Vance tore at his hair. "The whole damn world locked themselves in their homes for a year, and you know what someone doesn't need to go from their couch to the kitchen? A fucking evening gown!"

I could only blink at the rapidly deteriorating mess in front of me.

"Sales plummeted during the pandemic, and the company was forced to borrow heavily to stay afloat. The big bosses thought all they'd have to do is hold out. Soon, our customers and high-profile clients would come back, and we'd crawl out of the red again. But then the head of Caddell House Paris was hit with a sexual harassment suit that was cosigned by everyone in the fucking building! That pig even hit on the part-time cleaner's daughter. Her *twelve*-year-old daughter!"

I grimaced, stomach churning. "Fucking hell."

"Yeah, fucking hell!" he cried, spinning back the other way to resume his pacing. "The company paid out millions to buy them all off and get them to sign NDAs. And then if that wasn't enough, we were forced to recall the entire summer line because the bitch-ass textile company used Class Three fabrics to undercut the price."

"Class Three fabrics are flammable," I told Sunny, seeing his confused frown. "Highly flammable. As in, 'cannot be used for clothing under any circumstances' flammable."

"I see," Sunny replied. "But what I don't see, is what the fuck that has to do with my family. We didn't cause the pandemic, or hire a pedophile to run your fucking Paris house, *or* set supermodels on fire!"

"No, you just embezzled enough money from us to buy a fucking country!"

Sunny blew back. "Embezzled? What the fuck are you talking about?"

"Don't give me that!" Vance picked up his desk clock and flung it at the window, shattering it on impact. "The numbers just weren't adding up. Caddell House Cinco City is the flagship branch, but somehow, we were bleeding money worse than anyone, and we have been for years since before I took over.

"We didn't understand it until I finally hired a forensic accountant to go over the books. That's how I found out about your little fucking scam."

Sunny and I traded looks. He's just as confused as me.

"What scam?" he asked. "I have no idea what you're talking about."

"Maybe you do, maybe you don't, but just because you weren't the Merchant in particular who embezzled from us, doesn't mean one of your felon brothers and sisters didn't."

"Dude, enough with the accusations and just explain what you mean," I snapped. "Why do you think the Merchants embezzled from Caddell House?"

"I told you," he hissed. "We figured out the scam. It wasn't right away or even noticeable at first, but one day, we woke up and found out our expenses had tripled. The price of fabrics, buttons, buckles, sewing machines, you name it! Our individual suppliers kept raising the costs, and when we finally confronted one of them to tell us why, the truth spilled out," he spat, lips curling. "You, or one of your fucking family, threatened them all one by one. You told them to inflate their invoices, charge us more, and then give *you* the cream off the top. If they didn't, they'd regret it."

If possible, Sunny's "what the fuck?" face got even more screwed up. "What the hell? No, we didn't."

"Yes, you did! I have proof—"

"You have proof that we both got played and you fucking fell for it. The Merchants don't go after legitimate businesses or innocent people—period. We fuck sure don't intimidate random button-sellers!"

"You don't go after innocent people? Ha!" Vance barked, making me jump. "Don't make me laugh. What do you call what you've been doing to Caddell House for years! You've been treating us like your fucking Green Mart!"

Sunny's eyes narrowed to slits. "The deal our family has with Caddell is legitimate. My dad gave him a straightforward, *legal* investment with a *legal* contract that wasn't signed under duress. It was your original boss who offered our family a discount for life, and he did that of his own free will to say thank you. Don't you fucking dare turn a gift into a bribe. The Merchants have done a lot of fucked-up shit, and I'm proud as hell because we've only ever done it to people who deserve it.

"We didn't embezzle a dime from Caddell House, dumbass, so you better show me what proof you think you have saying otherwise."

Sunny advanced on him, blowing away his promise not to get closer. Vance scrambled to pick up the gun. Snapping up, he pointed it at Sunny just in time for my man to smack it away.

"Stop playing with that before you hurt yourself." Sunny plopped in Vance's armchair. "Well? Hurry the fuck up and show me this frame job."

Vance blinked from him to the gun lying across the room, and then he blinked at me like he expected me to tell him what to do.

"All of this is a huge, terrible misunderstanding, Mr. Hollywell," I offered. "Show us the accountant's supposed evidence so that we can figure this out."

"I... uh... okay." Never has a man been so defeated, and Sunny didn't even lay a finger on him. Vance flicked on the desktop and navigated to a folder tucked in a folder tucked inside another folder as I came closer, peering over Sunny's shoulders.

"All of our vendors and suppliers were given this account name and routing number to deposit the money." Vance clicked on a jpeg and the image filled the screen, blasting the slip of paper with the account name for all to see. "Do I need to read what it says to you, or do you want to confess now?"

"Confess?" Sunny forced through gritted teeth. "What I want to do is punch you in the fucking face, Hollywell."

"What?" Vance cried, jumping back. "It says right there! The account belongs to Bellisario Holdings!"

"Exactly, you dumbass! What kind of fucking idiot slaps their real name on an account full of stolen money?" Sunny stared at him in true disbelief. "What the hell is wrong with you? Did you spend too much time playing with your sewing machine in college, you forgot to take an actual lesson?"

"But—but—but— I—I—I—" Hollywell was well and truly broken.

Still, I had no sympathy for him. I shook my head, giving him the same disbelieving look as Sunny. "Come on, boss. Plain old common sense should've caught this one. Of course, the Merchants don't own this account. They've been ruling the city for decades. You don't stay on top for this long by being that stupid."

"But I..." Vance fell silent, slumping on his window seat. All the righteous indignation whooshed out of him, leaving nothing behind but a puppet with its strings cut.

"What else is in this folder?" Sunny asked, clicking around on all the documents.

"It's the... proof the... accountant... gave me..." Vance's voice got smaller and smaller.

"Fake," Sunny dropped, pulling up a pdf of account information and scrolling through. "Fake. Terrible fake. Fake. For fuck's sake, my name is misspelled," he burst out, smacking the screen. "This is the French spelling of my name, not the Italian spelling. I've taken a few hits to the head, but I still know how to spell my fucking name, Hollywell!" Sunny threw the pencil cup at him, making the man burst into tears. "What is wrong with you? Someone hands you a pile of manufactured bullshit, and just like that, you hop on board the train to aiding and abetting murder."

"I—I didn't mean—"

"Don't give me that. It was you, wasn't it? You put the trackers in our clothes, letting those bastards know exactly where my niece was. They almost killed her, Vance!" Sunny ripped out his phone and shoved his screensaver in Vance's face. Of course it was a big, cheesing, adorable photo of Tricky—his favorite girl. "This is who you wanted dead? Huh!? She your hated Merchant enemy too!?"

Vance took one look and wailed louder, sinking on the floor smashing his fists against his forehead. If Sunny was going for complete emotional castration, he nailed it.

I just shook my head at the pathetic mess that used to be Vance Hollywell, director of the great Caddell House. For all his wide-eyed shock and wet-his-pants bleating, Hollywell wasn't this stupid. If he had bothered to hold this *proof* under the slightest bit of scrutiny, he'd have seen for himself it was a load of garbage.

But the fact is he didn't bother looking deeper because he plain didn't want to. This accountant handed him all of his assumptions and prejudices wrapped in a bow. The Merchants were bad guys doing what bad guys do, so therefore, he was perfectly justified in doing whatever it took to get them out of Caddell House forever. That it also gave him a handy excuse to skip over the twenty million-dollar buyout was the cream on top.

Like I clocked the minute I met him, Vance Hollywell is a cheapskate.

My eyes narrowed, lighting on something as Vance blubbered to Sunny, swearing up and down that he didn't know anyone would get hurt, especially not an innocent little girl.

"Then what did you think would happen?" I sliced in, dropping down on the vacant chair and squinting at the screen. A PO box address tucked away at the bottom of the bank accounts taunted me, tickling a memory dancing out of reach. "When the Brotherhood approached you about the trackers, what did they say?"

"He—he said— They needed them to follow you to all of your hideouts and stashes—prove the Merchants were connected to criminal activity. It was all to gather evidence to finally put you on trial, I swear," he cried. "I didn't know anything about any bombings!"

"Why would they need to follow us around for evidence if *that* was your supposed evidence?" Sunny gestured to the computer. "Why didn't you just turn your proof of embezzling over to the police? Why didn't that forensic accountant make you?"

"He said there would be a huge scandal!" Vance climbed up on his knees, near pleading with Sunny. "He told me he'd seen a million of these cases play out in court, and even if you ended up in jail, the Caddell name would be forever tainted with the stink of theft and dirty money. We're buried under too many scandals and lawsuits already. We can't afford to lose the few clients we still have."

"Batavia," I whispered, still staring at that address.

"And let me guess," Sunny went on. "After feeding you that load of bullshit, he gave you the number of someone who could clean the whole mess up without a scandal coming anywhere near Caddell."

Vance bobbed his head, spittle coating his cheek. "Yes, I'm sorry. I didn't know. I swear, I didn't know anyone would get hurt!"

"How could you not know? Why didn't you see that this whole thing was shady right off the bat? You got in bed with criminals because you wanted to get out of bed with criminals!" Sunny shouted, seizing his collar. "Tell me how that makes sense in your small little mind!"

"Because they weren't!" Vance shrieked. "That's what I'm trying to tell you! I didn't know they were dirty! I didn't know! Dwyer didn't send me to a darkened corner in a back-alley bar! He gave me the number of two detectives who he promised would handle my case discreetly!

"I thought I was working with the cops. I thought they were undercover and—"

"Using you to illegally surveille suspects and ensure their case was kicked out of court as quickly as their asses were out of the police force?" Sunny finished, tone dead.

Vance broke down, wailing on the floor under the force of his immense greed, naivety, and stupidity.

"Batavia... Batavia..."

Scoffing, Sunny turned his back on the sad act soaking his shoes. His gaze sharpened on me. "Sugar Bum? What's wrong?"

"Sunny, I... I think there's more to this," I said slowly. "Much more."

"What do you mean?"

"I mean, Vance finds out there's something not adding up in the accounts and he just happens to hire a forensic accountant that fronts for the Brotherhood, giving them the access they've been praying for to build their money-printing machine?"

"Babe, this money-printing-machine thing is an insider you've got with someone else," he said, dropping down next to me. "I don't know what that means."

"Oh, right, of course. Basically, it's when the key to everything you've ever wanted just falls into your lap one day. There's no way that happened here. There's just no way *Vance* just happened to them. All of this had to be a setup from the beginning. A setup that's been years in the making.

"The only question is if this has always been a Brotherhood setup, or it's a trap someone else set and the Brotherhood jumped in and happily sprung it." My grip tightened on the mouse. "It makes me sick to say I'm leaning toward the latter."

"Kenzie, I'm not following this." Sunny grasped the chair and gently turned me around. "You're saying someone else embezzled from Caddell House, and the Brotherhood used that to drag us and Vance into it."

"That's exactly what I'm saying." I avoided his gaze, stomach sick with shame. "And even worse... I know who it was. I know who figured out who the Johnsons really are, and used that info to scam millions from innocent suppliers. I know who did such a stupid, clumsy job of leading a fake paper trail to the Merchants, they were found out by an enemy that's been hunting and fighting to uncover all of your weaknesses. And I know who offered you and Vance up on a silver platter all in the name of keeping his filthy money and seeing someone else go down for his crimes."

Sunny stiffened, his lips peeling back from his teeth. I saw in his eyes... that he knew too.

***

Genny

The darkness spun—twisting, entwining, crashing, and crumpling on itself. I burst out of it and vomited on the floor.

"—GH? FGH!"

Wheezing, I strained to lift my head. Voices crowded in, jangling my aching skull. *What the fuck happened?*

The last thing I remembered was running headfirst, Genny-style, into a mob of armed gangsters. The next, pain exploded in the back of my head and...

I cracked an eye open and immediately snapped it shut. The spinning world beyond my lids twisted my stomach, ejecting more vomit past my lips. I didn't need to remember what happened to connect the singing pain in my skull to the upset in my belly. Someone hit me hard enough to drop me into unconsciousness with a concussion as my going-away present.

"FGH? Can you hear me, boss?" someone cried. "Are you okay?"

"No," I groaned. "Not okay. Definitely... not okay."

Somehow, I forced my eyes open. Peering through my lashes, I took in the bland walls, bare floor, and the biting chill soaking into my wrists. I was chained up in the Brotherhood's house of horrors.

"Can you get up?" Shug asked.

Every ounce of my strength channeled into my legs. I might as well have been a newborn for how much I struggled just to lift my head. With it an inch off the ground and away from my spreading vomit, I worked on my legs, getting them under me enough so that I could use the chains to pull me up into a sitting position.

Rising up, my chest heaved—pumping and rolling with my strained lungs.

Shug, Bee, and Pixie breathed sighs of relief to see me up. All except for the silently crying girl in the corner. Of course she was crying. I told her I'd save her, and all I did was end up chained to the wall right next to her.

"Please, boss, tell me your brothers and your parents are on the way," Bee croaked. "They're right behind you, right? With the firepower?"

I clicked my tongue, shaking my head at the three Bees spinning in my vision. "Shame on you, Bee. Do I look like a fucking damsel in distress? Think I need my mommy and my big brothers to save me?"

"Uh... yes."

I blamed my mother for raising me so soft that I tolerated this disrespect. The woman just had to be all kind and loving and supportive, so I didn't get my prerequisite evil-villain, mommy-issues backstory. Now all my Cardinals think they're my fucking friends and equals, and damn me for always confirming it.

"I'm going... to let that slide, Bee, since you've been dealing with a traumatic... situation." My head lolled, almost dropping me back in my sick. "I don't need them to save me." My chains rattled against the wall. "Everything's going according to plan."

Chapter Four

Kenzie

"This makes no sense." Bane stalked in front of his wall of weapons, taking things down and concealing them within folds of his clothes to be found by no one but him. "Is Vance with the Brotherhood or not?"

"Not," I said firmly. "He's a pawn. A chess piece. One that they moved when the time was right, but were willing to sacrifice if the trackers were ever discovered."

"But he didn't frame us for the embezzling?" Bane took down a gun, examined it, rejected it, then put it back.

Sunny stretched out on the couch, holding me to his side while I dug and kneaded his bad shoulder.

"The embezzling started long before he joined the company," Sunny spoke up. "Doesn't make sense for him to take the job, discover someone cheated the company out of millions, and then frame us for it instead of finding and charging the person who actually fucking did it."

Bane gave us a look. "He might've if the person who actually fucking did it threatened him. Forced him to pin it on us or he'd lose his job."

I was shaking my head before he finished. "He doesn't have the power or authority to fire people. He didn't have that power over a junior designer, he definitely doesn't over the director of Caddell House Cinco City."

"He would if he was secretly in the Brotherhood," Bane returned. "Backed up by an army of psychopaths, you could deliver a lot of effective threats."

"Bro, if that shitfuck is in the Brotherhood, why is he living the good life in New York when he should be fighting the good fight here in Cinco with his brothers?"

Bane inclined his head. That was a good point.

"Guys, please," I rasped, rising up on my knees. "You don't have to dance around his name. You don't have to protect me. My broken-picker chose another fucking winner. Damien Frost, father of my child, used the Merchant name to scam millions out of innocent people. And because that wasn't enough for the greedy fucker, he seduced Talia for her money, and then destroyed my life when he thought I'd get in the way of it.

"You said you have to understand people to destroy them, but your enemies can say the same. The Brotherhood knew cheapskate Vance would jump on any opportunity to save Caddell House from more scandal and lost sales, so he sewed those damn trackers into your clothes instead of going to the real police.

"Just like they knew money-grubbing Damien would do what money-grubbers do, and trade his integrity, decency, and innocent people for a quick buck." I tossed my head. "Sometimes the money-printing machine isn't anything amazing, or clever, or impossible. It's just two weak men with shit morals for a backbone."

"Kenzie." Bane dropped down before me, taking my hand. "I admit that none of this looks good, and there's no question that deadbeat piece of shit deserves the ass-kicking of his life, but why are you so sure he's behind all of this? The Brotherhood already had a plant inside Caddell House—Madison."

"That woman scammed thousands off the pain and suffering of desperate mothers and kidnapped children," he said. "She could've just as easily stolen that money and blamed her hated enemies, the Merchants."

Another headshake. "Madison wasn't a plant. I worked with her, Bane. She's the real deal. Truly a talented designer, and that's something you can't fake. She earned her place in Caddell House, that much I know and..." I hesitated. "As crazy as this sounds, I don't believe she'd steal from suppliers or Caddell."

"Why not?"

"Because Caddell House gave her everything she lost when Daddy kicked her out the door," I said, gaze drifting off over his head as I pictured that terrible day in Madison's life. "Thanks to Caddell, she has money, prestige, the right address, and the right social circles again. She'd never risk losing that all over again by stealing from Caddell, and I know that because it's what her mother would do.

"And if there's anyone in this life that Madison hates and never wants to be, it's the mother that lied, cheated, and stole from everyone... including her own daughter. She robbed her daughter of a fancy privileged life, and then she robbed her of a mother." I spoke with the certainty brimming in my bones. "Madison hates her mother, and that's why she's been getting back at her by *saving* kids from versions of her mother for years," I said.

"I know your mom thinks Madison didn't hide her involvement in the Sunshine Adoption Agency because she's an idiot, but I think it's much deeper than that. She didn't hide because she's not ashamed. She truly believes she's the hero in this story, saving kids from poverty. Saving them... like she wanted to be saved."

I released a deep breath. "She can't pretend she's achieving her grand mission through scamming innocent people and stealing from Caddell, so no, Bane, it's not her."

Sunny broke out into a grin. "See, bro?" He rubbed my back. "I told you she's good."

"I know she's good." Bane smiled at me, sending my heart cartwheeling into my throat. "I've met her, haven't I?"

Sunny tickled me. I shot away yelping and giggling. "Tell him the rest, beautiful."

"The rest," I said softly, picking myself up. "The rest is Batavia. Damien did a fashion design certification program in New York after he graduated. He had an aunt who wasn't really his aunt. She was a close friend of his mother, so he grew up calling her Aunt Della. She moved to Batavia when he was in high school, and after he moved to New York, he'd drive up and drop in to see her.

"Batavia is the location of the PO box all the bank documents are connected to," I said. "Damien no doubt believed no one would connect Batavia to him because no one in Caddell even knew about his aunt that wasn't an aunt, or where she lived.

"No one but me."

"Hmm." Bane rocketed to his feet. "Well, that's all the proof I need to give that bastard the beating I owe him, so how do you want to handle this? Liam traced the number Genny called from and narrowed it down to a stretch of forest outside the city, but it's a wide radius. There aren't many cell towers out there, so we can't narrow it down. He's calling everyone, and I mean everyone, in to start the search, but we can't sit on this information.

"Frost stole the money, but somehow his theft became leverage against Vance to cover us in trackers. At some point, Frost got mixed up with the

Brotherhood, and whatever he knows about those faceless bastards, we need to know. He might even be able to narrow down our search."

"Agreed," I replied, sitting back.

The guys stared at me. I flicked between them, brows furrowing as the silence stretched.

"Wait, me?" I cried. "You're asking me how to handle this?"

"Of course, we are," Sunny said. "You're strangely opposed to me kicking his skull in and dropping him off the docks. You said he's your ex and you want to make him pay your way, so here's your chance, baby. What do we do now?"

My jaw worked. I wasn't expecting them to throw this to me, but I did understand why they did. I'd been entertaining Sunny's many violent fantasies against Damien, and then shooting them down as never going to happen. Damien ruined my life. He abandoned my daughter. If anyone was going to get revenge against him, they'd have to get in line after me.

Damien Frost was my problem to deal with, and now that I knew he was responsible for Sunny being thrown off a bridge, Liam and Elizabeth nearly being blown up, and Genny getting shot at and trapped in a burning building...

Now that I knew that, I was done with mercy.

I stood up. "You guys, go and save Genny. She needs you. But on your way, call down to the hangar and tell them to fuel up the jet. I'm going to New York."

***

Genny

Voices sounded from the hallway. I didn't have to strain to hear, all the shouting and carrying on they were doing made their conversation easy for all the woodland creatures in Elmshire Woods to eavesdrop.

"—bitch did something to Brother Abraham! She must've! He called down saying he trapped a Merchant rat and was coming down to dispose of her, then next thing we know, she's bursting through the door, Brother Abraham is nowhere to be found, and he's not answering his phone. She killed him," the guy shouted. "She must've killed him."

"Brother Abraham could never be taken out by some skinny little bitch, okay? It's just not possible!"

"Then where is he? Where are his guards?" another calmer voice asked. "Why is she here, and he's not?"

No one had an answer for him.

"From this point, we have to assume Brother Abraham, Brother Clark, and Brother Eugene are out of play. We also have to assume she called for help after taking them out. Her brothers and their empty-headed henchmen are on the way as we speak."

"I don't think so."

"Wake the fuck up," Calm Guy snapped. "Of course they are."

"No, because if her brothers were on the way, she would've waited for them," Shouty argued. "Blundering in here was a desperate move because she didn't know what else to do, or where else to go. Brother Abraham wouldn't have brought her here unless she was blindfolded, and she couldn't have gotten here on her own if she killed him before they hopped in the fucking car."

I gritted my teeth. I fucking hated the smart ones.

"She's on her own," Shouty confirmed—glee leaking into his voice. "Brother Abraham may have paid the ultimate sacrifice, but in doing so, he gave us our best weapon against the Merchants. As long as we have Genevieve Hunt, they can't touch us."

"You're right, Brother." Calm Guy was smirking his ass off. I didn't need to see it to know it. "You're absolutely right."

"Still, we've got to change locations," said Third Guy. "Just in case. We've underestimated the Merchants before and paid for it. Losing Brother Abraham for one."

"I agree," Calm Guy replied. "All right, here's what we do. Brother Sam, start moving out the guys, the guns, the food, the TV, the fridge, everything. The secondary location's got nothing. It's got less than nothing, so we'll need it all."

"Right." Stomping footsteps sounded Brother Sam's retreat, running off to follow orders like a good little dog.

"Brother Malcolm, arm the bomb."

I froze.

"We're only taking Hunt with us. She's all we need. If the Merchants blow in here looking for her, they won't resist trying to free all of these bitches like the heroes they pretend to be. While they're wasting their time sawing at chains, the bomb will tick down—taking them all out."

"Can't we take a few of them with us?" Brother Malcolm asked. "There are a couple tasty ones I'd like to sample again."

My lips peeled back from my teeth. *Oh, you'll get a sample of something all right. Straight to fucking hell.*

"I told you to stop doing that," Calm Guy snapped. "We're not thug rats like those fucking Merchants. We're better than them."

Oh yeah, so much better, asshole. You don't approve of raping innocent people but you're plenty happy to murder them.

"Hey, you said I couldn't touch them unless they gave me permission." Smugness laced that shit's tone. "And they all did."

Yeah, they gave "permission" after you beat the crap out of them.

"Answer's no. There's barely enough space at the other location for all the brothers. We're not giving up room so you have someone to play with. Just do what I say and arm the bomb."

"You do it," Brother Malcolm returned. "That shit makes me nervous. My hands will shake and I'll end up blowing us all away."

"Fuck's sake, fine. I'll do that while you get a blindfold and gag on the Hunt bitch. Put her in my car. We're moving her first—getting her far out of her family's reach."

More stomping footsteps announced that Calm Guy was off laying a deadly trap for my family by blood and by sisterhood. Only one pair of footsteps left.

Creaky hinges assaulted my ears, peeling my lips further back from my teeth. My snarl grumbled low and long as Brother fucking Malcolm towered in the doorway.

Rage filled me. I knew they were out there smirking their asses off, but seeing it on his long, pockmarked face made me heave.

Long, oily black locks hung over his face, casting shadows across his eyes. He was dressed nicely in a dark blue suit, but it looked wrong on him. The arms hung too low, the pants were too high, and the waist was the wrong size going by the cracked-leather belt straining to keep it from sliding down his hips.

Clearly, he grabbed the first uniform out of their Brotherhood Lost-and-Found Box without caring if it fit.

I raked him up and down, taking in everything from the oversized gold hoop in his left ear to the fading bruises on his knuckles.

"Well, well, Hunt. Don't you look ready to be served up and eaten?" He bit the air, moaning. "Yum."

"And don't you look like the mistake your mama still wishes came out the other hole?" I fixed my snarl into a mocking grin. "That's a real nice earring, Discount Pirate. Really brings out the vacancy in your eyes and the ugly on your face."

Bee, Shug, and Pixie laughed out loud. Never had a smirk been wiped off someone's face quicker.

"You hang on to your jokes, bitch, because that's all you've got! First, we're going to blow up your whores, and then we're going to waste your family. We'll see who's laughing when the Brotherhood rules Cinco, and the only thing you're running is my dick."

I rolled my eyes. "I bet that sounded all smart and menacing in your head. Stop running your mouth, you ignorant dumbass, and go and get your boss." I smiled wide. "Poor Brother Abraham is out there in the woods, bleeding, and crying, and shitting his pants."

Malcolm stiffened.

"If you hurry, you might just save him."

"You're lying," he barked, roaring up on me. "There's no chance you'd leave him alive, and there's even less chance you'd tell me if you did."

Another eye roll. "Of course he's alive. I killed his henchmen, naturally, but Brother Brammy I shot in the gut and left cuffed to a tree root. I had to," I said, shrugging. "Vito and Madison let slip just how important he is to the Brotherhood. I need to question him for info, but I also needed to rescue my Cardinals. There was no way I was driving back to the city with him and leaving them here, and there was no chance I'd risk him getting away while I pulled some serious heroics. Answer: Tuck him away until I'm ready for him."

Malcolm's eyes narrowed to slits. "Again, you wouldn't tell me this if that was true."

"Hmm, I'm pretty sure I would if I was captured, chained up, trapped in a room with Pirate Predator, and I wanted him to get the fuck away from me." I glared at him right back. "Yeah, I'd give up my best bargaining chip to send a rapist in the opposite direction. No question. Brother Bitch Abraham isn't worth being touched by the likes of you."

Malcolm crouched down, getting in my face. "You're going to want to be nice to me. No one said I'd be the one trekking off on your wild goose chase. I'll just send the new recruits into the woods while you and I get to know each other a little—"

He touched my thigh and I snapped forward, smashing my skull into his nose.

"Argh!" He roared, blood spurting through the air as he fell back—clutching his nose. His heels drummed the floor as he wailed, crying and carrying on like the little bitch he was.

"I told you not to touch me," I breezed. "This is on you."

"You stupid fucking whore! I'll kill you! I swear I'll kill—"

I dropped back on my hands and swung my legs out, clamping them around his throat. I didn't give him a chance to cry out. Wrenching my body, I snapped his neck—ending his wailing in one swift act of brutality.

Slipping free of him, I beamed at Bee. "I'll take that apology now. I'm no one's damsel in distress."

She granted me a wry smile. "I'll save my praise, FGH, since you're still chained to the same wall as me."

"Not for long." Propping my left foot on my right, I toed off my boot, then my sock. "Brother Dumbass told him to wrap me up and deliver me to the car." I stuck my wriggling toes in his pocket. "To do that, he would've needed the— Ah-ha!"

I withdrew my foot, clutching tight to the keys dangling from my toes. "We're getting out of here," I said, talking to my Cardinals and the battered girl in the corner who lifted her head, lips trembling when she saw the keys. "I'm getting you all out of here. I promise."

***

Kenzie

"You're not going by yourself."

"Of course I'm not going by myself." I cooed at Laurel, making her giggle as I strapped her in her car seat. "Laurel is coming and so is Sienna. Can't get any more not by myself than that."

"Kenzie, please," Bane spoke up. "Sunny's right. We have no idea what that shit Frost will do when confronted. He could try to hurt you or the baby."

"He's not going to do either of those things." The four of us were in Laurel's nursery. Sunny and Bane stalked me while I packed Laurel's diaper bag and got her ready to go. "The only good thing that man has going for him is that he's not violent. He'd never put his hands on a woman, and most definitely not a baby."

"Yeah, I bet you once thought he'd never frame a woman for fraud and abandon a baby," Sunny returned. "You were wrong then too."

"Ouch," I cried, poking his side. "Low blow, baby."

"Kenzie, I'm serious. This is Serious Sunny talking." He grasped my shoulder, making me slow down and face him. "A cornered rat is never more unpredictable than when the sirens are getting closer. Let me or Bane go with you."

"Baby, you can't." I gently stroked his cheek. "The Brotherhood is holding Genny in a Luca hellhouse. You know what those are like. You know guns, violence, and most likely bombs are waiting for you on the other side of the door. I won't stand for a single one of you to get hurt because you weren't all there guarding each other's backs.

"Liam needs you and Bane by his side, Genny needs all of her brothers, and I need to find out what Damien knows about the Brotherhood and the shadow people running it. Let me do this," I said firmly—urgently. "I can't back you up in a gunfight but I can do this. All you have to do is trust me."

"I do trust you, Lollipop Lips. I trust you more than anyone." His eyes hardened. "But I don't trust Damien Frost."

"That's why Sienna is going with me. She's my backup and I'm hers. We survived months on the street together. Damien is nothing compared to that."

Sighing, Sunny looked to Bane as if hoping he could talk some sense into me.

Bane assessed me, gaze unwavering.

He nodded.

"She can do this, Sunny." Bane took my hand and kissed my knuckles. "I should know. I trained her myself."

Sienna stuck her head in the doorway. "Hey, guys. We ready to go?"

"No," Sunny dropped.

"But, Sunny—"

"Not without weapons," he continued, flashing me a wink. "It'll give me great pleasure to picture you tasing that dickhead every time he gets mouthy."

Sienna laughed. "Oh, don't worry. He will and *we will*. And I'll most definitely record it for all of us to watch on movie night."

"This is why we're besties, SiSi."

I rolled my eyes at the both of them. Finishing up packing, I picked up the car seat, handed Sienna the diaper bag, and left the nursery just as Liam entered the living room. "Everyone's ready," he announced, face grim. "It's time."

"Good luck." I hugged and kissed Sunny, Liam, and Bane—holding each one tight. "Come back to me."

"We will," Sunny said. "This day is going to end badly for someone, but it won't be us."

I held on to those words as Sienna weaved through the streets of Cinco, heading for the hangar.

"Are you nervous?" she asked.

I shook my head, turning away from the buildings flashing by. "No. Not about Damien. I..." I sighed. "I realized something after confronting him in Caddell. I don't care anymore. I don't care about him. I don't love him. I don't miss him. I don't hate him. I'm not even worried about the effect his absence will have on Laurel, because he'll have no effect on her.

"She'll be raised with so much love and protection and safety around men who'd do anything for her. They wouldn't leave her for all the money in the world, so why should I give a shit about the man that would?"

"Me and the spirit friends agree with you completely, sis," Sienna replied, making us both bust out laughing. Laughter that ended quickly as the seriousness of that day filled us, but still, it was a good laugh. The cleansing laugh of two people who had well and truly... moved on.

Sienna turned the final corner leading into the hangar. The headlights lit up the large gray building, and the man leaning against it.

Sienna smiled. "We agree a thousand times. Why would anyone want Damien Dumbass Frost when you've got men like him on your side?"

He walked up as Sienna pulled into a parking space, grinning that enigmatic grin that always aroused and enraged me in equal measure. The grin of a man I'd spend the rest of my life trying to understand, but never would.

"So, how does this work?" I asked, grinning back. "Sunny calls you up and tells you I need an escort, and you drop everything, including your dislike of him, and come running to my side?"

"Didn't do much running," River drawled, hooking his finger through my belt loop. "Took a cab like everyone else, but the rest is pretty much spot-on."

"But I don't need an escort," I said as he towed me in, wrapping his arms around me. "I'm a big girl. I can take care of myself."

"Same thing I told him." River's voice was just as light as mine. "But Sunny shared his theory with me about the Brotherhood being a Leighbridge gang. Just because Leighbridge cops are always chasing me and mine out of the borough, doesn't mean I don't know all the players.

"I thought I could go with you when you talk to Damien. Float some names to him and see how he reacts. What do you think?"

I shook my head, still smiling. That suggestion was so reasonable, River knew I couldn't turn it down—which was the whole point.

"Sounds like a plan."

He tipped his head. "There's also the little matter of it not being safe for you guys to stay in Sunny's place in the city."

"What, why?" I asked. "Why can't we stay in Sunny's place?"

"At this point, we have to assume the Brotherhood knows everything about the Merchants, including the location of their second, third, fourth, and fifth homes. That's why Adeline and her husbands have moved out of their home upstate. That's why their oldest daughters and their families have cleared out and taken off somewhere that not even I know about," River said, tightening my shoulders. "No one is taking chances right now, and walking right through the doors of a penthouse that is one hundred percent being watched is a big fucking chance."

River rubbed my shoulders, smiling into my eyes. "They're probably watching the hangar right now too."

Shivers crawled up my spine. I shot in front of Laurel's door, my skin rippling with goose bumps. "My goodness," I breathed. "Are—are you sure?"

"It's what I would do." River gently moved me aside and reached in for Laurel. He held her close, car seat and all, shielding my baby so naturally and willingly with all the love and protection that once shielded me during the worst time of my life. "It's what I did when I considered the Merchants my enemies."

River nodded to me and Sienna, communicating silently for us to quickly and quietly get on the plane.

We did—both of us flanking River and Laurel and guiding them across the asphalt. Only when we were safely inside with the door closed and sealed did I breathe again.

"Where is your place?" Sienna asked.

I settled Laurel in a seat and gave her a bottle. Her eyes were already starting to get droopy. I had a strong feeling she'd drift off to sleep before we left Cinco airspace.

"How do you know it's not being watched too?"

"The Brotherhood isn't watching me." River reclined in his seat, but I didn't mistake this for relaxing. His eagle eyes scanned everything happening through the window. "I've no doubt that they know about me and my connection to the family, but they've long ago dismissed me as a homeless bum."

"How do you know?" That question came from me.

That grin danced on his lips, teasing out a dimple that I and only I got to see. "I just told you, baby. The most dangerous threat to the Merchants— The most effective and complete tool of their destruction has been standing in their face for longer than even the Merchants have known, but those assholes have spent all their time on useless assassins and sniveling fashion directors instead of coming straight to the only person they ever needed—me."

I was quiet for a long spell. "Do you still feel that way?" I asked softly. "I know why you do. Even more, I understand why you do, but I've been wondering if there's anything other than a common enemy that will bring all the men I love together."

River nodded slow. "Yes, there is, Kenzie—you. But not just because I want you. I can let it go because you and your story have helped me see things clearer than before."

"My story?"

River tipped his head again. "What happened between your mom, and your dad, and you."

Jaw clenching, I looked away.

"Your mom was willing to kill to protect you, and you were willing to die for your daughter, because that's what it all comes down to in the end—loyalty." River slipped his hand in mine, making me look up. "Adeline's loyalty to her dad. My loyalty to my mom. Sunny's loyalty to his mom. None of us were acting out of malice or hatred toward the other. Just the opposite, we were acting out of love, and that's why we were so fucking stubborn and hardheaded about it," he said with a laugh.

"That's why we refused to apologize or pretend we were sorry because I'll go to my grave protecting my mom and her memory, so... maybe I should finally fucking understand that my sister will do the same for her dad—the only parent who loved and protected her while the other was selling her to drug-dealing pedophiles."

My brows shot up my forehead. "Adeline's mother? She..." I trailed off, words failing me.

River just laced his fingers through mine, kissing my knuckles. "Adeline's idea of family has been small—just like mine. She believed she had to protect that family at all costs from everything and everyone, sometimes even from her own blood—and I believe that too." He sighed. "There are no right or wrong decisions when you're fighting for someone you love. They're the only ones you'll defend to your grave.

"All this time I've been wanting—demanding—that she regret choosing her father over me, but that's not fair," River whispered, wisdom beyond his years belying his words. "Because I didn't choose her over my mother, and your mother didn't choose that controlling abusive piece of shit over the wonderful and perfect you."

Tears filled my eyes.

"I keep bringing up your mother, Kenzie, because she's looking out for you again, by drilling sense into my thick damn head. The whole world believes she did wrong, but I know she didn't. She so very much didn't because what she truly did was fulfill the promise she made to you and Sienna on the days that you were both born—to protect you with all her strength and might from anyone who dared to hurt you."

I bit my lip hard, penning in sobs.

"Her love was punished. Her love was illegal," he said, voice thick, "but it was still right because you and Sienna had to come first—you just had to. If she can love two people so much that doing a terrible thing is still the right thing, then I can stop being such a fucking hypocrite. If your mom was right to protect you, and my mom was right to protect me, and I was right to protect her, then..." He gave me a lopsided, but resigned grin. "Maybe my sister can be right too, in protecting her dad—our dad. And I can understand that and I can let it the fuck go, because there's no one to protect anymore. There's just us, and I'm tired of fighting someone who never wanted to hurt me."

Clearing my throat, I rubbed my eyes hard. "That's very wise, River Redgrave. Incredibly, wonderfully wise."

He kissed me slow, then pulled back, drawing us both back into his seat and me on his lap. "I'm not saying me, Sunny, Bane, and Liam are going to be best buddies overnight, but I'm in this fight with them for real. They're my family and I'm going to protect them because they've done one thing right in their lives and protected you, Laurel, and Sienna."

I dropped my head on his shoulder, so happy I could burst. "Do you think this is a fight we can win? What if Damien is another dead end? I thought we had Vance, but he's clueless. I thought we had Madison but..." My sentence died thinking of the body the cops carried out of the gas station. The last thing I saw on the news before Sienna and I left for the hangar. "The Brotherhood is like water. We keep trying to grab them with our bare hands, but they slip right through."

"They're just people, Kenzie. Flesh and blood like you and me, and they make mistakes. They've *made* mistakes. Mistakes that are revealing them whether they like it or not," he said. "For all their self-righteousness, they aligned themselves with Luca Adams instead of putting him in the ground and freeing the women he abducted, so right off the bat, we know we're look-ing for a bunch of dead-inside monsters."

"I still don't understand that," I whispered, dropping my voice when I saw Laurel had drifted off to sleep as predicted. "Is hating the Merchants re-ally the only criteria for membership? They don't care who they are or what they do as long as they throw their weapons, money, and vengeance in the pot?"

I flicked to Sienna. She had taken a seat further back to give us some pri-vacy. "What do you think, Si? Do you think the answer really is as simple as Sunny said? The Brotherhood doesn't care about the women Luca tortured for the same reason Madison didn't? They—we—were too low class to live in the imaginary utopia the Brotherhood has planned for Cinco?"

"I can't say for sure." Sienna got up and crossed to join us. "All I know is that I've been feeling for a while that this enemy is someone connected to the Merchants. Someone who had crossed their path and has every reason to hate them. But it's an old grudge. A patient one. A grudge that's been fester-ing and growing in hate and malice, and even though mistakes have definite-ly been made, whoever's behind this has been planning this long enough to have considered every angle, and they'll make sure that the only one standing at the end of this war... is them."

I was glad that River shuddered beneath me, because I did too.

***

Genny

I stumbled on the steps, half tripping, half falling down. With a cloth sack over my head, it was amazing I was upright at all.

Clambering off the final step, a wrenching grip on my arm frog-marched me through a parade of shouts, arguments, and barked orders. The Brother-hood was clearing out as fast as they could, getting ready to take off behind the car that boasted me blind and gagged in the trunk.

"No, leave that! We won't have room for a TV."

"What are we supposed to do all day without a TV?" a weedy voice snapped back. "All we do is sit around waiting for orders."

"The TV stays. Take a fucking book if you're so bored."

From the grumbling, groaning, and bitching, no one liked that decision.

Wherever they were going, it obviously wasn't another Luca Hellhouse with plenty of rooms for his vile business, so maybe—hopefully—this was the last of Luca's boltholes, and all the women he kidnapped were finally found and could get back to the lives stolen from them.

"Whoa, look," someone cried. "It's that Merchant bitch. The stupid shit actually thought she could take us all on her own."

Raucous laughter ripped through the fussing and fighting.

"Poor girl's been sipping on her legend for too long. She actually thought she was some unbeatable badass." He raised his voice. "How'd that work out for you, sweetie?"

I was dragged out the door as a million cutting snapbacks sprung to my lips.

"They've been parking their cars all over the woods so that no one who stumbles on the house will think it's weird that thirty cars are parked on the lawn," Bee hissed.

I couldn't see her, but she was obviously big-time pulling off the ruse. As gross as it was, I had to strip that worthless sack's corpse and choose Bee to take his place. She was the only one tall enough, thin enough, and with hair short enough that a quick glance from the side wouldn't alert the brothers to the switch. With them so busy packing up and clearing out, and the sun beginning to set, I trusted they were too busy trying to clear out while they still had light to worry about what the guy lurking around next to them was doing. So far I was right.

So far...

"Brothers could be lurking anywhere in the trees," Bee said. "The car for this key could be anywhere. I'm supposed to know where it is and take you there. What now?"

"Calm, Bee. Just confidently march me off to the big blue van parked out in the open. That's the car I was brought in."

"They're loading their weapons into that van."

All the more reason that's the van for me. I worried my lip, thinking quickly. "Okay, just march me into the woods like nothing's wrong."

Bee veered us both toward the left. I held my breath waiting for someone to shout, shoot, or sound the alarm but... nothing.

"Okay." Bee tugged the sack off. "Now what?"

I looked around as I placed my back against a massive oak tree, giving myself one less position to defend. I could still hear the brothers, and dusk's light allowed me to partially make them out through the trees.

"Don't worry, Bee. The first step was getting out of that hallway. There was only one way out, and it was too dangerous having bullets flying around you guys. We're lucky no one got hit the first time."

"So do we wait?" she asked, peeling off her borrowed blazer and flinging it over a branch.

I wasn't too worried about anyone finding the man who used to own that blazer. There was nothing but empty closets in the hostage bedrooms. The brothers had no reason to go in looking for anything, because none of them kept a single thing in them. And besides, why would they need to go looking for Brother Rapist when they just saw him walk out the door?

"They said all the hostages are staying behind," Bee continued, "so once they leave, we can free them, get out of here, and the Brotherhood won't know a thing."

I shook my head. "Most of them will leave, but not all of them. A few will stay behind, hiding in the dark and the trees to wait for my family to get here. As soon as they all enter the house, they'll set off the bomb—making damn sure this time." I looked away from the guys loading guns into the van and met her eyes. "Gotta assume they'll do the same thing if they see me pop out of nowhere to lead the hostages out.

"Kaboom."

She flinched. Bee, short for Beatrice, may have been tall and thin, but that didn't mean she wasn't tough. Bee was a slick and slippery fighter. Just when you thought you had her pinned, she'd disappear from your hold and you'd wake up a minute later with her boot on your throat. If I was going to take on a dozen armed idiots and a bomb, she was who I wanted on my side.

"Okay, okay," Bee whispered, beginning to pace. "If we can't make a move because they're watching the place... and they won't make a move until your brothers arrive, then... then we have a very short window to crack some skulls open."

I smirked even as my head pounded with pain. "This is why you're my favorite."

***

Kenzie

I settled Laurel in the crib, smoothing down her wearable blanket. Ducking out of the room, I turned out the light and gently shut the door.

Padding out to the living room, I found River in the kitchen, standing over a boiling pot of something that smelled delicious.

I had no idea what to think when the third cabbie pulled up in front of the brownstone. River insisted that we keep switching cabs and take the most confusing route to throw off anyone who could've been following us. That meant we arrived at our accommodations well after dinnertime.

The first thing Sienna did when she stepped out of the car was head straight for the artists' café across the street, promising to bring back dessert when she was done. That left River and me to get the baby inside, feed her, and get her down for the night while River started dinner.

With my task complete, I finally had a chance to take a proper look around, and first looks said this place was swanky.

Hardwood floors, exposed brick walls, plush white carpets carving out the living room and the dining room, a huge sectional in front of the big screen, and everything in the massive kitchen was spotless from the marble countertop to the six-burner gas stove.

"Wow, River. This place is amazing. Is it yours?"

He shook his head as I came in and hopped on the countertop, watching him cook with interest.

"It's a friend of a friend's friend," he replied. "Well, it's their income property. They rent it out to people on vacation. I figured it was better to be safe and stay somewhere not connected to me or the Merchants."

"But does this friend of a friend's friend know we're staying here?" My brows popped. "We're not doing that thing where we break into someone's place because it's empty, are we? Because I've watched enough New York crime shows to be very scared of the NYPD, and I do not need them busting in here guns blazing with Laurel in the next room."

He laughed. "They definitely know we are here, Kenzie. You did watch me use a key to open the door, not a lockpick and rock." River dropped a peck on my cheek while leaning over to reach the spice rack. "Debs said it's cool since it's only for one night."

"Okay. Well, in that case, what are you making?"

"There wasn't much to work with, so I'm making Cajun shrimp and rice."

"Oooh," I crowed, kicking my feet. "Sounds yum."

River gave me a look out of the corner of his eye. "Have you thought about what you're going to say to Frost? How you'll confront him?"

"Oh, yes." My smile dimmed. "I know exactly what to say to Damien."

He squeezed my wrist—a quick and comforting gesture before returning to stirring the rice.

"Can I ask you something?" I heard myself say.

"Always."

"What's your plan, River? Long term," I clarified. "I know most of the crew are living in the Leighbridge shelters, and you're living there and running them now, but do you think you'll ever settle down? Have a home? A family?"

"Stop being the Rat King, you mean." River flashed me a wry grin. "I've thought about that a lot over the years. Thought about it even more after falling in love with you."

I flushed to hear him say that so easily. With another unhappy reunion with Damien on the horizon, I couldn't help looking back on our relationship more and more. And right then, I was thinking how rushed and thrown-away all of his *I love yous* were. Nothing like the sweet, honest, sincere *I love yous* from the man next to me.

"If I set up in a real house with a real job, a bank account, a mortgage, credit, and all that shit, well then, just like that, everything changes. I go from the Artful Dodger to the Fagin, and when that happens, my crew—the people who've been on my side and watching my back for years—will have nothing to do with me."

"You won't be the Fagin," I cried. "Fagin was a greedy miser who hoarded the wealth he forced children to steal for him—letting them live in squalor while he went all Smeagol over his gold."

River barked a laugh. "Smeagol?"

"Hey, if you can make literary references, so can I." We laughed again, but I sobered quickly. "It's not the same, River. You would never use and abuse your friends like that. You'd never stuff your face with everything while they sat at your feet begging for scraps of anything."

"I know I wouldn't. Of course I'd still look out for them, but—it's like—" He blew a breath, shaking his head. "Okay, it's like this. You know this theory you guys have about the leaders of the Brotherhood really being a rich prick, or a group of rich pricks, who's hiding in the shadows while letting their army of lower-class rent-a-thugs do all the dirty work?"

"Yeah," I said slowly. "What about them?"

"Well, if that's true, and to be honest, I'm betting that is true, then, it's a problem. A big fat fucking problem that this Brotherhood can't fucking see yet, or they never would've built their gang this way."

I could only listen and watch as River slathered the shrimp in seasoned butter, then tipped them into the sizzling pan.

"They've created a huge imbalance within the core of their gang. An *us versus them* distrust that will always be there no matter how scared the lower members are, or how much they're paid."

"Why would there be distrust?"

"Because they're not fighting the same fight, Kenzie." He trapped my gaze in his enigmatic pools. "On the surface it's 'Merchants' this and 'take the city back' that, but underneath, they have these two groups of people who don't face the same issues, so how can they be fighting for the same cause?

"Madison James wanted to keep preying on abused and trafficked mothers so that she could get rich selling their children." He scoffed, lips twisting. "For all that she told herself she was *saving* those kids, notice that she squeezed fifty thousand dollars each for her *heroics* instead of presenting herself as a foster care agency and adopting those kids out for free."

I blinked. "My goodness, I never thought of it like that, but you're right. I mean, if you're going to set up a fake fucking agency anyway, it could've just as easily been a fake government foster care agency that didn't extract a year's salary from everyone who came through the door."

"But she didn't," River continued, "because in the end, it's all about the money. With soulless roaches like that, it'll always be about the money. In the meantime, Joe Nobody at the bottom rung of the Brotherhood is probably the father of one of those kidnapped kids, and he joined to make enough money and get enough help on his side to track down his missing daughter.

"The very daughter taken by a fellow member he doesn't even know, because she's too good to go near the likes of him."

Even as my stomach heaved, I nodded. "I understand."

River came to me, positioning between my legs and grasping my hips. "I'm not going to pretend like every gang out there is some fairy-tale vision of camaraderie and brotherhood, but the ones that don't implode from the inside last because everyone is the same. They live in the same neighborhood, they hate the same people, or they're the same kind of scared and alone, so they're banding in with people like them to feel tough and safe.

"As weird as it is to pay him a compliment, Sunny went out and built the kind of gang that lasts, and he did it quicker and better than any of his siblings. Even better than his parents," he confessed. "Everyone in the Sons of Saint is the same. They're on the same level—man and woman. Art thief and forger. They're even on the same level as Sunny.

"Sunny may be the leader, and he may have more money than Midas, but at the end of the day, they want the same things and they're fighting for the same things. And when that fight gets dirty, Sunny will drop down in the mud right alongside them and take all the same risks.

"The minute I'm the guy in the mansion while my people are sleeping in the shelters..." He shrugged. "We won't be fighting the same fight anymore, Kenzie. And I won't be able to pretend otherwise even though I'll want to."

"River," I whispered, stroking his cheek. "I truly do understand. You wouldn't be able to lead them anymore. You'd become an outsider looking in on your family and... and no one wants that."

"They certainly don't want that twice."

I pressed my forehead to his, sighing. "So you won't move in with me," I said, saying clearly the topic we'd been dancing around the whole conversation.

"I want to," he ground out, holding me close. "You have no idea how much I want to go to sleep next to you every night, and wake up next to you every morning, but my crew was who I had when I had no one. They stuck with me through things that would break other people in half. I can't turn my back on them to run off with my hot-ass sugar mama."

I giggled.

"What about you?" he asked. "Can you handle dating a homeless bum for a little while longer?"

"Hmm," I hummed, pushing out my lips. "Let's see. Do you have a—?" I leaned over his shoulder, peering down. "Oh, yep. The cute-butt requirement is fulfilled." I sat back, beaming at him. "We'll make it just fine."

River cracked up. "Actually, I don't know," he mused, wrinkling my nose. "How can you be sure I met the requirement? You didn't get a very good look."

My brows shot up my forehead. "That is true. It would strongly behoove me to give that ass a good and proper test spin," I purred, draping my arms around his shoulders. "For the sake of the relationship."

Smirking, River nipped my nose. "I think you'll find that it's your ass that's about to get a hard and thorough test spin."

Heat exploded in my body, tearing my hardening nipples free of my balconet bra. I did not use the words hard or thorough, but I liked them much, *much* better.

River bent, dropping kisses on my collarbone, and the dizzying heat surging through my body skyrocketed. "But—but what about dinner?"

River turned the stove off in two quick snaps.

"And what about Sienna?" I blurted, head falling back.

"I promised I'd let her lease our newest, so-to-be-purchased location for a dollar a month," he dropped, "in exchange for three uninterrupted hours of Kenzie time."

I blinked. *I swear, every time I look away, my sweet and clever sister makes another move to build her entrepreneurial empire.*

"Seems like you and my ass had this date booked out in advance."

"Yep." River lifted me squealing over his shoulder, marching me off to the couch. The world spun as he tossed me down and then himself after me. "Got a problem with that?"

"Not a single one."

Just like that, our clothes came off in a flurry. Getting alone time with River was less than easy. I was hardly going to bring Sunny's hated half uncle back to his place to screw him on Sunny's bed, but River's room in the shelter was no more than a small cot in the office. Amazing man that he was, he refused to take up a proper bed that could go to someone who needed it more.

All of this left me in desperate need of River time.

My hands were everywhere. Threading through his locks, running down his abs, raking down his back, and squeezing his ass—pulling him ever closer to me.

I was drowning in River Redgrave—soaking in his spicy burnt-orange-and-sandalwood scent, barely hanging on to his arms holding me tight.

River kissed down my forehead to my nose, escaping the cliff of my chin and dropping down between the valley of my breasts.

I shivered under the burning trail, eyes fluttering—

"Oh!" I moaned, eyes popping wide as two fingers teased my lower lips, and then slipped past their entrance—finding a warm and eager welcome inside.

"Dammit, Kenzie, you're so freaking gorgeous," he growled. "Do you have any idea what you do to me?"

I moaned louder, legs spreading wider as he sunk in to the knuckles and spreeeaaad his fingers. "If it's anything... like what you do to me... you're a lucky man."

He chuckled, and was still chuckling when he wrapped his tongue around my nipple—sending delicious vibrations through the sensitive nub.

My back arched off the soft, plush fabric, transporting me to a world of pure, passionate, animalistic pleasure. Reaching between us, I palmed his length—feeling no shame at the naughty, shallow happiness I got at barely being able to fit my hand around the size of him.

Balancing on my heels, I got under him and pushed, flipping him unceremoniously on his back.

"Whoa!" he cried, blinking up at my smirk.

"Uh-uh," I teased, shimmying down his legs. "No interrupting while I'm working."

With that, I bent and swallowed his cock whole, ripping a grunt out of him.

I took River as deep as my gag reflex would let me, moaning around the warm, stretching girth of his twitching, happy dick.

"Fuccccckk, Kenzie," he grunted, tangling his hands in my hair. "I take back all the stupid shit I said. I'll move in with you now."

I giggled. Once again, I felt no shame at the shallow, dirty pleasure it gave me that I had so much power over such a powerful man. River Redgrave was putty in my mouth, and that's exactly how it should be.

My mouth went as far as it would go, then my hand squeezed the rest.

Bobbing, sucking, licking, dipping, and rubbing, I milked rough pants and hard grunts out of him with wild abandon. His thighs tightened, harkening the coming explosion.

One hard tug and he ignited, coming hard in my mouth. I relaxed and accepted all he had to give me.

River wrung himself dry, then collapsed on the couch, chest heaving. "Fuck, yes, baby, you're incredible."

"I know," I purred, swiping my tongue across his tip and standing it up for round two.

"What do you think about finishing your work up here?" River asked, tapping his lips. "Your seat awaits."

"Oooh. Yes, please." I crawled up his chest and sat on his face, not shy about it in the least.

If I was honest about it, and there was no reason not to be, this would be the first time River and I sealed the deal. Yeah, we hooked up before, but then a cop knocked on the window and broke that up fast.

It was funny because I'd known River twice as long as the other guys, but he was the last one I claimed for my own— Well, actually, technically Bane was still fighting his claiming, but he was a pin I was determined to knock down... and I get what I set my mind to.

But River...

River wasn't someone I was trying to get. River Redgrave was wild, dangerous, and unpredictable. He was a mystery stuffed with secrets, basted with doublespeak, and baked in an oven of hot, smoldering bad-boy enigmas.

Everything in me screamed to run away from wild and unpredictable because I needed to be the opposite. I needed stable and humdrum because a stable, safe life was the path back to my daughter, and finally having a home with her and my only family.

But then Sunny crashed into my life and brought Bane and Liam into it, and everything I knew about safe, stable, and the *right* kind of life went out the window. All of a sudden, I could finally see River for the stone-cold catch he was.

While Luca was a slimy, vile pig in a flesh mask, hiding his true nature from dozens of unsuspecting women, River was who he'd always been.

River never once tried to hide the man he was. Even though there was much he'd never told me, he also never lied to me. He welcomed me and Sienna, and gave us protection while other people refused us their spare change.

The truth was, River was always the man I was afraid to love, because I knew once I gave him my heart... he'd never give it back.

I rocked back on his tongue, eyes rolling up in my head as he latched on to my clit and sucked like he was trying to take the thing off and run away with it.

His fingers caressed a path from my hips and down to my middle. One, two, three, four fingers probed my pussy, stretching that happy hole wide. In went his long, thick, pink tongue.

"Ahh, yes," I whispered. Rising up, I bounced up and down on his face—impaling myself on his tongue and those naughty fingers.

I wanted to be all cool and demure about it, but who was I kidding? I've never been cool or demure a day in my life, and if I learned to be, it wouldn't be when one of the hottest guys I've seen was licking my pussy like a lollipop.

"Ah, yes, River, yes!" I shrieked—shaking and gyrating and riding him like the rodeo. "More! More! Deeper, River, yes! Baby, rub my clit! Rub my clit!"

He complied. The man got his thumb in there like a pro, vigorously rubbing that bundle of nerves *while* his fingers stretched me wide *while* tongue-fucking the crap out of me.

My screams quickly devolved into unintelligible nonsense. Heat rose beneath my skin, raising my temperature to a fever pitch. I doubled over—my lower belly contracting hard, trying to hold back the lit fuse burning down, down, down—

"Ahh!" My core exploded, bursting multicolored fireworks in my mind.

I came so hard, my spasming body tipped over and I fell off the couch.

"Shit! Kenzie, are you okay?"

"O-okay," I gasped, shaking as orgasmic wave after wave crashed over my body. "I am... very okay..."

River scooped me up. Sitting upright and feet on the floor, he propped me on his lap and kissed the hell out of me as the last traces of my orgasm shuddered out of my body.

Tongues tangling, fireworks igniting, we made out like lovesick teenagers—hot and sloppy and addictive, and so distracting, I didn't know my pussy was receiving another visitor until the sneaky slut let him in.

Moaning, my brows popped when River spread me cheeks and all, pushing me firmly down on his hardness. He held me still as he started pumping, springing off the edge of the couch and drilling me hard—all without breaking our kiss.

I cried out, pouring all my filthy words and desperate urgings for more, harder, and faster through his lips and into his soul. I had to be reaching his soul, because the man had found mine.

Small, afraid, and hiding in the deep, dark place it crawled into when my mother shot my father, and blew away the façade of my perfect dad and perfect childhood all in one act.

River coaxed it out and taught it to trust again, to laugh again, to believe in men again, to love again.

Yes, I loved River Redgrave. The truth was I always loved him... that's why he pissed me the fuck off. When I wasn't looking, the man talked me out of all my resolutions against love and made me his in every way before I could blink.

I dropped down as he pumped up—our bodies in perfect tandem. Our souls in sync. Our first time together, and still he knew my body like his favorite book.

His hands on my waist just the right kind of tight and firm. His lips the right pressure. His tongue teasing and delicious without choking me like Luca used to do. His cock *biiiiiggg* without being a pussy-ripper. Every single bit of being with River was right and perfect in a way it'd only ever been with three other men—Sunny, Liam, and Bane.

I broke away gasping. "River, I—"

"I love you." River smiled into my eyes even as he pumped faster, cracking my jaw in a silent scream. "I love you more than Romeo loved Juliet. More than Jack loved Rose. And more than hazelnut loves chocolate."

"I—I—" River struck that spot and all words and sense flew out the window.

I crested the peak, then went careening off—free-falling into a volcanic eruption of pure ecstasy. Each individual nerve ending caught fire and burned away, surrendering totally to River and my complete love for him.

He pumped once, then came inside me, painting my walls with hot ropes of cum.

We tipped over, collapsing in each other's arms—grinning at each other like lunatics.

"More than hazelnut loves chocolate, huh?" I giggled, kissing the tip of his nose. "Now that is real love right there. How can I top that?"

"You don't have to." He laced his fingers through mine, holding me close as the sweat cooled on our bodies. "You just have to love me back."

"I do, River." I pressed my forehead to his, closing my eyes while we descended into our own private world. "I love you."

***

Genny

Bee and I watched from the shadows as Calm Guy stepped out of the house—free and unweighted down by all the weapons, food, and even furniture the other brothers were carting out of the house as fast as they could.

I only knew he was Calm Guy because Bee matched the voice to the face.

"His name is Brother Edwin," she whispered. "He's in charge of these guys but we've heard him mention a Brother Abraham a bunch of times. I'm guessing that's who Eddy Boy takes his orders from."

I nodded, studying him. Edwin was tall and slim with shaggy brown hair, wide-set eyes, and a tattoo on his neck that I couldn't make out. None of that stood out, but what surprised me, is that he was young. He held some kind of authority over the others, but he looked no older than twenty-one. A simple glance told me most of the other brothers were older than him, so what about Edwin made him qualified to be the warden of this prison?

"I've met Brother Abraham," I spoke up. "We had a nice chat before I killed him. A stupid, ignorant, pea-brained moron, but he did do my girl Kenzie a favor, and murdered the bitch who threw her and her baby into the arms of a sex trafficker, so at least the man will have one good deed in his logbook when he's standing at the gates of hell."

"Wait, you killed Brother Abraham?" she hissed as we watched Edwin pause to talk to the men loading guns in Abraham's van. "What does that mean? If you took out their leader, does that mean— Is it over?"

I was shaking my head before she finished the question. "If Abraham was the true leader of the Brotherhood, these guys would care a lot more about the fact that I clearly murdered him and disposed of his body sometime between him driving me here, and me busting in there and blowing out their hideout. But look at them..."

We watched the brothers working quickly, efficiently, and coldly. Not a single soul was weeping and boohooing about the place over their blessed leader's death.

"I mean, they can't even be sure he's dead," I continued. "They're assuming he is, but Edwin didn't send anyone to check. Why? Because they don't really care."

Edwin ended his conversation and continued on toward a break in the trees.

"If Abraham was truly their leader, and they're sacrificing—and dying—to serve him, then they'd give way more of a shit than this."

Bee tipped her head. "You're right. This Abraham guy was higher up in the ladder, but he can't have been at the top."

"Did they give any clues as to who is at the top?" I gestured for her to follow as I stepped lightly, following Edwin's figure through the shadows. "Did they mention any other names? Did they report to anyone else?"

"Not that we could tell."

Edwin was oblivious to the two stalking foxes trailing as he left his men and protection behind, heading for wherever he parked his car.

"They said a bunch of names," she continued, whispering. "But whenever they had to check with someone or ask permission to do something, they only spoke of Abraham as the one to go to."

That didn't surprise me. "For as much as they hate the Merchants, the Brotherhood doesn't mind ripping us off."

"What do you mean?"

"Back in the old days, my dads structured their gang the same way. Members at the bottom of the ladder report to the rung above them, but they don't know who's above that person, and no one knows who's at the top." I flapped a hand toward the guys on the lawn. "Abraham was an enforcer. Tough. Violent. Brutal. But also fakely sincere and gentlemanly. He kept an iron grip on the foot soldiers, keeping them always off-balance by the fact they could never guess when he'd turn and slaughter them all.

"But whoever holds Abraham's leash... that's the question."

She clicked her tongue, tossing her head. "Hera, fuck them, but they're a weird, pointless gang. They don't trust each other. They don't like each other. They don't care when their fellow *brothers* catch a bullet in their head. I doubt they even know each other's real names. This must be entirely about revenge for all of those guys, because they're damn sure not enjoying each other's company for another reason."

I couldn't argue with a single thing she said. From how quickly and easily Abraham shot Madison in the face to how little the brothers cared when Abraham caught his own bullet, they called themselves brothers but they couldn't be further from.

The one at the top of the ladder may have thought they were clever ripping off my dad's old gang structure, but if they were really smart, they would've asked themselves why old Daddy Cash drop-kicked that structure into the trash.

A true crew lives and dies by loyalty and trust, and no one trusts a lurking, anonymous shadow. There was a reason the Merchants have ruled for decades, while the Brotherhood can't take us out with an army of assassins and trackers up our asses.

We're the best for a reason, bitch, I thought as Edwin unknowingly led us to the car our stolen keys belonged to. *And you're about to find out the hard way.*

"Malcolm? Malcolm, turn on the lights," Edwin called. "I can barely see a thing."

Bee tapped the key ring, making the headlights flash their signal about twelve feet ahead.

Silently, I signaled to Bee—giving her one last nod before she broke right and I broke left—disappearing into the dark.

Thud.

"Ow!"

"Who's that?" Edwin cried, whipping around. "Who's there?"

"Brother? Brother Edwin, it's me," Bee ground out—her voice deep and gravelly like that Malcolm shit. "I fell! I—I think I messed up my ankle."

"That Merchant bitch! Do you have her?" The man was going wild spinning back, forth, around and around with his gun—aiming at twigs and leaves. "Did she get away?"

"No, she's in the car— Ah," Bee carried on, selling it like a pro. "She's secure. Just help me!"

Edwin cursed. "All right, for fuck's sake. Just tell me where you are."

He stomped off in the opposite direction as I crept up to his rather modest four-door sedan. Climbing inside the backseat, I tugged my black sack back over my head and hid my hands behind my back for good measure.

I waited while Bee faked him out, discovering her ankle miraculously healed before Edwin could get too close and realize she wasn't who she said she was.

Noise sounded outside the car, signaling Edwin's return.

"—fucking fool wasting my time." *Slam!* "Hurry up and get in the fucking car!"

Shifting and shuffling, and then I felt a groping hand on my side.

"Safety first," Edwin taunted as he buckled me in. "You're our grandest prize, Genevieve Hunt. The key to our victory. Can't let anything happen to you."

"Awww." My hands flashed. As quick as my left rose to yank the sack off, that's how quickly my right flew at his face. "If only I felt the same about you."

Wide-eyed shock blew up his brows just in time for me to punch him dead in the nose, cracking the cartilage beneath my knuckles.

"Argh!" Edwin snapped back, bumping the back of his head against his headrest. He scrambled for his gun as Bee dove inside.

Ripping it free off his waistband, Bee leveled it between his eyes—her grip firm and steady staring down the barrel of her revenge against the soulless monster who chained her to a wall like an animal.

Chest heaving, nose weeping, Edwin slowly sat back, his gaze darting between me and the gun.

Smart guy. He knows I'm just as deadly.

"Now, then, Edwin." I reached around, grabbed his seat belt, and wrapped it around his wrists—securing him. "We don't have much time, so let's get straight to business. Where's the bomb?"

Edwin's throat bobbed with a hard swallow. "Okay, look, this doesn't have to go down this way. Let's all just calm down and—"

"—have a nice pleasant chat with the psycho mass murderer planning to bomb a house full of innocent people?" I finished—my voice just as calm and pleasant as his. "No, thanks."

His brow twitched. "No one in that house is innocent."

"Really? Please, tell me all about the sins committed by the random hiking couple that happened to knock on the wrong door? Please," I hissed, anger bleeding into my voice. "Explain how you're justifying in your sick and twisted mind that they deserved to be beaten, raped, and blown up."

Edwin's jaw tensed, eyes flashing. "No one wanted that couple caught up in this. Or those women that disgusting scum roach Luca forced into his business. *I* wanted to let them go! It was Brother Abraham who said they had to stay upstairs with the others. We couldn't risk them telling anyone about all the guys in that house in the woods who helped them."

"Well, Brother Abraham is dead now," I dropped without a twinge of conscience. "You're making the decisions now, and this is your chance to make the right one. Tell me where the bomb is and who's holding its trigger because"—I patted him down, checking all his pockets—"it's not you."

Edwin didn't move. He didn't say a word.

I sighed. "Look, I'm not going to mess around and lie to you. I'm going to kill you." My conscience wasn't disturbed by that either. "You call Luca a scum roach, but you're not better than him. You're clearly the one who was in charge of watching over these fools for Abraham, and even though you told Malcolm not to touch your hostages, you knew that he was.

"You knew he was beating and raping them, and you did nothing about it!"

"I didn't know!" he roared, calm façade breaking.

"Then, you should've! You should've given a fucking shit, and made sure those women and that man were protected, but the truth is, you didn't care what happened to their bodies, any more than you care about their lives!" I punched him again, ripping a scream from his broken nose. "For that, you're going to die, but here's the good news. You get to do one last good, kind, and moral deed before I send you to your maker.

"You can help me save the lives of those innocent women and man. You can be the hero you've been pretending to be, instead of going down as another deranged terrorist."

"Argh!" Edwin lunged at me, getting as far as the seat belt would let him—which wasn't very far. "Helping them means helping *you!* It means helping your slavish biker bitches and your rotten family! I will never—NEVER—help the Merchants!"

I blew out a frustrated breath, feeling the ticking seconds of my brothers, my Cardinals, and everyone in the house drawing down. "Fucking hell, we get it, okay! The Merchants hurt people. There was collateral damage in our bid to take over the criminal underground, and who or whatever you lost matters. Your pain matters."

He jerked—fury cracking with the shock of hearing me of all people saying something like that.

"You want me and my family to face the pain and damage we've caused? Fine. You want to kill us? Fine. You want to go to war with us? Fine!" I shrieked. "But take the fight to us! Fight us like a fucking man! Face-to-face! Out in the open!

"Enough of this skulking-around, stalking, planting-bombs, and cowering-in-the-shadows bullshit! Enough dragging innocent people into it and using them as shields, because you fucking know you won't and can't win without fighting dirty!"

"We will win!" Spittle showered the opposite seat. "Just because we're leveling the playing field, doesn't mean any of us are fucking afraid of you! We have a plan!" His eyes bulged out of his head. "We know all of your weaknesses, bitch! You've already lost, and the best part is"—Edwin laughed out loud—"you don't even know it."

My lips peeled back at the gleeful malice on his face. All I could see was Jill's bruised and bleeding face as she sobbed over having to beg for rape.

Right above his head, that woman was going through hell, and this fucker dares... to laugh.

"Bee." My voice was light—dangerous. "What do you say you and I show this fucker what we do to winners?"

The smirk that twisted her lips was a joy to behold. Because it wiped Edwin's away.

"With pleasure."

Chapter Five

Kenzie

I sipped my chocolate rooibos tea, trying to be as classy and ladylike as my companion, but what I really wanted to do was suck it down so I could skip to the part where I begged for more.

"This tea is delicious," I spoke up, slicing into the awkward silence. "Thank you so much for introducing it to my life."

Talia cleared her throat, and tried on a smile. "It's from an artisanal tea shop," she replied. "I'll give you the address. You must drop in while you're in the city."

"We absolutely will." I flashed her the same smile, then turned it on River and Sienna who were sitting on my other side—smiling the same uncomfortable smile.

There was nothing this visit was ever going to be except for tense. It was weird enough explaining to the doorman why he needed to call up to the penthouse, and then even fucking weirder than that when she actually let us in.

Now we were all sitting in her impeccable living room—a space as grand as Sunny's but as homey as Liam's—while the great, powerful, and successful Talia Barker sat stiff-backed in the sectional next to me. As usual, her hair was bottle-chestnut-red perfection. The brown freckles on her nose drew your attention to the brilliant jewel-tone emerald of her eyes; her mouth was a smashed cupid's bow, painted with light lipstick; and wrinkles at her temple did their job of proclaiming just how well she was aging.

Grinning at each other like loons, the silence stretched... and stretched... and stretch—

"So—"

"We—"

Talia and I spoke at the same time, and then cut off, murmuring *excuse mes.*

The front door swung open.

"Hey, hon." Damien stepped in and turned right for the coatrack, shrugging out of his five-thousand-dollar Caddell coat. "I know you asked me to stop by the pharmacy on the way home, but the line was out the door. The pediatrician said it's not an emergency, so—"

Damien finally turned. Lifting his head, he looked right into my eyes. "Kenzie?! What the—?" He took in Sienna, River, and playing on the carpet between us, Laurel. "What are you doing here! What is *she* doing here?!"

"Damien, dear, please stop shouting." Talia gently set down her cup. "*She*, as you can plainly see, is playing quietly with her brother. If little Laurel can do so, there's certainly no reason for you to be shouting and carrying on like a child."

Damien paled, going very still. "B-brother?"

Talia's frosty glare was her only reply.

I looked away from them and flicked down to Laurel. She indeed was being very sweet and gentle with the six-month-old baby lying on the blanket next to her and her toys. I believed she thought he was one of her dolls, because she kept poking and blowing Jeremiah kisses. Either way, it was the most adorable thing I'd ever seen.

So adorable, even Talia dropped her fake polite smile and flashed a real one whenever she looked at them.

It was a surprise when I stepped out of the elevator and got an eyeful of the playpen, baby toys, and spit-rag tossed over Talia's shoulder. I didn't realize they'd gone through with the adoption already, welcoming a sweet little bundle of chub into their career-driven lives, but in that instant, it made sense why she let me in.

Your priorities shift when you become a mother. All of a sudden, you care a lot less about covering and lying about your partner's faults, and a lot more about making sure the person you're raising a child with... isn't a monster.

"Darling." Damien surged forward. "Whatever that woman's told you, it's a lie," he hissed, not even doing me the courtesy of using my name. "Every single word of it a lie!" He scooped up Jeremiah, picking up and carrying him away from Laurel as if he couldn't stand for my daughter to touch his son.

And in that second, all lingering traces of affection for him burned away in a flood of white-hot hatred. Why in the hell did I hold back Sunny from carrying out those revenge fantasies against him? This piece of shit was never worth my mercy.

"I'll thank you not to be hysterical and get Jeremiah worked up before his nap." Talia plucked her baby out of his arms and placed him right back next to Laurel. Her gentle touch did not match the frost biting her words. "Now, Mackenzie is here to have a simple, civilized conversation with you about irregularities in the Caddell House financial accounts."

If I thought Damien was pale before, the man was Casper the Dickhead Ghost following that sentence.

"Considering you lied, framed, and abandoned her to raise a child alone, the least you can do is sit down, shut up, and answer her questions honestly."

"But—but, sweetheart—"

"Sienna," Talia continued, reaching behind her to grab a bottle off her side table. "Please give this to Jeremiah if he starts fussing. I'll be in my office—making a few calls to my colleagues and fellow fashion directors. It's time they know there was a fraud in the fashion world, but it wasn't Mackenzie Blaine."

My brows shot up, blowing as high as my eyes went wide. I wasn't expecting her to do that. I didn't ask her to do that, but my throat choked on my gratitude when I tried to tell her what it meant to me.

"But, Talia!"

She brushed past him, head held high.

"Talia, please, listen to me," Damien cried, shooting to her side. "I promise you, she's a liar. A crazy, obsessive lunatic who mistook my kindness for a crush. When I rejected her, she used her fatherless accident to try to ruin my reputation and career!" He grasped her shoulders as Sienna grasped mine—preventing me from leaping across and ripping his face off for speaking about my daughter that way. "She didn't get away with it the first time, don't let her get away with it now. She—"

"I know, Damien." Talia peeled him off her. "I've always known. About the cheating. About the women. About Vivica Rostov—the dancing whore currently living in an apartment paid for with my money."

Damien opened his mouth but nothing came out.

"But what I didn't know," Talia continued, "is that you're a fraud and thief as well, but, if I'm honest, it doesn't surprise me." She pointed to a door off the kitchen. "Right now, the only calls I plan to make are to fix a horrible mistake you forced me to commit. But unless you want me to also make a call to the police and a divorce attorney, you will sit down, cooperate fully with Mackenzie, and you'll do it without any more of your insults. Do I make myself clear?"

"I—I—" Damien's jaw worked, sweat dripping down his brow. "I... Yes, dear," he rasped. "Whatever you need."

River, Sienna, and I threw astonished, and pleased, looks at each other. It was so easy to see how Talia rose to the top of the Caddell food chain in only six years. The woman was a force to be reckoned with.

Turning on her heels, Talia stormed off to her office.

"Talia," Damien called. "Please, just know that I love y—"

She slammed the door shut.

Damien stood there for a long beat—not knowing what to do or say.

It was me who made the first move. "River, Sienna, would you guys mind keeping an eye on the babies while Damien and I speak in the dining room?" I bent down and smooched Laurel's cheek. "I love you, baby girl. Mommy will be right back."

She screeched some babble back to me in return—the picture of carefree and happy in the midst of a man's total and complete breakdown.

River caught my hand as I moved away. "If he doesn't listen and gets mouthy"—his gaze sharpened on Damien—"go for the eyes."

I laughed.

River didn't.

My chuckles dried up. *Goodness, is it a Redgrave trait that makes them deliver violent threats of maiming and death with such a perfect straight face?*

Putting that aside, I crossed to the dining table and claimed a seat across from Damien, flashing him a bland smile that he didn't return.

"Let me guess," he hissed before I opened my mouth. "You're here for child support. You think you can blackmail me into paying for a kid that's not mine? Let me set you straight right now, Mackenzie. That's never—"

I flapped a hand, waving his nonsense away. "Enough, Damien. I don't want child support from you. I don't want anything from you. Laurel already has a safe, loving family and more fathers than she'll know what to do with by the time she's a teenager." I looked him dead in the eyes. "The only example of men she'll have in her life is of honest men with integrity who never take the easy way out, so, of course, that excludes you."

Nostrils flaring, he bared his teeth. "Don't you dare judge me," he barked. "Whatever I am, it's still ten times more than you're worth."

Wealth and privilege had been good to Damien. Naturally, he always dressed well, but going from a five-figure salary to a seven-figure lifestyle meant his leather coats, black slacks, and polished shoes cost the same amount as his former salary.

On top of the new wardrobe, he filled out around the middle, sported a new swooshy haircut, and his skin looked amazing. Damien was absolutely thriving as one of the New York elite—

—and yet, he never looked more hideous to me.

Sitting there turning his nose up at me like I was the scum, when he was a cheating, lying, child-abandoning thief, and my only crime was loving the wrong man.

Amazing the lies people tell themselves so they can remain the hero of the story.

I rolled my eyes. "If that's what you need to tell yourself, Damien, have at it. But, if you don't mind, I'd like to get off your delusions and return to the point." Reaching into my bag, I pulled out the folder of documents and slapped it on the table. "You embezzled from Caddell House."

"What?! How dare—!"

"Save the outrage." I slid the folder over to him. "It's all there—including the PO box in Batavia. You bullied suppliers into inflating their invoices so that you could pocket the difference, and you did it all using the Merchants' name."

"That's not—" He flipped through the folder, bug eyes darting back and forth among the pages. "I didn't—"

"I don't work for Caddell anymore, so prosecuting you for your theft is up to them— Oh, I mean, it's up to Talia," I corrected, grinning away as he flinched. "I just want to know how and when the Brotherhood got involved."

Damien's head snapped up. I saw in his eyes that he recognized the name, but just as quickly, his face shuttered closed. "I have no idea what you're talking about." He tossed the folder back at me. "I didn't bully anyone, and I certainly didn't embezzle from my own company. You have the wrong guy—which you should've figured out on your own. It's not my name on those documents."

"No, it's Sunny's name on those documents." I shook my head. "Actually, it's his misspelled name. Seriously, Damien, you really should've looked up the correct spelling of Sole before you forged his name."

He shrugged. "I have no idea what you're talking about. I did no such thing."

I folded my hands on the table, the picture of patience. "Damien, would you do me a favor and look to your right?"

Brow wrinkling, he did as I asked.

"Good. Now, do you see that incredibly handsome and sexy-ass man who is currently holding and feeding your son? He's Adeline Redgrave's brother."

Façade crumbling, Damien turned an unhealthy shade of purple jumping up from his seat.

"Calm down," I said, crossing into his path. "River would never hurt Jeremiah. Why would he? When he's here to hurt you if you don't. Stop. Lying?" I hissed through gritted teeth. "Stop fucking around, Damien, and tell me everything you know about the Brotherhood."

"I—"

"Do it fucking now, or Sienna and I will take the babies for a little stroll through the park and let you finish this conversation with River."

We both turned to look at River—who was currently blowing raspberries on a giggling Jeremiah's stomach. I saw an adorable scene, but Damien...

He sat back down.

Reclaiming my seat, I flashed him another smile. "Now, let's start again. How did you get involved with the Brotherhood? What do you know about them and what they're planning against the Merchants?"

"I..." Damien glanced at River. "I know that I'm not a part of them. Whatever you're thinking, I'm not in the Brotherhood."

I leaned back, studying him. "But you know who they are."

It wasn't a question.

"Everyone knows who they are. Everyone who needs to know," he stressed, "knows who they are."

"But you're not one of them?"

"No."

"But you did steal the money?"

Damien squeezed his eyes shut, his jaw ticcing. "Yes," he forced out. "I took the money."

"Why?"

He flicked up, lips twisting. "Why not? I gave Caddell House ten years of my life, I've won two Phenomenal Five competitions, I was singlehandedly responsible for designing a line that gave Caddell House Cinco its most profitable year in twenty years, and do you want to know how management thanked me?

"They passed over me!" Damien punched the table. "They continually refused to promote me—claiming I was doing my best work 'where I was.' So why not?" he cried, throwing up his hands. "Why not take money they owed me anyway? There wasn't any harm in it."

"No harm?" My fists balled. "No harm in threatening innocent, hard-working people and making them believe they'd be the target of a criminal organization if they didn't comply with your demands? You call that harmless?"

Damien shrugged. "The Merchants demand a cut of everyone's business. They want their name on every con, bribe, and murder. They got their wish."

To say this man felt zero remorse for what he'd done was an understatement.

"So you wanted to get caught?" I asked. "Or I should say, you wanted the Merchants to get caught stealing from one of their most profitable, and legitimate business partners. That's why you did such a clumsy and embarrassing job covering *Sole's* tracks." I threw the folder back at him.

Damien caught it, and tossed it over his shoulder. "I told you, I've got nothing to do with that folder or those documents. I never left, or forged, a paper trail. Vance said it was better that way."

I stilled. "Vance?"

"Yeah, Vance," Damien said—his color coming back with his voice. "That's why we had the suppliers inflate the invoices all on their own. After Caddell paid, they'd give us the difference in cash. Our names weren't on anything, and if the IRS ever came sniffing around, all they'd find is a bunch of businesses taking in more money than they were reporting. It was genius."

"Vance?" I cried, leaning over the table. "Vance Hollywell?"

"Yes, Vance Hollywell." Damien looked at me like I was an idiot. "Who else?"

"He's been in on it with you from the beginning?" My mind conjured up Vance's performance in his office in a whole new stomach-turning light. "But he wasn't with the company when you started your scam. He didn't even live in Cinco!"

"He was born here. We went to school together, but then there was some trouble with his family. They were forced to leave the city, then my family left the city, but we stayed in touch." Damien blew out a sigh. "Enough that he loaned me some money—a lot of money—when I got into some trouble with gambling. I owed the wrong people money, but Vance helped me out.

"When I couldn't pay him back, he was cool about that too," he said. "Vance suggested I pay him and myself back by taking it out of Caddell's ass. They owed me anyway."

"So where is the money if it's not in Batavia?"

"Can't tell you where Vance hid his money, but mine is all in cash, and it's tucked away in my safe," he replied, glancing at River. "I'll tell you where if that means we're good."

My throat tightened. My body shook. "There was no forensic accountant. There were no phony cops who pressured Vance into putting trackers in the Johnsons' clothes," I rasped. "It was Vance who dummied up those documents and he purposely did a terrible job so that if Sunny ever came for him, which he did, he'd go searching for some empty-headed fool connected to Batavia—as in *you*.

"He set you up to take the fall for everything! But of course, he couldn't blame you for the trackers now that you're living in another fricking state, so instead, he makes up some bullhockey about forensic accountants and dirty cops—people he had to get involved with because of you."

If I expected Damien to rant, rave, and get upset over his friend's betrayal—

Damien shrugged. "Yeah, that sounds about right."

—my expectations were dashed.

"Are you serious? You don't care that your best friend set you up to take the fall for his scam?"

Damien rolled his eyes. "What am I? Five? Vance is hardly my best fucking friend. We were cool when we were kids, but what he actually was is my *most generous* friend. He was always the guy you could hit up for money, and he'd just give it to you. Sometimes he'd ask me to pay it back. Other times he wouldn't."

"And of course a leech like you would make sure you never lost his number."

He let the insult roll off his back. "I may be a leech, but I'm nothing compared to what Vance is. The guy, he— He just— He has no ego," Damien burst out. "He has no prejudices or opinions or morals. He's like a fucking chameleon. He's whatever he needs to be in whatever situation he finds himself in—putting on a flawless act—but when he goes home to his empty white room, he plugs himself into the wall, powers down, and recharges for another day of pretending to be human like the rest of us."

I shuddered, a real and chilling shiver crawling up my spine. *What a terrifying way to describe someone, but if Damien is right and all that sniveling, bawling, and wailing was nothing but a performance...*

"Terrifying is exactly what he is," I whispered. "He's so good, he's made me ignore my instincts twice. I swallowed every word of his bullshit because I didn't believe anyone could fake being that pathetic."

Damien shrugged again as he looked down. "So he forged these, did he?" He picked up some of the documents scattered on the floor. "Of course he linked it to the Merchants. It's always about the Merchants. Not much could make Vance feel something in his empty, amoral heart, but when you got him going about the Merchants..." Damien trailed off, shaking his head.

"He hates them," I confirmed. "I won't ask why. Plenty of people think they're justified in hating the Merchants because Adeline exposed the ledger, and then because she and her family won't let the criminal underground run around unchecked."

"I know what his reasons are." Damien turned away, staring out the window at the beautiful New York skyline. "I know they were strong enough for him to join the Brotherhood."

"What do you know about them?" River came over—sleeping baby and all—not able to keep himself out of the conversation any longer. "And why weren't your reasons strong enough to join?"

Damien swallowed hard, tensing right up. "Please," he said, holding out his arms. "Let me have my son—"

"Answer the question." River handed me the little sleeping bundle. "Now."

Damien relaxed to see me holding his son, instead of the brother of a dangerous mobster, but only slightly. "Fine," he got out. "All right? I'll tell you everything. Let's just all stay calm."

River claimed a seat. Leaning back, he spread out his hands as if saying *I'm the picture of calm, how about you?*

"I don't know much about the Brotherhood," he began. "Because I didn't need to know. Only those who need to know *know.*"

"What the hell are you talking about?" River barked. "Stop talking in riddles."

"I'm not—" He carded his hands through his hair. "I'm trying to explain!"

"Do a better job."

I glanced at my own baby while they argued. Laurel was very happily playing with her auntie, completely unaware of the drama unraveling around her.

"—names or people," Damien said. "I just know that the Brotherhood was founded by victims of the Merchants *for* victims of the Merchants. When I was around fifteen, I heard my aunt Della tell my mom that a woman approached her coming out of the grocery store." Damien dragged my attention back to him. "She told her that she knew my aunt lost her father during the riots on the Night of Tears. He owned a jewelry store. They busted in and looted the place. He tried to stop them and... I'm sure you can guess what happened."

We could.

"So this woman," he continued. "She went on about it being all the Merchants' fault. All Adeline's fault. She ruined my aunt's life and killed her father, and she was owed revenge. Revenge that this woman would help her get.

"My aunt said no."

"She said no?" I repeated. "Why?"

"Because she didn't blame Adeline or the Merchants. She never did. The store was looted by a band of violent, opportunistic psychopaths. The Merchants had nothing to do with it," he said. "But even if she did hold them responsible, Adeline already made it right."

River and I sat up straight.

"What do you mean?" I asked. "How—?"

The office door opened. Talia stuck her head out, found Jeremiah immediately, confirmed he was sleeping safe and peacefully, gave her husband a poisoned glare, then turned.

"Sweetie," Damien called. "Please, let me—"

The slam and click of the lock were deafening.

Slumping over, the end of his cushy life feeding off his wife's millions hit Damien like a battering ram.

And I couldn't give a shit. "What do you mean?" I demanded. "How did Adeline make it right?"

"She... uh... She..." He tossed his head, fighting to reclaim some of his dignity. "Adeline Redgrave started a charitable fund laundered through Our Lady of the Sacred Heart Cathedral. That fund has been giving money and support to victims of the Night of Tears, and even victims of the ledger, for decades.

"A few months after her dad was killed, the charity paid out her mom's claim when the insurance company refused to. And then again, when Aunt Della got accepted into Cinco University, the charity came out of nowhere and offered her a full scholarship," he said, blowing my brows up.

I glanced at River, but he was sitting there very still with a strange look on his face.

"Aunt Della didn't know it was her or the Merchants who were really behind the money, but she found out." Damien smirked. "I've only ever told you, Kenzie, about my sweet auntie who babysat me for free, and dropped in my dorm with care packages when I was in college.

"I never told you she runs a private cybersecurity firm and has contracts with the government."

"No, you did not," I muttered. "So, she dug into the records of the charity to find out who her fairy godmother was, and she discovered it was Adeline."

Damien tipped his head. "I don't know if my aunt ever hated the Merchants, but after seeing that name on the records, she definitely didn't hate them anymore. Honestly, I think that's what got to her the most," he said softly. "That Adeline didn't reveal herself. She didn't shout about it, ask for credit, or try to be anyone's fairy godmother. She just helped people. A grieving mother and daughter who had no one and Adeline just... helped them."

We were quiet for a long spell.

"Anyway," Damien said, tossing his head. "When the Brotherhood approached her, they didn't have the trigger they thought they did. She said no, and then she said no again, and then again when the woman approached her a third time. Each time the woman got angrier and angrier with my aunt—going on about her being a coward who doesn't give a shit about her own father." He chuckled. "Aunt Della backhanded her across the face and sliced her cheek open. She told that woman she and Adeline settled their business a long time ago, and she should settle her own fucking grudges instead of goading people like my aunt into doing it for her.

"That was the last time that woman ever came around."

I nodded slow. "That woman was so persistent because she wanted your aunt in particular for the Brotherhood. Or I should say, she wanted her skills, business, and expertise."

Damien didn't disagree. "And all she got was my mom and aunt laughing in the kitchen over glasses of chardonnay about the time a criminal organization tried to recruit my tea-loving, sweater-knitting, computer-nerd auntie."

"Hmm," I hummed, looking down at the baby. "But what about the Brotherhood? If your aunt used her skills to hack into a Catholic charity, then she must've looked into the same criminal organization that kept stalking her."

"Of course she did," he said, gazing out of the window. "After the Sacred Heart church, school, and clinic were all burned to the ground, and their accounts raided and drained of every cent."

My jaw dropped. "Excuse me? After it— After it was what?!"

"That's right. It's exactly what you're thinking and it was done by exactly who you're thinking," he hissed. "*That* is how much the Brotherhood hates Adeline Redgrave, the Merchants, and everything they touch, and that's why I'll have nothing to do with them. The Brotherhood would've rather my aunt and her mom been broke, homeless, and feeding off hatred in a cardboard box on a street corner than having been helped and supported by the Merchants.

"They'd rather every single victim be as lost in hatred and revenge as they are instead of taking a hand-up and moving on with their lives, and instead of giving them a choice, they made the choice for them—by stealing from a charity and burning down three buildings with seven people inside."

Eyes huge, I clapped my hand over my mouth—horror burning my bones. "How could they do that? What is wrong with these people! How could Vance join them?"

"I told you. The Brotherhood is looking for people filled with hate and vengeance, and that's Vance. The only time I ever see the real him these days is when the name Adeleine Redgrave comes up."

"What did he blame her for?"

"Revealing that his father was a vicious mutilator and serial killer named the Slasher," Damien dropped without tone or inflection. "After killing him, of course.

"When it got out that the Slasher was his father, life got bad for Vance quick. People assume that evil is genetic, or at least they treated him like it was," he said. "Vance's mom picked up and moved the entire family out of Cinco, and my old friend Victor Pais became Vance Hollywell."

"Only those who need to know know," I whispered.

"Yes," Damien agreed in the most civil conversation we'd had in years. "I knew if the Brotherhood ever found their way to Vance, they'd only have to ask him to join once. Or maybe it's the other way around. Maybe he's one of the founding family. I don't know. It's not a question you can just come right out and ask." Damien shuddered. "Not to a man like him."

"Wait," I said, holding up a hand. "Family? Why did you say founding *family* and not founding members?"

"Because that's what my aunt discovered when she went looking for the bastards who burned down the charity. The cops tracked down the arsonist and got him into an interrogation room, and it's that tape that she dug up," he said. "On it, the guy was ranting on and on about the just cause of the Brotherhood. He said Sacred Heart was evil. It was run by evil people, and it was up to the Brotherhood to free Cinco from the grip of the Merchants because the cops were too stupid and chickenshit to do it themselves."

Damien scoffed. "They called a police psychiatrist in pretty quick to talk to the guy because he had zero remorse. Couldn't give less of a shit that a priest, a nun, and three clinic nurses were among the 'evil' people he brutally murdered.

"The shrink came in and tried to determine if the guy understood right from wrong, and if it sunk in that he was about to get the death penalty for carrying out an act of domestic terrorism in the name of a fictional gang. He then replied, 'There's nothing fictional about my family, and you can bring on your fucking death penalty. I'll happily die for Mom and Dad.'"

"Mom and Dad?" I seized. "Who? His mom and dad?"

"No, that's just it. The guy was an orphan. His folks died when he was two, and then he bounced around from foster home to foster home. Bad ones," Damien stressed. "Wasn't very likely he built up an attachment to anyone in that parade of abusive, neglectful monsters."

My mind raced. "Could he have been avenging his parents' death? Did he blame the Merchants for losing them?"

Damien was shaking his head before I finished. "His folks died in a house fire. They got blackout drunk and passed out with the stove on. Not even the twistiest of mental gymnastics could've made that the Merchants' fault. No," he said firmly. "My aunt was sure Mom, Dad, and family all referred to the Brotherhood, and possibly the top leaders. Why? Because it's genius. How in the world do you find someone who only goes by Dad?"

I snorted. "Good point. Very good point."

Jeremiah started fussing—his face scrunching unhappily in sleep. Automatically, I started rocking him, gently murmuring to the baby until his forehead smoothed out and he settled.

"You're good at that."

"I had a lot of practice," I told the father of my child. "Alone."

Damien didn't reply.

"So the police interview tapes," I asked, veering away from that topic. "Was that all your aunt was able to dig up?"

"That's all there was. That same night, Leonard Stevens was murdered in his cell."

"Of course he was," I gritted. "Didn't matter that he was loyal to them—and insane. All that mattered is that he might talk. Who knows? Maybe just saying Mom and Dad was talk enough, and they killed him for it."

"We'll never know," he confessed. "He was killed before he could give up anything helpful, and the search of his apartment and workplace turned up less than nothing. The cops closed the arson case, and as for the murder case, I'm pretty sure no one looked too hard for that bastard's killer."

"How do you know? Your aunt told you all of this?"

He tipped his head. "She did when I came to her my junior year, asking if she could help me get a scholarship from Sacred Heart too. Just like I heard her say all those years ago. But the minute their name came out of my mouth, she freaked.

"She told me Sacred Heart was gone, and some very dangerous people made it gone. She told me not to go digging around and let it go. I kept demanding to know why, so she told me some of it, and then she told me even more when I accepted a job at Caddell House Cinco City and moved back," he said. "If anyone ever approached me to join the Brotherhood, I had to tell her immediately, so she could protect me, and finally see them pay for what they did to Sacred Heart."

I sat back, worrying my lip. "But... But if your aunt is still looking for the real people behind the Sacred Heart fires, then Adeline will be too. If she didn't find them already. Your sister may have tracked down members of the Brotherhood years ago and had no idea," I told River, grasping his arm. "Did she ever talk... to you... about...?" I trailed off at his headshake.

"There's a lot my sister and I haven't talked about," he said simply.

"Well, then we fix that." I got to my feet. "Now."

Crossing to Damien, I put his baby in his arms, and then went to pick up mine. "Let's go, Si. We've got to talk to Adeline, and tell the guys what's going on. Sunny in particular is going to want another conversation with Vance Hollywell." I quickly rushed to Talia's office and knocked on the door. "We're leaving now, Talia. Thank you so much for your help. We've got everything we need."

She opened the door as I turned away. "Thank you for coming, Kenzie, and... I'm sorry."

Pausing, I met her eyes. "I'm sorry too."

Five words, and inside, I felt the gaping wound that was ripping longer, and infecting deeper... finally begin to heal.

River, Sienna, Laurel, and I were almost to the door when I heard—

"Kenzie, wait," Damien called. "Listen, about how I handled every—"

"Save it," I sliced off. "If I ever see you again, it'll be because I'm pointing and laughing at you while you're living in a dirty tent under an underpass—crying over the child you never get to see." My glare pinned him through. "So you better fucking hope I never see you again."

With that, I shut the door—closing the book on Damien Frost forever.

"Let's go, baby girl." I kissed my baby's soft cheek. "Your daddies can't wait to see you."

***

Genny

"Hit it."

We roared through the trees. Bursting on the lawn, Edwin's shrieking was the backdrop to my and Bee's raucous laughs.

"Right!" With Edwin's hands strapped to the wheel, and my hands holding the straps, I jerked him and the car to the right, careening straight for twin pairs of bugged eyes in the headlights.

We mowed those bastards down like bowling pins, taking them out before they even had a chance to think about their guns.

"Hey!"

"Who is that?"

"Merchants!" someone shouted. "Take them out!"

"Noooooo!" Edwin thrashed, straining to get free.

"Where's the bomb?" I roared, yanking his arms to the left—veering straight for the four brothers packing the last of what they needed into the van.

They dropped the television they were ordered to leave behind and snatched the guns out fast.

"Stop! Stop!" Edwin nearly pulled his shoulders out of their sockets trying to wrench free. "Get me out of here! Get me—"

Bang! Bang! Bang!

Bullets ripped through the windshield.

I was behind the driver's seat. Bee was hunched down under the dash, keeping Edwin's foot firmly on the gas. The only ones in clear range of the bullets were—

"Arrggghhhh!" Edwin wailed like a bitch, screeching as a bullet ripped open his shoulder. "Stop shooting! It's me! It's me!"

Our shooters dove out of the way, fleeing in way of a coming crush death between two vehicles.

I yanked Edwin's hands to the left, veering away at the last second.

Thump!

The car popped off a human speed bump and kept rolling, speeding through the shouting, fleeing parade of brothers.

"Where is the bomb!"

Running for the porch, the brothers finally got some sense in their heads. Taking their positions against the porch railing, they aimed—right at their blessed warden's head.

"Nooo!"

"Where's the bomb!?"

Bullets rained on the car—shattering the windshield, blowing away the rearview mirror, punching holes in the hood.

Edwin was franticly jerking and jumping in his seat, desperately trying to drive away from certain death. "Stop! Please!"

"Tell me where the fucking bomb is, Eddy!"

"It's— It's in the—" A bullet shot his middle finger off. It went flying as blood sprayed the dash, soaring over the seat and landing beside my boot. "Ahhh!"

His scream shook the heavens.

"Oven!" he sobbed, thrashing side to side like he could create a wind to blow the bullets away. "IT'S IN THE OVEN!"

"Who has the trigger?" I ducked, cursing when a shot took out the headrest—taking a piece of Edwin's ear. I wasn't sure whether to call these guys good shots, or bad shots. "Trigger, Eddy? Now!"

"You fucking ran him over!" he screeched. "Help me! Stop shooting and help me! Get me away from this bitch!"

"You don't need them to help you." Leaping forward, I grabbed the wheel and jerked sharply away from the porch, the brothers, and the bullets.

We raced through the gunfire raining down on us, speeding fast for the tree line and the scant cover it'd grant us.

Edwin sobbed the whole way. "I'll k-kill you, you filthy Merchant... cunt. I'll kill you for this!"

I laughed. "Save it. Your threats would go down a lot better if I couldn't smell your urine-soaked pants from here. So much for dying before you ever helped a Merchant. You—"

The car heaved.

Insults lodging in my throat, I choked on them as the car leaped off the back wheels, ejecting me through the windshield. It crossed my mind as my head banged across the hood that the brothers weren't as empty-headed as I assumed. They finally got smart, and blew out the tires.

I crashed onto the ground, pain jarring my bones and making every nerve in my body sing with agony.

"FGH?" voices reached me from far away. "FGH?!

Noise, sound, light, stars, thudding stomps, and piercing bullets twisted and spun in the air, chasing me into dizzying darkness.

"Get me out... stupid fucks... Help me!"

I strained to sit up. To figure out which way was ground and where was sky, so I could get my hands on the right one.

"FG— Argh!" Shifting shapes scrambled in my vision. "Get off me!"

A thud rumbled the ground. Something, or someone, fell down beside me.

"—find my finger! I need to get to the hospital," Edwin bleated. "Take me to the hospital!"

"What do we do with them?"

"Kill them!" Edwin bellowed. "Bury their bodies in the fucking woods, then bluff Hunt's fucking, disgusting, shitbucket of a family. We'll tell them we have her, and they'll have no reason not to believe us, so KILL HER!"

My vision cleared. Three—five—ten men surrounded me and Bee, their guns trained on our heads.

As quick, and clever, and resourceful, and beautiful, and perfect as I was... not even I could see a way out of this one.

"One last ride, Bee." I held my best friend since middle school's hand. "I'm glad we made it our best."

She smiled. Lips parting, she made to say—*what?* I'd never know.

Gunshots rang through the night, ending our last goodbye.

Chapter Six

Kenzie

Sienna pulled away from the hangar, putting an end to our adventure in New York.

River, Laurel, and I sat in the back. My baby was between us, kicking her feet and cooing at nothing, while my boyfriend leaned against the window—bearing the same silence that followed him on the plane ride.

"River?" I spoke up. "Is everything okay? You've been really quiet since we talked to Damien."

"Can't help it," he replied, voice soft. "We went there to prove what a dick Frost is, and instead he showed me what an ass I am."

"You? What are you talking about?"

He sighed. "I'm talking about Sacred Heart church, school, and charities. I'm talking about the school that hired Mom as a teacher, let her enroll me in the school with free tuition even though we weren't Catholic, gave her such amazing benefits she jumped up and down gushing and laughing when she read the employments doc in the kitchen, and then covered all of her medical expenses when she was diagnosed with the cancer that took her away from me.

"All of that," he croaked, "was Sacred Heart."

"Oh, River," I breathed, clapping my hand over my mouth. "Adeline? But... But all of that was from before—"

"The paternity test." River's voice was flat. Dead. "She did all of that for me and my mom before she knew I was her brother. Back when she thought my mom was nothing more than a cheating, gold-digging liar.

"What is that, Kenzie?" he burst out. "What do I do with that?"

"Well, I..." I reached for him. "You did say that Adeline had been keeping track of you two. She was the first one there when you lost your mom and had no one. I guess it's not a surprise that no matter how she felt about your mom, if there was any chance that you were her brother, she had to make sure you two were okay.

"For her sake and for her father's sake," I whispered, seeing the muscles in his neck tense. "Loyalty, baby. She couldn't have lived with herself if she let you or your father down in that way."

"But why didn't she say!" River slammed his fist on the door armrest. "All those times I called her a hypocrite. Accused her of not giving a shit about me until a piece of paper told her she could. Yelled that she was the worst kind of fake—acting like she was family above all when she tossed me out on the street, and the whole time—the whole time!—she did more for me and Mom than a-anyone." His voice cracked. "And she didn't fucking say.

"Why?" he ground out, spinning to me. "Why?"

My heart broke seeing the pain and anger in his eyes. For years, his anger and malice against his birth family defined him. It drove him to find a new family, and tear down the one before. All of those reasons and justifications were being ripped away from him, and with them gone, what was left except two hurt people who kept pushing away what they both wanted most.

"I don't know why," I murmured, stroking his cheek. "But if I guessed, I'd say it's because she didn't want you to feel like you had to be grateful to her. Relationships based on gratitude, and owing each other, are imbalanced right out of the gate.

"She wanted you to love her for her, and..." My mind scrambled to find the right words—the words that would rid the man I loved of the sorrow clouding his eyes. "And she wanted you to be angry," I cried. "Because if that's what you felt—angry, betrayed, abandoned—then she didn't want those feelings invalidated because she anonymously gave your mom a job and health insurance.

"Because those two things don't wash away the fact that she wasn't there. You lost your father and your sister, and she... she..." The truth came to my lips unbidden. "She hates herself too, baby. She hasn't tried to stop you punishing her, because she believes it's no less than she deserves.

"She didn't say because she loves you, River." I cupped his cheek, catching a stray tear on my thumb. "And she can't forgive herself for hurting you."

River roughly cleared his throat. "Yeah, well..." He kissed my palm pulling back. "That's something to think about."

"It's something to talk about too." I laid my head on Laurel's car seat, letting my baby poke me and tug on my hair. "Will you tell her that you know?"

"Have to," he replied, resuming his staredown with the city of Cinco. "She'll know I know when we tell her everything Frost told us. Family, man." River shook his head. "The stuff they do. The things they drive you to. Wouldn't surprise me if that psycho Leonard Stevens was avenging his mom and dad in some way.

"I wouldn't put it past the Brotherhood to lie and fake that the Merchants were behind the house fire that killed his parents—all to manipulate him into burning down Sacred Heart and killing seven innocent people.

"It's insane the lengths we'd go for our parents. To avenge them. To get justice for their memory," he said. "You want to turn a person into a monster or a petty, vengeful asshat. Just tell them someone hurt his mommy."

I froze, my smile for Laurel freezing on my face. A thought occurred to me. A terrible, awful thought. "Or..." I whispered. "Their daddy."

"—zie?"

I snapped out of it, Sienna pulling me back to reality.

"Kenzie, are you okay?"

"I'm fine." I fixed my face, smiling back at Laurel. "I'm just worried. I've been calling and calling the guys, but no one's answered. They all went to rescue Genny last night. We should've heard something by now. Plus, I need to tell them everything Damien told us. They need to know Vance Hollywell is the most dangerous brother we've come across."

She nodded. "He put the trackers in the clothes. He came closer than anyone in their goal of taking the Merchants out for good, and he did it all while hiding in plain sight."

"He must've known that you guys would've gone straight to Frost to confirm his story," River put in, putting aside his tumultuous family drama. "And he also must've known that Damien would tell us the truth. Seriously, what incentive did he have to lie and make himself an enemy of the Merchants, all for a guy he only used for his money?

"Vance knew he was cooked the minute you and Sunny walked out of his office."

"But we did walk out of his office," I reminded. "Giving him plenty of time to get away, plan his next move, or all of the above. Even more reason—"

My phone went off, buzzing against my thigh. I lit up when I checked the screen. "Bane," I cried. "Guys, it's Bane. One sec." I answered on the third ring. "Bane, finally. Are you okay? Is Genny okay? I've been calling you all morning."

"Kenzie."

Something in his voice stopped my words in its tracks.

"Kenzie," he croaked. "Last night... Last night was... bad."

***

The Night Before

Genny

She smiled. Lips parting, she made to say—what? I'd never know.

Gunshots rang through the night, ending our last goodbye.

"Ahh!" I threw my hands up, flipping over and covering Bee as bodies rained down on us.

Edwin, the nine-fingered wonder, dropped like a stone, and that hard fucking head dropped right on my gut.

"Ow!"

"I think what you meant to say, baby sis"—Bane's car roared onto the lawn, bringing a hail of bullets pouring from the passenger's side—"is thank you."

"Get these assholes off me!"

"Close enough."

Headlights blinded me—flooding the forest with squealing gears and honking horns. The cavalry had arrived.

The brothers still cowering on the porch kicked off, returning fire at Bane's car, then Sunny's, then Liam's, then about a dozen fucking cars of people I didn't know, but didn't have to. The Scourges, the Sons of Saint, and Liam's Prissy Sissys—he refused to name his gangs, so I did it for him.

They all came.

"'Bout fucking time," I snapped, kicking free of my would-be assassins like the damsel in distress I was not. "I summoned you hours ago!"

"Yeah, and I begged Mom to reverse the adoption and give you back to your birth parents," Sunny shouted back, bitching me out shamelessly as he rolled out of his car, crouched behind the wheel, and shot over the hood—picking off brothers one by one. "So we've all got things to be disappointed about!"

"You're the one who's fucking adopted!" I tugged Bee free of her load and dragged her behind the busted, shot-up car. She tossed me a wink and a grin when I tossed her my gun. Nothing was taking her down.

"Daddy Sin can't have kids," I called. "Sterile since birth— Oh, whoops! Mom made me promise not to tell you."

"That's not fucking true! You're lying. Liam, is she lying?"

"Will you both get a fucking hold of yourselves?" our big brother shouted at us. "This is not the time!"

"Notice he didn't say no," I taunted as I took off across the lawn. I had to get to that bomb, but there was always time to fuck with Sunny.

I had my priorities in order.

Skirting around the house, I busted in through the back door. As suspected, all the brothers were outside facing certain death. No one stayed behind to hang around in the kitchen.

I hurried across the linoleum, turning my nose up at the mountain of dirty dishes, empty takeout containers, and the ant trail happily taking advantage of it all. It's clear this cabin used to be a nice, swanky place with a bamboo island, quartz countertops, and stainless steel everything.

Unfortunately, it fell into the hands of human waste, and that human waste loaned it out to the scum of the earth.

I skidded to a stop in front of the oven. Slowly, carefully, I opened the oven a fraction, peering inside.

I breathed a sigh of relief seeing the bomb exactly where Edwin said it would be, then I breathed another sigh to see there were no surprises or tripwires—which was another reason why these Brotherhood clowns were so hard to take seriously. If it was me setting the bombs, I wouldn't miss.

Ever.

I dropped the oven door down all the way, took a proper look, and cursed. "Of course the little shit forgot to mention he put it on a timer."

It wasn't urgent. The timer was still counting down from twenty-eight minutes and forty seconds. That gave the brotherhood plenty of time to clear out, but it wouldn't have given me and my bros enough time to unchain all the hostages, clear them out, and then search the place for information. Or even worse, if we had held back and waited for the bomb squad to drive miles out of the city, the whole building would've gone up with my Cardinals and the hostages inside.

"You thought you were being smart, Eddy." I carefully lifted out the bomb. "But you're dead and dumb." Placing it on the counter, I thanked all the deities above that my mother fell in love with a knife-throwing carnie, a neck-snapping boxer, a duplicitous conman, and a bombmaker. "It's like you wanted to make sure your daughters grew up with all the necessary skills."

Standing back, I studied the device.

I half expected something crude and homemade to match the halfwit energy infesting the place, but I wasn't surprised that the bomb was the opposite. We'd long ago figured out that the Brotherhood was well-funded. They had enough money to buy the good stuff.

But too bad for them, so did my dad.

"All right." I clicked my tongue, poking around the kitchen for something sharp. "A remote activator with a secondary initiator. You'll try to distract with all the useless show wires sticking out of the top when the wire I really need"—I plucked a knife out of the drawer by the sink—"is on the bottom."

Knowing this didn't make my job any easier. Unless I wanted my face blown off, I couldn't just flip the thing on its head. A fact that the bombmaker knew—hence their decision to put all the wires that needed snipping in a place I couldn't snip.

"Too bad you were wrong."

I slid one corner off the edge of the counter and carefully removed the screw with the tip of my knife. After that one was out, the other three soon followed. I lifted the device off the bottom plate, and rested it half on the corner with the other half balanced on my fingertips.

Crouching down, I looked inside the guts of the thing, meeting with half a dozen wires—all white.

It wasn't like the movies where psychopaths did their victims a favor and color-coded the *cut me, cut me* wire, and that was the first thing my father, Killian, taught me.

This wasn't a game, or a movie, or a joke. There was no room for guessing. I needed to know what every part, component, and wire did, or I needed to get the hell out of the way and let someone who did take over.

"Don't worry, Daddy, I was only pretending not to listen to your lessons, because you're super funny when you're mad. I remain your best student"—I picked out a tied bundle of three wires and sliced through the one in the middle—"and your favorite kid."

Sliding the bomb back, I stood up, smiled at the blank display no longer counting down, and dusted off my hands. "That's how it's done."

I didn't waste any more time. I took off upstairs with Malcom's key in my pocket and freed everyone.

"It's time. We're getting out of here," I called over my shoulder, leading the stampede down the stairs. "Just hang back a minute. Got to make sure the cleanup is done."

"Thank you, thank you." The silent, crying woman broke from the pack and hugged me, squeezing me to pop out all my jelly. "Thank you so much. I don't know what I would've done— One more day and I swear, I would've— I would've—" She burst into tears.

"It's cool," I said, extracting myself from her hold. "All a part of the service."

With that, I took off before anyone else got it into their heads to hug me again. Nothing against them, but I had a thing about hugs ever since someone used one to literally plunge a knife in my back.

Another reason I didn't let bitches like Brother Abraham call my biker gang *little*. I fought, bled, scratched, bit, and killed to lead these women and rule my borough. Nothing little about it.

Taking off out the back door, I rounded the house to find the scene I was expecting.

My brothers standing around like proud, self-congratulatory peacocks while their people did the cleanup.

"Genny," Liam said, inclining his head toward me.

I rolled my eyes. "You can be less like our dad, you know, and jump up and down hugging, kissing, and crying at seeing me safe and sound."

"Maybe later," the dickbag replied, striding off toward the porch.

"Your turn," I called, holding my arms out to Bane and Sunny. "I'll lift my lifetime ban and allow you to hug me just his once."

Neither one moved.

"Put your arms down, woman," Sunny said. "I love Angel more than life, but what the hell were you thinking letting her talk you into running at the Brotherhood with nothing but a tampon? You had us punched in the face for going off without you, and we at least had weapons!"

I shrugged. "Because you need them, baby brother. I'm lethal with or without. As you can see."

Sunny was walking off, shaking his head before I finished.

It was Bane who came over, hugged me, and dropped a kiss on my head. "You keep joking," he murmured, resting his chin on my head. "But Mom knows that you walked into the hands of a homicidal, Merchant-obsessed cult with no weapons or backup... and she's waiting for you."

My grin wiped off my face. "Yeah, we should go."

With the brothers dead and the bomb defused, we quickly cleared out the house and loaded up the cars and trucks with the hostages.

"We'll hang back," Bane said, jerking his chin at his silent band of Scourges. "Sweep the area. Tear apart the van and their cars for info, and clear the house."

"You should do that in the morning," Sunny suggested. "Scoping out their territory in the dead of night? Who knows what other little surprises they've got hidden around these woods?"

"We'll risk it." Bane tossed me the keys before going off to talk with his men and women.

I cast them a curious glance while I followed Bee and Shug to his car.

We mostly kept our gangs and our business separate from each other. We ran different boroughs and had different interests, so there was no need for mixing.

Liam laundered big money through dozens of high-end Leighbridge businesses. Bane manufactured weapons. I dealt mainly in protection. Harlow was a dangerous borough with innocent people being preyed on every minute of every day.

The Cardinals were basically a lethal, and very attractive, private security company—except we didn't charge the people we protected. I took my fee from the stupid bastards who messed with them.

As for Sunny, he had a piece of every criminal racket in his borough. As long as they paid up, they lived.

All that said, I didn't know much about the people my brothers trusted with their lives, but I knew even less about the Scourges. Bane didn't talk much about his business because except for my bomb-making dad, Killian, none of us knew a thing about manufacturing weapons. And even if we did want to talk to him about it, the hermit freak was always off hiding in some hole in the woods.

Honestly, there were times when I saw more of Melanie—the Scourge who delivered our monthly shipment of guns and ammo—than I did my big brother, and she wasn't one for chat.

Melanie would oversee the delivery, reject an offer for a beer or drink, resist all attempts at small talk, and then take off without a *goodbye* or *see you next time.*

I've always said the people we recruit for our gangs are a reflection of ourselves, and going by Melanie—Bane's reflection was closed off, enigmatic, serious, and an expert at saying only what he needs to—no more, no less, and never anything that revealed the real him. That reflection...

...was spot-on.

Strange, but familiar, thoughts swirled in my head as I followed Liam's car down the dirt road—finally on the path back to my city.

I've known Bane my whole life, but the guy was no less a mystery to me than when he used to lean over my crib, trying to hide all the vegetables he didn't want to eat in my stomach. Sure, he was a good man and a good brother.

Growing up, he helped me with my homework, never picked on me, beat the ever-loving shit out of my first boyfriend when he bragged about every detail of our sex life to the whole school, and he always let me know when and where to find him when he moved—even if he didn't tell Liam or Sunny.

He was the Cadillac of big brothers, but fake, plastic books with lines painted on the sides were more open than him.

He never talked to me about his hopes, dreams, nightmares, worries, pain, trauma—nothing. The only people in my family who could ever get a window into that was our mom, and his dad, Baris Alexander. And even though I'd never say anything this shit-embarrassing out loud, that used to hurt my feelings like a knife to the heart.

It was like Bane thought they were a family of three, and the rest of us were just a bunch of cool people who lived in his parents' house and refused to leave. I always figured that was why he moved out of the compound a week after our folks did. What was the point in staying in the family home... when his family didn't live there anymore?

Of course, Bane never said anything of the kind, and he'd likely deny it up, down, and sideways, but in this life, there were just some people who only had so much room in their heart, and so little unconditional trust to dole out. And Bane's was all used up... until Kenzie.

I don't know how that little curly-haired, hot piece of ass did it, but she blew into our lives and made us a family again. She made Liam believe in love again. So much so that Liam trusts her with the being he's most protective of in the whole world—Elizabeth.

She got my playboy, never-takes-anything-serious, hopping-from-a-different-bed-every-night little brother talking about marriage, commitment, and getting all of his sports cars fitted with car seats. And most amazing of all, she brought Bane home.

Let's face it, the guy could've moved back to the woods a long time ago, but he stuck around for one reason and one reason only—Mackenzie Blaine.

The woman reduced the three most dangerous men in Cinco to a bunch of drooling chimps slobbering on her heels, and it was my privilege to witness it.

"—GH?" Bee poked my shoulder. "Hey, you okay?"

"I'm good," I replied, coming to.

Bee was in the car with me along with Shug, Pixie, and other forced inhabitant of their cell—Debra. She still didn't have much to say other than the thank-you she gave me after rescuing her, but I could see something in her eyes that likely hadn't been there for a long time.

Hope.

"I was thinking... we need to make some changes." Once it was out of my mouth, I knew it was right. "The Cardinals need to change. I created us to protect Harlow, but when you guys needed me, where the fuck was I? We're family," I stated. "You're just as much my family as those dickheads. Next time... I won't get there too late."

Bee blinked at me, then shifted around—sharing a look with Shug and Pixie. "Wow, boss, that's... that's really—"

"—fucking sappy," Pixie finished. "Yikes, Mom, you gonna tuck us in every night too?"

"Kiss our boo-boos?" Bee mocked, puckering her lips. "Read us a bedtime story?"

"Fuck you all to hell," I replied, setting them all off laughing. "I knew I'd regret saving your asses. Just didn't know it'd be this soon."

"Knew we'd regret it too," Shug rebounded. "What is it with you Merchants? Always trying to love and protect somebody. Keep it in your pants, woman."

I rolled my eyes so hard, I almost veered off the road and crashed the car. If these jerks were a reflection of me... well, then, everything my enemies have said about me over the years was one hundred percent true.

Bee caught the corner of my vision, tossing me a wink.

It also meant I was a pretty lucky woman.

"Fine. You guys also too good for my money and food?" I asked. "Chino's burgers on me?"

"Oooh, yes. I'm starved. Can't wait for—"

Bang!

A hard force slammed into the car, nearly popping it off all four wheels and flipping us into a ditch.

"What the fuck was that?!" Bee shrieked.

But I didn't. I knew what that was.

Headlights blasted my mirrors, beaming into my eyes. Through the shifting shadows I made out a black car with heavily tinted windows just as it revved up to ram us again. But that wasn't the problem— Or, it wasn't the only problem.

The other one was the half a dozen black cars trailing our attacker through the dark, backwoods roads.

I slammed the horn, sounding the alarm through the entire forest. "Go!" I roared. "Get the hell on! Drive!"

Whether they heard my commands, or my honking did the job—Liam's car shot into the night, his taillights racing off into the distance.

I hit the accelerator and my window blew out, showering my face and lap in glass. "Get down!"

Bee, Shug, and Pixie hit the deck, covering their heads as a barrage of gunfire rained on Bane's car.

The silly, short-sighted dumbass hadn't taken Liam up on his offer to give Bane's car the bulletproof upgrade. Bane claimed he didn't need all that when he spent all his time in the woods and barely drove.

"How'd that work out for you, dumbass?!"

The car rammed my bumper, and the car spun out of control—ripping the wheel out of my hands. Screams tore through the backseat as we careened off the road, spinning three-sixty around and slamming the back end of the car against a tree.

Debra freaked out, the white of her eyes neon lights of terror and helplessness. "No! No, no, no!"

A pack of rushing headlights blew past us, chasing Liam, Sunny, and the others down the dark road, but six didn't.

The cars squealed to a stop, kicking up and wave of dirt and sand, and surrounding us in seconds.

We were on a narrow road with barely enough room to call it a two-way street. Even if the guys wanted to turn back and help us, they had no chance with the shithead bastard parade blocking the street.

We were on our own.

"Get us out of here," Debra screamed. Pouncing on my chair, she shook it like she was trying to dislodge the last drops of milk from a carton. "Don't let them take me again! Drive! DRIVE!"

She didn't have to tell me. I jammed the key in the ignition, my foot a brick on the accelerator.

Rrrrrr-rrrr-rrrr

The engine sputtered and spat at me, refusing to turn over.

Rrrrrrrrr-rrrrrr

Shadows spilled out of the cover of the blinding headlights, converging on the car.

"Down!" I ordered, ducking my head as the first shot blew through the window, exploding glass on a screaming Debra.

"No! Leave us alone! Please!" She was still shaking and slapping at me, trying to grab for the wheel. How the bullets were missing her was nothing less than a miracle. "Get away! Get—"

"Bee!"

Bee didn't need another word or clue. Her fist flew up, smashing into Debra's face.

Blood spurting on the dash, the woman flew back into her seat and slid down, folding over on top of Shug.

It wasn't the kindest way to get the woman to calm down and cover herself, but it did the job.

"Enough," someone shouted, ending the gunfire in a blink. "We've made our point."

Footsteps approached as I jammed the key in like a dick—twisting, yanking, and praying for it to go off.

"We know it's you in there, Merchant bitch. This is your one and only chance. Throw your keys out, then your weapons, and then slowly get out of the car," she said. "Do it, or we'll keep up target practice until we get the high—"

Vrrrroom!

The engine roared to life.

I didn't waste a moment. I slammed the accelerator, bowling over a hard, screaming object that bounced off my hood and went flying to hell.

"Stop her!"

"Kill her!"

The gunfire resumed anew.

I couldn't lift my head to see, but a hard, jarring crash let me know I collided with car number one. Bellowing, I jammed on the pedal—forcing the car out of the way and roaring onto the street.

I jerked the car around, my head snapping up in time for me to confirm I was pointing in the opposite direction of Liam and Sunny, and heading right back toward the cabin.

I didn't slow down.

There was no way I could follow behind the guys now. With the Brotherhood behind them and behind me, all they had to do was box me in and get it right that time. I couldn't take the chance.

"Hurry up! After her!"

Headlights out, bumper scraping up half the road, driver window and windshield blown out, and one of the passengers unconscious in the backseat. I prayed to Loki, Hera, and all the gods in between that this bullet*un*proofed piece of shit had a little bit more fight left in her.

"Come on!" The car fought me, wobbling dangerously out of control when I tried to push the speed past sixty. "Come on!"

Wind rushed through the gaping hole—whipping, stinging, and watering my eyes. I couldn't see a thing for blinking and squinting, and my destroyed headlights weren't helping.

I couldn't see the turn or the cabin or even if it was coming up. I couldn't—

Bang!

A car slammed into me, trying to finish what a tree and their bullets couldn't.

Bang! Bang!

"FGH?" Pixie shouted. "I don't want to stress you, but if I'm going to go out with a middle-aged woman on top of me, I'd prefer it be because I choked on caviar while she was licking my pussy! Do you have a plan or not!"

"Me? A plan? I thought you didn't need Mama's help?"

"Really?" she screeched. "You're giving me shit now!?"

I shrugged. "Might be my last chance." Jerking the car to the right, I heard a shout and squeal of tires when their attempt to ram us again went wide. "But you want a plan? Fire back, aim for the tires—or the heads—but don't you dare fucking die! I'm not going through all of this just so you guys can go and get yourselves shot!"

They didn't need any more instructions. Twisting around, they pointed their guns out the window and fired blindly and wildly—anything to slow down our tail.

"Come on," I hissed, squinting through the gloom to find the cabin. Who knew that only minutes after leaving the horrible place, I'd be desperate to go back. "Come on! Where are you? Where—!"

There!

In a split, waterlogged second, the headlights from one of the cars chasing us revealed a branching turnoff on the dirt road.

"Brace yourselves," I shouted, then yanked the car to the right, swerving onto the natural, grass-covered driveway.

I was honking the horn before we came into view. "Bane! Bane!" I bellowed. "Make yourself useful and take these bitches out! Ba—!"

Edwin's abandoned car roared up on me, bursting into my vision. I slammed the brakes and—

—nothing.

"Hold on!"

We crashed head-on—slamming into Edwin's car at full speed. Pain exploded in my temple—its final parting gift before dropkicking me into complete and total darkness.

Chapter Seven

The Next Morning

Bane

"Kenzie," he croaked. "Last night... Last night was... bad."

I glanced back at the bed where my sister lay sleeping. Our Mom held tight to her hand, stroking her cheek and murmuring softly to her.

"First, I need to know if you're still with River."

"We are," she replied. "He's sitting right next to me. Why? Do you need to talk to him?"

"I do. Hand him the phone for a sec, if you don't mind."

"Okay."

Shuffle, and then my uncle's voice came through the speaker. "Yeah?"

"Oxtail. Rice and peas."

"Understood," he replied without skipping a beat. "Hey, Si. Can you pull over here? I'll drive."

"Why?" I heard Kenzie ask. "Is something wrong?"

More murmuring, shuffling, car door slams, and then my girl's voice was back in my ear.

"Bane, what's going on? Are you all okay?"

"What's going on is we got to Genny and took out the brothers—or so we thought," I said, stepping out of the bedroom. "Turned out they called in reinforcements who caught up to Sunny, Liam, and Genny on the road.

"Genny had to spin around and drive back to me. The Scourges blew her pursuers away but Gen..."

"But Gen what?" Kenzie cried. "What happened?"

"Genny got into a crash." I slid down against the wall, fists balled at my side. "She hit the dashboard at full speed. Our parents and the doc are with her now, but she's got a broken nose, two black eyes, three broken ribs, and a severe concussion."

"Oh no— How is—? Did she—? Is she okay? Is she going to be okay!"

"The doctor said she's going to be fine," I replied, hearing a whoosh of relief from her end of the phone. "But she's out of this fight, Kenzie. She needs complete and total bedrest. Mom will tie her to the bed if she needs to.

"The Brother-fucking-hood didn't break us, but they did weaken us."

"But as long as you guys are okay," she said firmly. "We're never weak as long as we have each other."

Even with everything going on, I smiled.

I liked Mackenzie Blaine talking about us as a *we*. I liked it a whole fucking lot.

For fourteen years, I kept my resolution to stay out of serious relationships, and I did it without much trouble. No matter how much I liked a girl, those feelings just furthered my resolve. Loving them meant *never* risking their lives and their futures by dragging them into my crazy, dangerous world.

They deserved a guy who could give them everything—a home, love, family, and protection—with heavy emphasis on the protection.

I glanced back at my sister's bedroom door. *But protection's the one thing I can't promise. I couldn't even unload my clip fast enough to protect Genny—the baddest badass I know. How can I protect sweet, yummy Mackenzie and her beautiful baby girl?*

I knew the answer to that. I knew the reality. I knew the life expectancy of the typical gangster and a gangster's wife, but for the first time ever... I didn't give a shit.

I didn't care about the odds. I didn't care about reality. And I could give a flying shit about my inability to control fate.

I wouldn't give up Mackenzie, Laurel, or Sienna because nothing was going to happen to them. I would protect them. I'd keep them. I'd give them a home, and family, and everything they could ever ask for, and a bunch of things they didn't ask for, and as for love...

"I'm so sorry, baby," Kenzie whispered. "I can't imagine how stressed you are right now. Don't worry. We're on our way back right now, and I promise, as soon as I get you alone, I'll do something about that tension."

My chest thumped as hard as my dick. Who the fuck was I kidding? If me keeping Mackenzie isn't her choice, then me loving her isn't mine. She blew down the barbed wire fence around my heart, and took what she wanted.

"I believe I'll take you up on that," I said simply. A man could only engage in so much phone sex when his parents were literally on the other side of the wall. "How did your talk with Frost go? Did you kill him?"

"Killing him was never on the itinerary." Her voice was flat.

"It should've been."

"Something tells me if I had come at him with a knife in front of his wife and infant son, he wouldn't have been so forthcoming," she said. "Bane, I got it all wrong—again. Vance Hollywell is with the Brotherhood. *Deep* with the Brotherhood.

"Damien definitely stole from Caddell House, but Vance was in it with him. Vance dummied up the documents knowing he could use them to pin it all on Damien if it ever came out. And it worked."

I hummed. "Didn't work that well," I mused, heading for the door out of Genny's apartment. "I'm going to go kill him now."

"Considering he's the reason Sunny was thrown off the overpass, and Tricky almost got into a car with a bomb underneath it, I'm really not all that interested in Vance living through the night, but you have to know," she said. "This guy is... slippery.

"He takes manipulative, gaslighting sociopath to a new level. He was willing to throw his friend to the wolves without a second thought, and he gave the performance of his life when we confronted him. Sunny went in there to beat the shit out of him, and instead we walked out feeling *sorry* for *him*.

"He's been a step ahead of us this entire time," she said, once again thrilling me with her use of *us*. "We've got to assume he's ready for our next move."

"I'm sure he is." I made it out to the hall and headed for the stairs. "That's why I'll shoot first and ask questions later."

"Damien had more to say," she continued. "He told me that his aunt was recruited by the Brotherhood when he was a teenager. She turned them down—big-time—but they were persistent."

"Wait? A teenager?" I said, stopping in my tracks. "But the man is in his thirties."

"Exactly. Bane, the Brotherhood has been around for a long time. A very long time."

I frowned, unease drilling into my bones. "I don't understand. How can they have been around all this time and we're only hearing about them now? How did they stay out of our radar?"

"I don't think they did. They've likely been on your parents' radar for a while, they just weren't calling themselves the Brotherhood back then," she said. "Damien told me that his aunt suspected the Brotherhood was behind the fire that burned down Sacred Heart Charities."

And then I truly froze—standing there in front of the elevator with my finger hovering over the button. "The Brotherhood did that?" I hissed. A rage I'd never felt burned a hole in my chest. "That was my grandfather's church. It was my father's home after his mother was forced to give him up. My parents spent a fortune rebuilding it after miserable fuckers went and burned it down the first time, and now you're telling me after all of that, it was the Brotherhood that went and burned it down again?"

"I'm sorry, baby, but if everything Damien and his aunt suspected is true, then... yes," she said softly. "That's exactly what I'm saying."

I spun around, heading back the way I came. "I've got to tell my folks. There's no doubt they hunted down whoever set the fires, but I was a kid when it happened. They didn't give me any details."

"Then, you should also tell them that Aunt Della got as far as Leonard Stevens and a police interrogation video where he bangs on about setting the fires in the name of his *family*. They leaned on him for names, but he claimed that he'd never betray *Mom* and *Dad*. His parents died when he was a toddler, so Damien and Della figured Mom and Dad were leaders of the Brotherhood, and that was just another way they were ripping off the Merchant family," she said. "By pretending they are a family."

"They might be right. There are plenty of criminal organizations that keep it in the family, but they don't make their members call them Mom or Dad unless they're their actual mom and dad. Going by those titles could be the leaders making some kind of creepy point, because everything with them has to be."

I could sense her nodding on the other end.

"There's one more thing," I went on, letting myself back into Genny's apartment. "You're on your way back but you need to know the compound is on *guest* protocol."

"Guest protocol? What does that mean?"

I cursed. "Sunny was supposed to explain all this to you. Real quick, there are different levels of security depending on who is home. When it's just the family and staff, then we can move from floor to floor with just the elevator and stair codes. When we have unvetted guests in the building, the elevator and stair doors need both the correct code, height, and weight to open or move."

"Height and weight? What do you mean?"

"As in, if someone got their hands on Sunny's floor code, when they got into the elevator and put it in, they wouldn't go anywhere. The floor and wall sensors would note that no one of that person's height or weight has been put into the system as having access to Sunny's floor."

"Wow. No wonder people say the Fairfield has better security than the NSA."

"And that's just guest protocol," I mused. "On hostile enemy protocol, the elevator would seal itself with the intruder inside, then fill with a toxic gas and kill the fucker."

"Fucking hell!" she cried. "Wait— Are me, Sienna, and Laurel in the system? Does it know *we* aren't hostile enemies?!"

"Of course it does. Your heights, weight, gait, voices, and even your DNA have all been entered as family. Even the combinations of all of those have been entered," I said. "So Sienna holding Laurel will come up correct on the sensors. It'll know the extra weight she's carrying is our baby girl."

"Goodness," she breathed, but I could sense her relaxing. "You guys don't mess around."

"We can't. Our parents raised their children here. Liam is raising Tricky here. You, Sienna, and Laurel live here. It *has* to be safe from our enemies because the one time it wasn't..." I trailed off, knowing I didn't need to go on.

Because the one time we let someone that we thought was safe in the same building as Kenzie and Laurel, they were kidnapped and thrown into the hands of a soulless trafficker.

"I understand," she whispered, "and... thank you."

"No one is ever going to hurt you, Kenzie. If I've got to exterminate the entire human race to ensure it, you will be safe."

She chuckled. "Now that sounds like something Sunny would say."

"What can I tell you? The guy gets his best traits from me."

Now she was full-blown giggling, which put a smile on my face. I loved Kenzie's laugh more than the smell of gunpowder in the morning.

"But, wait," she said. "Why are we in guest protocol?"

"Because last night Liam and Sunny led the Brotherhood on a high-speed chase through the streets of Cinco, and then I broke the land-speed record racing Genny here and into the hands of the doctor. All that meant we didn't have time for a pit stop," I confessed. "We had to bring the Cardinals, the Sons of Saint, the Scourges, Liam's crew, and the freed hostages here."

"Ah, I see. But why are they still there? Is it not safe to leave the building?"

"No, it is not." My feet carried me away from Genny's bedroom and over to the window. Peering down, I saw them clear as day—no matter that I was fifty-feet up. "They're all camped out around the building, Kenzie. In the cars parked on the street. In the cafés across the building. In the street-facing hotel rooms. And even on top of the buildings, with their sniper scopes pointed right at our windows."

"Snipers?!"

"We've counted seven so far. They've got all the exits and all of our balconies covered."

"Fuck's sake! How— Why— How can they just do that? They can't do that! Call the police!"

"Reinforcements are on the way," I chirped. "So no worries about that, but I'm just telling you so you know why River is currently driving to the secret, underground entrance that leads into the building. No one can go through the front door right now.

"But that's even if you want to. I understand if you'd rather bunk up with River right now."

Kenzie hesitated. "I know you guys have security covered, but I don't want to freak out every time Laurel crawls in front of a window. I think we will take a little detour, and then just River and me will meet you at home," she said. "This will give River a chance to talk to the former hostages. Let them know there's help and a place to stay if they need it."

"Cool. See you soon."

We exchanged our greetings, then hung up. A second later I was pulling up Sunny's name and sending him a text on my way to Genny's room.

Me: You got played. Hollywell's a fucking liar. He's in the Brotherhood.

Sunny got me back immediately.

Sunny: I never get played. I put a tracker on his phone while he was bawling and throwing himself on the floor. He made an interesting pit stop on the way to work this morning. He's still there as it happens.

Me: Where?

Sunny: The rooftop of the Overton building. Right across the street.

I tensed, glancing back at the glass doors leading to the balcony. The Fairfield had been outfitted with sniper-proof glass a long time ago. That didn't make it any less unsettling that the man who used to design our clothes was outside with a gun waiting... for us to give him a reason.

***

Kenzie

"Are you sure you guys will be okay?"

"We'll be fine." Sienna settled Laurel in her stroller and tucked her blanket in around her. "I've got bottles, diapers, money, and this stroller lies flat for naptime. We'll be good for hours."

I hesitated outside the entrance to the park. Of course, I trusted my sister with my baby. I just hated the idea of the three of us being apart when the Brotherhood had officially lost its mind. Chasing the guys through the streets? Surrounding the compound with snipers?

There was no way I was putting Sienna and Laurel in the middle of that craziness.

"My phone is on and fully charged," I said. "If anything happens. If someone even looks at you funny, just call me and I'll be here." I thought about it. "Also run."

Sienna laughed like I was kidding. "Kenzie, relax. Your future is a shifting, shadowy kaleidoscope on your best day, but mine and Laurel's are clear. No one is going to hurt us. No one wants to." She gave me a look. "The two of us haven't been collecting mortal enemies for the last four decades."

Laurel shrieked her agreement.

"True. Very true," I mumbled. "But these Brotherhood psychos are everywhere, and they might get it into their heads that messing with you could get them close to the guys. That's exactly why Luca took me and Laurel that night."

"Ehh, not really. That's why they took *you*. That shit-shitting bastard only took Laurel too because she was strapped to your chest," she pointed out. "You're the one Liam, Bane, and Sunny are in love with. You're the target of Gen's girl crush. You're the leverage against them, not us.

"And if you think about it," Sienna continued. "It's being next to you that puts the target on our backs. Now that you're taking off and leaving us to our Auntie/Neice Day, we're probably the safest we've been all day."

A snort sounded behind me, making me snap my narrowed eyes to a laughing River.

"Thank you for laying that out for me, sister dear," I gritted. "If you're finished telling me how much you won't miss me, I'll go now."

Sienna laughed in my face. "Bye, Kenz, love ya."

With that, she strode off with Laurel, leaving me shaking my head.

"Can you believe her?" I muttered, stomping off to the car.

"Nope. I can honestly say your sister is one of a kind. There has not nor will there ever be anyone like her." He jogged ahead of me to get my door. "That's what I love about her."

"I'm finding that quality less endearing at the moment," I snapped, setting him off laughing at me too.

Soon we were on the road again, driving in the opposite direction from the Fairfield. It was in the car that I remembered there was something else I wanted to tell Sienna before she got on my nerves and I forgot.

"Where is this secret entrance?" I asked, typing out and sending my text to my sister. "How far away is it?"

"About a mile. Cinco City is rotten with underground tunnels from back in the Prohibition days. The majority of them aren't on any official maps or schematics, because of course they're not. That would've defeated the purpose," he said. "The trick is to find one that isn't caved in, or already occupied by the unhoused of Cinco." River dipped his head. "Then you've got to make sure no one else discovers it.

"But the Merchants went another way, and built their fucking own."

My brows shot up as my phone beeped Sienna's reply. "They dug their own secret Prohibition underground tunnel."

"Yes, they did." He shot me a grin. "And you're going to love where it leads."

Ten minutes later, I was standing on the sidewalk—blinking up at a familiar logo.

"Caddell House?"

"Yes."

"This Caddell House?"

"The very same."

"The same Caddell House that I worked in for years is parked on top of the entrance to a secret tunnel?"

"Yes, ma'am."

He kept answering me clearly, but he still wasn't making any sense.

"Why?" I blurted.

"Didn't you ever wonder why the Merchants invested in the fashion industry of all things?" River asked. "All of their other businesses are a front for criminal activity. There's no chance for them to do that with Caddell House unless they rip off their designs and sell them as knockoffs, and to do that, they'd need a warehouse full of people sewing those clothes for terrible pay—which they would never do," he clarified.

"So what happened is Killian Hunt bought the building first." River gestured to the grand structure before me. "Then, and this is the real genius part, he invited every business school in Cinco to participate in a scholarship program/contest. Whoever came to him with the best business plan would win a hefty amount of startup money, and the first floor of this building"—he pointed—"to house said business.

"Jonah Caddell won."

"That is genius," I breathed, shaking myself at the wonder that produced Liam and Genevieve Hunt. "That way it would never look strange if Killian or the Merchants popped up in Caddell House one day. They are the landlords, investors, and business partners—of course they belong."

River tapped his nose, winking at me. "Plus, with security on the door making sure people who *don't* belong stay the hell out, they never have to worry about an ambush waiting for them on this side."

"Genius," I said again. "I know I'm still in the apprenticeship stage, but I'm really looking forward to the part where I start thinking like an evil criminal mastermind. Hanging around you guys is truly a master class in leaving your enemies blinking in your dust—wondering where it all went wrong."

River took my hand, leading me inside. "Baby, you just say the word. You can take my master class any time. Trust me, there's plenty I want to teach you." He winked at my reddening face. "And even more I want you to teach me."

"That is not what I meant, you dirty perv."

River's smirk was wolfish. "Yeah, it was."

It really was *not*, but he got a giggle out of me all the same.

Together we stepped inside the cool, ordered lobby. I expected River to turn left for security, but he walked right up to the receptionist.

She was a gorgeous creature decked out in a gold, shimmering Caddell sheath dress and matching gold pumps.

I knew about the shoes because they were currently on her desk, wrapped around her feet.

"What?" She leaned back on her chair, not bothering to look up from her phone.

"Is Mr. Hollywell here?" I asked, stepping forward.

"Nah. He's out sick," she said to her phone. "All appointments with him are canceled for the rest of the week."

Figures.

"That's fine, I'm here to pick up my order," River said. "Oxtail, rice and peas."

I grasped River's arm, shaking my head at him. "What are you doing? This isn't—"

"Yeah, whatever." Without looking up, she reached into her desk drawer, pulled out two visitor badges, and tossed them at us. "They're good," she shouted at the security guards. "Let them through."

I shook my head walking off. "No wonder the Blonde Bandit made this place her bitch."

River cracked up. "You can be honest, Kenzie. How much does Genny love that nickname?"

I think it was the danger we were heading straight for that made us overly chatty and giggly, because I couldn't help but crack up too. "She's already shown me the design for her soon-to-come Blonde Bandit tattoo."

"Underneath the title is there a drawing of her getting her ass kicked by a bunch of doodling seamstresses?"

"Hey!" Outrage dropped my jaw. "I'll have you know that we're much more than doodling seamstresses."

Actually, now that I think about it, that's a surprisingly simple yet accurate term for what I do all day.

"We're designers," I barked, shoving that thought aside. "And we're tough. More than tough enough to take on the Blonde Bandit."

He clicked his tongue, walking past the guards and their waving metal detectors like they were nothing but moving mannequins. "Sorry, baby, but I don't buy it. You'll have to show me how tough you are."

"Oh yeah?" I walked through next, my brows bouncing up to my hairline. "Is that right?"

"That's right. I challenge you to a wrestling match. Tonight. Between the sheets." He nipped my nose, making me squeak. "No one leaves until we declare a... winner."

I think I said something in response, but by the time my brain came back online, I missed it. I was no virgin. I had the fruits of sexual reproduction to prove it, but that didn't mean I was used to being with guys that said exactly what they wanted, exactly how they wanted it, exactly when they wanted it.

The guys I was used to dealing with would just text me a series of crude emojis when they wanted me to take my pants off. One guy even did it when I was lying in the bed next to him.

Being with decent, and sexy, guys really had a way of putting your past loser parade into perspective.

River's fingers curled through mine, pulling me close.

I wasn't shy about laying my head on his shoulder—drinking him in. Yes, we were walking into a dangerous situation, but if I was going to do that with anyone, I'm glad it was with River.

We didn't say much as he led me on a familiar path through the halls of the junior designer offices. I half expected to hear Lyla barking orders at everyone, conveniently forgetting that they weren't her assistants, because she didn't have assistants.

But a surprise meeting with my nemesis was rescheduled for another day. I didn't see Lyla or her usual crew—sans Madison of course.

Unless that's why they're not here. Because a close friend of theirs was murdered in a gas station basement.

I winced, my grip tightening on River at the horrible thought. I hated Madison James with the hellfire of all levels of Hades. I wanted her to suffer pain and misery like no one ever suffered before. That woman threatened my life, my safety, my body, and my baby with a sociopathic malice that was truly frightening. I had no sympathy left in me to care about her fate—

Or so I thought.

No, I didn't feel bad for the Madison James who was killed by the crazy violent cult leader she refused to give up.

I felt bad for the little girl she used to be. For the child who was happy and loved in a beautiful home with her family by her side, and her friends all around her. Then one day, through no fault of her own, it was all gone.

Her father tossed her away, and then her mother committed suicide—leaving her all alone with her pain, bitterness, and resentment until it festered into hate. And instead of healing and finding joy in her amazing talent, wonderful job, beautiful home, and the band of harpies she called friends... she found the Brotherhood.

No, they found her. They tracked her down and weaponized her hatred against the people I love. How many people have they done that to?

"I wish we had more information on the Brotherhood and how many people they've got on their side," I mused allowed. "Every time we think we've struck a blow, a hundred more swarm out of the sewer." My eyes darted around. "And they seem to be everywhere and everyone. Hell, I worked for Vance and I had no idea he was another reptile in a human suit."

I tipped my chin up, gaze tracing the strong line of his jaw. "That old ledger...? Whatever happened to it?"

"The ledger?" He turned furrowed brows on me. "That old thing? Adeline dumped it on the world decades ago. It's worthless now."

"Maybe not. Everyone who needs to know knows," I said. "Well, how does the Brotherhood know who needs to know? If they tracked down Della by digging up the list of the deceased from the Night of Tears, then don't you think they would've started with victims of the ledger dump first?"

"Yes," River replied. We rounded a corner, and the noise of the busy hall fell away—leaving us in the silence that surrounded the entrance to the basement. "Yes, they would. But we're talking hundreds, possibly thousands of people. That must be why it took the Brotherhood so long to make a move. It took this long to get to all of those people."

I tossed my head. "I know that. Sunny and Liam said the same thing, but that's not what I was thinking of. *Today* the Brotherhood has an army of people willing to trade in their weaponized hatred for actual weapons, but what about twenty-five years ago?

"I mean, a gang doesn't start out with a thousand devoted members. It starts with one person. Maybe two or three. Who say 'hey, let's start a gang today,'" I said, even as River chuckled at me. "A gang that has a very specific purpose, and is therefore going after specific people. So, if their only place to start is by ambushing random supposed Merchant victims in grocery store parking lots, they couldn't have been as organized or well-funded as they are now. They didn't have an army of minions to do it for them."

"Kenzie, what are you getting at?"

I stopped him with his hand on the doorknob. "I'm saying there's a reason why Brother Abraham was the only upper-level name we knew about until Damien told us about Mom and Dad. He knew about Mom and Dad because he had info from two decades ago when the Brotherhood was smaller and weaker.

"When they knew so little about the Merchants' history and their interests that they didn't know about Sacred Heart Charities until Della told them." I grasped his shoulders. "River, what I'm getting at is in the beginning, the founders of the Brotherhood had nothing, no one, and no resources other than a list of names. So what do you want to bet they approached the people on that list... in person?"

Understanding blew up on River's face, tensing his shoulders. "Fucking hell, Kenzie. You're saying the ledger isn't a list of Brotherhood members. It's a list of people who've met and spoken to the real masterminds behind this war. The Mom and fucking Dad who started it all."

Expression grim, I nodded. "What if Mom is the woman who spoke to Della again, and again, and again? Harassing a tech genius because she didn't have one in her growing crew, and she couldn't afford to hire one."

He goggled at me. "Baby, that's brilliant. Why the fuck didn't Sunny, Liam, Bane, Genny, or even I think of that!" River swooped down and kissed the crap out of me. "You can stop calling yourself an apprentice, because you have officially graduated to sexy genius—outthinking everyone from criminal masterminds to your dumbass boyfriends."

I swatted his thumb. "You're not dumb. I just realized that getting inside the mind of a ruthless sociopath doesn't work so well for me, but getting inside the mind of a victim does." My hands slid down the dips and valleys of his muscled arms, drawing him close to me. "I thought about what I'd do if I'd gotten away from Luca too late—after he ripped my whole world away.

"If I wanted to take him down with no money or resources, I'd start with tracking down the other women he hurt, and convincing them to join me. And I wouldn't hide my face while I did it."

River stroked my cheek—his touch soft and soothing, he spread warmth, love, and reassurance into me without needing to say a word.

But still saying everything.

"We couldn't do this without you, Kenzie, and I'm not just talking about this war with the Brotherhood. All of it," he whispered. "Everything you've healed, put right, and made better just by walking into the room... none of it was possible... before you."

Tears stung my eyes. A million replies sprung to my lips, but the only one that mattered was...

"I love you."

"I love you too." He kissed me. "Now, let's track down the number of the infamous Aunt Della and get a description of the woman she smacked the shit out of. Something tells me she hasn't forgotten her face."

My lips found its smile again. "Let's do it."

Together we took off down to the basement. My surprise at finding out there was a secret tunnel entrance under Caddell was nothing to discovering that entrance was marked with a sign saying, ***Danger: High Voltage. Keep Out Under Pain of Death***

"That's a sign that would keep me away."

We cut down on the joking as we entered the dark, concrete tunnel.

I expected a dark, gloomy space with steam rising up from nowhere to conceal the rats waiting to jump out at me.

I expected it, but that's not what I got.

The tunnel was shockingly well lit with a string of exposed hanging lightbulbs leading the mile ahead. There was nothing but gray on gray, but it was clean, smelled fine, and there wasn't a rat in sight.

Holding hands, we began the trek leading to the family I just found, but refused to ever give up.

"Why are we going there when they could all evacuate through these tunnels?" I asked. "The Brotherhood would sit around all day waiting to attack no one."

River shook his head. "No one knows about this tunnel except for immediate family. If it gets out, they'll have to brick it up and never look back. Besides, as scary as it is to have snipers on the front porch, there is nowhere in the city safer than the Fairfield. Nowhere," he pressed. "That building is one of the many reasons why the Merchants have ruled unchallenged for forty years.

"It's where they sleep, shower, and eat. It's the only place they're vulnerable, and it's the only place no one but the Merchants can get in."

I quieted, accepting that the guys had a plan to get everyone out of the building safely. Trust was all I had to go on, so best to keep it in over supply.

The mile felt like it stretched into five as we walked through a tunnel of gray on gray. There must have been nothing but solid concrete, dirt, and gravel above us because the bustling Cinco sounds were nothing. All I could hear were my own thoughts, and all I could think about was Laurel and Sienna out there walking through the park. Hera, help me, I hoped they were safe, because I had a terrible feeling that—

"It's starting," I whispered. "The Brotherhood's final endgame, River. They're done losing little battles, and now they're ready to win the war."

Meeting my eyes, he said, "I agree."

***

Bane

I opened the trapdoor, reaching down to help Kenzie climb in.

Gazing up the ladder, she smiled at me and it about punched me in the gut. *Gods, she's beautiful. A thousand painters could try a thousand times to paint her beauty, but in the end they'd break their brushes and run off crying.*

Her perfection is a gift of nature, and it cannot be replicated.

"Hey, love." Climbing up, she captured my lips before she was even out of the hole—swiping her tongue against my entrance, then plunging in.

I let her think she was in charge for all of two seconds, then tangled and wrestled her tongue into submission—drawing a soft, heart-pounding moan from her.

"Ahem," a dry voice interrupted. "I'm still down here, you know."

Kenzie broke away giggling. "Sorry, baby. Let me help you." Pulling herself the rest of the way out, she reached down to draw River in after her.

The natural ease, and sizzling heat, between them came through loud and clear. Whatever happened between them in New York cemented their relationship. Somehow I ended up sharing a woman with my brothers and my uncle, and I still don't know how that happened.

I had no problem with my parents' relationship, but I never wanted it for myself. I never wanted *any* relationship for myself. But here I was with my father's words echoing in my head.

You can love a woman so much that their happiness becomes everything. The reason you live and breathe. The reason you get out of bed in the morning.

So if another man and another love can give her that happiness, then they're not your rival or your enemy. They're one of the smartest men on earth, because they see in her what you see.

My dad wasn't always able to speak to me growing up, but when he did, he said words that lived in my head forever.

River looked me in the eyes as he climbed out, closed the door, and kicked the rug back over it. I could see the tension in his shoulders and challenge in his eyes, waiting for me to have shit to say about him and Kenzie. I could also see Kenzie standing behind him... and the expression on her face.

I held out my hand. "I'm sorry, man."

River frowned. "You're what?"

"I'm sorry for how everything went down between us. I'm sorry that I was part of the reason you didn't feel welcome with your own family. I thought I was protecting my mom but..." I blew out a breath, shaking my head. "But my mother has never needed protecting. What I should've done was have your back. And from here on, I will."

He leaned back, considering me. "I... Thanks, man. I appreciate you saying that, and for what it's worth"—he took my hand—"I'm sorry too."

"I've got to admit I took it to the next level by going after you guys and your businesses the way I did. Pantsing you all on the playground, showing you up, and making you cry like bitches," he mused. "All I can say in my defense is that it was very easy and incredibly funny."

"River!" Kenzie cried, making him laugh.

"But that's all in the past now," he continued, shaking my hand warmly. "Let's just leave it there, and focus on the real enemy."

"Agreed." I made for the door, taking my Kenzie along with me. "So does this mean I've got to start calling you Uncle River now?"

"Egh, no." River fell in step with us, exiting the first-floor linen closet that served a dual purpose. "It's still weird as hell to me that I've got a nephew who's five years older than me."

"As weird as dating that old nephew's girlfriend?"

Kenzie snapped her head up. "Girlfriend? Did you just say girlfriend?"

"Yes, I did. You got a problem with that?"

Kenzie gave me a smile so beatific I almost kicked my own ass for waiting this long to make her this happy.

"No," she whispered, rising up to kiss me. "I don't have a problem with that at all."

"What now?" River asked. "Who is going to pick off all those snipers and chase the assassins from your doorstep, if you're all locked down in here?"

"What do you mean who?" Kenzie spoke up.

We came out of the back hallway and crossed under the staircase, making for the old servants' elevator.

"Haven't you called the police?"

I shook my head. "We don't call the police."

"Don't?"

"Don't," I said firmly. "Calling the bomb squad down on the gas station was a one-time necessity. Dozens of innocent lives were at risk. But we're criminals, Kenzie. The cops aren't on our side. And they shouldn't be, because then they'd be dirty as hell.

"If we get them involved, they'll use that as leverage to put us in the same cell as the Brotherhood. It's not worth it." I rubbed her arm soothingly. "Not even now."

"But then what are you going to do? You said it was being taken care of. That's why I told Sienna it would only be a few hours. She and Laurel can't wander around the park all day and night."

"They won't have to. Trust me. It is being taken care of right about..." I checked my watch. "Now. We can go up and watch if you'd like."

She glanced at River, who winked at her. "Uh... okay."

We stepped up to the elevator, and on the imperceptible pressure plate beneath the floor. The doors opened automatically when I pressed the button, welcoming home our family.

When we got to my floor, I let them both in, then straight to my coffee table and the pair of binoculars I left on it. Handing it to Kenzie, I gestured for her to follow me to the balcony doors.

"Are you sure it's safe?" she asked, staying rooted to the carpet.

"I'm sure. The best sniper in the world tested it with the best weapons on the market," I assured her. "The most she was able to do was crack the glass. We're safe."

Trusting me, Kenzie stepped up beside me.

"You see there on the roof of that office building?" I pointed. "There's the one assigned to me."

"Assigned to you? What does that mean?"

"Look."

Edging closer, Kenzie put the binoculars to her eyes and leaned forward—peering out the glass to—

"Ahh!" she cried, shooting back. "He waved at me! He fucking waved at me!"

"Creepy, isn't it." My tone was light—almost amused. "He's been waving at me all morning. Making sure I know he, and his gun, are there."

She shivered. "Creepy is right."

"Keep looking. It's about to get even more interesting." I squeezed her arm, letting her know I'd be right back, then I ducked into my office and got two more binoculars. One for me and River.

We all had them for this very reason. It wasn't the first time an enemy got it into their heads that they didn't need to break into the Fairfield to kill us. All they had to do was wait until we stepped outside.

Together the three of us posted up against the glass, staring at the assassin as he stared right back at us. We watched him wave. We watched that five-fingered wave become a one-figure salute, and then we watched him lift both middle fingers high for the double fuck-you.

"Dick," Kenzie muttered, making both me and River laugh. "What's about to happen? Because I don't—"

The dickhead sniper suddenly jerked—the whole of him flopping like he was electrocuted. In a blink, his hands dropped, falling over the side of the roof and dangling there. Nowhere near his trigger.

"Done."

"Done?" Kenzie looked from me to him. "What do you mean done? Did he—? Is he dead?!"

"As the proverbial dodo."

"But how? Who?" She dropped her binoculars, not wanting to stare at a corpse for a second longer. "I thought all of the Sons of Saint, Cardinals, Scourges, and Liam's people were stuck in here with us."

"Yeah, they are." I winked. "But not all of the Merchants are."

She flicked to River. "I'm guessing you know what that means."

"Yep."

Kenzie sighed. "Am I ever going to know all of your secrets?"

"Yes, but only when dropping on you means you'll make that cute, shocked face."

"You are so—"

Boom!

"What the—?!"

Boom! Boom! Boom!

Kenzie fell in my arms, screaming as explosions ripped through the deceptive calm Leighbridge morning.

"Don't worry, baby. That's just the sound of the trash getting taken out." I rubbed her back. "We can't call the police on them, but we can blow up all those sneaky shits lurking in the cars that ran my sister off the road, and when the cops, fire trucks, ambulances, and news crews rush in to pick up their pieces, we'll walk everyone out the front door." I beamed at her. "Not even the Brotherhood will try to pull something in front of all those journalists and first responders."

She gaped at me. "That—that— I don't know if that's brilliant or terrifying. Who came up with this plan?"

I grinned wider. Her jaw dropped further.

"Again, terrifying but... brilliant, baby."

"I thought so." I dropped a kiss on her nose. "So, if you want, you can tell Sienna to find a comfortable spot to wait all this out." Sirens and ambulance blasts hit the air, backing me up. "As soon as we're sure the Brotherhood has cleared out, and we've got everyone safely home, they're safe to come back."

"Okay, okay," she said softly, rubbing her arms. "That's not so bad, but I really don't want to be away from Laurel for that long. But I also don't want her in a building surrounded by exploding bombs and waving gunmen."

"Whatever you want to do." My voice was gentle and non-pushy.

River stepped forward. "Kenzie, why don't you go and be with Laurel and Si? If this all takes too long, you guys can book into the Marchmont Hotel for the night." He stroked her cheek. "You know the place."

She nodded. "I do, and that's a good idea, River. Thank you. I think I'll take you up on it."

I flicked between them. "What's up with the Marchmont?"

"I did right by the owner, so he always keeps a room open for me—just for this reason," River explained. "Too many times my crew has had young mothers or pregnant teenage girls join because their parents threw them out onto the street.

"A tunnel under a bridge is nowhere for a pregnant girl, or a mother with an infant. I always put them up in the Marchmont until we find a better, safer, arrangement for them."

"Yes," Kenzie said softly. "I've stayed at the Marchmont before. The owner and his wife are truly wonderful people. They and River took amazing care

of me, my sister, and my baby until I found a way to get Laurel off the street."
She gave me a wry look. "But then you already know how that worked out."

"I'll walk you out through the tunnel and drive you all to the hotel," River said. "I'm just sorry you've got to do that whole trek again."

"I'm not. I wanted to come with you when you spoke to the women they rescued from Luca's hellhouse. I think they'd all feel a lot more comfortable if they heard from another one of Luca's targets," Kenzie said. "I can vouch for you. I can also let them know about Madison and the Sunshine Adoption Agency.

"If they had kids that were taken by that demon couple, they need to know the FBI is working on locating their children as we speak."

"Hearing from you would help them a lot," I agreed. "There are four women, and one couple that knocked on the wrong door when they got lost on their hiking trip. They're all in the rooms on the first floor. The doc has already checked them all out, and Sunny's chef served them all breakfast, so now's a good time to talk to them."

"There's something else," River said, stopping us when Kenzie and I made for the door. "Kenzie, I know we have to check the list of ledger victims anyway to make sure we get descriptions of them all, but seeing as we already know the name of the woman who has seen one..."

She cringed. "You want me to call Damien and get his aunt's number."

He shrugged. "If she works with the government, her number and address will be unlisted. You've got to hit that deadbeat piece of shit up for the info."

Kenzie heaved a sigh. "I know I do, but that doesn't mean I have to like it. Ugh," she groaned, pulling out her phone. "I'll try Talia first. At least she's less likely to immediately block my number the minute it comes on the screen."

"Want to fill me in?" I asked as we set off. "Why are you calling up deadbeat pieces of shit?"

"Kenzie pointed out that the leaders of the Brotherhood were a small-time outfit fifteen-plus years ago. An outfit after very particular members. They would've approached victims of the ledger dump who held a grudge against Adeline, and they would've likely done it face-to-face."

I shot up straight. "So those people all know what the true leaders of the Brotherhood look like! Just like my dads Saint and Killian had to recruit my father, Bane, without the masks. It was just the two of them in those days. They couldn't outsource recruitment until much later. Same for the Brotherhood.

"Kenzie, that's fucking genius! Why didn't any of us think of that?"

"The woman's amazing," River said matter-of-factly. "She came into our lives to bring us to our knees in shock and awe."

Kenzie laughed even as she blushed. "Stop it, guys. It was just a stray thought. Hopefully it pans out."

"I'm hoping the same thing, because I spoke to my parents about Sacred Heart Charities," I said. "They got as far as Leonard Stevens, and only that far. After he was murdered in his cell, Killian picked his life apart but there was nothing. No clue as to who he was working for, or proof that he was working for anyone other than what he said in the police interview.

"My folks figured he must've been talking about his bio mom and dad. That maybe he convinced himself that they didn't die in a tragic accident, and they were actually murdered. He was avenging his own delusions."

"But of course, there was no way to find out what he was thinking after he died," Kenzie said. "But what about everything else that's happened to the Merchants in the last twenty years. As in attacks that seemed random and out of nowhere. Attacks like the one on the movie theater. Maybe it wasn't a rival gang." She met my eyes over her shoulder. "Maybe it was the Brotherhood, trying to destroy another thing the Merchants created to help the community.

"If those psychos would burn down a church, school, and clinic with innocent people inside, they'd have no trouble going after a theater."

"That's true," I said simply. "That's very true."

I thought back as we rode the elevator down. My parents only let us children into the full details of their business when we turned eighteen. We knew they weren't law-abiding citizens before then, naturally, but all the information didn't come until we were adults. I knew about some past attacks that none of our main enemies claimed credit for, but I doubted I knew about all of them.

The service elevator dinged for the first floor, spitting us out. I took them through the back entrance into the first-floor main hallway.

The Fairfield used to be apartments with penthouses on the top floors. My family took over the penthouses, but the bottom floors remained empty apartments that came in handy for times like this—giving our allies a place to stay.

Kenzie walked up to the first door on the left and knocked.

"Who is it?" a voice called.

"My name is Mackenzie. I was hoping I could talk with you for a minute."

The door opened a crack. A pale, bruised sliver of a face peered at me from under the door chain. "Who are you?"

"I'm a friend of Genevieve's," she replied. "You're probably scared and wondering what comes next, and that's why I'm here. The family isn't going to throw you out onto the street to fend for yourself. We'd like to help you, if you'd let us."

She shifted enough for me to see it was Debra—the woman Bee was forced to give a five-fingered sedative. But she was also the woman who came to in the crash, and ripped and yanked at Genny's crumpled driver side door just to pull her out.

"What kind of help?" she asked.

"This is River." Kenzie pointed him out. "He runs a homeless shelter here in Leighbridge with an open bed if you need it. Along with food, clothes, doctors, and therapists on hand. Did— Do you have children?"

Debra shook her head.

"Do you know how long you... were in the house?"

"I... I think it's been..." She dropped her gaze, eyes watering. "I think it's been seven months. Maybe more."

"Okay," Kenzie said gently, moving in a little closer. "Then it's likely your job has found someone else, and your apartment—if you lived in one—has been rented out. We can help you track down all of your things. We can speak to your old boss, or help you find a new job. Whatever you need, you just let us know."

I stood beside Kenzie, just marveling at her.

Maybe it was the big sister in her. Maybe it was motherhood. Maybe this was just who she was. There was something about this gorgeous, sweet woman that made you feel safe and cared for. When Mackenzie Blaine said you could count on her... you believed her.

"Why?" Debra rasped. The door shook in her hand, bumping up against her cheek. "Why would you do all of that for me? Why would you care?"

"Because Luca Adams kidnapped my child and tried to sex traffic me," she replied, popping Debra's brow up. "He was a monster. Truly the lowest form of reptilian slime, and he would've destroyed my life if the Merchants hadn't rescued me. Now I'll make it my life's mission to destroy his.

"Luca wanted to bring pain and destruction to every woman that crossed his path. I want to make sure his legacy is just as much a failure as he was."

Debra was quiet for a long time.

"Thank you," she said softly, "for sharing that with me. I do believe you want to help, but I'm a grown woman in my forties. I've been taking care of myself for a long time, and to stop now would mean admitting to myself that I let those men make me helpless, and like you, I will prove them wrong."

"I understand." Kenzie didn't push her. "I'll leave you in peace."

"Wait, no," Debra cried when she turned to go. "That name you said. Luca Adams. I heard the men say it while I was in that place, but I never knew who that was. Did he do this to me? Was he the reason I was taken?"

"That house was owned by Luca Adams, yes. He was the leader of a sex-trafficking and child-kidnapping ring."

"And you knew him?"

"Too well."

Debra closed the door in our faces. Thudding and the clinking of metal on the other side, and then the door flew open. A hand beckoned. "Please, come in. I want to— I *need* to know who did this to me."

***

Kenzie

I gestured for the guys to stay behind, then stepped in, letting Debra close the door behind me.

I looked around the apartment in surprise, but I really shouldn't have been. Nothing about the Merchants should've surprised me by that point.

When Bane said all the lower-floor apartments were empty, I expected them to be empty! Instead what met my eyes was a leather sectional, full kitchen, big screen on the wall, dining table with Debra's half-eaten breakfast, and a patio entrance that showcased a group of firefighters spraying down a burning car.

The whole place was nicer than my first apartment, and no one even lived here full-time. But then, what seemed like waste turned out to be good fortune. There were dozens of people trapped in the building now. It'd be ten times more uncomfortable if there was nowhere for them to sleep and eat.

"Please, sit," Debra said softly. "Can I get you anything?"

"Of course not. You don't have to serve me or worry about being a gracious host right now." I dropped down in an armchair. "I'm the one who's here for you."

She gave me a wry grin. "You're right, but I can't help it. Feels strange for you to be taking care of me. You're so young. Young enough to be my daughter."

"Only if you had me when you were three."

Debra barked a laugh, then caught herself—as if startled that her body remembered how to do that. Taking a seat across from me, she smiled. "Three, huh? You're a little charmer, aren't you. I'm not in my twenties nor do I look like I am, but I thank you for the compliment. It's nice of you to give me one considering..." She gestured to her face. "No one else will for a long time."

I didn't wince, but I wanted to seeing what those beasts did to her face.

Everything below her honey-blonde hair and above her chin was a riot of black, blue, purple, and green bruises. Her left eye was half swollen shut. Her lips were split and scabbed over in four places. Her nose was crooked, and she had a scar across her cheek—telling of a cut that sliced deep.

"I..." I halted, trailing off as my eyes went back to that scar.

"They would've approached victims who held a grudge against Adeline, and they would've likely done it face-to-face."

"Each time the woman got angrier and angrier with my aunt—going on about her being a coward who doesn't give a shit about her own father. Aunt Della backhanded her across the face and sliced her cheek open."

"Yes?" Debra prompted, snapping my eyes up.

I swallowed hard, mind spinning. It could be a coincidence. There had to be hundreds, maybe thousands of people with a scar on their cheek. It wasn't proof they were the psychotic leader of a murder cult.

But she's in her forties. That means twenty years ago when the Brotherhood started recruiting, she was in her twenties. That's more than old enough to begin carrying out a vendetta.

"I was wondering," I began, schooling my face. "If you don't mind sharing, how did you end up in the house if you didn't know Luca? From my experience, and the experience of the other women I've spoken to, he preyed on mostly single mothers in his apartment buildings. He wined and dined them—us—first, made us believe he loved us, and then he walked us willingly into hell."

"Did the other men who work for him do the same thing to you?" I asked. "Does he have a whole team of guys out there pulling the Casanova Cunt routine?"

She snorted. "Casanova Cunt. That's a good one, and it sounds like the bastard earned that title and more, but no. No creepy landlord preyed on me, or convinced me he loved me in exchange for chaining myself to a wall. I'd never fall for something like that.

"No, I lived right here in Leighbridge when I was taken."

Wrong. Luca hunted exclusively in the poor neighborhoods of North Quay and Rockchapel. Practically a different world from where the other part of the business, the adoption agency, was located. The man couldn't sell kids in their own neighborhood. Too high a chance they'd be recognized.

"I'm a criminal law attorney," she explained. "I own my own practice on Martindale Street."

Wrong again. Luca never would've taken a high-profile person with a mess of clients and employees who would miss her.

"I live— lived," she rasped, pushing out those fake fucking tears. "I lived in a penthouse on the west side, near the galleries. One morning I was in my building parking garage, heading to my car to leave for work. I heard a noise behind me, but before I could turn to look, I was struck on the back of my head and everything went dark." She choked on a sob, clapping her hand over her mouth. "I woke up in the house."

Eeeeehhhh! Three strikes, you're out. Luca never targeted rich women living in penthouses, and he didn't go around bashing people over the heads in a place where he could be seen. He was always careful. So careful he only went after poor, abandoned women that no one would miss, and no one would believe.

And that's not you, Debra Whoever-The-Fuck-You-Are.

"That's awful. I'm so sorry." I pulled out my phone. "But I'm starting to get a horrifying picture of what happened. If you were in criminal law, you must've gotten tangled up in a case that involved Luca's business in some way. That's why he targeted you."

She gasped. "Oh my goodness, you must be right. If only— Who are you texting? I'm really not ready to tell my story to everyone."

"Oh, of course not." Someone somewhere should give me an academy award for acting. "I'm texting my sister. She's watching my baby while all of this craziness is going on."

Debra nodded, smiling in understanding.

I smiled back.

Me to Bane, Liam, Sunny, Adeline, River, Sienna: It's a trap! The hostages aren't hostages at all. They're with the Brotherhood, and this was all a trick to get them into the building. We have to get them out!

"I know you said that you don't need our help, but is there anyone we can call for you?" I asked. "Parents? Friends? Brothers? Sisters?"

She shook her head the whole way through. "My parents are gone, and I don't have any brothers or sisters. I'm embarrassed to say I didn't have any friends either. I was one of those pathetic married-to-the-job lawyers, and look what it got me? No one even noticed when I disappeared." Debra swallowed hard, lips quivering.

It was everything in me not to roll my eyes. "I'm sure people noticed. Your children will have noticed."

"What? No." She rubbed her eyes, brushing away the crocodile tears. "I told you I don't have any children."

"Are you sure?" My expression was wholly and entirely neutral. "So there's no one out there who has a reason to call you... Mom?"

Debra's brow twitched—so quick and gone in a flash that I almost missed it.

Almost.

"No," Debra said, pulling on a confused mask. "There isn't. Of course there isn't. If I had children, I'm pretty sure I'd know."

"The Brotherhood."

"What?" She blinked at me, overdoing the puzzled act. "Who is—?"

"They're the people who held you hostage in that house. They're who Luca worked for. I know you've got to respect attorney-client privilege, but did any of your cases involved the Brotherhood?"

"I... uh... Oh, let me think." She paused, scrunching up her face like she was thinking about it. "No. Sorry, no. That name doesn't come to mind for me or any of my colleagues."

"That's all right. It doesn't really matter now." I gestured out the window. "The Brotherhood is finished. Wiped out and exterminated like the infestation they were. Now, all the people they preyed on can get their lives back, and be happy." All the smiles I was forcing was making my face ache. "That's all I want for you, Miss Debra. For you to be happy again."

"I will be." Another lone tear traveled down her face. "As long as there's breath in me, I'm not beaten."

I stood up, not able to stand her presence a second longer. "I won't take up any more of your time." I crossed to the door. "Enjoy the rest of your morning."

"Wait—"

I didn't. Throwing open the door, I stepped out and came face-to-face with River and Bane.

The scream trapped in my throat.

My boyfriends knelt on the floor, their hands both bound with stolen curtain cords from the drapes, and steak knives pressed to their throats.

Four women and one man held them down—all of them bearing faces more beaten up than ground beef.

"He—!"

A hand seized me from behind, snapping me back against a soft chest. I didn't have time to think before a flash of silver flew across my vision, and dug into my throat.

"Don't scream. Don't fight. Don't think," Debra hissed. "Just do exactly as I say. Understand?"

Carefully, I nodded—feeling the blade's merciless kiss.

"Reach into your pocket and take out your phone. Show me the text that you sent."

I didn't fight or argue or hesitate. Tugging out my phone, I showed her.

Debra swore foully. "Fuck! She warned them! She warned them all! How?" She shook me, opening more cuts on my neck. "How did you know!"

"The scar on your cheek was my first clue," I spat, hatred burning my throat. "The next was your pride."

"Pride? What the hell are you talking about?"

"You couldn't stand to *lower* yourself to the likes of me and the other survivors of Luca—women who were seduced and manipulated by that cockroach. So you fed me all that garbage about being some high-powered attorney attacked in a penthouse parking garage." I scoffed. "Didn't anyone ever tell you that the key to a good lie is not to embellish?"

"My lie was good enough," she hissed, strangling the blood out of my arm. "It got me and my brother and sisters into the most secure building in the world. Ha! You Merchants are so simple, it's pathetic. Running around pretending to be heroes saving the day. All the while never looking back at the trail of bloodshed and bodies in your wake. All I had to do was bleat and cry out of a battered face, and they swallowed it hook, line, and sinker.

"Down!" She shoved me to the ground. "Kill her if she moves."

My chest burned listening to her footsteps retreating back into the room—no doubt to get some curtain cords for me. "I'm so sorry," I whispered to Bane and River. "If I hadn't insisted we come down here—"

"—they'd have turned on me when I came down here alone to escort them out of the building," Bane said. "This is not your fault, Kenzie."

"Yes, it is. Because she forced my hand." Debra knelt over me and bound my hands. "Things are about to get very unpleasant very much ahead of schedule." She shoved my phone in my hands. "Send another text. Tell those Merchant scum that I'm in charge now, and they're not to do anything until they receive instruction from me. No moving, thinking, breathing, or fighting. And make sure they know I can slit your throat much faster than they can test me."

I looked at Bane and River.

They both tipped their heads ever so slightly. *Do as she says.*

I typed out the text and let her see it.

"Good. Send it."

I did so, then it was plucked out of my hands. I heard the sound of her crunching it beneath her shoe.

"Move." Another shove. "All of you."

Two on one, the bastard brothers marched us down the hall, their knives firmly pressed to veins that didn't like to be cut.

Bane was forced ahead of the pack.

"Open it, and don't think you can trick me." The entire way Debra moved had changed. Gone was the terrible actress pretending she had human emotions. Her tall figure towered shoulder to shoulder with Bane, and standing up straight you could see the purpose in her walk, and the hard, corded frame beneath loose, borrowed clothes.

"I know the Fairfield is loaded with security measures no one could ever see coming, but if we're surprised, I promise you my hand will slip, and your little fuck toy will die."

"Don't call her that." Bane's voice was as light and jovial as it always was. The man was not in the least bit cowed. "We're all enemies here, but there's never a need for misogynistic insults."

"You don't give the orders here." Debra withdrew the knife and stabbed me in the arm with a quick, shallow jab.

"Ahh!"

"Hey!" Bane and River shouted.

"I do," she said over our noise. "I'll decide what there's a need for."

Bane glared at her, lips peeling back from his teeth as a dark, ferality dimmed his eyes. "You're in." He threw open the hall door. "Fuck off into that swarm of cops and SWAT teams. I beg of you."

She laughed. "Thank you for the suggestion, but I have a better idea. You go out there and evacuate Thatcher and everyone on your security team. Now," she barked. "They're all out the front door in two minutes, or I paint the walls with her blood."

Bane took two steps.

"Uh-uh." Debra hauled me around River and his captives.

I clutched my arm, just trying to breathe. And think.

"That's far enough," Debra said, keeping Bane half in and half out of the doorway. "Tell them."

Bane's jaw clenched, his muscles ticcing. Releasing a hard breath, he said, "Thatcher, clear out. You and the whole team."

"Excuse me?" Thatcher's deep voice replied. "Why—?"

"Take the back way, but go now. All of you." Bane's expression was hard. "Now."

There was a tense silence in which Bane did not speak, move, or twitch. There was no doubt Thatcher observed that his behavior was odd. And why would Bane be acting weird after coming out of the hall filled with all of the hostages unless—

"Very well." I heard shuffling, Thatcher giving the same order, and then heavy footfalls.

We waited in tense, pained silence until the back door slammed in the distance for the final time.

"Now, out!" She shoved me, moving the knife to my back. "Walk, and don't try anything."

I stumbled out into the lobby, my arm singing with pain.

Debra forced me to the vacated security booth and put the knife back to my neck, strangling me against her.

"Put the brother in the closet," she ordered. "Adeline left the bum to rot on the streets, so she obviously doesn't care about him. Keep all your knives on the son."

River shouted—loudly and profanity-laden—as he was shoved roughly into the cleaning closet. My heart ached as they shoved not one but two front hall couches in front of the door, trapping him in that dark, windowless room.

I wanted to believe there was another secret entrance in there leading to a way out, but the tunnel we came through was solid concrete with only two entrances on both ends—and neither one was in that cupboard.

Task done, all five of the bastards followed their leader's orders, and pressed their tips in a perfect ring around Bane's neck.

"Now, here's what's going to happen. I know that right now you've got the whole family in the building for the big reunion," Debra crowed. "Everyone except for your oldest sisters, but they'll be easy enough to track down when this is all over.

"You're going to call all of them down here right now, and I mean all of them, Genevieve and that little brat, Beth or whatever her name is, included. Unarmed goes without saying. The longer it takes for them to show up"—she stabbed my other arm—"the more time I have to poke holes in your girl-friend."

"Stop!"

"Ahh," I cried, tears springing to my eyes. Overwhelming, burning hatred flooded my soul at this scheming, worthless bitch, but amidst that, I only had one thought.

My sister truly is psychic.

Sienna said the safest place for her and Laurel to be today was far away from me, and I thanked every deity from every culture and religion that they both were.

"You don't need to prove how *tough* and *serious* you are by torturing an unarmed, innocent woman," Bane barked, loading his words with scorn. "I'm not resisting!"

"She's not fucking innocent!" Debra's growl assaulted my ear. "No one that has anything to do with your filthy family is, so get on with it!"

Silently, Bane typed out his text and showed it to his captor.

He read it, nodded to Debra, then ordered Bane to hit send.

There were six elevators in the lobby of this apartment building turned family home, and all of them dinged their tune as the most infamous family in Cinco City exited their confines.

Sunny, Liam, and even Genny. Pushed in her brother's borrowed wheelchair, Genny strained to keep her bandaged head up as one of her fathers wheeled her into the lobby, followed by Adeline, Killian, St. John, and Baris.

"Yumi, Maryann, check them for weapons," Debra demanded. "If even one of them is packing so much as a paperclip, cut off Alexander's finger, then— Hold on, where's the girl?" Debra said, noticing the missing member of the family. "I said everyone!" She positioned the knife perpendicular to my throat. "Bring your daughter down here right fucking now or—"

"There is no place for me to *bring her down* from," Liam said—tone smooth like honey. "Elizabeth is not in the building. I didn't want her sitting alone in the apartment while we focused on getting Genny safely home, so I sent her and Fuller off to the beach for the weekend."

Debra hesitated, sharing a look with her compatriots. "You're lying. This is some stupid, father's love attempt to hide her from me, and—"

"I don't need to hide my daughter from you." His shiny, cold eyes dragged the room temperature down fifty degrees. "As assuredly as I can see your hand shaking from here, you're no threat to my child, because if you even thought about hurting her, I'd rip your head off your shoulders with my bare hands and stomp your worthless skull in until your blood and brain matter stuck to the shit on my shoes."

Debra was shaking, and truly, so was I. I'd never, *never*, heard Liam speak this way before. Not just the threats, but the vicious way he delivered them—as if the violence he would visit on her was a fact of life.

Lions eviscerate zebras. Eagles tear the heads off fish. And Liam Hunt brutally murders anyone who threatens his daughter.

These were just the facts of life...

...and it made me love him so much, my knees weakened.

I spent the morning in the presence of the shittiest father to ever walk the earth. How lucky was I to have the love and the heart of the best.

"So as I said," Liam continued—cool and calm as the two women patted him down and tossed his phone across the room, "Elizabeth is not here, and I can very easily prove that to you, but anymore talk of bringing my child into a hostile situation will cease immediately—for your own sake."

Living, choking hatred bled from Debra's pores. "Cold, hard Liam Hunt, so desperate to follow in his daddy's footsteps—if you could remember which one of your mother's manwhores he even is.

"You're not in charge here, you bigamist's bastard," she hissed, leveling the knife on him. "I am."

Liam, Sunny, Bane, and their parents exchanged a look... and burst out laughing.

I gaped at the lot of them. *What the hell is funny?!*

"What's funny?" Debra screeched, echoing my thought. "Why are you laugh—? Stop that! I said stop! Wilson!"

Bane's captor moved so fast, Bane's laugh was still in the air as the knife slashed across his forearm—tearing through flesh and muscle.

Bane growled, eyes popping and veins thickening on his neck. He clapped his hand on the weeping wound, glaring at Wilson with a venom that would put me on the ground if it ever came my way.

I had no idea how the dick was still standing.

"What happened?" Debra taunted as the room fell silent, leaving only River's muffled shouts in the background. "Not laughing now, are you?"

"Oh no, we very much are," Adeline replied. Her smile was wide, even pleasant. "I'm sorry, dear, but it's quite hilarious that you think you're being so clever and smart when in fact, this is the stupidest thing you've ever done in what has surely been a pointless, trainwreck of a life."

Now my bulging eyes were on her. What life were the Merchants living that they could laugh and insult the mad people holding knives to their brother/son and his girlfriend's throat? This kind of blasé calm in the face of violent madness was just something I could never comprehend.

"How in the world could you ever think you could take charge in our home? On our turf?" Adeline pushed out her lips, gazing at Debra in convincing sympathy. "Has no one ever taught you the first rule of dealing with assassins?

"You never chase a snake into its den."

I couldn't see Debra's face, but I imagined her expression wasn't too pleased going by her tightening grip on my throat.

"I wouldn't be too sure of yourself, or the Fairfield's famed security," Debra spat. "This isn't your den anymore. It's mine." She flicked the knife in Bane's direction. "Bring him."

Debra dragged me out of the security booth so that her buddies could shove Bane in.

"Log in to the building security system and shut it off. All of your door codes, elevator codes, pressure plates—"

Bane's and Sunny's heads snapped up, surprise clear in their eyes.

"Yeah, that's right," Debra crowed. "I know about those. Just like I know about the poisonous gas, the security for Liam Hunt's island home where I bet sweet little Lizzie is having her beach vacation, and the hidden tunnel leading to Caddell House."

The Merchants exchanged looks again, but these weren't amused.

"What do you say to that, Adeline? Want to lecture me some more on my ignorance?"

Adeline didn't reply—her pinched expression as deafening as her silence.

"Log in and turn it off," Debra said, "and don't try anything, Alexander. I told you, if I'm surprised, my hands will slip."

Bane gave her a look that would've boiled her head. "I can log in but I can't turn off the system. Only the developer knows the code, and that was by design. If no one in the family knows, then none of us can be forced into doing what you're doing now!"

"Let me worry about that. Just do what I said."

Flicking from her to me to his family, Bane sat down.

Wilson and Debra—and I—were shadows over his shoulder, tracking his every twitch and keystroke. As ordered, Bane pulled up a program called *Cofre*. He logged in, then Wilson grabbed his desk chair and flung him back. A hard shove sent me flying too, right into Wilson's hold.

"You all thought you were so clever." Debra sauntered up to the desktop, flipping the knife on her palm. "Hire a security expert in complete secrecy, allow him to choose the shutoff code, and then send him on his way. No one would know the important information he holds in his head. No one will even look his way."

"And no one can," Liam sliced in. "He died over a decade ago, taking the code with him. He was—"

"—shot in his home," Debra finished. "The police claimed it was a burglary gone wrong." She smirked right in his face. "I think they wrote that on the report to make his wife feel better. It was kinder than telling her I didn't take a damn thing when I tortured him for hours until cutting things off finally made him loosen his lips."

I goggled at her. "What the fuck! What the hell is wrong with you?!"

Debra blinked at me, holding her hand to her chest like *who? Moi?* "Not a thing is wrong with me, Mackenzie Blaine."

I shivered at her casual use of a name she shouldn't know.

"What you should really be asking is what is wrong with your pals here? How could they have been so stupid as to let an outsider walk out of here with the code to their security? And of course, because they've never known the code, they've never been able to change it any time in the last ten years. So this..."

Bending over, she pulled up the main screen. Clearly displayed across the top was *GUEST MODE*, but beneath it were some of the modes Bane talked about. Family Mode, Hostile Enemy Mode, Natural Disaster Mode, and even a Cops Mode. At the bottom beneath all of that was a red button we all knew well:

SHUTDOWN MODE

Debra clicked it and a warning box appeared on screen.

Warning: If you proceed, all camera feed, entrance codes, exit codes, door alarms, panic buttons, and all existing security protocols will be disabled.

Confirm you wish to proceed with shutdown?

I internally screamed as she typed it in. *Don't work, don't work, don't—*

SHUTDOWN CONFIRMED

"Still works," Debra finished, straightening up.

Still and heavy silence hung over the room. Even River fell silent in the closet, his banging coming to a halt.

Adeline stepped beside her daughter, drawing Genny close and stroking her hair. My friend did not look good at all. She needed to be in bed resting. But then... I didn't think any of us were doing too well either.

"What do you want?" Adeline asked simply.

Debra scoffed. "It's incredible to me that you even have to ask. You have ruined and destroyed so many innocent lives, you lost track of your body count decades ago. You can't even remember our names, which we haven't changed!

"Wilson," she cried, pointing to him. "Jillian, Yumi, Natalya, Maryann, and Debra. The names our fathers gave us before you took away theirs!"

If understanding was dawning on Adeline, she wasn't giving it away on her face. None of Sunny, Liam, and Bane's parents gave a sign that they had a clue what she was talking about.

"No?" Debra stepped out, facing the Merchants head-on. "What about you, St. John? Don't you remember Racer, Viper, Gunner, and Hawk?"

The man shrugged. "Not even a little bit. Why? Should I?"

I could hear her clenched jaw cracking from where I stood. "You should. You should remember shooting my father in the stomach, cutting out his tongue, and leaving him to bleed out in a back-alley dumpster. You should remember my father, Donald Seward!"

Another shrug. "Nah, doesn't ring a bell. But if I did all of that to him, you can rest assured the cockless bastard son of a gas station toilet seat deserved everything he got and more." The impossible man smiled—smiled!—right into her eyes. "I hope that puts your mind at ease."

Debra snarled. Lips peeling back from her teeth, I wouldn't have been able to pick her out of a lineup with ten other feral animals. She charged him, knife high—then jerked to a stop.

"No," she shrieked, stumbling back. "You're trying to provoke me. You want me to throw myself at you with a weapon you can easily get off me, and then it'll be hostage against hostage. Threaten to cut my throat too, and Wilson will let your little boy go."

Saint hummed. "You're not completely stupid after all."

"You think you understand that now, but trust me," Debra said, moving well back from the family of assassins. "You'll underestimate me again, and it'll be the last thing you ever do."

"We don't underestimate you," Adeline broke in, "and we do remember you. *I* do. Your fathers were Merchants who attacked me and Saint, and tried to hand him over to the Kings to be tortured and murdered. During this attack, your father, Racer, put hands on me, and Saint found that..." She stroked her husband's cheek. "Hard to forgive.

"But none of that excuses the pain and grief you all feel at losing your fathers. You have every right to be angry and hurt, and to even want some semblance of justice, but whatever you think you're going to do here today won't give you that. The only thing that will happen is that you'll become even worse monsters than we could ever be," she dropped, the motherly tenderness leaving her voice as quickly as the chill set in. "And your fathers will still be dead."

"We could never be as vile as you," Debra forced through gritted teeth. "Never."

"No? Then why is that innocent girl who has nothing to do with this and never hurt you, or anyone, in her life bleeding and terrified in the grip of that brute?" she flung, pointing at me and Wilson. "Why is my daughter, who risked her life to save yours, being treated as your enemy? Why was my son, who was born after your father met his end, and has never even met you, attacked just for the crime of being my son? And why are you, Little Debbie, the girl who stands here today because we never visited your father's sins upon you... so desperate to lay hands on a six-year-old girl?

"Tell me how in your sick little mind you justified bringing a child into your vendetta, and then tell me how you think that makes you better than me?"

"We wouldn't have hurt her," Wilson blurted. "We're not monsters! We just want you to pay for—"

"Shut up, Wilson!" Debra barked.

"But, Deb, they—"

"I said be quiet! Don't you dare justify yourself to that scum-trash viper. Adeline Redgrave can fancy herself all she wants on her imaginary high horse, but someone started this fight, and it sure as fuck wasn't us.

"What happens to little Lizzie Hunt is not the Merchants' concern anymore," she dropped, turning away, "because you'll all be dead."

Debra snatched a paper tray off the desk and threw it on the floor. "Now, enough chat. Get all the phones into the basket. Get the unlock codes for them while you're at it.

"Wilson, bring everyone up to the thirty-fifth floor—including the girl and the other Redgrave." I assumed she meant me and River. "That's Sole and the nanny's floor. Tie them all up in the living room, I want them where I can see them at all times. Then, search the nanny's apartment and make sure he's not lying about her and the kid being here.

"If the nanny is here, kill her," Debra commanded without a trace of feeling. "We don't need her for the auction."

"Auction?" I croaked.

"Oh, that's right, didn't I say?" Debra spun on me with a bright smile. "Adeline is quite right about our beef being with only her and Saint. The others did nothing to us. They didn't kill our fathers. *But*," she stressed, "this little family of soulless criminals have done plenty of horrible things to plenty of other people, so, we're going to keep Adeline and Saint, and auction the rest of you off."

Blood drained out of my face with every word. "You're insane. No wonder you were best friends with that disgusting shitstain Luca."

Her eyes narrowed. "I was far from that scum's *friend*. Luca Adams was the lowest form of trash, but he was a necessary evil to get us this far. He hid the scale of his trafficking operation from the Merchants so impressively,

Sunny boy here thought he was nothing more than a lowlife, and low-level, pimp.

"We needed his many boltholes, and the victims chained within, so that we could hide among them and get here. But you can trust this, girl, I did not mourn his death."

"Oh, well, that makes it okay, then," I chirped, sarcasm dripping from my lips. "You just sat back and did shit all to help dozens of women forced into sexual slavery while their children were sold to the highest bidder, but at least you *didn't approve.*"

Her eyes flashed. "You mean like you sat back and watched your father abuse and subjugate your mother until she was forced to shoot him in the face?"

I blew back, eyes wide.

"That's what I thought," she taunted. "There's plenty of hypocritical bitch to go around, so I suggest you shut your mouth."

I breathed hard, chest heaving against the arm locked around my chest... but I shut my mouth.

"Good." She turned her back on me. "Now, as I was saying, the auction begins tonight at seven o'clock on the dot. It took many years, countless fortunes, and endless recruitment to get where we are now. My financial backers required proof that we could achieve our goal of dismantling the biggest, and deadliest, criminal syndicate in history.

"And for a long time, we couldn't provide that proof... until Sacred Heart Charities erupted into flames." She grinned at Adeline's narrowing eyes. "Even though none of you were inside, unfortunately, the fact that we were able to unearth one of your money-laundering operations, burn it to the ground, and get away with it—proved we were a serious threat.

"The money started rolling in."

I gaped at her. "But— You didn't unearth anything! You badgered some poor woman into joining your deluded revenge plot until she was forced to spill about the charity to get you to leave her alone. Oh, and don't forget the bitch slap!"

Debra shrugged. "Regardless, that day marked the changing of the tides. The first of our serious investors pledged their support and membership, and now the brothers and sisters of the inner circle are due their reward.

"Of course, they all can't have a piece of you. Hence, the auction. Revenge goes to the highest bidder."

"Inner circle?" I repeated. "Highest bidder? But what about all those brothers and sisters outside the inner circle? The ones who've been cannon fodder for you? Who were cut down and killed for your fake rescue!"

Debra looked at me in amusement—as if I was a cute little puppy that kept yapping.

"Don't they get their revenge?" I asked. "Isn't that why they joined you?"

"It's so cute that you're worried for them, but you don't need to be, they will also share in our victory. In fact..." She tipped her head to Natalya. "Send for them all. Every brother and sister in the lower tiers.

"The Fairfield is now theirs. Their home. Their reward for our victory." She turned that smirk on me. "Also let them know that their new apartments are currently filled with all the gangbanger trash that threw their lot in with the Merchants. If they want to move in, they'll have to shoot the previous tenants."

"No!" Sunny shouted.

"We'll supply the guns," Debra finished, ignoring Sunny completely.

"You—!"

"Enough," Debra cut me off. "Bring everyone upstairs like I said, but use the stairs and go one at a time—keeping the knife on their throats the whole time. Be ready for them to try something, and kick them down the fucking stairs with a slit throat if they do."

"Shouldn't we wait for Abraham's toy soldiers to get here?" Wilson asked. "They would've warned their people to be ready to attack the second they got this girl's warning. And they would've deleted those warnings off their phones so we wouldn't see them."

Considering, she nodded. "You're right, but we can't hang around here like sitting ducks either. Not with only a couple of steak knives to defend ourselves. There are guns stashed all over this hovel, and we need to get our hands on them. Now."

"What about the old servants' entrance?" Yumi spoke up. Underneath all the bruises, I could see she was an attractive woman with bright, mahogany eyes; full lips; and skin that was black, blue, and green, but otherwise didn't know a single pimple, pockmark, or blemish. "There's a servants' staircase and elevator too. I bet they didn't let any of their hired thugs near either. Anything to protect the location of their secret tunnel."

"Good idea," Debra replied. "Take them that way. And remember, if you find anything living in Bellis— Excuse me, make that *my* new apartment, kill them. We're all going to get nice and comfy until the auction begins—"

"No."

Debra went very still. "Excuse me?" Slitted eyes burned me. "What did you just say?"

"I said no," I repeated. "None of this—not a single thing you're doing—makes any sense. Why in the hell would you want to hang out for hours in a building filled with your enemies that just had all of its defenses taken offline? Especially after you just acknowledged that the Merchants likely put out calls for help far and wide?

"The door to the parking garage is literally behind you. Why wouldn't you shove them all into trunks, drive out from under the noses of half the Cinco police force, take them to some secret location that you control, and have your precious auction there? Why—?"

"Wilson, gag that bitch. I've had enough of her running her mouth."

"Don't—!" That was all I got out before he clamped his hand over my mouth.

I shouted, argued, and struggled as loud as my guys as the dragging began—hauling them none-too-gently to the doors leading to the hidden servants' entrance.

"Wilson, leave her with me," Debra said when he tried to yank both me and Bane by our bad arms. "Take Alexander to his floor first and make him turn over his stash of weapons and ammo. Go by elevator, so you can meet us in the staircase with the weapons. Break his kneecaps if he tries anything, but don't kill him.

"He's the smartest bastard Redgrave popped out. He'll go for a higher price than his siblings."

"Why can't we all use the elevator?" Maryann asked.

"Too dangerous to be alone in an enclosed space with them. Plus, for all we fucking know, pushing all the buttons on the elevator releases the poison gas." She jerked her head at Wilson. "I'm only letting him go alone because he's a black belt, Alexander will be tied up, and the Blaine girl is staying with me. Alexander might try to fight back, but if everything isn't how it should be by the time I get up to my new apartment, I'll slit the girl's throat without a second's hestiation.

"Now, no more arguing. We need to move."

Wilson shoved me down in the desk chair. I was forced to watch while they took the people I loved away. River was last to go. Forced out of the closet, Natalya wrapped his dreads around her forearm and pressed her blade to his throat, dragging him hunched-over and shouting across the room.

"Stop that!" I screamed. "You're hurting him."

"His pain is the least of your problems right now," Debra hissed, turning on me as the door swung shut—leaving us alone in the prettily decorated lobby. "You know, when the name Mackenzie Blaine appeared on our radar, I looked into you and found the disappointing, embarrassing history I expected to find of slum trash that offers her ass to be passed around among the Merchant boys.

"Failed daughter, failed mother, failed thief, failed person." She spoke like we were having a light, breezy, casual conversation. "So I'm more than a little surprised to find that even though you are all of those things and worse... you're not stupid. In fact"—her eyes sharpened on me—"you're surprisingly quick and insightful."

"Okay..." I edged away from her. "Why are you saying this?"

"Because you figured me and my brother and sisters out while your Merchants were still choking on my lies, and you were spot-on. There is no reason for us to stay in this building. In actuality, sense says we should stuff those shits in the trunk and leave this building immediately."

I swallowed hard, eyes darting around the room. "Then, why don't you?"

"Because I can't," she said, slowly coming around the desk. "For more than a few reasons, and the first and most important... is the ledger."

My brow crumpled. "The ledger? You mean the old ledger that Adeline made worthless decades ago? That ledger?"

"No. I mean the one Adeline Redgrave started when she and her husbands took control of the underground. In their little black book are the names of every syndicate, gang, outfit, and criminal family in Cinco—along with all the heaps of dirt they've got on them to keep them in line.

"It's somewhere in this building, and it was heavily protected, until I turned off the security system of course." Step. And another step—coming closer than I ever wanted to be to this rotted hellwhore. "It would've taken long enough even with all of us searching all forty of these fucking floors, but that's why I needed that little brat, Lizzie Hunt. Adeline wouldn't have dared dick me around if I had a knife to the throat of those big crying eyes and bouncing blonde curls."

My jaw dropped, horror leadening my bones.

"Although, I suspect Hunt is lying, and she is somewhere hidden in the Fairfield, because I've had people watching this place for the last week, and they would've alerted me if the nanny took her away.

"But as it is, even if we don't find her by auction time, as long as she's in the building, I have the leverage I need to force Adeline into giving me that flash drive."

"H-how?" My voice was nothing but a thin croak.

Debra blinked at me. "Why, the bombs, of course. Before Vance Hollywell met with what was no doubt a grisly end—" She winced. "I wasn't expecting the Merchants to shoot up and bomb the avenue, and I dare say, neither was he. But anyway, before he died, Vance waved in a crate of explosives into Caddell House's loading dock under the label *fabric*.

"Once the Merchants are secure, Maryann and Yumi will bring the bombs in through the tunnel," she said, plopping herself down on the desk like we were a couple of friends shooting the shit. "Then we'll blow this shithole to hell."

"After the auction," I whispered—understanding hit me like a brick to the face. "After you've tricked your rich friends into paying you millions for Merchants that they'll never get their hands on. You'll kill the whole family, their gangs, and even your own. Your *investors* will think it was an accident gone wrong, because why would you kill your own fucking people, but really, you're burying the Merchants and the Brotherhood in the same grave—only to run off with the money and the black book to build an empire even bigger and stronger on their ashes.

"And the only hope you'll give Liam, Adeline, Sunny, Bane, and Elizabeth's family is that they can save Tricky from their fate."

She tapped her nose, winking at me. "See? Smart."

"Yeah," I gritted, "so smart, I know that you couldn't give less of a shit that your people will die in the explosion too. I bet you never cared about the *lower-tier* members of your cult. Their revenge means nothing to you. It's always been about yours."

"Ours," she corrected. "Me, Wilson, Maryann, Yumi, Jillian, and Natalya. The children of Donald Seward, Liam James, Adrian Westwood, and Noel Harvey. Our fathers were friends just like we were. And they all died on the same day, destroying our worlds in the time it took St. John to pull the trigger.

"The six of us are the Brotherhood, and we always have been," she said, rising up. "Waiting, planning, training, and recruiting an army of no-nothing thugs. Those thugs will keep the Sons of Saint, Scourges, and the rest of them in our trap, and if the Merchants sent for backup, when they storm the place, they'll end up in our trap too.

"Worthless cannon fodder the lower members may be, they're still vital as a means to this end—the end of the Merchants, and the rise of the Quay Street Boys." Debra smiled almost tenderly. "That's what our dads called themselves when they were young."

"Wow," I dropped. "That's a stupid fucking name."

Debra barked a laugh. "It's not the best, I admit it, but they were seven. What can you do?"

"Seven, huh? That's only a year older than Elizabeth."

She flashed me an irritated look.

"She's just a little girl," I burst out. "And if she is hiding somewhere in the building, then she must be terrified. As terrified as you were when your father went out into the night to live the dangerous life that he *chose*. But Tricky didn't choose any of this. Leave her out. She's just a—"

"For fuck's sake, save your breath," she snapped. "Of course I'm not leaving her out of this. The girl dies too. She has to. Look what happened when the Merchants got all soft-hearted and left me, Wilson, Maryann, and our friends alive. We grew up, hunted them down, and destroyed them. I can't have little Elizabeth Hunt doing the same to me one day."

I looked that beast in the eyes. "Adeline is right. You are worse than she could ever dream of being."

Debra's grin melted away. "A man gave her a little boo-boo on her fore-head, and she had him brutally murdered. That was all it took for her to leave six innocent children without fathers. Don't you fucking dare defend *Saint* Adeline or her partner-in-hell, St. John. Their death toll would put the Civil War to same.

"No matter what I do. No matter how many people I kill, I will always be an angel compared to that demonic bitch, and her loyal hellhounds."

I leaned in, sneer on my lips. "If you really thought that— If you really believe you're the angel and they're the sinners, why are you hiding like a maggot in shit? Why have you *been* hiding for over twenty years? Why have you been selling this lie to your investors and followers about dismantling the Merchant empire, when all you really want to do is steal it?

"Face it, Deb-Deb, you're nothing but a spineless, cowardly embarrass-ment." I spit on her shoes. "At least your fathers faced Adeline and Saint like men and died on their feet. While your big plan is to scuttle around tunnels like a roach in between hunting down a first grader.

"You're pathetic. Your little grudge is pathetic. Your half-baked revenge plot is pathetic. And you can trust me on this, hellwhore, the Merchants will stop you."

Debra weathered my speech in stony silence. "Hmm. Well, as valid and important as the opinion of a trashy, homeless slut is, if you don't mind, I'm going to toss it on the pile with the other worthless shit that's dropped out of your mouth."

I smiled mirthlessly at her. "If that's true, why did you tell me all of this?"

She hummed, leaning in. "Honestly, I just wanted to tell someone. I'm about to pull the biggest heist and coup in history, and no one is going to know or see it coming."

"The Merchants will see it coming."

"How's that?" She picked her knife off the counter. "It's not like you're going to tell them."

I shot up, backing away from this crazy fucking woman. "What are you doing? You said I was going upstairs with the others."

"I only said that for the benefit of your boyfriends." She stepped into my path, blocking my escape. "By the time they realize you're not joining them, they'll already be gagged and bound to the coffee table. A lot less shouting and fighting back that way."

"You don't have to—"

"Argh!" She lunged, the blade slicing through the air—falling in a graceful arc for my neck.

Chapter Eight

Sienna

I sat near the entrance to the park, claiming a shady spot on the bench.

Laurel snoozed next to me. A mix of a bottle full of breastmilk, a leisurely stroll, and a warm, muggy day sent her drifting off into her nap.

I smiled at her little cherub face as the call rang out and then ended in Kenzie's voicemail.

My sense that something was wrong heightened with every missed call.

First, a cacophony of sirens and flashing lights blew past the park—making that jogger on my left trip and nearly end up in the bushes.

I hopped on my phone along with everyone else in the park, and found the news alert about explosions outside the Fairfield. That they said *outside* the building and specified that all structures on the avenue were still standing undamaged, was the only reason Laurel and I didn't go flying through Leighbridge.

Still, if everyone inside the Fairfield is fine, why isn't Kenzie picking up the phone?

My eyes flicked up, peering through my lashes at the well-dressed brunette woman who showed up at the park halfway through our visit, parking herself on a bench not far from the playground.

To the normies, there was nothing strange about the young, attractive woman taking selfies of herself in the park.

But to me, my senses alerted me to the danger from the second I laid eyes on her. And they only got louder when she followed me and Laurel out, then stood on the sidewalk—seemingly waiting for a cab, but letting no less than three drive past her without flagging them down.

Releasing a long slow breath, I closed my eyes—letting knowledge and truth come to me.

A fuzzy, shifting vision unfolded in my mind.

I was sitting on the same bench with Laurel sleeping next to me. Suddenly a car pulls up, driven by the same jogger. They say something to me—I couldn't tell what. But the focus on their moving lips makes me miss it when the selfie woman sneaks up behind me, jams something in my back, and forces me and Laurel into the car.

The car takes off and drives us to—

I frowned, face crumpling. *The Fairfield?*

Cloudy and fuzzy though the vision was, I saw them driving us straight into the Fairfield's parking garage, which opened for them despite the state-of-the-art security system.

They blow in, jump out, lock the doors behind them, leaving me and Laurel trapped inside, and then—

BOOM!

I jumped, my scream blasting against my clenched teeth. Bolting off the seat, I grabbed Laurel's stroller handles and half ran down the path into the park just as the green car I saw in my vision turned the corner and headed for us.

"Wait?" someone called. "Excuse me, you with the stroller! I need directions to— Shit!"

I picked up the pace, heart shotgunning into my throat and choking me. *What do I do? What do I do?!*

I always trusted my visions. Always. Ever since that day Mackenzie left on her bike to the grocery store and came back with ten stitches holding the vicious gash in her arm together. The guilt I felt at not stopping her from going that day, ate me alive for weeks.

Now when I saw something, I didn't waste time questioning it. I acted. And what I saw was that if there was any place in the world Laurel and I shouldn't be that day, it was the Fairfield.

But that's where Kenzie is, and she's not answering her phone! She has to get out. They all need to get out!

I craned my head around, peering up, up, up at the forty-floors-high skyscraper towering over Cinco City. The Fairfield was still there. It was still standing, but the frustrating thing about my visions was that I didn't know for how long. That explosion could be timed for an hour from now or a month. It might not even be a literal explosion. Could just be a warning of certain danger awaiting me and everyone in that building, and lots of terrible weapons could achieve that.

"But none of them are fucking getting near my niece!"

Just as the words left my mouth, I flicked down... and looked right into the eyes of Selfie Girl.

She spun away, quickly veering to the right and stopping at a water fountain like that's what she meant to do all along, but it was clear. She was following me with whatever was in her oversized tote bag. The only thing stopping her from pulling it out was a park full of witnesses.

"Oh, no. No, no, no, no."

Thanks to that rotted pile of fish guts, Luca, I wasn't a stranger to running through the streets, trying to get away from shady people. But Mackenzie and I never had to do it with Laurel. By the time Luca's thugs caught up to us, Laurel was safely with the woman who kidnapped her—which was still weird to say.

Charlie Mayberry was a kidnapper, but she also protected and cared for Laurel when we couldn't, and I'd hate and appreciate her for that for the rest of my life.

But now there is no Charlie, and Kenzie's not here. Laurel is depending on me to protect her. Kenzie is depending on me to protect her. And I'm fucking depending on me to protect my niece, so I have to think of something. Think!

A group of joggers came down the path toward us. I opened my mouth to ask them for help, then cut myself off—tossing my head. I couldn't do that. If Selfie Lady really has a gun, then what was an innocent Good Samaritan going to do to stop her, other than get seriously hurt? Or killed.

No. I had to keep far away from her so that pulling out that gun at all would be pointless. Her targets are already gone.

"Come on, come on," I hissed.

Another park entrance loomed ahead of me. Through the scant amount of distance between a kissing couple, I saw that green car parked right outside—waiting.

"Oh, Hera, no..." I white-knuckled the handle, sweat beading on my forehead. I wasn't getting away from Selfie Bitch. She was herding me exactly where she wanted me to go. "Oh, gods, what do I do? What do—? No, what would the Merchants do? Neither Sunny, Bane, nor Liam would run from some skeezy Brotherhood bitch, so think! If they were here, they'd—" I snapped my head from side to side. "They would—"

I glanced at a little girl blowing bubbles, and a thought came to me. I scrambled inside my purse, pushing Laurel's stroller with my stomach.

Mackenzie was a typical type-A, do-everything-herself eldest sister. Even though she was dating a whole bunch of filthy rich guys, she refused to take money from them. Matter of fact, she was already talking about opening an online shop for clothes, now that she'd been fired from Caddell House for the second time. She didn't like the idea of getting money for nothing.

But I was one hundred percent fine with it.

Before we left for New York, Sunny slipped me a fat wad of hundreds. Either it was to make sure we had a place to stay in case River's plan fell through, or it was to pay for the hitman to take Damien out. Didn't know, but I damn sure didn't do the "oh, no, I couldn't" dance. If the right hitman came along, I wasn't going to let lack of funds give Damien one more day to live that he didn't deserve.

"And look at that…" I gave that bitch the side-eye as I plucked out the money. "A hitwoman did come along."

Slipping off the rubber band, I raised the money in the air and let the wind whip and pull at it, snatching the money away from my fingertips.

Hundreds rained like confetti, falling all over the path, and landing on the joggers—

"Hey! Hey, look," one of them shouted. "It's money! There's money everywhere! Look!"

It was like being in kindergarten when the bell rang for recess.

Joggers, picnickers, kissing couples, and even the mother of the bubble-blowing girl snatched up her daughter and stampeded for the trail—swamping the money confetti flying through the park.

"Whoa— Watch it!" Selfie Bitch was knocked sideways, nearly stumbling over her feet and rolling down the hill into the pond. She righted herself and tried to fight free of the crowd. I lost her in the pack of joggers.

"Hey—!" Her shrieks echoed through the park, even louder than the jubilant cries for free money. "Let me through! Keep the damn money, and let me through!"

Her grasping hand appeared between two oiled-up bodybuilders. Head following, she clawed her way out—her face a mask of rage and thunder.

"Stupid, trashy bitch!" she screamed, dropping all pretense. She bolted for the stroller—ducking and dodging eager parkgoers. Yanking Laurel's stroller away, she ripped off the blanket and—

Nothing.

There wasn't a thing in Laurel's stroller. Not my niece. Not her diaper bag. Not even a pacifier.

"Wha—? Where?" Selfie Bitch twisted around, scanning all the running, shifting faces for me and the baby. "Fuck!"

I crouched behind the bush, watching the stupid fool freak out. Laurel fussed against my shoulder, less than pleased at being rudely awoken from her nap.

"I'm sorry, baby girl, I've got you." I soothed her, gently rocking her back and forth. "You're okay now. You're—"

"My baby," Selfie Bitch shrieked. "Someone help, she took my baby!"

My eyes bugged.

"Some skinny, brunette crazy woman stole my baby! Help me! Please!"

"Okay," I croaked, scrambling to my feet. "She's not that much of a stupid fool. We've got to get out of here."

I spun on my heels, and ran. No hesitation. No looking back. I held my niece close and ran as fast as I could, picking up speed when someone shouted and pointed at me out of the corner of my eye.

I bolted out of the south entrance, coming out on the street that led to River's homeless shelter. I almost went that way, then stopped.

No, if they know about me and Laurel, then they know about River. Besides, homeless shelters aren't known for being locked-down vaults. Being open and inviting to everyone is kind of the point!

"Oh, gods, oh, gods, oh, gods." I bounced from foot to foot, holding Laurel close. What was I supposed to do? If I couldn't go back to the Fairfield, and I couldn't go to my friends in River's crew, where could I take Laurel so she'd be safe.

"You!"

Selfie Bitch booked it hot on my heels, bursting out of the entrance and heading straight for us. She scrabbled in her purse, tugging out something that glinted silver in the sunlight.

I spun around. Slipping the diaper bag off my shoulder, I smashed it across her face.

Her head snapped all the way around, spraying blood from her nose like a fountain. She screamed, collapsing on the ground and setting off a wave of giggles from Laurel. Her gun skittered into the dirt.

"Don't fuck with me, bitch." Balancing the baby, I hefted out the massive rock I had shoved into Laurel's bag. "I'm the mean sister."

I dropped the stone right on her head.

"Ahhhh—!" The rock bounced her skull off the concrete, splitting it open and showering the stone in blood.

She stopped moving.

I didn't stick around to lord my victory over her. Only too aware of that green car and the fact it could come around the corner at any minute, I took off for the sidewalk and flagged down a cab.

A short, Asian woman with a kind smile peered at me through the rearview mirror. "Where to?"

"Uh... I uhh..." I tugged out my phone, pulling up Kenzie's number. I had to try her again, and keep trying her until—

I lit on the last text I sent her. *That's not a bad idea. Even if the Brotherhood ripped apart my and Kenzie's lives, they'd never in a million years think to look for us there.*

"Just a minute." I pulled up my web search. "I need to get the address."

Finding what I was looking for was easier than it should be. All too blessedly soon, the address flashed on screen.

"1526 Bay Breeze Court."

She tipped her head. "On the way."

The car pulled away from the curb, joining the flow of traffic just as the green car jerked to a stop next to the bleeding woman. A dark-haired guy climbed out, rushed to her side, and shouted for help as we turned the corner and disappeared.

***

I stood on the sidewalk outside the apartment building, bouncing Laurel in her carrier.

Thank goodness my sister was always prepared for everything. We lost her stroller, but Laurel was still perfectly happy kicking and cooing at strangers with me strapped to her back.

I blew out a hard breath. "I'm going to need your help on this one, baby girl, okay? Turn that cute up to maximum."

"Da!"

"That's right, Laurel." I stroked her cheek. "This is all to help Da."

Steeling myself, I walked straight up to the doorman. He took one look at innocent little me with my cute baby niece, and waved us in with a smile.

"Hello," I said, stepping up to the receptionist. Her nametag read Mrs. Cole. "I don't know her apartment number, but if you call up and say Mackenzie Blaine is here to see her, she'll let us in." I told her who we were here to see.

Severe silver glasses and sharp brown eyes looked down at me even though she was sitting—until she flicked to Laurel.

The baby smacked her little fists on the counter, screeching and babbling her good time.

The stern mask cracked like an egg, letting loose and wide, an awwwing smile. "Sure. That won't be a problem."

Nice job, Agent Laurel. Mission success.

"Please, have a seat," she said, gesturing to the leather couch tucked between two fake leafy plants. "Help yourself to some lemon water."

"Thank you."

I helped myself to a lot of lemon water—gulping down two cups before Mrs. Cole picked up the phone. Sprinting around the park scared out of my wits dehydrated me something fierce.

"Miss Blaine." Mrs. Cole set the phone back on the cradle. "You can go up now. Apartment 403."

I thanked her and made for the elevator.

All the way up, I counted and recounted the ways this was a bad idea. I was going off a random text from my sister that she sent after a random idea occurred to her. She didn't have any more proof than I did that I had a right to be here.

But I also had a right to walk through the park with my niece on a bright, sunny day without worrying about assassins chasing me. Or at least I thought I did.

So right now was a time to take a leap of faith, and take a chance on a safe place to hide out where no one from the Brotherhood or even Mackenzie would think to look for us.

The elevator dinged open, and I came face-to-face with Lyla Dawson.

"What the hell are you—?" She cut off, blinking at me. "Oh. You're not Mackenzie. You're the other one. The sister. And..." Lyla stared at Laurel like she'd never seen a baby before. "What do you want? Where's Mackenzie?"

"She's not here." I stepped off the elevator which forced Lyla to step back, letting me in the hallway. "I used her name because I knew if you heard Mackenzie Blaine was here to see you, you'd be too curious to send her away.

"It worked."

Lyla scowled. "Yippee for you. You got as far as my hallway. Now you can turn around and leave. I've got nothing to say to you." She gave me her back.

"You don't want to know why I'm here? Why I came all this way just to talk to you?"

Lyla slowed ever so slightly. "Don't need to. I know why you're here. You want one more taste of the indoors before you're out on a street corner, shaking your ass for loose change. Did you know your sister got fired—again? And guess who manages the Johnson account now?" She tossed a smirk over her shoulder. "Me."

"Well, that's a bald-faced fucking lie. The Johnson account was closed the same day Vance Hollywell wrongfully terminated my sister to hide his crimes. And even if it wasn't, the Johnsons wouldn't buy so much as a button from Caddell House now. The business relationship is well and truly destroyed."

I shook my head at the surprise on her face. "See that, Dawson? That's why I'm here. Your desperate need to show up my sister, even if it means resorting to lies, it's just... exhausting," I burst out. "And if it is for me, it has to be for you, and it definitely is for Kenzie.

"Don't you think it's about time we all just say what we need to say?"

She sniffed, lips curling. "I have no idea what you're talking about. I have something to say to you. Matter of fact, you're a trespasser. Fuck off before I call security."

"Okay, but before you do, do you mind if I change your niece's diaper? The kid dropped a serious poop in between us running from our lives to get away from a gun-wielding psycho cultist, and even though all I want to do is take her home to her mother, said home isn't safe for either one of us right now. I assume the rest of the gun-wielding psycho cult members have something to do with it."

Lyla gaped at me, her hand on the door—gripping it mid-slam. "My— My niece?" she rasped, stuck on two words in a mind-blowing speech. "You mean *your* niece?"

"No." I spoke clearly, erasing the distance between us. "I mean yours. My sister figured it out this morning when she was talking to her boyfriend about family. How they can get under your skin and dig a vengefulness out of your soul that not even your worst enemy can touch.

"But with you, Kenzie had no idea why you declared yourself her worst enemy all those years ago. She didn't know you. She had nothing to do with you. And she never did anything to hurt you. But then, it wasn't about what Kenzie did to you. It was about what my mom did to our dad."

"Stop it." Hard, shiny eyes filled with rage. "Shut up. You have no idea what you're talking about."

"Then, tell me I'm wrong. Tell me we don't share the same dad, but before you do, let me say straight off that I'll know you're lying." Blunt was always the way to go. "Now that I know what to look for, I can see my dad's eyes and nose on your face clear as day.

"So how about it?" I asked, pointing to a giggly Laurel. "You going to let me change this baby or not? And before you answer, remember that saying no makes you a bad person."

"I— I don't— We're not—" she sputtered, stumbling over my sudden subject change. "Yes, fine. Change her, but I didn't—"

I blew past her before she could change her mind.

Stepping inside Lyla's lair, I was mildly surprised to see that it was a total mess. Nice enough for a Leighbridge loft with its sleek designer-picked leather furniture, the detached staircase leading up to a plush loft space, gorgeous art prints covering the walls, and a kitchen so nice you'd take your wedding photos in it... if it wasn't for the mass of dirty dishes spilling out of the sink, the dried bits of meals past sticking to the countertops, dirty clothes strewn all over the place, and coffee rings on every single surface.

But all of that only got a passing glance from me. My attention fixed on the photograph snuggled amidst the art prints of a young Lyla cheesing with her arms around my father.

"Yeah," I said, gesturing to the picture. "I'll definitely know you're lying."

She shot past me as I made for the living room and laid Laurel down on the carpet.

"You don't know anything!" She tore the frame off the wall. "You can't just come in here, call me a liar, and—and— say whatever bullshit you want! If you had a single clue—"

"I've got more than a clue, Dawson." I was calm getting out the diaper supplies. "My father treated my mother terribly. It's hardly a surprise that he cheated on her too. It's also not a surprise that you loved him. He was good at that," I said softly. "Making people love him.

"It fed into his malignant narcissistic fantasy that his goodness was measured by all the people he could dupe into *believing* he was a decent, charming person. That way he could be as monstrous as he wanted behind closed doors, and think it all balanced out—"

"That's not true! Don't you dare—!"

"Don't yell," I sliced in—voice light as can be. "You'll scare the baby."

She flicked from me to Laurel—who was staring at the shouty, red-faced being in curiosity—then, shockingly, lowered her voice. "It's not true," she hissed. "He wasn't a monster. Don't you dare call him that. I knew him."

"I knew him too."

"You know what your psycho murdering mother told you to say." She darted to her couch, perching on the edge and leaning over to growl in my face. "It wasn't enough for her to kill him. She had to destroy his memory and reputation too. Turn him into a monster so that she could be the victim—even though there were never bruises or scars on her, but there is a coffin around him!"

I was chill in the face of her fury, focused on cleaning Laurel and slathering her in diaper cream. "Not all abuse is physical, Dawson."

"Yeah, your crazy mommy tried the same argument at her trial—"

"—and it didn't work," I snapped, anger beginning to bleed into my voice. "It wasn't enough for the judge or the jury that he forced her to drop out of college when she miscarried their first baby, convincing her that it was all her fault working and studying when she should've been taking care of herself and the baby.

"They didn't care that after he guilted and shamed her out of an education, he then sabotaged any attempt she made to get a job. Making her late to interviews. Forcing her to drop shifts for every fake emergency that popped into his head. And then when she got pregnant with Kenzie—forget it. Her working days were over.

"And then, of course, since he was the only one bringing in the money, he was the only one who could control it. She wasn't even allowed to know the passwords to the bank accounts," I flung. "He made her beg, plead, and justify every fucking cent he gave her.

"But now," I cried, "you're asking *why didn't she leave him? Why didn't she ask for help?* Well, who was she supposed to go to for help, Dawson? He alienated her from all of her friends and her family. The bastard wouldn't even give her the money to buy a plane ticket home for her mother's funeral. And when her uncle tried to send her the money himself, our dear blessed dad broke her phone, all the computers in the house, and... he bought that gun."

She gaped at me, eyes wide.

"And he pointed at me in my crib and told her that if she ever left him, he'd kill me, Kenzie, her, and then himself."

"That—that—" Lyla shook, eyes watering. "That's not—"

"It's the same threat he'd make to her countless times, even after she gave up hope of ever leaving. He just had to keep her in constant fear and terror for the lives of herself and her daughters. Because she believed him. She believed that if she ever took us and ran, he'd hunt us down and kill us all." I pinned her through, the silence so heavy even Laurel stopped cooing and watched us solemnly. "So she endured it all... until he turned his abuse on Kenzie."

My own eyes started stinging. "My psycho mother, as you call her, told all of this to the jury and the judge, but that wasn't enough for them, and they sentenced her to twenty years in jail. Two decades of her life stolen. Her kids taken from her. Everyone picking apart her life and her actions, even though they have no idea what it was like to live through what she did. And on top of that, she's never even held her granddaughter.

"You wanted someone to be punished and to suffer for the death of that evil bastard, Dawson, well, what do you call what my mother's been through?" I barked. "Because any sane person would call that punishment. Anyone would say that she is suffering!

"But that's not good enough for you. You can't get to my mom, and you can't make my dad answer for the things he's done, so all that rage, and pain, and grief, and confusion got blasted at Kenzie, and you never even gave her the chance to know why."

Her lips trembled, tears running down her face.

I sighed, rocking back to finish putting on Laurel's diaper. "Look, I know it seems like I came here to yell at you and make you feel bad, but I really didn't. I came here... to welcome you into our family."

"Wha—what?" she croaked.

"You're my sister. You're Laurel's aunt." I picked up Laurel and plopped her on Lyla's lap.

The woman squawked like I threw a koala bear at her, claws first.

"We're here. We're free. We're sisters. So let's stop letting ghosts drive us apart."

"I—I don't—" She goggled at Laurel, eyes wide at her babbling like the baby was dropping f-bombs. "I never said that I believe you. I *don't* believe you! If my father was anything like the man you're talking about, I would know. He put me to bed every night. I saw him every weekend. He—"

"Take her back," she cried, holding Laurel out to me. "I don't know anything about babies, and she's not my niece—no matter how many times you say it."

"She is your niece, and you do believe me." I got up and moved to the armchair, leaving her to hold a giggling Laurel who was kicking and bouncing like this was a fun game. "You believe me because even though you have so many terrible things to say about my mother... I bet yours didn't."

Lyla tensed, her lips pressing tightly shut.

"Did your mother say she was crazy? That my father *would never do those things*? Or even that she misses him and wished that he was still here?"

Deep, piercing silence echoed from her half of the living room.

"I know your mom got married. What's your stepdad like? Is he anything like the guy who used to take you to the movies, water parks, and for ice cream, but never let you pick the movie, said that only little sluts wear two-piece bathing suits, and made you eat the same ice cream as him, even though you hated pistachio?"

Silence.

"And if you ever dared to argue with him, he'd cut the trip short, throw you in the car, and spend the whole ride berating you for being a rude, ungrateful brat until you promised through your tear- and snot-covered mouth to never have an opinion of your own again?

"That guy, Dawson. Is that the guy you don't believe was abusively controlling?"

She didn't utter a word.

"I know you believe me," I said, voice firm. "I know you believe your mother, and I know you believe mine. What's really bothering you is that you believe us all... and you love him anyway."

Lyla flinched, pulling Laurel in reflexively.

The baby automatically laid her head on her shoulder.

"You think that makes you a bad person, but it doesn't. It really doesn't," I said, seeing the look on her face. "Love isn't something that we can control. After all... my mother loved a bad man too.

"The only thing that makes you my father's daughter, Lyla, is taking your anger, pain, and insecurity out on Kenzie. That was very Eddie Blaine of you."

She flinched again, jerking back like I slapped her.

"But you don't have to be like him anymore. Eddie Blaine was such an evil, abusive jackass, he destroyed any chance at having a real, loving family that would've *willingly* stuck by his side.

"What about you? Because this is the moment where you choose. Do you want two sisters who will put the past aside, and support and stick by you through the good and the bad? Do you want the cutest, cuddliest niece ever born using you as her pillow all the time?

"Or do you want to keep seeking love and validation from someone who wasn't capable of it when he was alive, and can't give it now that he's dead?

"Your choice."

Lyla was quiet for so long, I almost thought she fell asleep with her eyes open. She was so still.

"Kenzie won't," she whispered so softly, I had to lean in. "She won't forget the past. She won't... forgive me."

"Yes, she will. I know because"—I took out my phone—"of this."

I passed her my cell with the text Kenzie sent me displayed loud and proud on the screen.

Kenzie: Everyone keeps asking me why Lyla hates me so much when we don't have history, but River just made me think maybe it's not about our history. Maybe it's about something way more twisted and illogical: family.

Do you think it's possible that our dad had another daughter, and that daughter is Lyla? If it is, we have to find out for sure. I can't imagine how lost and alone she's felt all these years. We've got to let her know that everything is going to be okay and that

"Us Blaine sisters stick together," Lyla read—the final words of Kenzie's text a thin, raspy croak.

Lyla took one look at me, and burst into tears.

I let her cry, knowing she was getting all the comfort she needed from the family peacemaker. Laurel chewing on her expensive, designer shirt and covering it with drool was the first step to letting the healing begin.

After a long while, she straightened and grabbed for the tissues on her coffee table. She had to toss aside her strewn bra to get to them.

"Okay," she said, clearing her throat. "Let's say I'm interested in... things being different between us. What would that even look like?"

"It looks like brunch, Christmas vacations, shopping for fabric with Kenzie, going hiking with me, movie nights on the weekends, and getting to watch Laurel grow up. But that's later," I said, getting to my feet. "For today, it looks like you babysitting Laurel for a few hours while I get my sister and everyone I love out of the Fairfield." I glanced out the window, clocking that rising tower easily in the distance. "I feel in my bones that she's in danger, and I can't sit by and do nothing."

"Wait— Me? Babysit? I can't do that," she cried. "I told you, I don't know anything about babies, and I just met this kid. I—"

Bang! Bang! Bang!

"Open up!" blared through the door. "I know you're in there!"

We bolted off the couch.

"Quick!" I snatched her hand and tore for the bathroom. "Get inside the bathroom! We—"

The door flew off the hinges, banging into the opposite wall and rattling the whole apartment.

Selfie Bitch flew in—the neon-red bump on her forehead as stark and glaring as the murder in her eyes.

"Good little hiding spot." Her gun flew up. "But not good enough."

Chapter Nine

Kenzie

"I only said that for the benefit of your boyfriends." She stepped into my path, blocking my escape. "By the time they realize you're not joining them, they'll already be gagged and bound to the coffee table. A lot less shouting and fighting back that way."

"You don't have to—"

"Argh!" She lunged, the blade slicing through the air—falling in a graceful arc for my neck.

My training with Bane kicked in, almost like he was right next to me, speaking in my ear.

"First thing you do if someone attacks you with a knife is fucking run. But if getting away isn't an option, block the hit with your forearm—

I snapped up, smashing my forearm against hers and catching the blade just a millimeter from my jaw.

"—they'll recover from the block quickly, so you need to be quicker. Strike them somewhere so sensitive that any hit will put them on their ass: nose, eyes, throat, and groin for men—"

My fist was already up and flying, smashing into the bitch's throat.

She gasped, eyes bugging, and stumbled back.

"—if you can, run away, and even more if you can, get the knife, then run away. You don't want to be chased by a twice-as-angry fucker with bruised balls and a knife."

My heart jackhammered out of my chest—running on fear and pure adrenaline. I didn't recognize the girl who grabbed Debra's wrist and smashed it on the armchair, popping the knife out of her grip.

It skittered out of her hand under the security desk, and I dove—dropping down and scrabbling under it.

"Argh! You stupid slut!" Fingers tangled in my hair and yanked me back, exploding pain in my skull.

"Ahh!" I screamed, stumbling over my feet.

"If someone grabs your hair, don't try to yank away. You'll just rip all the hair out of your scalp. Lean into it, not away."

"Leaning in sounds good to me," I growled. Throwing my head back, my skull collided with something that crunched under the force.

"Ahhh!" The grip on my hair disappeared.

I spun as Debra flew back, clutching her gushing, broken nose. I didn't give her a chance to recover from this one.

Snatching up the computer desktop, the cords I unplugged under the desk easily came through the hole when I swung—cracking her over the head.

Debra dropped like a stone, but I kept swinging.

Bang! Bang! Bang! on her skull, smashing the computer over and over again until the screen shattered—covering her in plastic, glass, and blood.

I stumbled away, gasping around the heart throwing up in my throat. "Ugh," I cried, grabbing the knife and running for the elevator.

Sunny, Liam, Bane, Genny, and their parents would be kept alive until after the auction, but the Sons of Saint, Scourges, Cardinals, and the Prissy Sissies—sorry, baby, but it has such a nice ring to it—were in grave danger. I had to save them from an ambush, then get them to help me ambush the Brotherhood!

"...aggh..."

I froze.

Groans echoed in my ears, coming from one source and one source alone. Debra—

"...help... help..."

—was still alive.

I stared at her weak and limp hand, scratching uselessly at the carpet. I stared... and I didn't move.

I knew what Sunny would do in this moment. I knew what Liam would do. I even knew what Bane would do, and what he would say. Bane would tell me to run and keep running until I found a safe place to hide, and wait for him to rescue me. Wait for him to save me like everyone has had to do my whole life—save helpless little Kenzie.

But if it was them, they'd kill her.

Slit her throat like it was nothing at all, and then they'd march right upstairs and wipe out the rest of her friends like ants on the counter.

Merciless killers or not, it was just common sense not to leave a psychotic killer free to get right up and try again. And this psychotic killer really took the cake.

Debra was insane with revenge. She wanted to kill a six-year-old child just to eliminate the chance she might grow up to be as insane with revenge as her. She had a school, a church, and a charity burned to the ground with innocent people inside. She sat back and let Luca prey on innocent women and children, just because his business would be handy for the day they laid a trap against the Merchants.

She was evil to her core. Any goodness or humanity in her rotted away and died out long ago.

I have to kill her, I thought, taking a step. And then another. *She's obviously the leader of these nutbags. Without her, they'll scramble, and that confusion will give my guys the edge.*

She tried to kill me without a second thought. I stood over her, gazing blankly into her fluttering eyes. *If I'm going to be a Merchant, I can't just think like a criminal mastermind—*

"N-no..." she croaked. "Don't— P-please... don't..."

—I have to act like one too.

"But I'm not a Merchant," I whispered, knife dropping to my side. "I'm just Makenzie Blaine... and that's more than enough." I smiled coldly into her bloodstained eyes. "I don't need to kill you to stop you, Debra Dumbass.

"You're going to lose because you're a failure. All you've ever done since the day you were born till this morning when you woke up curling your mustache, muhahaha-ing over your dastardly plan finally coming together—is fail.

"You're stupid, arrogant, and pathetic," I said to her flashing eyes and quivering lips, "and today, all that hate in your heart is finally going to bring you down like a tranquilized elephant. So buckle up, Deb-Deb"—I snatched her phone out of her pocket, undeterred by her weak attempt to slap me away—"the fuck toy is about to make you her bitch."

"Give that... back—"

I forced her flapping hand onto the screen, opening the phone with her thumb.

"Stop—"

Thud!

"—nice digs." A group of four guys and three women strolled right into the lobby, entering through the back door. "I could get used to living like a Merchant."

"No, living like a brother," one of the women corrected. "All of this is ours—"

I shoved the phone in my pocket and bolted up when they came into view—our eyes connecting in an instant.

"—now." A youngish woman with a bald head covered in tattoos blinked at me. "Uh-oh, what's this we have—?"

"Kill her," Debra screeched.

I flung the knife at them.

"Agh!" they cried, throwing their hands up and scattering like bowling pins.

I bolted for the servants' entrance.

"Stop her!"

"Kill her!"

"Shoot her!"

Bang! Bang! Bang! Bang!

Bullets rained down around me, blowing out the door's window. I fell against it in a shower of glass and pain—my injured arms screaming at me. The stab wounds weren't deep, or even bleeding that much, but they hurt like a Debra. All I wanted was to jump into a tub of ice and not get out until I was pleasantly numb.

And that's just exactly what I'm going to do when my baby is in my arms, my guys are all around me, and our home is vermin-free.

I burst through the door and locked it behind me. It was as low-tech as low-tech security came, but right then, I was very glad that no one could take old-fashioned steel and brass offline.

My attention lit on the fire alarm. I fell on the thing, jamming it down as hard as I could—

Nothing.

"Come on," I hissed at the strobe alarms attached to the wall. "Light up! Sound off! Do something!"

They didn't do a thing, clueing me in to the horrible truth that the fire alert system was also hooked up to the main security system, and it was also offline.

Bang!

My head snapped up, getting level with the gun peeking through the busted window. The brother adjusted his aim to try again.

I took off, racing around the staircase and the little cover it provided, to fall on the elevator.

"Open!" I jammed the button.

Thud! Thud!

"Get that door open!"

Thud! Thud!

"Hurry up!"

"Open!"

The elevator dinged, chirping its arrival.

I forced inside and jammed it shut again, screaming when I heard my offline brass and steel fail me.

"Get after her!"

A flash of moving, shoving bodies appeared through the slats of the stairs. I flung back against the wall, stabbing that stupid close button like my life depended on it—because it did!

"Close!" The doors slowly inched back together. "Fucking close!"

They raced at the elevator, blasting it with their guns.

I fell to the ground screaming, covering my head as a chorus of ricocheting metal played its deadly tune.

Through my arms, I saw the tattoo lady break from the pack. Sprinting across the concrete, she jammed her hand in the way of the doors, triggering the automatic safety feature that made them reopen at the first hint of obstruction.

"Agghhhhh!"

The metal closed shut on her fingers, breaking all the little bones with audible, and horrifying, crunches.

Or not.

Her screams bounced through the stairwell and leaked into my little windowless box, stirring the faintest dredges of sympathy for her.

It looked like taking all the security measures offline really got rid of *all* the measures. Poor little Tattoo Lady shouldn't have been so eager to get a gold sticker from Mom. Now all she was getting was a cast and, oh yeah, blown up—Mommy Deb's final gift to her loyal followers.

"Wow," I breathed, chest heaving as the elevator rose... taking her hand with it. I looked away as we left her floor behind, and took her fingers with us. "Shake it off, Blaine." I slapped my cheeks, beating back the shock. "You've got her phone. Do something clever with it!"

I flicked down, wondering just what the hell that was.

Natalya clearly had time to summon the lower-tier brothers in between tying up my boyfriends and their family. Should I send them a text from Debra telling them there's a change in plan?

I immediately rejected that idea. All it would take is another *where the hell are you?* text from Natalya, and they'd all hop back in their cars again. I had to do something to disrupt their plans because they already had two-thirds of what they needed before moving on to the blowing-us-all-up stage of the plan. Once they—

The answer hit me like a brick to the head.

Pulling up her text messages, I found the group message between her and her buddies easily—it was labeled *The Quay Street Squad*.

"Stupid fucking name," I muttered, typing quicker than fast.

"Debra": That fuck-toy bitch throat punched me and ran off. She's loose somewhere in the building with a phone she stole out of the security desk.

I hit send.

A flurry of texts lit up the screen.

Wilson: What!?

Maryann: Fuck! Where is she!

Yumi: What do we do?

Jillian: Are you okay?

"Debra": I've taken worse hits to get to where we are now, and I'm fuck sure not going to let her get in our way. But we don't have time to look for her, and the girl, and the flash drive. We need to speed this up, but first, where are you? Are the Merchants secure?

Maryann: They're secure. They wisely didn't put up a fight on the way up, especially when Wilson traded our knives for guns.

Wilson: Alexander has a treasure trove. I couldn't take it all with me, but I did throw all the ammo out the window. The guns are useless.

I cursed. *You're not as stupid as I want you to be, Wilson.*

Wilson: I'm waiting for the elevator now.

Yumi: And I've got the Merchants tied up with muzzles pressed to their brain stems. We're good.

"Debra": Good. Here's the plan. We're moving the auction up. It goes off within the hour. Yumi and Maryann, start bringing in the bombs.

I stopped the elevator on a random floor and let myself out, allowing it to continue to Bane and Wilson.

Yumi: Now? We can't.

Maryann: Because of that designer bitch?

Wilson: We can't move it up. They'll want immediate delivery of their Merchants as soon as the money goes through. We can't deliver until we've got the flash drive.

"Debra": We'll have the flash drive, and you can thank the designer bitch. Adeline's bastards are obsessed with her. They'll do anything to stop me from "torturing" her.

The wave of smirky, winky faces I sent was obscene.

"Debra": Wilson, just tell Bane to give up the flash drive, then put me on the phone. "Her" screams will do the rest.

Wilson: You're a genius. But what if he figures out it's not her?

"Debra": Every scream sounds like another. He won't risk it. Just do it. But first, put your phones on do not disturb. Block all unknown numbers. We don't want the real designer bitch to pull something with her stolen phone.

Wilson: Got it.

Maryann: Done.

Yumi: Done.

Natalya: Got it.

Jillian: Done. Now get that flash drive. Let's finish this.

I took a deep breath, shaking out my limbs. I was nervous, jittery, and sweaty like a criminal in an interrogation room with the key evidence in her back pocket. I had a very tight window to escape unscathed before it all blew up in my face.

Debra's phone rang.

I allowed it to ring a minute, prepping myself for the performance of my life.

"—where the flash drive is, Alexander." Wilson's snarl bled through the speakers. "Or she'll regret it."

"I have no idea what you're talking about." Bane was chiller than ice-cold soda. "We don't have some little digital black book. My family learned their lesson about hanging on to ledgers a long time ago."

"Is that so?" Wilson's voice got louder. I assumed he was holding the phone closer to his mouth. "Debra?"

I took a deep breath, and screamed. "Ahhh! Ahhhhh! No, stop! Please! Ahhh!"

"Who is that? Kenzie? Kenzie, is that you!" The calm tone was gone.

"Ahhh! Ahhhhh!" I screamed my lungs out, ripping my throat to shreds. "Help me, Bane! Help!"

"Stop! Stop it!" Bane roared. "Leave her alone!" Grunts and the sound of struggling came through the speakers. "Get your fucking hands off her!"

"Ahhh!"

"Where's the flash drive!" Wilson bellowed. "Give it up, and your girl gets to keep most of her fingers!"

"Arggh!" My chest caved in hearing the agony in Bane's voice. "This isn't her fight! She has nothing to do with this! Stop!"

I just kept screaming.

"Flash drive!" Wilson sounded strangled, like he was fighting to peel a strong and determined grip off his neck. "Give it up!"

"Let her go!" *Thud!* "Let her go, and I'll give you whatever you—"

"Debra, gouge out one of her fucking eyes! Maybe that will loosen Lover Boy's tongue!"

My screams ratcheted higher.

"Nooo! It's in Liam's apartment," Bane burst out. "In his bathroom! It looks like a regular stick of Chapstick, but the bottom twists off and the USB is hidden inside. No one would ever look at it twice."

Wilson laughed. "Thank you very much for that information, Alexander.

"Deb, did you get all of that?"

"Ahhh—*eugh*!" I cut my scream off at the knees, falling eerily, deathly silent.

I held the phone away from my mouth, and covered it for good measure—disguising it to match Debra's raspy, smoker's voice. "Got it, Wilson. On my way now."

"Kenzie? Kenzie! Answer me! Say something, baby, please," Bane roared. "Oh gods, what did you do?! What the fuck did you do?!"

I hung up, unable to hear the despair in his voice for another second.

I hated that. I hated every single fucking second of it, but I had no choice. The Brotherhood had two of the three things they needed to destroy almost everything and everyone I loved. They had the Merchants, and they had the bombs. The only thing left for them to get their hands on was the flash drive, and once they did, they'd have zero reason to keep any of us alive.

I had to get to it first.

Sprinting away from the servants' elevator, I ran across the hall to the main one, and fell on the button—jabbing the hell out of the thing.

Wilson, Natalya, and their group were all closer to Liam's apartment than I was. All it would take is one of them popping down a floor or two, and checking out Liam's bathroom for themselves, and everything I did would've been for nothing.

There was also the little matter of the Brotherhood moving in, and Debra being loose—and pissed—in the building. The minute she met up with Wilson and her crew, the game was up.

"Hurry up!" I screamed at the panel telling me the elevator was only on level six.

Once I have the flash drive, I'll separate the lock from the key. Without the flash drive, the Brotherhood can't steal money from their rich brothers, murder their poor brothers, and fake their deaths before stealing the Merchants' empire.

It's not enough to save my guys, but it'll put a serious knot in Debra's plan, and she'll have to play by my rules to unravel it.

The elevator dinged, finally letting me on board. I rode it to Liam's floor, then burst out—tearing across the hall.

With the security disabled, his front door swung open at my touch, not even faking a fight. I shut it behind, then peered around the cluttered, but clean space.

Elizabeth's toys scattered about the living room. Her crayons and scribbled pictures dominated the coffee table, her stuffies were plenty comfy on the couch and armchair, and her—

I choked, seeing her blue cup poking out from beside the armchair. The half-drunk remains of her unicorn smoothie had melted together to form a purplish-grayish mush. A mush that clearly revealed a little girl had been in the middle of drinking it before her father picked her up and rushed her away.

Liam never would've left that sitting there all night. He lied to Debra. Tricky is hiding in the Fairfield—

I darted into the living room, snatching up the cup and tossing it into the sink.

—and Debra cannot know that.

I rinsed it out and threw it in the dishwasher. Heart racing, I skidded back into the living room, scooped up her drawings, and swept her crayons into the coffee table drawer.

Sunny may not have informed me of all the security measures, but Liam did. Unlike Deb-Deb, I knew exactly where Tricky was.

She was hiding in the panic room concealed behind her closet. The same room Liam showed me, and told me to hide in with Laurel if anything ever happened.

The panic room was the size of a bedroom itself. It was well stocked with nonperishable food and juice boxes, it had a little bed for her to sleep in, there were plenty of toys for her to play with, there was a fully functional bathroom and shower, and it even had a television. An introvert could hide out in there for two weeks, and think they died and went to heaven.

The trouble was that if the security was gone for the entire building, it was gone for the panic room too. Normally, after Tricky went inside, no one but Liam would be able to enter the code to open the door to let her out. Without the computer-controlled locks, that door... was just a door.

Nothing could stop Tricky from walking right out, and nothing would stop Debra from going right in.

I made for the hallway, reached the door to Liam's room, then blew right past it.

Debra wasn't getting her hands on that girl. If she tried, I had a feeling I'd have no trouble accessing my homicidal maniac side.

I burst into Tricky's room and went straight for her closet. Throwing aside her clothes, I found the little notch in the wood that opened the panel. I pried it open, revealing a metal door about as tall and wide as a kitchen island. Big enough for an adult or child to crawl in.

Beneath the metal latch was a keypad. Going by my hunch, I tugged on the latch and the door gave way, swinging into the panic room.

"Tricky?" I crouched down, sticking my head inside. "Are you here, sweetie? Everything's going to be—"

I lifted my chin, and my nose bonked against the cold nip of the muzzle.

Chapter Ten

Sienna

Selfie Bitch flew in—the neon-red bump on her forehead as stark and glaring as the murder in her eyes.

"Good little hiding spot." Her gun flew up. "But not good enough."

Selfie Bitch screeched—wide, cloudy eyes rolling in her head. She choked on a sob, weakly pounding and clawing at the arm around her throat.

The tall, glamourous woman dragging her around by the neck dug the muzzle deeper into her temple. "You should've tossed that phone the minute you realized you were being followed, Sienna Blaine," she continued, chatting to my bugged eyes and hanging jaw. "That's most likely how they found you, because it's how I found you.

"Speaking of..."

She shook Selfie Bitch, jiggling her beneath her ample bosom. Even without the gun, she was an intimidating figure. Her long, waist-length braids started black at the roots, but turned bloodred as they flowed to her tips. Knee-length boots balanced on knife-tipped heels, and I wasn't kidding. Her stilettos were literal blades—honed to kill with a single kick.

Her tight, designer dress hugged her voluptuous curves in all the right ways—screaming that she had money and a fine ass with the same breath. The breath that whispered against her full lips; wide, fawn eyes; pointed nose; and long, cheek-tickling lashes. I guessed she was about late-twenties.

"Why were you following her and the kid?" she demanded, half-throttling Selfie Bitch. "Answer me, or I'll shoot you in the head."

"Ah!" Lyla screamed. Taking Laurel, she raced to the bathroom and locked them both in.

Smart move. Laurel did not need to see the end of Selfie Bitch.

"I was f-following her b-because..." Something told me the head injury was slowing her down as much as the violent new stranger. "We were ordered to... follow her, the brother, and the girlfriend from the hangar. Make sure they all... went to the Fairfield," she croaked. "But they split up."

"How many of you were tailing her?" the Glamazon asked.

"Just me and—and my boyfriend, Nathaniel."

The guy in the green car.

"Why does your boss want them at the Fairfield?"

She tried to shake her head, then thought better of it—going for slumping in the Glamazon's hold instead. "Don't know," she got out. "I just... got a text from Mom last night. We never get direct texts from Mom, but when she speaks... you obey. It said to go to the hangar. Wait for the Merchants' plane. Then make sure everyone on it made it back to the Fairfield... in time for the auction."

"What auction?" I demanded.

"All the Merchants are being auctioned off." Pained eyes found mine just to glare at me. "There're even bidders for the Rat King, your thieving sister, that baby, and you."

"Me, Kenzie, and Laurel? What the fuck? And you're okay with that?" I cried, roaring up on her. "It never occurred to you that some anonymous creep who wants to buy two women and a *baby*, doesn't have good intentions!?"

She smirked at me. "Why should I give a shit what happens to you? The Merchants didn't care when they destroyed my father's business and took his clients, suppliers, and merchandise. We lived in a homeless shelter for two years while they got even richer, living in their mansion in the sky!

"You're on their side, you can meet the same fate." She shrugged even though she was bent at the waist with a gun decorating her forehead. "Not my fault you want to fuck around with scum, but won't pay the consequences for it."

"She could say the same thing about you," the Glamazon mused. "But there's more, isn't there? You took a big risk chasing a woman and a baby through a crowded park in broad daylight. You seriously risked twenty-five to life just because someone sent you a text?"

"You don't understand," she hissed. "That's your problem. You could never understand what the Brotherhood is trying to achieve! The auction is going to pull in millions of dollars. Tens of millions of dollars. Maybe even hundreds of millions! And when it does, Mom and Dad are going to split it equally among all of us."

The Glamazon and I shared a look.

"They're going to what?" I asked. "Among who?"

"Everyone in the Brotherhood. All the brothers and sisters," she gasped. "While all the Merchants did was take, take, take. The Brotherhood is different. It's *better*. Today, wealth will be redistributed on a scale the world has never seen before. And with that money, we the brothers, are going to destroy the cesspool the Merchants made of Cinco City, and build something new and beautiful in its place."

"Right..." the Glamazon drew out, looking down at her captor like she was nuts. "And that's why you couldn't let these two get away. The more *products* up for sale. The more money in your pocket."

"You make it sound so sordid! All empires are built on blood, pain, and death! This one must be too, when we rise, we'll create a fairer city for—"

"Yeah, yeah, yeah." The Glamazon twisted, wrenching Selfie Bitch's neck with one hard jerk.

She let her body flop to the floor—dead.

"Disgusting hypocritical bitch." Glamazon kicked her away. "Wants to rant about a better world while hunting down a baby just so she can deliver her into the hands of a trafficker. It's insane how terrible people convince themselves they're not. I mean it," she said, tucking her gun into the holster concealed by her boots. "Insane."

I gaped at her. "Uh... hi, and... thank you."

"No problem, but if you really want to thank me, you'll toss your phone battery into the garbage disposal. She said it was only her and her boyfriend following you, but she could've been lying."

I was moving before she finished. Hurrying to the sink, I ripped out the battery, dropped it down the disposal, and stomped on my phone for good measure. "Thank you again." I turned to her, leaning against the counter. "But who are you? I can sense that you're not here to hurt us, but why are you here at all? Who sent you?"

She eyed me, grinning. "My name is Gianna Cross, daughter of Gianna Cross." She rolled her eyes. "After two boys, both named after our father and grandfather, my mom made a big stink about how women should be able to name their daughters after them just like men do with their sons, so here I am. Gianna 2.0," she said, doing a little spin. "But, that's off the topic. The Brotherhood isn't the only one tracking you, Sienna. Did you really think my cousins would let you fly off to New York with Uncle River without making sure someone was watching your backs?

"Of course, River can more than handle any threat, but then you guys split up, so I stayed on you and the kid, while River went off with Mackenzie."

It was hella weird having this perfect stranger talk about me and my sister like she's known us for years.

"Speaking of, where did that woman rabbit off to with my baby?" Her sudden soft and cooing voice shocked me. "I've been waiting weeks to chew on those cheeks. Bring her out here. Let me hold her."

"I... uh... okay." Crossing through the kitchen, I knocked on the bathroom door and told Lyla it was safe to come out. "But why keep it a secret? Why didn't Sunny tell us about you?"

"Because Sunny promised your sister no more bodyguards after the last one... you know."

I winced. I definitely knew.

"Obviously, he wasn't going to put someone else on you that he didn't trust absolutely, but he did have to get someone." She flapped a hand at Selfie Bitch. "Whether your sister likes it or not, you need a bodyguard."

"You just saved me and her daughter. Trust me, Gianna Jr., she is not going to be unhappy to see you."

She laughed. "I prefer Gigi, but good to know. I've been wanting to meet the woman who tamed Sunny's, Liam's, and Bane's hearts. So many others have tried and failed, but Mackenzie Blaine succeeded."

Lyla cracked the door open. "Is it safe?"

"It's safe," I replied.

"Okay, good." Lyla stepped out, took one look at the body on the floor, and shot back inside with a sleeping Laurel—her scream trapped behind her teeth.

Gigi rolled her eyes. "Calm down, woman," she called. "The cleanup crew will take care of this within the hour. Until then"—her gaze pinned me through—"you and I have an auction to stop."

***

Kenzie

"Tricky?" I crouched down, sticking my head inside. "Are you here, sweetie? Everything's going to be—"

I lifted my chin, and my nose bonked against the cold nip of the muzzle.

Fuller snatched it back. "Oh my goodness, I'm so sorry, dear." Taking the gun away, she helped me up. "Are you okay? I'm so relieved to see you."

Fuller hugged me tight. Over her shoulder, I observed Tricky calm and content, sitting on her bed watching television while drinking her juice. Sitting next to her were Nadine and Hendrix—Sunny's cook and Genny's doctor.

The Merchants rushed all of their employees to the safe room, protecting them from a fight that wasn't theirs. Meanwhile, Debra and her cronies were planning to blow up all the people who fought and died to get them here.

It amazed me that woman couldn't see who the real monsters were.

"I'm okay," I said, pulling back. "I only came to make sure Tricky was safe, and to let you guys know that security is down for the whole building. Right now, that door will open for anyone, so if it does... be ready."

Fuller exchanged looks with Hendrix and Nadine.

"We'll be ready," Hendrix said, putting her arm around Elizabeth. "But what do we need to be ready for?"

"Five women and one man. They pretended to be hostages of Luca so that they could get in here, but they're actually the leaders of the Brotherhood," I said. "The same Brotherhood that is currently moving into the building. They've decided they live here now."

"Goodness gracious," Fuller breathed.

"I'm going to take away something they desperately want, but that will only strengthen their determination to find leverage that will force me to give it back"—I flicked to Tricky—"but if I don't, you have to get out of here. I'll text you why."

Fuller tipped her head, expression solemn. She understood me perfectly.

"Go," she said. "Finish this."

She didn't need to tell me twice. Waving goodbye and good luck, I ducked out and headed fast for Liam's bathroom. On the way, I typed out the full explanation to Fuller that I didn't want a little girl to hear.

I spent many a night, and many a morning, with Liam Hunt. I knew his bathroom like I knew his bed—and I knew that tube of Chapstick. I'd even seen the man use it! In every way, it looked like a harmless moisturizer. I never looked at it twice.

Entering the bathroom, I padded across the marble floor, peering around for the slightest shift or shadow.

Liam's his and hers sinks already had a few of my things claiming half of the space. I crept to his side and drew open the counter, finding the Chapstick lying innocently among a spare tube of toothpaste, dental floss, and shaving cream.

I paused reaching for it.

My guys were smart. They had tricks hidden up their sleeves even when they were naked. What were the chances this was some kind of horrible trap that Bane wanted the bastard who hurt his girlfriend to spring?

A strong chance, but what choice do I have but to spring it? I won't be able to trick Wilson again. Debra's minions have likely already carried her concussed self up to Sunny's apartment. She's berating her Quay Street Squad right now for falling for a few texts and some screams.

I took a deep breath. "Here goes everything..."

Picking up the Chapstick, I uncapped the bottom and tipped it over—dropping a little rectangular metal device on my palm. It didn't burn or blow up, so maybe there was no trick. I had what the Brotherhood came here for, and as long as I did, I had leverage.

It was obvious Debra and her partners made a lot of promises to their members that they had no intention of keeping. They convinced their rich Leighbridge "investors" that they were destroying the Merchant empire that held them back, but what they were really going to do was steal even more of their money, fake their deaths, and then replace the Merchants' boots on their throats with their own.

As for their "lower-tier" members, they were the army six people needed to take on a criminal organization as big as the Merchants, but their deaths were assured the minute they joined up.

If they weren't so blindsided by revenge, they'd realize that they didn't need the flash drive to build a criminal empire. They already fucking did it, and when they stole the auction money, they'd be able to do it again ten times over.

But that wasn't the point.

The point was always to steal it from the Merchants. To destroy everything they've built, reduce it to ash, and build their hate and vengeance on their graves. They had to take away what their fathers died for, and no other outcome would do.

"And you won't have that outcome without this." I slipped the drive into my pocket. "All that pride and arrogance, Deb-Deb. It's made you so stupid, you can't see you already pulled the greatest coup in underground history, but you're going to mess it all up because you're a dumbass."

"Who's a dumbass?"

I jerked, stomach shotgunning into my throat as I spun around and came eye level to that smirk.

"I'll take that flash drive." It was snatched out of my pocket before I could move. "Now."

***

Bane

"Kenzie? Kenzie! Answer me! Say something, baby, please," I roared, Kenzie's screams echoing in my ears. "Oh gods, what did you do?! What the fuck did you do?!"

Click.

The call ended, leaving me with only the eerie silence that prefaced its end.

"No, no, not Kenzie, no," I gruffed, panting hard. My chest constricted—fighting the metal band tightening, tightening, tightening around the whole of my body. A roaring beat and battered against my eardrums, drowning out the world. The only thing I could hear clearly... was her screams.

Wilson peered around just to smirk in my face. He had me shoved up face-first against the door to my own apartment with my tied hands wrenched so far over my head, a rough jerk would dislocate them both.

"Hey, don't make that face," he mocked. "Just think, Debra wanted to do that to your niece to get you to give up the flash drive—which even I thought was going too far. This was a much better compromise. Better the woman you've only been fucking for a few months over your own family, right? Right?" He laughed.

He fucking laughed, and the red mist descended.

"Argh!"

Balanced against the door and his own hand, I kicked back—striking him so hard in the testicles they reascended.

"Ahhhh!" He dropped, clutching his crotch.

He hit the ground and I turned on him, stomping him again, and again—howling my rage.

Red-faced, Wilson flashed, caught my foot, and flipped—knocking me off my feet and bringing me down on top of him.

He reared to punch me and I headbutted him, crushing his nose under my skull. Blood spurted, carried farther on the gush of wind from his bellowing roar.

I dove, flipping head over ass off of him. Lying beside his head, I forced my legs around his neck, and squeezed.

"N-no—" He croaked, punching and clawing at my thighs. "St—op! St—"

I wrenched to the side, snapping his rotted neck in two.

I kicked his fucking corpse away, getting to my feet and snapping my binds over my knee.

"They're dead." I kicked in my door, and pulled off the wall the weapons too heavy, impractical, and attention-grabbing for Wilson to fling out the window. "They're all fucking dead."

Loaded up, crushing despair followed me out the door—choking the air out of my lungs. I promised I'd protect her. That knowing me and being in my family's orbit would never put her in danger. I promised her... and I failed.

I kicked open the door to the back staircase, praying I'd meet one of them on the stairs.

No one dared to cross my path, but the staircase wasn't empty. A cacophony of voices bounced up the walls and assaulted my ears.

Laughing, jeering, celebrating, and congratulating themselves on breaking into my home, holding my family, friends, and crew hostage, and moving into the apartments dear old Mom and Dad stole by volunteering to be beaten and chained to a wall—all the while ignoring the innocent women who did not willingly sign up for the experience.

I'd be going down there to kill them twice, but first—

"Debra."

I hefted my double-headed battle-ax, and cleaved the doorknob in two.

It clattered to the floor, coming apart and making its twin on the other side fall on the carpet with a dull thud.

Storming inside, I didn't pause at Liam's door. I shoved it open and caught a flash of someone running past the entrance to the hallway—no doubt headed for Liam's bathroom.

For decades my parents, then my eldest brother, kept that flash drive safe. And I gave it up with one phone call.

I'd do it again for Kenzie. I'd go back and sell out everything my family's worked for *better* if it meant my girl didn't spend her last moments in pain.

I crept to the door of Liam's room, hearing someone rummaging around inside. The door swung open on oiled hinges.

My ax led the way, screaming out to split open Debra Seward's skull.

Sunny was named Demone on the streets for the unhinged smiling psycho he unleashed on his unsuspecting victims. River was the Rat King for building the biggest, fastest-growing gang in all of Cinco—with a crew that was anyone, everywhere, always watching, always listening, and always on the move.

But I was Bane—by birth and by reputation, because when I had prey in my sights, I don't stop. I don't sleep. And I don't feel remorse as I relentlessly hunt them down, following them to the ends of the earth to extract every ounce of agony and regret from their flayed bones.

It wouldn't just be Wilson and Debra who met their violent ends that day. I would sweep through every floor of the building, and separate from the necks the heads of every brother who entered this building.

And then I would hunt down every brother outside of this building.

And then I would kill the silent, greedy rich fuckers who funded them.

And then I'd mutilate the people who didn't join, but knew about it and didn't stop it.

And then I'd destroy the apathetic fucks who overheard a rumor about the Brotherhood and shrugged it off.

And then I'd kill all of their friends.

And then I'd go back, find their graves, dig them up, salt their bones, piss on them, then light them on fire.

There'd be no memory that the Brotherhood ever existed, because no one would be able to hold on to that memory with their brain matter smeared on my battle-ax.

I pressed the ax to the bathroom door, quietly pushing it open.

I almost dropped it.

"—you won't have that outcome without this." Mackenzie Blaine, whole and untouched, slipped the drive into her pocket. "All that pride and arrogance, Deb-Deb. It's made you so stupid, you can't see you already pulled the greatest coup in underground history, but you're going to mess it all up because you're a dumbass."

"Who's a dumbass?"

She jerked. Spinning around and came eye level with my face-splitting grin.

"Because I'm pretty sure it's me for ever thinking you'd let that psycho witch get the better of you." I dropped my weapons. "I'll take that flash drive now." I plucked the drive out of her pocket. "And you'll take this."

Hooking through her pants, I snapped her to my chest and kissed the crap out of her.

Tangling in her hair, pulling her close, breathing her in, pressing her soft lips to mine—all the rage, hatred, and vengefulness in my chest disappeared, chased away by a magic that was Kenzie's.

She melted into me instantly, moaning softly as I broke through her soft, pillowy shield, and tangled with her tongue—wrestling it until she surrendered more moans.

She broke away gasping. "Wow," she breathed. "If that's the way you kiss me when you discover I'm not dead, I've got to pull that trick on you more often."

"You already got a man killed for it, baby." I nipped the tip of her nose. "You may not want to risk it."

Kenzie sobered quickly. "Wilson?"

I nodded.

"Well, I'm not shedding any tears for him."

"Good. Don't." My voice was harsh to my own ears. "Then tell me I don't have any tears to shed for Debra either."

She shook her head. "I had a chance to kill her, but I couldn't do it. It's one thing to act in self-defense or the defense of people I love, but slitting the throat of some bitch who's just lying there? That's not me," she said seriously. "I hope you can understand that."

"I can understand that just fine, Kenzie. You don't have to be my clone for me to love you so insanely and dizzyingly much, it'd be my pleasure to kill all the bitches you leave lying on the floor"—I cupped her cheek—"if it means I never have to go through the pain of losing you again."

She pressed her forehead to mine, smiling softly as her eyes fluttered closed. "I'm so sorry I did that to you. I had to make it real for Wilson and you. So that you would give up the drive, and Wilson wouldn't come looking for it if he believed Debra had it covered.

"If it helps," she mused, pushing out her lips. "The drive was immediately taken from me, so my cruel plan fell apart instantly."

I laughed. "Sorry, babes, but the Brotherhood is willing to kill and torture for this drive. The last place I'm hiding something so dangerous is in your pocket."

"But what do we do now?" she asked, peering around my shoulder. "Jillian, Yumi, and the other shithead bastards are going to be wondering if it worked and *Debra* got the drive. And that's only if the real Debra hasn't walked through the door and revealed it was all a trick.

"Plus, she lied about everything. Debra told me, before she tried to kill me, that all of this is just a stall," she cried. "The auction. The Brotherhood moving in. All of it. They just want us all in the same building so that the bombs they're parking all around the foundation will take us all out and make the world believe they died while actually—"

"—they're off on a beach somewhere with millions in the bank and the flash drive in their hands," I finished. I cursed, tossing my head. "It's smart. It's very fucking smart. And it explains everything. Why they recruited in secret. Why they waited so long to attack. Why they hid their identities from everyone, including the members of their own gang. Why they structured said gang the way they did. And why they made sure that we—their prey—never discovered they were a threat until it was too late.

"This was always how it was going to end. They were always going to kill their accomplices and fake their deaths, but when they take over the underground, they'd have an edge we never had. With our ledger, they'd rule from the shadows without the threat of anyone hunting them down, threatening them, or coming after their families. How could they?

"They're dead."

Kenzie swallowed hard, stricken. "They're evil bastards, but they're not stupid. They have the perfect exit strategy. Or at least they did until I screamed on the phone. Without the flash drive, they're stuck. They won't be ruling any underground, so again, my love, I ask, what do we do now?"

Mind spinning, I drew Kenzie out into the living room. There were a million and ten things we could do and should do, but what were the odds of the two of us doing those things when all those people I heard banging on downstairs were armed and ready to stop us.

"What we need to do is get Tricky out of here," I heard myself say. "But there's no safe way to do that. They're all over the servants' entrance, and the Brotherhood knows about the tunnel."

"What about the front entrance?" she asked. "The cops, fire trucks, and ambulances are still down there blocking the street. If you walk right out there with Tricky, they're hardly going to run out in front of all of those cops and stop you."

I was shaking my head before she finished. "The first thing they're going to do with their toy soldiers is position them at all the entrances and exits—in between them picking off the Scourges, Sons of Saint, Cardinals, and Liam's crew one by one. We can't risk carrying Tricky all over a building filled with armed psychos, but she can't stay here either since those armed psychos are going to blow up the building!"

"They won't blow up the building until they've got the drive," she soothed, stroking my arm. "That's something at least. It gives us room to breathe. And room to figure out a way to warn your gangs." She looked around. "I tried the fire alarm, but it very much does not work."

"Nothing works now that the security system's off."

She gave me a look. "Yeah, I figured that out. But is there any chance you know the numbers of all of your *employees* by heart?" Kenzie held up her borrowed phone. "Or even better, have a group chat?"

I gave her a look. "No, and no. Besides, we can give them a heads-up, but I won't tell them to fight. If they go head-to-head with the brothers, they'll kill each other in the shootouts, and that's exactly what Debra wants. All of us dead. I won't play into her hands."

"But they still need to know—"

The phone went off in Kenzie's hand, making her jump. She turned the screen to me—wide-eyed. It flashed one name on the screen: *Wilson*

I could practically hear her thinking, *I hope you've got a plan, because time's up!*

"I left an ax and flail in there," I said. "Get those for me, baby, while I have a little chat with Willy's ghost."

She didn't fight me.

Moving into the kitchen, Kenzie went the other way while I hit *Accept*.

"You bitch! You killed him! When I get my hands on you—"

"—you'll apologize for calling me a bitch, I'm sure." I dropped down at the kitchen table, kicking up my feet. "Because it's an insult to me and your friend Wilson—pretty much saying that a big, tough guy like him was taken down by a little bitch."

"Alexander," hissed a voice I'd remember for the rest of my life.

"Debra."

"Where's your little girlfriend?"

"She's safe—despite your worst intentions. And she let me in on your little plan." I took out the drive, examining the sleek, unimpressive surface in the light. "I'm happy to hear you're not going to sell me off to some foot-sniffing pervert, but I'm not too pleased that you're going to blow me up."

"Oh, don't worry about that." She added some jaunt to her fury. "I've got a much slower and more inventive death planned for you now."

"And I've got a deal for you," I replied, getting right to the point. "The flash drive—I have it, and I'll give it to you."

She fell quiet. I could hear her suspicious mind turning from the other end of the phone.

"You'll give it to me?" she repeated. "And what do you want in return?"

"Simple. Evacuate the building. Let all the kids go, and leave the adults to work this out amongst ourselves. All includes everyone in your gang and ours—Scourges, Cardinals, Sons of Saint, everyone." I glanced out the balcony window. "I'll be watching from the window. Once I see them all leave the building, I'll hand the drive to you. Just like that."

She made a production of humming, like she was considering it. "Let your gangs go *and* my brothers? Why would you care about my people?"

"I care that you lied, exploited, and used these people, only so that you could bury them in the same grave as mine. Kenzie told me all about your recruitment requirements. People and children who lost everything on the Night of Tears. Innocent people who caught the shrapnel of the ledger-dump explosion.

"Regular people that you've weaponized and filled with hate, all to make you rich and powerful, and them dead. I've done a lot of questionable things in my life—frankly, I've done all the questionable things—but I would never do that.

"As for my people, they're not fucking dying because the children of a bunch of traitorous pieces of shit can't comprehend that their bastard fathers got what was coming to them," I growled, setting her off too. "So let's compromise. Let them go. I give you the drive. Simple."

"No," she sliced in before I finished. "This isn't a compromise. It's a trap. There's no way you trade the key to your success for a bunch of worthless thugs. It doesn't make any sense. Why aren't you asking me to release your family? Or let your little niece skip out the door?"

"My niece isn't here," I lied, eyes flicking in the direction of Tricky's room and the safe room. "And I know you wouldn't let my family go for anything, not even the flash drive. But as you said, they're just a bunch of 'worthless thugs.' You don't care about them. You don't care if they live or die. You definitely don't care more about them than you do the drive, so what's the problem?

"Let them go, and I'll give you the drive, Seward," I blared. "Seriously, how is this a conversation?"

"I have no assurances that you'll give up the drive!"

"My family is your assurance! You're still holding them hostage. I'm obviously not going to fuck you around when you've got guns trained on my brothers, sister, and parents."

"Hmm. That is a good point. I do have guns trained on everyone you love," she chirped. "So how about I shoot one of them every ten minutes until the drive is in my hands?"

"You can't trick me with that empty threat. I know you need them alive for your auction. You're not shooting anybody."

"I don't need all of them alive. I'd be more than happy to have my fun with one or two of them. You're all going to die after the auction anyway, so what difference does it make if I shoot your little brother and sister in the head now?"

I took a deep breath, reining in the side of me that no one got to see—not even my family. If I learned anything from my father, it was that it was always better to be the calm, silent one against a brash, loudmouth idiot. If they run their mouth long enough, they'll give you the rope to hang them.

"I'll tell you what difference it'll make. If you refuse my generous deal and lay a finger on Sunny or Gen, I'll take the meat tenderizer sitting one foot next to me, and smash this drive into a million pieces." I beamed. "You won't be shooting anyone then, will you? Because then the auction is the only pay-day you're going to get."

"You— You wouldn't do that!" she barked. "You'd never break that drive. Without it, the Merchants are finished."

"Let's test that theory. Let's switch to video call. You put the phone and your gun to Sunny's head, and I'll put mine up to my big, spiked, metal hammer. You'll be able to see me smash this sucker to bits two seconds after harming an unarmed, unresisting man. Deal?" I taunted, voice as jaunty as hers. "Shall I switch over to video now?"

"No," she hissed. "All right, Alexander, let's both calm down. Thanks to your girlfriend, I've got an auction kicking off in an hour, and a splitting fucking headache. Let's both of us not get off-track and do something we'd regret."

"What's that supposed to mean?" Kenzie came into view, holding the weapons. "Do we have a deal or not?"

"No deal. No one leaves this building—including you. All of those fools who think they're in my Brotherhood will die. Your brainwashed thugs will die. And *you* will die, Alexander. Right next to your mommy, your shared slut, and your tucked-away niece. You're trapped in here with the rest of them—you're trapped in here with me—and it's only a matter of time until I find you and pluck that drive out of your bloody fingers."

"It's only a matter of less than an hour," I corrected lightly. "You're timing your explosion for the middle of the auction, yes? How else are you going to make your rich members believe you're dead? They'd have to witness it themselves, or they'll hunt you and their millions to the end of the earth.

"I grew up in this place, Seward," I said. "I know all of its hiding places, and believe me, I can hold out for a lot longer than an hour."

"Do it, then." She laughed. "Hide-and-seek was always my favorite game growing up. Or in your case, cat and mouse."

I smirked. "Haven't you ever watched Saturday morning cartoons? The mouse always wins." I hung up, dropping my grin immediately. "She didn't go for the deal. She won't release anyone, not even for the sake of getting the drive without a fight. We're moving to plan B."

"What's plan B?"

"Darling, may I have that ax?"

She handed it over. I took it, stood up, went into the living room, and swung on the hardwood—splitting it like a cleaver. I whacked it over and over, showering the floor and couches in splinters.

"I have a question," she shouted, covering her ears and eyes. "Why?!"

I chuckled. "Because as much as I love the idea of beheading my enemies like a feudal lord"—*clang!*—"I'd rather not bring an ax to a gun fight."

I got the ax under the floorboards and pried it up, revealing the floor safe Liam tucked away.

"Wow," Kenzie said, dropping next to me as I typed in the combination. "Just when I think I scratched the top layer and found all of your secrets, you dig up a safe."

I flipped it open, revealing my big bro's stash of cash, gold bars, knives, guns, fake passports for him and Elizabeth, hard drives, and even a satellite phone. I loaded up.

"If only he was stashing another way out of here too." I glanced at the door. "I've said so many times that the Fairfield has one security weakness—there's only one way in and out of these apartments."

"You think they could be waiting out there for us?"

"I know they are." I jerked my chin. "Someone tried the door handle in the middle of my conversation with Debra. They were checking to make sure it was unlocked."

"What!" Kenzie shot away, ducking behind the couch. "What do we do? Why haven't they come in?"

"Because they don't know what's waiting for them on the other side. Wilson emptied my apartment of any useful weapons. They haven't touched this place." I jerked my chin. "Whoever is out there will wait until they've got enough backup to storm inside, which is why"—I dropped my voice—"you need to get into the panic room now."

Her beautiful face crumpled into a stubborn frown, and I already knew what she was going to say before she spoke. "Not gonna happen, Alexander. I'm not leaving you to face that creep and his *backup* all by yourself."

"May I remind you, my sexy protégé, that I am trained in all weapons and nearly every form of martial arts, and your only expertise is the plaited braid stitch."

"Not true. I'm also an expert at knitting, and I'll show you where I'm about to shove those needles!"

I snorted, grinning at her even with deadly threats outside the door. "Mackenzie Blaine, I would never dare underestimate you. You are more than tough enough to handle those bastards. You *did* handle those bastards by yourself, with no weapons and no help on the way. I know you can face them..."

My grin melted away. "But I can't face ever losing you again. Kenzie, when I thought she killed you, I fell so far, I planned to murder everyone in this building... and then myself."

Her eyes widened. Lips parting, she made to speak, and couldn't.

"I cannot possibly convey how uninterested I am in living without you, so please," I said, tucking the last gun through my waistband. "Stay here where I know you're safe."

Coming out from behind the couch, Kenzie came over and rested her hand on mine. "Bane, who are you lying to right now? Me or yourself?"

I blew back. "What?"

"If you really believe that I'm strong enough to face the Brotherhood by your side, why are you telling me to hide? And if you really think you're enough of a weapons master, martial arts badass to take them all on by yourself, why can't you protect me if I do need it? So which is it?" she demanded, folding her arms. "Are you lying about how tough I am, or how strong you are?"

I gaped at her. *Damn, she really turned that around on me, didn't she?*

"I'm not lying about anything," I cried. "I just don't want you in harm's way. That's a very natural wish for a boyfriend!"

She shrugged. "Well, I'm not going anywhere, so"—Kenzie plucked one of the guns from my waistband—"let's do this."

"I—"

The door burst open.

I whipped around, squeezing off two shots and dropping the brother before the battle cry left his throat.

"Arggh!"

I grabbed Kenzie and we dove over the same couch, dropping down hard and grabbing each other as bullets ripped through the furniture—raining fabric and down on our heads.

"There's no point hiding, Alexander! Mom says you've got something of hers, so bring it and yourself out from there. Do it without a fight, and we'll deliver you to Mom with a lot less holes."

Kenzie leaned over and kissed the tip of my nose. "I've got an idea. Stay down."

"Wha—? Don't!"

"I'm standing up," she called. "Don't shoot." Kenzie raised her arms and stood. Her hands weren't empty. "Because if you do, I'll shoot this."

I goggled at her. The woman was standing out in the open with her gun pressed against one of Liam's floor-safe hard drives.

"What the hell's that?" one of the goons shouted.

"It's what your mommy so desperately wants. She wants it even more than me and Bane. That's why we came up here and busted it out of the floor," she said, nodding at the mess we made of my brother's living room. "We don't want to fight, and I'm one hundred percent sure you were told not to kill us anyway, so here's what we do: Bane and I will walk nice and slow to the elevator. Once we're inside, we'll throw the hard drive out to you, then let it whisk us away. Everybody wins."

Raucous laughs filled the room. I snarled, peering around the couch and training my gun on the two men standing half in and half out of the room—waiting for them to give me a reason.

"That's cute, sweetheart, but you're wrong. We were told not to kill Alexander. You're fair g—"

"Think, dumbass," she snapped. "If you kill me, I'll drop the drive, and Bane here will destroy it before you have time to jump over this couch and stop him. Then—oh yeah—he'll kill you. Let us both go, and at least you'll win big points with Mom."

I saw them exchange a look amongst each other, and then to whoever else was waiting out in the hall.

"But... Mom would kill us if we just let you go," he ventured, actually considering a trade for a useless hard drive that was no doubt filled with nothing but boring tax and accounting information for Liam's businesses—dirty and legitimate. "She specifically said she wants Alexander."

"You're not letting us go. There's nowhere for us to go. Either way, the Brotherhood has the building locked down, so all you're doing is making us someone else's problem." She clicked off the safety. "We have a deal or not?"

A long, tense silence smothered the room. I fought with everything in me not to grab Kenzie and pull her out of the line of fire, but if her play was going to work, I couldn't make them jumpy. I had to—

"Fuck it, fine," said the sandy-haired one with an eagle tattoo on his neck. "Deal. Throw us the drive and we'll let you go."

"Fuck that for a joke," I barked. "All of you, aim your guns at the floor and back away from the door. Do it. Now!" I blared when they didn't move.

Cursing, Eagle Tattoo and his friend disappeared from the doorway. Murmurs, swears, and shuffling footsteps followed, along with my jaw-hanging disbelief.

That worked? It actually worked? Everyone said to let my blue balls lead me to the woman of my dreams, and damn, were they right. Kenzie Fucking Blaine wasn't just the whole package, she was the US and all the international post offices combined.

"Stay behind me," I said, rising up.

I kept my gun trained in front of me, stepping lightly and slow toward the front door.

Kenzie glued to my back, clutching the hard drive.

We stepped out to a parade of seven men and seven muzzles.

"I said guns pointed at the floor!"

"I don't think so." Eagle Tattoo's knuckles whitened on the handle. "After you throw us the drive and those doors close, we'll point at the floor."

"Everyone, just be cool and clear the way." I glared at the two guys standing between us and the elevator. "Stand over there with the rest of them."

The two guys glanced at Eagle Tattoo, who nodded. Thus, began our dance.

We stepped. They stepped. We moved. They moved. Kenzie sneezed. They jumped, fingers twitching on the trigger.

Step by step, we inched down the hall—Kenzie and the drive shielded behind my back while seven guys aimed their guns at my head, not knowing the drive they really wanted was in my pocket.

The elevator dinged open at Kenzie's touch.

"Inside and against the wall," I told her.

She darted inside, plastering herself in the corner beside the panel.

"She's in, now give us the drive," Eagle Tattoo shouted.

"Steady." I reached my hand back. Kenzie placed the drive on my palm and I held it up, backing inside. "When I'm in, I'll toss it out. That's the deal."

Step. Then another, taking me over the threshold.

"You're in," he barked, rushing me. "Now give us the—"

I flung it over their heads, snapping seven noses in the air. I jammed the *close* button and plastered myself against Kenzie, gritting my teeth as bullets ripped through the closing doors.

"Stop shooting!" Eagle Tattoo ordered. "Mom said not to kill him! Besides, we've got it." His laughter slipped through the narrowing crack. "We've got the drive."

I hit the button for the thirty-ninth floor, then drew back—checking her over. "Are you okay?"

"I'm okay," she rasped, visibly shaking. "I don't think I'll ever get used to people shooting at me, though."

"I don't want you to get used to it. I want it to stop." I dropped my forehead against hers, smiling. "But you were brilliant. Absolutely brilliant.

Fuck's sake, woman, how many times a day are you going to leave me in awe of you?"

She giggled. "The limit does not exist."

I kissed her slow, nipping her bottom lip pulling back. "I'll make out with you later tonight when I've got you naked in the shower. Right now, we've got to find somewhere to lie low and run down the clock."

"Can we?" Kenzie walked the elevator numbers racing up. "If Debra doesn't find us and the drive before the auction, won't she just push it back? I only tricked the others into moving it forward so that they'd be too busy explaining it to their backers, and wouldn't have time to go searching for a bleeding, moaning Debra."

"She could push it back to the original time," I admitted, "but if she does, she'd have to explain what the hell's going on and why she keeps changing her mind. It'll come off like she doesn't have as much control over the situation as she told them she does, and the last thing you want to do before asking people for millions of dollars is show weakness."

"That's true." Kenzie worried her lip. "But is there somewhere we can lie low?"

"We'll find out." The elevators slid open and a thick, hulking mass of muscles and cheap cologne filled the entrance. I clubbed him with my gun before he got out a shout.

Kenzie and I shot back, letting the lug fall forward inside the elevator. I gestured for her to step out while I pulled him all the way in, smacked a random floor, and stepped out. The doors closed and carried him away.

"Keep an eye out," I whispered, motioning for Kenzie to follow. "This floor doesn't have apartments. It's where the old fitness center and clubhouse used to be. It also leads to the rooftop terrace. I figured it'd be light on security since both those rooms are empty, and the terrace doesn't look like it has anywhere to hide."

"Then why are we hiding here?" Kenzie looked between the glass-paneled walls, giving a clear view into the stark bare rooms. There was no chance of hiding in there. They were two big fishbowls. "When that guy wakes up, he'll just come back up and give us matching brain injuries, then!"

I laughed. "I said it doesn't look like there's a place to hide, but I played hide-and-seek with my brothers and sisters in this place for years." He winked. "They never found me."

Walking her out onto the terrace, I breathed in the warm, muggy Cinco morning. The sky was so clear and beautiful, shining down on a living nightmare.

My family was in more danger than they'd ever been in. We were trapped in a building that was about to blow up. Kenzie was separated from her sister and daughter, and the only thing I could do about it was hide like a little bitch.

All I wanted to do was storm Sunny's apartment, but even though they needed proof of life for their little auction, they didn't need to prove they didn't torture and shoot us a bit first. There were a lot of horrible things Debra could do to my family before I even got close to wiping out her and her cronies.

What I needed to do now was play it smart, stay hidden, and wrench away the upper hand. The more desperate she gets, the more mistakes she'll make.

Together, Kenzie and I stepped out from under the cabana and took it all in. The terrace was always my favorite place growing up. Just more proof that I belonged outside.

The entire perimeter was shrouded with plants. Mostly to give us our privacy, but also to make it feel like we were in a breezy, verdant jungle. All the chairs, chaises, and tables were angled around the firepit, and memories of long nights laughing and roasting marshmallows with my family filled my head.

I had a good life, and a great childhood, but now... I gazed at Kenzie. *Now I have something to live for that isn't making weapons and making money. There's a life with Kenzie and Laurel waiting for me after this fight, so what do I want that life to look like?*

"Over here," I said, shaking away my heavy thoughts. "This is where we hide."

Kenzie followed my finger. "Bane, you're pointing at a bush."

I cracked a grin. "I'm pointing at a fake bush sitting on top of a huge, man-sized flowerpot. All of these plants are fake," I explained, grabbing hold of the plastic fronds, "and all of these pots are empty. We climb in, put the bushes back over our heads, and no one will know a thing."

"Oooh, sneaky. No wonder your siblings couldn't find you."

I swept out my hand. "Milady."

Dropping a peck on my cheek, Kenzie swung her leg over and climbed inside. I carefully placed the bush cover back on, then hopped inside of mine...

...and waited...

...and waited...

...and waited some more.

Thanks to Debra's phone, I was able to keep track of how long I spent cowering in a big flowerpot while my enemies invaded my home and held my family hostage.

It went off in the middle of me checking the time for the sixth time.

"Hello?" I chirped.

"You shitfuck, bigamist bastard swine!"

"Debbie, love, is that you? What's going on? You sound upset."

"Thought you were so clever, tricking my guys into giving me a hard drive filled with baby photos of that blonde brat?!"

I laughed. "I actually didn't know the drive had photos of Tricky, but you should give them another look. Maybe her sweet, chubby cheeks will melt the ice around your desiccated heart. Once it gets some room, I'm sure it'll grow, my green Grinchy friend."

"Where is the drive?" she forced through gritted teeth.

"It's safe."

"Really? As safe as you are in those oversized chamber pots?"

I froze.

"I hope so, because if you don't stand up and hand it—and whatever weapon you're carrying—over to me right now, I'll put a bullet in the fuck toy's head."

I didn't pause. I shoved away the fake bush and stood up—in the middle of another parade of goons and guns.

No less than six brothers trained their guns on me. The same number that surrounded Kenzie.

She gazed at me in misery. *I'm sorry,* she mouthed, knowing what I'd have to do.

Debra stormed past the empty clubhouse. Or at least, she tried to. It was better to say she slid along the clubhouse windows, straining to look tough and intimidating with a massive bandage stuck to her forehead, and dried blood running down the side of her face. Yumi had to walk by her side, holding her hands out to catch her when she inevitably fell on her ass.

I smiled back at Kenzie, tossing her a wink. *Nice job.*

"Give me the drive," she bleated. "Now."

I knew when I was licked. I passed over the gun and the drive—not saying a word.

Debra claimed it with a smirk that turned my stomach. "Take them both."

A fist flew at my face.

Pain exploded in my skull, then the world went dark.

Chapter Eleven

Kenzie

The guy with the eagle tattoo dragged Bane over the threshold and threw him none-too-gently at River's feet.

Adeline cried out, straining to get to her limp-and-unconscious son, but the binds around her wrists were replaced with proper shackles that attached to the metal around her ankles and bent her in half. They were doing too good a job keeping her exactly where she was.

The same guy grabbed me out of his friend's grip and sent me flying, making me trip over Bane and tumble head over feet into the entertainment center.

"Fuck's sake," Sunny burst out, thrashing against his irons. "What's your problem? You don't have to be that rough!"

I might've said something about the thin-skinned dickhead being pissed because he got duped so hard, and so easily, but Debra had me gagged the minute I jumped out of my flowerpot. Breathing hard, I righted myself—leaning against the glorified television stand.

Bane wasn't telling anyone the truth of what Debra, Jillian, and the rest of them planned to do here either. Even if he recovered from that hit in time, there was no chance because they gagged him too.

"Five minutes," Jillian called. She, Natalya, and Maryann were rushing about the place—moving tables and chairs, setting up laptops, and shoving the Merchants and River onto the sectional. Adeline, Saint, Cash, Brutal, Mercer, an unconscious Bane, Liam, Sunny, River, and then an injured Genny were placed on the couches—lined up in front of the webcams.

Bane was treated to a set of handcuffs, but they didn't bother with me or Genny. Genny wasn't going anywhere, and as for me, Natalya's gun pointed at my head was keeping me still.

Yumi helped a wobbly Debra into Sunny's armchair. I wouldn't lie, I felt a twisted sense of pleasure at dropping that bitch so hard, she could barely stay upright.

"You can go now," Debra said, flapping a hand at the brutes who carried me and Bane in. "There are plenty of Merchant worshippers in this building who still need killing. Get to it."

Eagle Tattoo hesitated. "Maybe we should stay, Mom. It's ten of them against five of you. Let us even the odds."

She shot him a piercing look. "Don't you dare argue with me. We don't need your odds, now get out!"

One of the guys behind Eagle Tattoo pulled his phone out of his pocket. He tapped his screen, read it, and scowled. He grabbed Eagle Tattoo's shoulder. "A bunch of the Sons of Shit are acting up."

Sunny whipped around, shouting obscenities and violent promises at them that they ignored.

"They're fighting to take back the third floor," the guy continued. "We have to go down and help them."

"Three minutes," Jillian warned.

"Do that," Debra agreed. "Go down and stamp out those roaches. Make sure nothing and no one interrupts this auction." Her expression softened. "This is it, Brothers. After all this time. After everything we've sacrificed, we're finally taking Cinco City back from these murderers. This is your victory lap. Let no one take it away from you."

Eagle Tattoo beamed. "Yes, Mom. Thank you."

Together, all fourteen of them tromped out the door—leaving us alone with *them*.

Debra's smile evaporated like a puddle. "Finally. Those stupid, ignorant cunts," she spat. "I know we needed bodies, but couldn't we have invested in a better, and smarter, class of criminal?"

Natalya laughed. "A smarter class of criminal wouldn't have believed us when we promised to 'redistribute' the wealth of Leighbridge, and share all the auction earnings equally."

"That is true," Debra crowed, setting them both off laughing.

"Two minutes."

"Okay, okay." Debra sobered quickly. "Are the recordings ready to go?"

"Ready," Yumi confirmed, setting five different recorders on the table behind the laptops.

"Are the bombs set?"

"They're set," Maryann confirmed.

"Okay, the auction is on a timer with the highest bid at the end of five minutes the accepted bid. That gives us fifty minutes to get through them all. We want as much as we can milk from these fools, so we don't blow the bombs until minute forty-eight. That way we still make a little something from the invalid," she said, waving at Genny. "All of you need to be seen moving, talking, and being in this room until minute twenty.

"After that, they'll only hear our voices, but they'll be too busy focused on the auction to care about us. That'll give us more than enough time to get out, go through the tunnel, and drive away. Don't worry"—she held up the drive—"we're all packed."

"Ten seconds," Natalya said, gun steady on me even as she watched the clock. "Nine, eight, seven..."

"For Wilson," Debra said.

Her friends nodded. "For Wilson."

"—three, two, one."

From my side view, I saw the screen flick on, and the show begin.

Debra sat up high in her chair as her buddies followed her direction—moving around the room and providing the proof of life and presence that would sell the lie that they died here in the explosion with the rest of us.

"Welcome, Brothers and Sisters," Debra began. "It's taken a long time. Months for some, decades for the faithful, but at long last, we've finally done it. We've cracked the Merchants' famed security and put them where they belonged"—she detached the webcam and turned it around—"in chains."

"Now," Yumi took over, leaning over Debra's chair. "I know we promised the entire family, and that promise will be kept. With these ten neutralized, it won't take long to track down the final two siblings, and the daughter of Liam Hunt. As soon as we have them in hand, they'll also be put up for sale. But for now, we won't let this opportunity pass to offer you the main set."

"The original leaders of the Merchants," Jillian announced, "the children chosen to lead their criminal empire after they stepped down, and the Rat King."

"Let's not waste any more time," Natalya chimed in. "We begin with Adeline Redgrave, daughter of notorious gangster and fixer, Oscar Redgrave. Oscar and his gang, The Lords, were the original creators of the ledger. Adeline was its final owner. Her knowledge of the Cinco underground spans her generation, and the one before. As such, the minimum bid to own her is twenty million dollars.

"Brothers and Sisters, enter your bid in denominations of millions," she said, popping my brows to my hairline. "Meaning, the only acceptable rising bid from the base price is twenty-one million and higher."

Debra leaned forward and fixed the camera directly on a curled-lip, glowering Adeline. "Begin."

Debra tapped a button, which popped a huge five-minute timer on the screen that was big enough for me to see. The rest of what was going on was hard to make out. It kind of looked like she was in an old-fashioned chat room with no faces, no real names, no locations, and no trace. All there was to see were usernames floating through cyberspace.

She frowned. "Everyone, you can begin placing your bids. The auction has begun."

Behind her, Yumi and Jillian were moving around uselessly, pretending to have a conversation. They paused their charade to peer over her shoulder.

"If you accept the opening bid, simply type *accept*," Debra said. "Twenty million dollars for the underground queen of Cinco City herself. You can keep her or ransom her. Either way, we're practically giving this old bitch away."

More seconds passed with Debra's forehead crumpling further and further, fashioning deeper grooves between her temples.

"Why is no one bidding?" Natalya hissed.

"Shh!" Debra snapped back. In a louder tone, she said, "Twenty million might be a bit high. Just this once, we'll lower the starting bid to seventeen million dollars. That's seventeen million dollars for Adeline Redgrave—the architect of the Night of Tears, and many more tragedies since."

I could see the clock ticking down, but I wasn't seeing a flurry of activity on her screen. Going by the confusion on all of their faces, neither were they.

Debra tapped a button on the laptop. I guessed *mute*. "Yumi, you did call and confirm the new time, yes?"

"Of course, Deb," Yumi cried. "Everyone confirmed twice over. Maybe there's something wrong with the feed. Or the audio."

"There's nothing wrong with the feed," Jillian gritted. "*I checked everything twice over. Maybe the bid is still too high.*"

"We can't come down again," Natalya argued. "The minimum bid is the bid. End of. I bet they're just waiting until the last second to rush their bids in. That's what everyone does."

"Good point," Debra agreed. "We've got little more than two minutes. We'll get our money."

One minute left.

"All right, this is a good time to start getting your bids in."

Thirty seconds left.

"Don't let a smart strategy become a losing strategy." Debra forced a laugh. "Waiting until the last second can be risky, so let's start throwing in those bids."

Ten, nine, eight, seven, six...

I counted down the seconds right along with Debra, Natalya, and the rest.

Frozen smiles plastered over shocked and confused faces.

No one bid a cent, did they? Not one lousy cent.

Debra spun the camera around, then smashed the mute button. *What the fuck?!* was written all over her face. "What the hell just happened? Why did no one bid?"

"I—I—uh—" Jillian stumbled all over herself. "Maybe—maybe the real problem is that no one wants some washed-up, geriatric queenpin," she burst out. "Adeline and her concubines have been out of the game for years. We should've started the bidding with Hunt." Jillian shot behind Liam. "This man owns half of Leighbridge. Tell them that control of him, means control of all of his businesses. And to ensure that control, we'll throw the daughter in for free."

Debra snapped her fingers, nodding at Jillian. "Good idea. Liam Hunt it is. Let's try this again."

I looked at Liam as Debra fiddled with the camera and reclaimed her composure.

My love met my eyes—hunched and shackled as he was—and winked.

A wink? Was that really a—?

And then he smirked, erasing all doubt.

These monsters were talking about selling him and throwing his daughter in the bag too like she was a free toy in a kid's meal and he was... smothering a laugh?

"Hello, again, everyone. Your message came through loud and clear," Debra began. "We're pushing against noon, and you're tired of appetizers, you're ready for a meal. Next up, we have Liam Hunt. Not only does he own half of the businesses in Leighbridge, he also co-operates the gunrunning business he inherited from his grandparents' circus. Those very guns are designed and manufactured by the second-eldest Merchant son."

She swung the camera to Bane, who was beginning to stir.

"Those businesses will be *your* businesses," she claimed, turning back to Liam, "and we'll throw in Hunt's daughter for free to ensure his cooperation. Now, let's start the bidding at twenty-five million doll—"

The door swung open, letting in Eagle Tattoo and eight of his friends.

Mute.

"What the hell do you think you're doing?!" Debra was apoplectic—which really wasn't good when you have a head injury. "Get out of here!"

They didn't move.

"Why should we leave?" asked a guy with brown, shaggy hair, and a thick beard. "We're all a part of this auction. We all want it to succeed. We'll stay."

"You get the fuck out of here, or you won't see a cent! I told you—" She flicked down. Hurriedly, she unmuted the mic. "No, no, there's nothing wrong. A few uninvited guests but nothing to be concerned about."

"The bidding for Liam Hunt begins at twenty-five million dollars." She started the timer. "Now."

I craned my neck to see. There were a few chat bubbles on the screen which I assumed were the bidders asking about the interruption, but now the chat had no activity.

At all.

Debra muted again. "I don't know what the hell has gotten into all of you, but you need to leave this room—"

A snort swung every head around, including mine.

Bane straightened up. Rolling his head, he shook away the aftereffects of the hit, and laughed his ass off.

Hehehehehe, came through the gag, and it set Liam off.

He cracked, barking a laugh which made Genny giggle a funny, high-pitched, loopy-on-painkillers giggle. She fell over on River who caught his niece on his back, shaking her and himself as he guffawed.

And then the whole family was gone.

Full-on, chest-wracking, belly-shaking, eye-watering laughter filled the room, and all anyone could do was stare at them.

"What's wrong with you?" Debra barked. "What's funny? Stop laughing. I said stop laughing!"

Eagle Tattoo raised a hand. "If I may, Mom, I'm fairly sure they're laughing at all of you. I bet they're thinking *if only you five were a better, smarter class of criminal. Then you could've pulled this off.*"

Debra, Yumi, Jillian, Natalya, and Maryann went very still.

"What are you talking about?" Debra rasped. "Why would you say that?"

Eagle Tattoo cocked his head. "You don't know?" he replied over the Merchants' laughter. "Hmm. I guess we're not the ignorant cunts after all. That's still you."

"Where did you hear that?" Debra shrieked, shooting up. She wobbled and fell back down, clutching her head.

Her friends had her covered. Scrambling for their stolen guns, they aimed them at our visitors—all of them including Natalya.

"If I may," Sunny chimed in, grinning away. "I believe I have a little guess as to where they heard your true feelings about them. I'm going with YouTube. Is that right, gentlemen, or did someone just send the link direct to your phone?"

"Direct to my phone," Eagle Tattoo replied, pulling out his cell. "But they got it straight from YouTube, so solid guess. I'll give you full points for it."

Eagle Tattoo tapped his screen and Debra's voice filled the room.

"Finally. Those stupid, ignorant cunts. I know we needed bodies, but couldn't we have invested in a better, and smarter, class of criminal?"

Debra paled. "What is that?! Turn that off!"

"A smarter class of criminal wouldn't have believed us when we promised to 'redistribute' the wealth of Leighbridge, and share all the auction earnings equally."

"I said turn it off!"

Eagle Tattoo turned it off, but his stony face went on to say even more.

"That wasn't what you think," Natalya blurted, lowering her gun. "So let's all just calm down. We weren't talking about you. We were talking about the Merchants."

Shaggy Beard silently tapped his phone.

"This isn't a compromise. It's a trap. There's no way you'd trade the key to your success for a bunch of worthless thugs."

"Worthless thugs, huh?" His smile didn't reach his eyes. "That's funny because when you said this, you were speaking *to* the Merchants, not about them. So if you weren't speaking about them..." His voice dropped the temperature thirty degrees. "You must've been speaking about us."

"Where did you get that?" Maryann broke in, surging forward and making all of their guns fly up. "Have you been recording us? Spying on us?!"

"Get a fucking clue, woman," Adeline snapped, "and look at where you are?"

"What?" Maryann whipped around. "What does that mean?"

"Take that gag out of my son's mouth, and I'm sure he'd be happy to tell you."

"We're not—"

Eagle Tattoo reached over and pulled the gag out of Bane's mouth without missing a step.

Bane coughed. Shaking his head, he rose up—shining his beaming smile on the room. "Thank you so much for the assistance. Now, where were we?" He turned on Debra. "Oh, yeah, you were about to get those cuffs and that gag off of Kenzie."

No one moved.

"Do it, or I won't tell you why your timer just ran out, but no one put in a single bid in your ridiculous auction."

Their eyes snapped to the screen. By their blown brows, I knew Bane was right. No one bid for Liam.

Natalya took a step toward me, then stopped.

"Do it," Bane growled, eyes flashing. "Before I lose my patience."

Unarmed and handcuffed, but Bane still gave the air of being the most dangerous man in the room.

Slowly, Natalya ungagged and released me. "Don't move." She trained her gun between my eyes. "She's free, but she's not going anywhere until you tell us what's going on."

"I'm sure Kenzie can help you out with that," River chimed in. "Baby, what's the first rule when dealing with assassins?"

I blinked. "I... uh... It's... that you never corner them in their home. Because they're the only one who knows where all the weapons are hidden."

"Ding, ding, ding, ding, ding!" Sunny sounded off. "What does she win, Bane, other than a vigorous bout of blisteringly hot sex tonight?"

My cheeks caught fire. I knew we had bigger problems right then, but did he have to say these things in front of his parents?!

"I'll tell you what she wins, brother, she wins that look of utter befuddlement on Debbie's face, because she still doesn't get it."

"Get it?" Debra flicked from him, to the laptop, to the standoff in the middle of the room. "Get what?"

"You don't get that there is no reason on earth that we'd ever shut down the Fairfield's security. No reason ever. So if that day ever came, we'd have to be under extreme duress, and that's the security protocol you automatically triggered when you typed in that shutdown code. Extreme Duress Mode."

"Ex— Extreme Duress?" she croaked.

"That's right. Now, I bet your next question is: what is Extreme Duress Mode? And that's a great question," he cried, enjoying himself immensely. "I don't just make weapons. I also dabble a bit in cybersecurity, and Extreme Duress Mode was a stroke of genius on my part, if you don't mind the brag.

"When the building is on Extreme Duress Mode, it does turn off all the standard security measures, but it also *turns on* every hidden camera and speaker stashed in every single room in the building."

Debra was white as a sheet. "C-camera?" Slowly, achingly, she tipped her head, gazing up at the ceiling fan above her head.

I don't know if there was a camera in there, but it'd be a great place for one.

"After those cameras and speakers turn on, a link to the live streaming feed is instantly sent to every Merchant—everywhere."

"We're worldwide, baby!" Sunny crowed.

"That includes our oldest sisters, our aunt Gianna and all of our cousins, the whole circus fam, and every one of our trusted friends, family, and allies." Bane smiled into her blown eyes. "They've all seen and heard everything you six have done here since you typed in that code.

"And going by the fact that your auction is bust, and your members have guns pointed at you right now, they shared with them and the rest of the world that you planned to take their money, fake your deaths, and blow them all up."

A deep, suffocating silence spread through the room, broken only by my giggling.

"This is hilarious," I shrieked, reddening Debra's and Maryann's cheeks. "Decades and decades of planning, and you blew it all up like the dumbasses you are. Here it is! The better, smarter class of criminal in action!"

"Shut up!" Debra roared. "This isn't possi— This doesn't make any— This is a trick! It's a Merchant lie, and you're falling for it. You're all falling for it," she shouted at the webcam. "We've been working, and fighting, and dying, and planning to get to this moment for years, and just because some random sends you a YouTube link, you're willing to throw it all away? This is Merchant trickery, please wake up and see that!"

"So, it's all a deepfake trick?" Eagle Tattoo said, expression blank. "You weren't planning to run off with the money, and kill us all right along with the Merchants?"

"Of course we weren't," Jillian said, going for a soft, motherly tone. "You know we weren't. The Brotherhood has been there for you when no one else was. We are your family. *They* are your enemies. There shouldn't be a question of who you can trust."

"Hmmm," Eagle Tattoo hummed, bobbing his head. "So, then, maybe you can explain the bombs we watched you two carry in through that secret tunnel you never told any of us about. Because Brother Emily just found one stashed in the lobby linen closet, and she says there's nothing deepfake about it."

Debra's lips peeled back from her teeth. "Proud of yourself? Think you got an upper hand on us because you finally used your big-boy brain after the truth was handed to you? How's this, Brother Cunt, *you don't matter.*

"Your lives don't matter. Your piddly-ass little problems don't matter!" Spittle flew over the screen. "Saint killed our fathers! He killed them! Then he threw them out like garbage! They will pay for that. Nothing matters except them paying for what they did to our families!

"You should be thanking me," she shrieked. "You were too stupid, broke, and worthless to bring down the Merchants, but now, thanks to us, you'll be a sacrifice to the greatest coup in underground history. You must not know what a favor is, because this is what it looks like! I'm giving your pathetic lives meaning. I'm—"

Eagle Tattoo shot her in the face.

I screamed as Debra blasted back. Folding over, she tipped over the side of the couch and dumped on the floor—dead.

"No!" Maryann charged them, bullets flying.

The brothers let loose—firing on Maryann, Natalya, Jillian, and Yumi.

I hit the deck at the same time the Merchants did. Shackled and restrained, they tipped off the couch, taking Genny with them.

Sunny and Liam rolled on top of their sister as Bane pounced on me, covering me as the firefight ripped through the once peaceful, happy home.

An eternity passed before the shooting stopped, or at least that's what it felt like. Through the circle of Bane's arms, I strained to see who was still standing, and who wasn't.

Yumi bled on the coffee table, the laptops crushed under her body...

...Natalya slumped against Sunny's armchair...

...Maryann was still and unseeing at Eagle Tattoo's feet...

...and Jillian—

"Please," she rasped, kneeling on the floor with her hands up. "This was all Debra's plan, not mine. I never agreed with the decision to kill you all and steal the money, but she wouldn't listen to me. We've built something great with the Brotherhood. The gang that brought the Merchants to its knees.

"We don't have to throw that all away. Together we can start over," she cried, eyes wild and rolling in her head. "All you have to do is kill the Merchants, and we can walk right out of here with their digital black book! It's everything we need to rule the city, so just kill them. Kill—"

"Nice try," Eagle Tattoo said. "But you were laughing just as loud as the rest of them about the dumbass thugs catching a bomb."

She growled. "You *are* dumbass thugs! I'm giving you the chance to have everything you want! Fucking take it, you—!"

Beardy shot her twice.

Jillian flopped over, and he shot her again—making sure.

"You don't give us anything," Eagle Tattoo said. "We can get what we want all on our own."

A chill climbed my spine, chasing out all the laughter and victory that was in the room only minutes before.

Bane rose as their eyes, and their guns, turned on us. "What are you going to do?" Bane moved out in front of me—shielding me. "For the whole world to see?"

Eagle Tattoo peered around the room under the watchful eye of the cameras. "The real question," he began, tone even, "is what were you going to do? We heard you on the phone with Mom, saying that you'd trade that drive to get both your people, and us, out of the building?" Shrewd eyes narrowed to slits. "Was that real, or a trick for the cameras?"

"Those are real bombs, Ethan—and yes, I remember your name now," Bane said to his raised brows. "It would've been a real explosion, and you would've been really alive and safe from the danger if Debra took my deal and let you out of the building, so yeah, that's more than enough real to prove it wasn't a trick."

Ethan shared a look with his friends. "Why? Why would you care about saving us?"

"Because I get it now. *We* get it now. We thought we were doing good. That we were making Cinco safer, better, and stronger for everyone—the underground and the rest—but we were fooling ourselves." Bane unlocked the cuffs and flung them away like they were little more than an annoyance. "In a lot of ways, we were no better than Deb-Deb and her buddies. Using threats and force when we didn't get compliance. Treating you like you were no better, and had no more value than our enemies."

Ethan's jaw clenched, ticcing a wild beat. But he didn't interrupt.

"You wanted to make us take notice? Make us listen?" Bane got up and crossed over to Debra's body, completely ignoring the guns that flew up to follow him.

Taking the drive from her pocket, Bane put it on the table, took off his shoe, and smashed it.

"We're listening," he announced over my bug-eyed shock, and his mother's proud smile. "No more threats. No more blackmail. If you want to work with us, we'll sit down and talk partnership—equal partnership. But if you want to be enemies..." He grinned, shrugging. "Well, then, pick the time and place and we'll show up with our own guns. I'm sure it'll be fun."

Ethan stared at him. What he was thinking, I had no idea. He didn't let an iota of it show on his face.

"I'm sure it will be," he said, lowering his gun. "Because we'll be all squared up then. You saved our lives. We spared yours." Ethan nodded to Beardy. "Tell the brothers to move out. The Fairfield is Merchant territory."

Just like that, they turned to go—all of them texting and calling their brothers and sisters, telling them to leave the building.

"I'll see you at that time and place, Bane." Ethan put two fingers to his temple and saluted him. "We'll settle that old score."

Bane waved heartily. "Looking forward to it, brother. But don't be a stranger in the meantime. Do a few drive-bys on me to let me know you're thinking of me."

Ethan actually laughed out loud, his guffaws echoing down the hallway.

"Why would you say that?" I bleated. "Stop joking around with violent, homicidal murderers!"

"Ahh, Ethan's all right," Bane said, waving my words away. "He's just pissed because he used to run the biggest underground weapons business in Waterford until I raided him, killed half his guys, and put his ass in a coma."

I just goggled at him as he rescued the key to the shackles from Natalya's pocket and got to work freeing his family.

"I'm never going to get used to being a Merchant, am I?"

"Nope."

Sunny, Liam, River, and Bane came over to me, wrapping me safe and warm in their arms.

"But the good news is," Sunny said, kissing my forehead. "You have a life-time to try."

Epilogue

"Shh."

"Why?" Bane returned, peeling off my shirt. "No one else is around."

"I don't know." I giggled, tugging at his belt. "We just have to shush."

"Oh, well, I know what will help with that." Bane captured my lips, gently guiding me back onto the seat.

I let him be as gentle as he wanted, but I was far from it—ripping his belt loose, tugging down his pants, and half ripping his boxers off his body.

It was wild to me how eager I still was for him after five years of Bane having fun with my body like I was his personal jungle gym, but I couldn't help it. Every time was like the first time for me—I couldn't get enough of him, Sunny, River, or Liam.

Bane kissed down the valley of my breasts, making only two pit stops to suck on them *hard*, and turn the poor nubs into hardened, desperate pebbles.

"Ahh, baby, yes," I moaned, back arching off the backseat.

How we got into the car to drive to the party, but only made it as far as the cliff, was anyone's guess.

My love, Bane, still preferred to be outside in nature instead of stuck in the city. That led to his buying another cabin in Elmshire Woods, but this one sat at the base of a gentle, sloping cliff that provided the most beautiful view of the thriving city below.

We were currently screwing each other's brains out and ignoring that view completely.

Bane bit my panties and dragged them off with his teeth, tossing them somewhere over the passenger's seat. "My goodness, woman, you just get finer with age. Every fucking day, more sinfully gorgeous than the last."

"Don't say that like I'm old." I poked him with my toe. "I'm only twenty-eight. You're the one walking through your thirties."

"And Liam's the one doddering into his forties."

I laughed. "No one is doddering anywhere. But you can," I said, spreading my legs like the wanton minx I was. "In this pussy."

"I'll take you up on that." Swooping down, Bane buried between my legs and latched on to my clit, sucking on the thing like he was trying to take it off.

"Ahh!" I cried out—electricity zipping through my body and lighting the world on fire. Heat, and love, and lust, and five years of breaking through each other's walls to build something whole, wonderful, and all ours—came to life under my skin.

I kicked, wiggled, and bucked under his ministrations, helpless to his expert tongue and its relentless dipping and diving into my well—turning the heat in my core up to maximum.

Bane reached up and captured my breasts, tweaking and tugging my nipples as if I wasn't enough of a helpless mess.

"Yes, baby, more," I breathed, anchoring my foot against the headrest, and rocking back and forth on his tongue.

My eyes rolled back in my head when one hand dropped back and his finger joined the party, pressing against my puckered entrance and slipping inside. "Holy flipping fuck that's good." I smacked his ass with my foot, making him chuckle and send vibrations through my out-of-control core. "Don't you dare stop!"

He most definitely did not stop.

Bane's other hand surrendered my nipple only to claim my clit. He rubbed hard—just the right amount of friction and pressure to make me—

"Ahhh!" I snapped my back in half, coming so hard I slipped off the leather and wound up flopping and jerking on the car floor—riding the delicious crashing waves that tossed me back under every time I tried to catch my breath.

Grinning, Bane picked me up—seating me firmly on his lap as I rode the ride down, gasping and panting on his chest. "My goodness, man, you give good orgasm."

"You know I aim to please, baby." He kissed the crap out of me, swiping his tongue across my lips, then plundering my mouth—reducing me to more of a mound of boneless jelly. "Now, giddyup, cowgirl."

I blushed. Once—just once!—I decided to surprise Bane with a sexy cowgirl outfit complete with fake sidearms. The man lost his mind and took me right there on the floor while I was still figuring out the lasso. I was screaming his name with my fake gun fucking my pussy within ten minutes.

I'd been his cowgirl ever since.

"Okay." I nipped his nose. "But only because there's a little outfit you'll be wearing for me tonight."

"Fine with me. You know the Savage Prince motto." His smirk set my body ablaze. "*Whatever gets Mackenzie Blaine's thong off.*"

It was their motto. Sunny even shouted it one time when he got in a bar brawl with some jerks who were hitting on me and Sienna, and ignoring our clear requests to go away.

I couldn't help rolling my eyes and loving Sunny more when I thought of that.

Rising up, I didn't waste any time and impaled myself on his dick—letting the magnificent beast between his legs stretch me in all the right ways.

Throwing my head back, I released a deep, long, satisfying moan—the two of us safe in our little, quiet, foggy world.

Bane held me close, peppering my chin, neck, and breasts with kisses as I moved, bouncing up and down on his lap.

Our moans mingled. Our breaths fogged the mirror. Our fingers threaded together—secure, firm, and forever.

I found that spot and impaled myself on it as rough as he drilled me, pumping in time to my bouncing.

"Yes, yes!" My moans were screams. I released his shoulders and pressed against the roof, balancing on the balls of my toes and widening my knees to receive him deeper, faster, and *harder.*

"I love you, Kenzie," he grunted. "I've always loved you since the day I nearly blew you up with my bazooka. I went into the woods to escape from love... so you came and found me."

I might've said something sweet and gushy back, if not for my core tightening so hard it snapped in half, igniting my orgasm and exploding it through my body.

Bane jerked, then he came too—spilling inside of me as we both screamed, grunted, and moaned under the shockwaves.

"Wow," I panted, slumping over his chest. "I think we just topped our personal best."

"Really?" He pulled me closer, kissing me all over. "What about Paris? We blew the lights out in the City of Lights that night."

I smothered a laugh. We really did cause a power surge and take out the lights in the whole building that night. But it wasn't my fault that we fell out of bed onto a power cord.

"And what about Tanzania?" His grin was wolfish. "You screamed so loud, you set off half the animals in the jungle."

"Okay, let's agree on top three, then."

"Definitely top three."

My phone went off.

"Lollipop Lips, where are you?" Sunny answered. "Did you forget you're bringing the cake?"

"Wait, what? I was supposed to do that?" I cried. "But look at the time. Everywhere is probably closed."

"Probably. So you better get your clothes back on and think of something."

I swore, hanging up the phone. "No more basking in the afterglow. Turns out we were on cake duty."

"Shit."

We hurriedly got dressed and got back on the road.

We went all around Leighbridge, begging three different bakeries to stay open later to give us something, anything, that resembled a birthday cake. The final guy finally took pity on us when Bane offered him ten thousand dollars.

And by took pity, I mean he ran back into the kitchen so fast, he left a him-shaped cloud of flour in his place.

Bane and I relaxed in a booth, talking, laughing, and making out while he worked—just enjoying each other's company.

Soon, he returned with the most expensive cake in the world, and we left for home—my home. I thought that every time I found the Fairfield in the skyline.

I'm home.

We pulled inside the parking garage, climbed out, and headed inside, waving hello to Thatcher on the way in.

The noise from the party hit us before we turned the corner for the terrace, finding our whole family laughing and dancing under the stars.

Adeline, her husbands, and their oldest daughters chatted around the fireplace while they took charge of s'more duty—melting, assembling, and putting them on plates as fast as the kids were snatching them up and devouring them.

Sunny, River, and Ryker manned the grill on the other end of the terrace, having a heated argument over grilled meat and vegetables. Three people could not be least alike, or argue more, but I'd never seen a friendship stronger.

As strong as Ryker's relationship with his girlfriend of two years—

"Kenzie, there you are. It's about time. You see, folks, this is what I have to deal with?" Lyla said, pausing to kiss Ryker's cheek before coming over to chew me out. "Running a business with someone who doesn't own a clock."

"Haha." We exchanged warm kisses on the cheeks. "Last I checked, that business is one of the most successful fashion boutiques in Cinco, with another one opening in New York this summer, so it can't be all bad."

She grinned, winking. "It's bad enough."

"No one believes that," Sienna spoke up. "The only person Lyla loves more than Kenzie is Laurel. Right, Mom?"

Our mother smiled at all of us as she sat next to the fire—happy and free. The last bit in no small part due to the heartfelt pleas delivered to the parole board by Lyla and her mother. "That's right. I'd swear you two were twins if I didn't witness myself that the doctor only pulled one baby out of me that day."

We laughed, broken only by Laurel running up and jumping on Sienna's lap. "Yes, Auntie?"

"Oh, I was just saying how much your auntie Lyla loves you."

"That's right I do," Lyla cooed, holding out her hands and catching Laurel when she ran giggling into them. "Who's my favorite girl? Huh? Who does Auntie love more than anything?"

"Me! Me!"

My heart melted into a puddle watching my sister with my perfect girl. Every day I pinched myself, but Laurel remained a high-energy, rambunctious five-year-old—racing throughout the Fairfield like she ran the place and everyone in it.

"Baby girl, did you finish your packing?" I asked. "We're going to visit your brother tomorrow, remember?"

Yep, the next day, we were jetting off for Laurel's monthly weekend with Damien, Talia, and Jeremiah. Damien still wasn't father of the year, but after adopting Jeremiah, he finally started to wake up to what a massive asshole he'd been.

One weekend every month wasn't much, but Laurel looked forward to it just as much as Damien, Talia, and Jeremiah did.

"I did it, Mommy," Laurel confirmed. "I did it all myself."

"Oh, really?"

Liam slid up to me, tossing me a covert headshake. He may have been forty years old, but the man was lean, hard, sexy, and gently graying like the fine-ass silver fox daddy he was. "Not a chance," he muttered. "What she means is she supervised me packing her bag all by herself."

I laughed. "That sounds about right. And thank you," I said, kissing him hello. "I missed you."

"You better have," he growled, kissing me harder. "It's been a whole six hours since I got my hands on you. You better have missed me so much, we need to go downstairs and do something about it."

"Oooh." I shivered. "Yes, please."

"Mom." Elizabeth pushed between us, snapping me back to reality. "How come I don't get to go with Laurel to New York?" Her pout was out in full force. "She's my sister, and sisters do everything together. Like you and Auntie Si and Auntie Lyla."

Liam and I exchanged smiles over her head. We'd been having trouble explaining the family dynamics to Elizabeth, and why she couldn't stay overnight in the home of a guy my guys still hated with all their guts. But even so, I loved how close my girls were. They loved each other the way Sienna and I always loved each other. They had each other's backs—forever.

"You are absolutely right," I said. "So how about this? Tomorrow, you, Laurel, Jeremiah, me, and Daddy are going to spend the whole day together in Central Park. Sound fun?"

"Yeah!" She ran off. "Laurel, did you hear? I'm coming too!"

"Are Damien and Talia on board with that?" Liam asked.

"Yeah, I already cleared it with them. They're actually looking forward to having some alone time. They're going to make a date of it."

"That's good. It means Frost won't be there," he mused. "And his death is delayed another day."

I rolled my eyes, chuckling. It may have been a long time ago, but Damien Frost hurt me, and that was something my guys would never forgive.

I rested my head on Liam's shoulder, and then my arm around River when he came over, dropping a kiss on my temple.

So much had changed in the last five years since we faced our biggest threat. After Bane destroyed the drive, new alliances were made and new bonds forged, but all wasn't forgiven.

Many people—former Brotherhood members and others—rose up to challenge the kings, as determined to topple them as they'd always been. And even though my heart stopped every time they went out to face those threats, my guys always came back.

They wouldn't admit it, but I put their endless winning streak to the new and most important alliance they made, with River.

It took time, but a year after taking down Debra and her people, River officially joined the Merchants. So officially, he moved into the Fairfield, and brought all of his people with him—getting his second family off the streets and into the dozens upon dozens of empty apartments that were waiting to be filled.

Now I went to sleep every night under the same roof as all the guys I loved more than air.

"Are you two done slobbering all over each other?" Genny stormed over and plucked the cake box from my hand. "The birthday girl's waiting."

Taking Liam's and River's hands, we trailed behind her—smiling huge as Genny took out the one-year birthday cake, and set it down on her daughter's highchair.

The curly-haired, brown-eyed beauty shrieked in delight as she tore into it, not bothering to wait for the singing.

I sighed, smiling at baby Marceline. Was that her birth name? We had no idea, because as promised, when Genny decided she was ready to have a baby... she went out and stole one.

Seriously, one day she simply went out and came back that night holding a two-month-old Marceline. She introduced us all to our new baby niece, and that was the end of that. No questions were allowed, and they were ignored when asked.

"Happy birthday to you, happy birthday to you..."

But even so, we didn't care. No matter what happened, we knew that Genny did not and would not steal a baby from a family who loved and wanted her, so however she came to be with our family, we knew she was right where she belonged—with all the other wonderful misfit toys.

The Cardinals. The Sons of Saint. The Scourges. The Prissy Sissies. The Rat King Crew. The Savage Princes. The Merchants.

Our family.

My heart burst looking around at all the people I loved most in the world.

"My family."

***

ABOUT THE AUTHOR

Ruby Vincent is a writer and lover of contemporary, fantasy, and paranormal romance. She loves saucy heroines, bold alpha males, and weaving a tale where both get their happy ever after. Be sure to check out more of her books on her <u>website</u>.